STARLION

Thieves of the Red Night

LEON LANGFORD

Leonard Leroy Langford Jr.

CONTENTS

One
The Green Night   1

Two
Shooting Stars Over Space City   6

Three
Lay Down the Law   14

Four
From Olympus on Down   19

Five
The Thieves   30

Six
Lay Down the Law [The Blue Giant Remix]   40

Seven
Bullies in Orbit   49

Eight
H-Town Crown   60

Nine
Fort Olympus   70

Ten
Meet, But Don't Greet   81

Eleven
Astra Inclinant   89

Twelve
The Battalia   99

Thirteen
The Hierarchy   108

Fourteen
Coliseum 7: Repel // Demons   121

Fifteen
Coliseum 7: Double-Barrel Fireworks   133

Sixteen
Coliseum 7: Raise Your Head   142

Seventeen
Ambrosia Cupcake Bomb   148

Eighteen
The Dead Don't Hunt   157

Nineteen
The First Strike   161

Twenty
Astro Day I: Rose Dawn   168

Twenty-One
Astro Day II: The World Today   180

Twenty-Two
Astro Day III: Crescent Cutter   195

Twenty-Three
Astro Day IV: Sparkle Five   209

Twenty-Four
Astro Day V: HUSH MODE   212

Twenty-Five
Astro Day VI: The Thieves Part 2   221

Twenty-Six
Astro Day VII: The Second Strike   230

Twenty-Seven
Alone Across the Rubicon   241

Twenty-Eight
[Young Lions] X [Rubicon]   256

Twenty-Nine
The Thieves Part 3   282

Thirty
The Third Strike   303

Thirty-One
BAD MOON RISIN'   316

Thirty-Two
The Red Night   326

Thirty-Three
Red Titan Rock   342

Thirty-Four
Regulus   355

Thirty-Five
Kingdom Come   365

STARLION

CHAPTER ONE

The Green Night

A green thunderbolt tore across the sky.

Like coiling serpents, green bolts of energy swirled in the heavens over Houston. The moon and stars had been swallowed by midnight nimbus clouds, whose celestial energies began to detonate deep within their core. Thunder rumbled through the green tempest like a foul, rotten hurricane.

On the streets below, a glowing figure walked across the pavement. Its body was composed of vibrating jade energy as if it were the storm made flesh.

The figure raised its arm, and a blast of emerald light erupted from its palm. In one instant, houses bowed, buildings surrendered, collapsing into monuments of smoke and rubble. Sidewalks were uprooted, streetlights were bent into L shapes, and the faces of brick buildings were blown to concrete dust. Then, in another instant and another flash of green, a chain reaction of citywide destruction plowed through Houston, ripping foundations from the sky and into the hellscape below.

A Houston Police Department squad car ripped around the corner, heading towards the destruction. Its wheels tumbled across crumbled brick and mortar, crunching debris under its weight. At the wheel was Officer Irvine and sitting terrified in the passenger seat was Officer Davis. Officer Davis, a lifelong Houston resident, peered out at the broiling destruction that coated his city. Block after block, home after home, and building after building were simply gone. Davis surveyed the once-familiar skyline but saw burning chasms where he remembered

1

homes. Officer Irvine glanced at a photo of his daughter on his dashboard, then back out at the destroyed city before him.

"My God, what did this?" Davis asked aloud.

"It has to be an Esper," Irvine replied, his stoic calm cracking a bit.

"But what kind of —STOP." Davis' reply was interrupted as he threw his hands up. The two turned down 31st Street, and standing in the middle of the road was the mysterious figure. It had two arms and two legs. But the human resemblance stopped there because its body seemed chiseled out of jade with viridescent light pulsating from its seven-foot frame.

It was a star in the shape of a man.

"Back up," Davis whispered, before exploding, "Back up, now."

Irvine snapped out of his shock then slammed the car into reverse. He stomped on the gas and rocketed backward. Davis snatched up the radio and shouted into the mic, "We have a Vesper on sight. I repeat. We have a Vesper on sight."

The glowing figure, a titan of storming green energies, took a step toward them and raised a hand as – CRUSH. The police car smashed to a halt as a toppled streetlight hooked into its undercarriage. Irvine slammed on the gas repeatedly. The car's tires squealed in protest. The car was a lost cause; it was trapped. Irvine and Davis exchanged a glance. They both agreed this was their last breath. Irvine looked from Davis to his daughter's picture, then to the light storm flaring just beyond the windshield.

The Green Titan's body flared with energy, before the lights dove back into its diamond body, coalesced into its palm, then burst in a flash of rolling green light. Both officers turned away from the blinding mass heading their way as – THOOM. The blast impacted their car, shaking it wildly, smashing the windows, and sending waves of broiling heat over their huddled forms. Just as suddenly as it began, it ended.

Davis was the first to open his eyes, blinking in amazement... He was alive. Irvine cracked his eyes open, and the first thing he saw was his daughter's photo, floating into his lap. He picked it up and gently cupped it in his palm.

"Ir–Irvine…" Davis stuttered. "It's them. It's the Olympians."

Irvine raised his head, and his breath escaped his lungs. His heart filled with relief and resolve as his gaze fell on the backs of seven imposing figures standing between them and the Green Titan. Even though he couldn't make out their individual faces, he knew them.

The world knew them.

The world's seven strongest Espers – the Olympians.

The Olympians, like all heroes, wore elastic bodysuits under a set of chrome shoulder pads, which covered their torsos, chests, and necks, and rose up to a set of retractable plates that formed a mask right under their eyes. Mighty gold stars embellished the center of their suits. While their suits unified them as one force, their differences in appearance were drastic. One had shaggy, blue hair. Another was feline in appearance with orange fur and pointed ears. It stood beside one other that had a shield at her side. To her left was a man with only one arm. Behind that one was another wearing a hood over its head.

Irvine and Davis perked up as a soft, commanding voice found their ears telepathically. "*We'll take it from here, Officers.*"

The two officers' eyes widened at each other, and Irvine stuttered, "Did you hear–"

"*Run. Now.*" The disembodied voice came to them, both comforting and commanding. The tallest of the Olympians faced them, his eyes focused and hard. There was a flash of red energy in the man's eyes, and he spoke without moving his lips. "*Go. Please.*"

The two officers didn't think twice. They opened their busted car doors and sprinted away through the destruction, leaving the Olympians to face the Green Titan.

A green thundercloud swirled above the Olympians, roaring with pent-up energy that seemed to move in step with the Green Titan. Hurricane-strength winds swelled off of its body while jade-tinted chain lightning looped recklessly through the black clouds above.

Though it had no eyes, mouth, nose, or ears, the Green Titan could sense them behind the diamond slate that covered its face. Maybe it sensed their energies, their presence, or maybe even their intent. Its body bristled and simmered with pulsating force.

Like a storm cloud or a tornado the area around the Green Titan swirled, kicking up hot dust and debris. Then with all of its supernatural might the Green Titan blitzed the Olympians and became a streak of green. The Olympians met the Titan in the middle, their mighty energies coming to bear and boiling forth.

As they impacted, a bright, hot, blinding light split forth from the city of Houston, searing high and mighty until it pierced the green clouds and starlit heavens above.

"It makes you believe that anyone can be a hero, you know?"
- *Jordan Harris*

CHAPTER TWO

Shooting Stars Over Space City

10 YEARS LATER

The seven Olympians stood still in the center of Houston. Moonlight and starlight reflected off their chrome bodies as men, women, and children surrounded them, or rather, surrounded the statues of the seven Olympians.

Though ten years had passed since that horrible, destructive night, the memory of the Olympians was immortalized in a series of seven statues that formed a half-circle around a slab of gold and black marble. The marble was inscribed with the hundreds of names Houston had lost that night. An epitaph carved into the face of the marble read, *"TO THOSE WE LOST ON THE GREEN NIGHT."*

Set directly in the marble in the middle of the etched words was an opaque crystal reminiscent of a full moon, which memorialized that night and the souls who passed with it. The memorial of the Green Night haunted the middle of a park in the heart of the city. What was once a dozen city blocks, then a field of fire, was made into a park where new life grew from the depths of the old.

Jordan Harris always found the memorial park a somber place to reflect – to gather himself, his thoughts, his fears, and his young hopes. Though he was only four on the fateful Green Night, certain scars have a way of following you through the years. At fourteen Jordan found that same pain lingering in his chest as he gazed at the memorial. Jordan stood in front of the seven, curiously searching the eyes of the men and women looking down on him.

"It's a shame, right?" a soft voice emanated from behind him.

Jordan suppressed the urge to jump and turned around to see a young girl with striking black hair and a pale face looking back at him. She was fourteen or fifteen, close to Jordan's age, yet her eyes carried a wisdom of someone three times her age. In her hand was a bouquet of flowers. She passed Jordan and placed them at the feet of the Olympians.

"I just came to pay my respects," she said softly.

"Me too," Jordan replied.

The girl rose from her silent prayer and examined Jordan for a moment. Jordan wore all black with gold trim: black jeans, black turtleneck, black jacket with gold cuffs and designs running along it, and a pair of sneakers, the Zeuz Airwalkers – also black and gold. Even though she said nothing, Jordan felt her analyzing him, studying his frame, his clothes, his intentions. Inside a pair of worn black tactical gloves, Jordan felt his fingers squirm. The gloves were just a bit too big for him, but he didn't mind. They were special to him since they once belonged to one of his favorite heroes.

"You look like you're a hero yourself," she mused.

Jordan smirked. "Not so much. But I'm working at it."

"Oh, a little vigilantism?" She smirked too. "I respect that."

Jordan froze. *Wait? Was she joking? Did she figure that out just from seeing me?*

His thoughts were interrupted when the device in Jordan's ear buzzed to life: "Calling all cars. Calling all cars. We've got a Vesper on sight – possible 10-90 at City Bank."

Jordan tensed at the words as he recalled, *10-90? That's a robbery in progress.*

The girl leaned in, studying the sudden spike in his stature. "Are you okay?"

Jordan paused, shook it off, and straightened. He scrambled to put a lie together. "Yeah," he said. "I just–I just get emotional when I come here. To see them and know what they did to save the city." Yet in his rush to lie Jordan found a nugget of honesty. "It makes you believe that anyone can be a hero, you know?"

"Heroes come in all shapes and sizes," the girl said. She cast another glance at the monument, its seven heroes, the hundreds of lost names, and the crystal in the heart of it.

While standing behind her, Jordan reached under the collar of his turtleneck and pulled it clear over his nose and mouth, leaving only his eyes exposed. His disguise was a mock imitation of the half-masks that official heroes wore. Hearing the rustle of his clothes, the girl turned back to Jordan, just as – *THUMP.* She reflexively turned away as a soft pop and a gentle burst of wind blew past her. She froze.

Jordan was gone, and only shimmering specks of golden light were left in his wake.

Jordan stood above the city of Houston. The black clouds of the night served as the backdrop to a series of glittering lights inside towering buildings. Perched atop one of the high rises, Jordan dared not look down. Moving from the highest point of one building to another was a usual occurrence, but it still gave him chills and a bit of vertigo to look down four hundred feet. Jordan preferred to think of it as hopscotch – with really high stakes.

He perked up as static echoed in his ear again. This was what he'd been waiting for. "Calling all cars. Calling all cars. We've got a 10-90 confirmed. Vesper currently on foot. Calling in Esper support on – " *Pshhh. Pshhh.* The device hissed. Jordan tapped his ear a few times, trying to get reception.

"C'mon, c'mon. Give me the address," Jordan huffed.

The voice came back in a patchwork of words, "Calling – cars – all – cars – 10-90 – Vesper – on – foot – Esper support –Avenue." Jordan bit his lip in frustration, then perked his ears up as a familiar sound echoed in the distance.

Sirens.

"There we go," Jordan mused.

Jordan searched the inky horizon and saw flashes of red and blue lights moving in the distance. Not too far from him, by way of the crow – or as Jordan preferred – by way of *hopscotch between buildings*. This was Jordan's specialty. He took a deep breath through the collar of his turtleneck and jumped off the edge.

He dropped freely for a second. Those four hundred feet of pavement below raced to meet him before he felt it activate. Like all Espers, Jordan was different from the average human. As all humans are born with trace amounts of stardust in their bodies, Espers were born with more – at least thirty times more. These Plasma Crystals, as they were known, collected in the bases of their necks, tied them to the universe, and gave them the power to alter it.

In the old days, Espers were called Gods, but these days they were just called superheroes.

Jordan felt a rush of bio-electricity course out of the base of his neck, flowing in every direction, snapping through every neuron, and finally flowing out of his body to connect to the gravitons in the air. Like daggers of light, his eyes flashed gold with plasma as it spread throughout his body. As his body became his own again and was under his full control, so were the gravitons around him. Jordan snapped the gravitons under his feet, and with a single thought flicked their polarity.

In mid-air Jordan rotated ninety degrees and went from falling down the building's face to running across its face. The view itself would be surreal for most. Suddenly the world went from upright to sideways. But Jordan loved it. He had read how runners feel a certain nirvana when they're in the zone as their minds go blank, and it's just them and the road. That's what he felt every time he found himself running across the Houston metropolis.

As he ran he felt his prized gloves sliding down. He pulled them back on, tight against his knuckles. While the gloves were a bit tattered from his various vigilante volunteerism efforts, they had a special meaning in his heart. They were a birthday gift, a really expensive birthday gift. They were signed by the hero, Kinetic Jordan's idol. And written in gold ink across the back of the right hand was the phrase, "Be Your Own Hero." Jordan peered down at the phrase and felt the familiar words of encouragement flood him. He leaped across the faces of the buildings, and as cold air and city lights blasted him, he realized he had never felt more alive.

Jordan rolled his collar down and let out an exuberant shout, but his voice cracked in the middle of it. He shook it off.

Ugh, Zeus, I hope no one heard that, Jordan chided himself as he pulled his collar back up.

Jordan reached the edge of the building. He rattled the gravitons under his foot, juggling them with his mind, crushing them underfoot, snapping them to his will, until they combusted. Jordan used the controlled gravity burst to fling himself like a projectile across the street and landed mid-run along the face of another building.

He heard a pop under him and looked down. Beneath his shoes and the golden light permeating from under his heels the glass had cracked. And beneath that was a terrified woman who went from making ordinary pasta in her kitchen to seeing an unbelievable masked teenager standing on her window.

"Get out of here, you Vesper," she shouted.

"Sorry. My bad. I'm a hero," Jordan shot back.

"Get the f –" Her shout was lost in the night as Jordan sped off toward the sirens.

Collecting more gravitons under his feet, he took off, sprinting down the face of the building, careful to avoid the windows. As his own energies from his Plasma Crystal met the ambient energies of the gravitons, they sparkled like golden fireflies, briefly leaving a trail of stars in his wake. Like a parkour artist on fast-forward, Jordan leapt from building to building in a dizzying display of flips, twists, and starlight.

Graham Grey never saw himself as a criminal, but necessity and circumstances beyond his control had forced him into a life he never wanted. Nonetheless, crime was just something he was good at. Ever since the Green Night, ever since the death of most of the Olympians, ever since crime had been on the rise, he found himself fighting for more and more. It was as if the dark corners of the world and the dark corners of his mind saw the passing of the greatest heroes as a sign that they could do whatever they wanted, or needed, without fear of being stopped.

He paid no mind to the increasing internal monologue of his own guilt or to the rising sound of the cop cars closing in on him. The bags of money in hand felt lighter than he imagined. While robbing the bank was the first step, the second was just as important – getting away.

A pair of cop cars skidded to a stop at the end of the block. Graham skidded to a stop too. He whipped around and saw another pair of cop cars coming his way.

Not now. Not. Now. Graham tapped into his Plasma Crystal, felt a familiar rush of plasma coursing through his veins, then tapped into the electrons in the air, before Graham snapped his fingers and a green wave burst from his thin frame that rippled through the area. The bulbs in the streetlights swelled before popping. The batteries in the police cars whined then burst. The electronics within range creaked and moaned as the electrons inherent in their bodies were extinguished.

Jordan was mid-leap across the city when the static ended, and the voice came back clear and more urgent than before, "Calling Esper sup –" Then it went silent, just as the lights about four blocks away went dark after a flash of green. Jordan felt a chill burrow through his stomach and creep up to his chest.

*Green plasma...*Jordan privately seethed, shaking off flashbacks to the Green Night. Jordan landed hard on the top of a building. Then in a burst of gold he was back in the air and closing in.

Graham saw the flash of green, then darkness. It went from a dozen streetlights and multiple flashing police lights to just moonlight. He capitalized on the officers and their disabled cars to bolt down an alley.

However, he failed to notice the shimmering golden streak above him.

Graham, bags in hand, rushed down the alleyway only to be met by the streak of gold that was suddenly crouched at the end of the alley.

Graham sneered, "Who are you?!"

Jordan rose from the ground and stared him down. He used the first few seconds to coach up a little self-confidence: *Okay, hero pose. Be intimidating. Shoulders high, back straight, lean back, don't blink. Is that sweat? Sweat in my eye? Ow. Ow.* Jordan stood up straight and tried to make his frame look as intimidating as possible even though Graham was clearly a few inches taller than him. Graham took a few seconds to study the kid: no bodysuit, no shoulder pads, no mighty star in the middle, no worries.

"Oh, you're nothing but a kid playing dress-up," Graham chuckled. "I gotta get outta here."

Ugh, I'm out of breath too. I need something easier to breathe through...Wait, did he say something? Jordan breathed heavily behind his collar, trying to maintain good posture after running and vaulting over several city blocks.

"Out of my way," Graham shouted, obviously for the second time. Green plasma surged down from his neck to his left arm, and burst out of his palm in a pillar of sizzling viridescent energy.

Why can't they just go quietly? Jordan sighed. He exploded gravitons underfoot, throwing himself up and over the blast. Then he manipulated another set of gravitons that sent him diagonally to meet the right wall of the alley. In a third burst, he ricocheted off the right wall to land on the left. In a dizzying display of light and gravity defiance he zigzagged between the walls and brought himself face to face with Graham, fists pulled back and ready.

With no choice but to abandon their cars, the officers charged to the edge of the alleyway. Officer Jons was ahead. With his gun drawn, he led his fellow officers to the mouth of the alley, when, in a flash of golden light, Graham was vomited from the alley and sent tumbling past the officers, end over end into the street. The officers paused. Graham stopped too but that was because he was unconscious. What didn't pause were the dollar bills that had been blown into the air.

Officer Jons glanced at the nearest officer, who stammered, "I think we got our Esper backup."

Jons rounded the corner, his firearm leading the way. Jordan, with his face mask up and gold light pulsating off his body, was trying to regain composure as the bills rained down around him. Jordan didn't dare take one, no matter how much he wanted the extra cash for lunch tomorrow.

"Vigilante," Jons hissed.

Jordan nodded at him: *Yeah, you're welcome, dawg.* With a final gravity burst under his feet, Jordan turned himself into a projectile, rose high above the alley, and left the streets of Houston below.

CHAPTER THREE

Lay Down the Law

Fourth Ward was one of the many historic wards in Houston, Texas. It was near downtown and also close to the Houston Museum District. It touted the position of being trapped between the city proper and the tourist attractions. While the Bakers Apartment complex wouldn't be featured on any museum trip or brochure, it was a part of the Fourth Ward that Jordan called home.

Jordan knew it was late, and as he hopped down from an adjacent building, he earnestly hoped his sister was asleep or still on patrol. He crawled across the face of his building, using the gravitons to simultaneously pad his steps and keep him locked onto the brick face. He was thankful to find his window still open, and he ducked inside of his room. Jordan hit the bare wooden floor with a thud.

Zeus, I really need to work on that landing.

Jordan turned and closed the window behind him. As it latched closed, he felt the weight of the world leave his shoulders. Another night of heroism—or vigilantism as the law saw it—was done. Now, if only he could get some sleep before school tomorrow.

Jordan used his left toe to pry down the heel of his right sneaker to free his foot. The smell hit him, and he gasped hard. He kicked off his other shoe and flung it to the side and into the corner. Jordan then removed his prized signed gloves and slipped them back into their display case on his dresser. Also decorating his dresser were a number of collectible hero figurines including Kinetic, Lion Force, MegaTon aka the strongest hero in the US, and finally a figurine of the number one hero,

Kurikara. On the ceiling was a constellation of plastic glow-in-the-dark stars, forming the Regulus constellation, a pattern of stars that formed a lion. Jordan looked up at the lion on his ceiling. It watched over him at night, the way he saw himself looking after the city.

I'm happy I kept my collar up. If those officers had seen me, I...

Click. Suddenly the lion disappeared as the lights came on. Jordan stopped. There was an officer standing in the doorway. Jordan didn't move. The officer glared at him with scorn, her eyes focused and angry. She had brown skin – the same as Jordan's, and brown eyes – also the same color as Jordan's. She had his nose too and most of his genetics because Officer Khadija Harris was his older sister. Full-time cop, full-time sister, and right now she was going to lay the law down on him.

"And where have you been?" Khadija asked, already knowing the answer.

"Uh...out," Jordan replied softly, already knowing where this was going.

Khadija looked over his black and gold digs. It matched the black and gold outfits of various hero posters covering Jordan's walls.

"Doing..." Khadija prodded.

"Nothing," Jordan scrambled to spit the word out.

"Oh really. So the call I heard on the radio earlier about a golden Esper vigilante wasn't you? Again?" Khadija said the last word as if it burned her. Her rage was just simmering, rising slowly.

"No. No way."

She pressed harder. "They said he was 5'3."

"I'm 5'7," Jordan shot back

"Yeah, maybe after a growth spurt." She checked his shoes in the corner. "They also said he was wearing sneakers." Khadija walked over and picked them up. "Beat up, black and gold Zeuz Airwalkers to be specific."

"Okay, I can explain –" Jordan began.

Khadija threw a shoe at him and yelled, "What did I tell you?"

Jordan instinctively dodged the shoe, burst gravity under his feet, flipped and reversed his body to pin himself on the ceiling. Golden light on his heels kept the gravitons reversed and his feet stamped to the ceiling.

"Jordan Maxwell Harris, get down here," Khadija shouted up at him.

"Khadija Maxwe –" Jordan was interrupted by his second shoe sailing toward him.

"Don't make me grab a ladder and come up there." Khadija picked up his prized gloves in their protective case.

Jordan sucked in air across his teeth. "Wait, wait."

She paused.

"Those are my signed Kinetic gloves. You got those off eBay for me."

Khadija stopped and considered. "You're right, those were expensive." Khadija set them down but immediately grabbed a figure of the Olympian known as Lion Force, half man-half lion, and tossed it toward her brother.

"He's expensive too." Jordan swiveled from the ceiling in time to catch the figure and land hard on his butt. He caught the toy only to sacrifice his position of safety. It was now Khadija who looked down on him.

"What did I tell you about using your powers?" she snapped.

"I know, I shouldn't, but..."

"But what?"

"But people needed help." Jordan sighed. "There was a mugging on Highland, then a carjacking on Sanderson, then a robbery on 5th –"

"You're not helping your case, J," Khadija interrupted him. "I gave you one – one rule, J – do NOT use your powers. Don't reveal them. Don't show off. Don't use them – ever. We have police officers and professional heroes to take care of that."

Jordan had endured this before and as tired as she was repeating herself, he was tired of hearing it. He looked to the floor, to the plastic hero in his hand, and then to the scuffed oak floor he had just collapsed on.

"Do you understand me?" Jordan was silent, so she repeated louder. "I said, 'do you understand me?'"

Jordan nodded. Despite his powers, a nod felt like the only thing he could do.

"I want to hear it," Khadija continued. "If–if the police or, Zeus forbid, a real hero, catches you out here doing this vigilante mess, you're going to jail–where they'll tattoo a scarlet V on your face. Do you understand that?"

"Yes, ma'am," Jordan muttered.

Khadija took a stilted breath, looked him up and down again, and sighed. "You are my brother. I love you. You've got a Gift, but that gift comes with consequences if you abuse it."

She knelt down next to him and took his hands. Her hands in his, she shook them as if to shake life back into them. "I'm gonna need a reply, J."

"Yeah, I gotcha," he grumbled. Khadija accepted that as the best she would get for now.

"All right," Khadija continued, "now brush your teeth, take your musty behind to the shower, and get in bed." Khadija, still holding his hand, helped him stand, then patted the back of his head.

As Jordan left the room and into the hall, he heard Khadija call out, "And you better not have left this window open all night."

Jordan suppressed a yelp and dove into the bathroom.

After a brisk shower to wash away the night, Jordan found himself in bed, playing on his phone. Though the memory of Khadija's latest scolding was fresh in his mind, it also brought up other memories that were tied to it.

The first time he snuck out. The first time he was too afraid to go out and slept in his vigilante gear all night. The first time he ran home after losing a fight, and how he scrambled up the face of the building, threw himself inside, and cried. Luckily he was alone then, but more than anything that night he wished she had caught him if only to comfort him after scolding him, of course. If only she was there, or if only their parents were still with them. But their parents weren't; they were long gone. Now, they were merely names etched on the marble plaque for all Green Night mourners and rubberneckers to see. Jordan found himself flipping through his phone, found the bookmark he had saved years ago, and clicked it open to reveal the list of hundreds of people that had died that night.

Jordan stopped on a pair of names: JOHNATHAN HARRIS / JULIA HARRIS.

Then he looked from them to a photo on his dresser featuring four-year-old Jordan, his parents, and twenty-year-old Khadija. It was from a Halloween party where they were all dressed as various heroes. Though he could barely remember it, he recalled small glimpses of his parents. He could see those same similarities in Khadija: the gentle booming echo of his dad's voice, the way his mom would massage the back of his head when she carried him. All of those distant memories could be brought back but not his parents.

It was Khadija's voice and the touch on the back of his neck he remembered the most when she told him. The day after the Green Night she told him how they were caught trying to flee the fight between the Green Titan and the Olympians. They didn't make it. He had buried his head in her shoulder and cried. He wasn't sure for how long, but she had been there, holding him, reassuring him with her father's voice and her mother's touch.

Jordan held his gaze on the photo with his parents' smiling faces for a moment then turned away from them. He turned off his phone, set it down, and looked up at the Regulus constellation above him. Looking down at him was a lion comprised of the very stars that composed the universe – that composed Espers – that composed him. Jordan put a pillow over his head and fought against the faint memories of his parents and of that night. He closed his eyes, and despite his best efforts he dreamed of them.

CHAPTER FOUR

From Olympus on Down

The bell buzzed, signifying only five minutes until homeroom.

Jordan shuffled his beat-up black-and-gold Zeuz Airwalkers down the hall along with the masses of other high-schoolers. Some walked and talked while some walked and played on their phones. Others scrambled to eat breakfast as they walked. Some managed to do all of those things at once. Yet all the students worked together to form a wall Jordan couldn't pass. Jordan resisted the urge to leap over them for three main reasons.

One – Espers were forbidden to use their powers in school. Two – his sister would take his phone and ground him for life if he revealed his actual powers. And three – Jordan was honestly more scared of his sister than the law.

Jordan accepted the morning pace and made his way through the congestion. The halls of West Memorial High School were painted with various historical figures running chronologically through history. From Zeus standing on Mount Olympus to Julius Caesar glowing with light in Rome to Napoleon on a winged horse to George Washington hovering over Washington, D.C.

Jordan pushed through a throng of students and reached his locker. He twisted in the combination, opened it up, and was greeted by a parade of professional hero memorabilia. Much like his room, the door and the inside of his locker were a celebration of heroes. Most notably among them was Kinetic. Black heroes were not uncommon in the world, but Kinetic was by far the most popular. He donned a hulking

6'3 frame, bald head, with piercing eyes behind a half-mask that covered up the lower part of his face. With his muscular body and piercing stare, he didn't need much to seem intimidating. His costume was a flashy purple and gold that highlighted his stout frame.

Kinetic was known for his purple bodysuit with gold lining and a gold set of shoulder pads that rested on his bowling ball-sized shoulders. The purple plasma he exuded wafted off his body like royal flames which matched his purple bodysuit. What he lacked in stealth he made up for in color coordination. Then again, at 6'3 and 280 pounds of muscle, stealth was hardly worth considering.

Pictures of Kinetic in various action poses and in the midst of battle surrounded by purple plasma decorated Jordan's locker like a collage. Most of the photos featured him throwing a torpedo-like knee into an unfortunate opponent. His Gift allowed him to charge kinetic energy behind his blows, so taking a knee from him was, in fact, like taking a torpedo to the chest. This attack was later coined the "Impact Knee" by the press and fans alike. While Jordan considered bringing his signed gloves, he didn't want to risk them being stolen. As Jordan grabbed his first set of books for homeroom, he was greeted by Nathan, who had the locker under him. Jordan heard him coming before he saw him. Nathan walked with the use of elbow crutches that made a distinct click as they moved. His crutches were decorated with stickers of various professional heroes and heroic organizations.

"Jordan, what's up?" Nathan asked as he pushed in beside Jordan.

"Chillin', man. What's good?" Jordan responded as he finished taking his books out of their locker.

"Dude, guess what I got," Nathan countered.

Though Jordan was exhausted from last night's adventures, he was suddenly spiked with energy.

"No way...You got it?"

Nathan adjusted his backpack around his crutches as he talked. "It came in the mail last night."

Jordan could barely compress his shout of delight. "Lemme see. Lemme see."

Nathan reached into his backpack and gently retrieved a Kinetic action figure still in its box.

"Yoooo," Jordan called out, forgetting those around them, even as his peers rolled their eyes at his childish outburst. Jordan went into overdrive, looking at every inch of the figure.

"It's a first edition Golden Age Kinetic," Nathan rattled off. "Sixth scale. Fully posable. With twenty points of articulated detail."

Jordan gawked and repeated the facts as if in a trance, "Sixth scale, posable, twenty points. And heads. He comes with different heads." Jordan mentally compared this epic find to the all-too-familiar posters and memorabilia that colored his life.

"Look at that face," Jordan exclaimed. "They got the eyebrows just right – and the scar. He's even got the scar over the left ear he got from the Battle of Detroit, when he fought Typhon. The attention to detail. The purple plasma glowing around him. You can even pose him doing the Impact Knee."

Nathan chimed in. "It comes with two heads and two sets of arms for when he's using his kinetic manipulation." Jordan looked inside the box and indeed, a set of plastic molded to mimic purple plasma flames was inside, which matched the same lavender aura in the photos.

"I'm gonna show it off today at the club," Nathan chimed, "but I wanted you to see it fir–"

THUMP. Nathan was suddenly bumped from behind, and the box went flying. Jordan caught Nathan and steadied him before he could fall. Even though they both suspected, they both turned to confirm that it was Trevor. Trevor was a student-athlete, meaning he was part-student, part-linebacker, and full-time Vesper to kids like Jordan and Nathan.

"Oops," Trevor said with sarcasm.

Trevor kicked the box down the hall where it flipped and slid under the feet of marching students.

"Hey," Nathan called out.

Jordan paid Trevor no mind and went after the box. "I'll get it. Don't worry about it."

Jordan pushed past the students and made his way over to the box. It was certainly not in mint condition now. One of the cardboard corners was ripped open, another corner was dented, and the protective plastic film was warped. Jordan reached down to pick it up when Trevor's foot came down hard on top of Jordan's hand.

"Trev, c'mon. Let me go," Jordan snarled.

"What do you say?" Trevor teased.

Jordan bit his lip, not wanting to play his game but also not wanting to risk damaging his friend's new figurine. As Trevor leaned down on Jordan's hand, Jordan could feel the cardboard and plastic giving under his palm.

"Please," Jordan spat out, hating every letter and syllable of it. Trevor took in the eyes watching them and smiled, enjoying his victory. Jordan looked down, not wanting to see the judgment.

"Say..." Trevor paused, "I'm a cape-dragger."

Jordan's ears burned with embarrassment. The word cape-dragger was a play-off of the phrase "knuckle-dragger." While "knuckle-dragger" related to primitive humans, "cape-dragger" was an insult for Espers, referring to the humans who would cling onto the capes of Espers; in other words, you were just a wannabe hero, a fake, a person who only brought the real heroes down.

Jordan fought the urge to activate his plasma. It was like pushing against the tide. He could feel the energy coursing through him at the impulse to make Trevor pay. Jordan bit his cheek and fought like Hades to keep his composure.

"I'm – I'm not saying–" Jordan stammered over his words. They were caught in his throat, which had gone dry from humiliation when Trevor activated his own plasma, which was seafoam green. Jordan could sense it like a current of electricity when the two tapped into each other for an instant.

Trevor sent plasma down to his foot, increasing the density and strength. The box flattened under Jordan's hand, and Jordan gritted his teeth, trying to simultaneously protect Nathan's action figure and his own hand from being broken.

"Say it," Trevor sneered. Jordan looked down at the figure and the stone-cold eyes of Kinetic looked up at him and seemingly admonished him for his weakness. He was no hero. Just like Khadija said, just like he heard the police say last night after stopping Graham, just as Trevor stood over him now – he wasn't like Kinetic at all. Jordan for all intents and purposes was...

"I'm a cape-dragger," Jordan admitted.

Trevor scoffed at him, enjoying the confession. The sound of a teacher's voice echoed from the depths of the hall, "Hey, hey, get to class. What's going on?"

"See ya, dragger," Trevor smirked, retracted his plasma, and headed to class behind his friends.

Jordan cradled the flattened box holding Kinetic, much like his own fragile self-esteem. He gathered himself as best he could. Nathan as fast as his crutches could carry walked over to Jordan.

"Hey, man..." Nathan tentatively approached.

"Sorry, I thought I could help," Jordan sulked.

"It's fine, it's just a toy. The box is ruined, but my parents didn't pay 500 dollars for a box, right?"

Jordan quietly looked at the floor.

"J, it's fine," Nathan added.

"Yeah," Jordan whispered, more as a conclusion, and less of an agreement. "C'mon, let's just get to class."

Thankfully, the day passed quickly and without further incident. Soon Nathan and Jordan found themselves amongst like-minded hero fans in the art room. It was an after-school club where fans of heroes came to talk, admire, and trade everything hero-related. Two dozen teens were gathered in the room and sitting at desks in clusters of different conversations.

Nathan took front and center of the classroom, and despite his small frame he managed to silence everyone with a, "Yo, yo, shut up and welcome." The teens quieted down and faced him.

"I hereby call this meeting of the Esper Heroes Club to order," Nathan continued. "I've got a limited edition Kinetic figure to show off later, but I thought we'd start with watching a video Jeremy made. It's a project he did for history last year that he eventually dropped online and it's getting a lot of views. So, I figured we'd do our part to watch it, give him some views if that's cool with y'all?"

The group murmured in agreement, and Nathan nodded to Jeremy, who was standing by his laptop. "All right, Jeremy, you're good."

One student used her Esper powers. After she snapped her fingers at the light switch, the switch flipped, and the lights went off. Jeremy used the remote to bring the projector to life. Nathan squinted in the glare of the lights. "Wait, wait, lemme move before I'm blind too."

Nathan scurried out of the way of the light and took a seat next to Jordan. For a second nothing happened as the screen went from blue to black.

Then a voice cut in behind the darkness. It was clearly a teenage boy's voice mimicking an adult. Everyone quickly recognized the familiar voice as Jeremy's.

"Long ago..." his voice cracked hard. He paused, cleared it with a rolling cough, and tried again. "Sorry. Long ago, when man was first born, he, like humans, was made of trace amounts of stardust."

The black screen was suddenly filled with glowing white lights, like stars in the night. The stars then coalesced around each other and took a crystalline form. Jeremy continued, "But a select few were born with an extraordinary amount of stardust. This material gathered in a crystal in the base of their necks and gave them powers beyond the normal man. They were called Espers."

The screen pulled back from the crystal to show the cartoon outline of a man, with the crystal embedded in his neck. The man glowed and flexed light off his body.

"I drew that for him," Nathan called out. The teens snickered at the crude drawing. "I know you love it," Nathan added.

Jeremy hushed Nathan then turned up the volume on his own voice as the video continued.

"Espers are able to utilize the powers of the stardust to activate their Gift and perform a number of abilities." The cartoon outline imitated throwing a thunderbolt, and as it did his illustration morphed into Zeus throwing a bolt of lightning.

"The first Espers were Zeus and the Olympians." Zeus and the Olympians appeared on screen, standing together on Mount Olympus. "Then their kids were born, Ares, Hermes, and most famous of all Hercules." There was a round of light applause from the teens as a drawing of Hercules appeared on screen. He was shown battling a number of foes with his super strength, finally leading to him wrestling the Nemean Lion and killing it.

"Hercules," Jeremy continued, "used his Gift to perform a number of legendary feats, including slaying the Nemean Lion. In short, this Esper was the first professional superhero." The image of Hercules wearing the Nemean Lion's skin as a throw transformed into a man wearing a cape overlooking the city. The lion's golden fur seemingly melted into the trademark golden armor sitting over the hero's skin-tight bodysuit, and the crossed paws of the lion became the star emblazoned on the suit's chest.

"Espers and humans still co-exist today, and we humans are grateful for those Espers who shaped society for the better. George Washington, Kinetic, Joan of Arc, and yes – even the legendary seven Olympians who fought on the Green Night." On-screen, there was a flash of green light, and the footage jumped into grainy news footage from that fateful night ten years ago. Within the chaos of Houston, the seven Olympians fought against the Green Titan. Each of the seven shined with different plasma colors as they swarmed around the Green Titan, who released an artillery of green beams that split Houston asunder.

Jordan flinched as he watched the video of a building topple in the distance. Rolling clouds of fire and smoke washed over the battlefield where the Olympians continued the battle against the Green Titan. A gulf of despair crushed down on his shoulders and swallowed him just as the rolling clouds of destruction rolled through that night. Jordan looked away as another building fell in the distance.

Jordan had long wrestled with anxiety. He saw it as an invisible monster with a hundred hands trying to wad him into a ball. Even now he felt it pin his breath to his lungs with one arm, nestle and twist his throat in the vise of his other arm, while the other ninety-eight arms fought to take his legs out from under him. Jordan wished his own control over gravitons could free him from this grip.

"That night, the seven strongest heroes in the world came together to prevent a calamity. Seven walked in, but only two walked out," Jeremy narrated as the footage cut to two injured men stumbling out of the fray.

They were swarmed by doctors and medics who attended to them and peppered them with questions. The larger of the two men was Titanus, who had bushy blue hair and strong Viking features: a face that saw one too many battles, a body honed by war, and the type of circles under his eyes that came from one too many difficult choices. The smaller man, known as Red Wing, had one arm and leather-like skin. He looked like he was made in a lab to be a quintessential Texan. He could have been a true cowboy in another life with that permanent tan and an admirable swagger. He had the lean body of a runner and beard stubble that framed his sunbaked face and trailed down his neck.

"Titanus and Red Wing were the only survivors. For a while, it seemed there were no more heroes – until other Espers stepped up to the plate, including Kinetic." To another round of applause from the teens, Kinetic appeared on screen, stopping a runaway car by throwing his knee into it. As the car made impact with his hands, kinetic energy in the form of purple light rushed down his arms and into his knee, which he drove into the front of the vehicle, smashing it to a halt. "And the number one hero...Kurikara of Japan." Footage featuring a golden figure walking calmly out of a flaming building followed. The teens gleefully cheered at the footage.

"Like their ancestors before them, they fight villainous Vespers and continue to make society a better place." The video concluded with pictures of Zeus descending from Mount Olympus. Then it panned to Hercules wearing the Nemean Lion as a cloak right before showing

George Washington's own cloak flying behind him as he flew across the Delaware River. It panned to the Olympians battling the Green Titan then finally to Kinetic and a host of other heroes whose faces were obscured by the half masks. The video ended, and the group hooted and hollered.

Jordan applauded lightly. His own fears and pain from last night, and his loss from ten years ago, flooded back into him. He felt his chest tighten and at least a hundred hands pressing down on his shoulders.

"Thanks, Jeremy," Nathan said. "You've got how many views now?"

"Going on three million," Jeremy announced proudly.

"Well, three million and one now, thanks to us," Nathan chimed. "Thanks for sharing. And next up is my – oh no." Nathan looked around frantically, before revealing, "My Kinetic. It's in my locker. I'll be back."

Jordan took this chance to put some distance between himself and the painful reminder of the past. He shot up out of his seat. "I'll go with you," he said. Nathan gave Jordan a knowing look and waited for him to follow.

Once out in the hallway, the friends walked in uncomfortable silence for a beat. Nathan was unsure how to proceed. Jordan wanted only to catch his breath and clear his mind. Nathan blurted out bluntly, "You know I don't need your help, right?"

After a pause Jordan replied, "Yeah, I just –" He paused again. "I just needed to get out."

Nathan studied Jordan for a beat, then nodded in understanding. "I – I noticed."

Jordan risked a glance his way, and Nathan returned it with a kind smile.

"I sort of felt the same way, you know? I saw my apartment go up in the flames in that video and uh –"

"I couldn't breathe back there." The words were out of Jordan's mouth before he could catch them. Like a painful memory thrashing loose it just slipped and spilled out.

"I get it," Nathan said softly. "When I saw it, the weirdest thing happened. I felt a pain in my legs. Like...I guess it's a type of phantom pain, you know?"

Jordan nodded without looking his way. "Yeah, I've heard of it."

Nathan nodded too. "I broke my leg in four places that night and – yeah, it sucked."

"I still think about my parents, you know? I think about 'em every day. Every time I see that footage I wonder how I could have saved them if I had been there." Jordan struggled behind a lump in his throat.

Nathan put a hand on his shoulder to comfort him. "We were kids, man. There was nothing we could have done."

Jordan nodded. "Yeah."

"C'mon, let's get Kinetic and make some people jealous," Nathan joked.

Nathan limped off. Jordan paused for a beat, calming himself, collecting himself, and coiling his emotions back underfoot. He exhaled to decompress then went after Nathan. As he did, he passed by a painting of the planet Earth, with murals of the seven Olympians surrounding it.

"Calling all cars. Calling all cars."
- Emergency Dispatcher

CHAPTER FIVE

The Thieves

That night, like many others, Jordan found himself simply floating.

It was a technique he learned years ago when he felt his chest tightening, his breathing short, and his mind too focused on the past. After his parents passed and his sister took up more patrols on the police force, he often found himself alone. In the quiet of the night his thoughts and past traumas swirled without mercy, so he had to find a way to quiet the noise – to fill the void. It allowed him to stretch, to be limber, to unfurl his limbs and his body and breathe easier. Up high in his room, floating, seemed to be one place where the hundred arms of his anxiety could not reach him.

Jordan found that freeing his plasma that was naturally attuned to the gravitons in the air allowed him to drift. By tapping into his Plasma Crystal, letting it freely disperse plasma into his veins and into the area around him, he could let go of what held him down, literally and figuratively. As his plasma reached out to touch the world around him, it mingled with the ambient energies and produced tiny golden lights that danced around him like fireflies in slow motion.

The second part was just as important, and this was blocking out the noise – or the static storm of silence. To block out the noise of his own mind and the noises from just outside his window he'd plug in his headphones and simply listen to music. Lo-fi Hip Hop was his favorite – an ambient noise, with a drum beat and soft repetitive chimes.

He breathed in tune with the chime. It helped regulate his breathing. An absence of breath was always the first sign that the multi-armed monster within Jordan was near. A short gasp, a twist in his chest, the thump under his collar bone, and a series of over-bearing triggers sent it climbing hand over fist to reach him.

As he drifted alone in his room, Jordan rose until he was face to face with the ceiling and seemingly within the safety of the Regulus constellation. The lion of his night, the lion of his stars, the thing that seemed to help always keep the monster at bay when his thoughts had roamed too far, stood guard. The collection of plastic glow-in-the-dark stars and glow-in-the-dark ink on his ceiling was a project he and his parents did long ago. While much in his room had changed over ten years, this was one decoration he chose to never replace. It was their sign to him that, just like the stars, they were watching over him.

Jordan let his plasma flow, let the music buoy his thoughts as he slipped free from the bonds of Earth and man. He drifted much like how people enjoyed simply drifting in a pool or down a river. It was his own form of relief, but he was jarred from his refuge as – THUMP.

Of course Jordan could only float about eight feet in the air before he thumped his head against the ceiling. His concentration broke; the golden lights in the room evaporated, and gravity came rushing back. Jordan landed hard on his butt. "Ow," he groaned as his headphones dropped out of his ears.

As the music drifted away, Jordan heard a familiar static filling the void. He rolled over and listened to a voice from under his bed. Jordan crept closer and pulled out a shoebox where he had stashed his police radio, a special set of wireless headphones he had tuned to tap into the local police dispatch.

From the cloud of static a voice rang out, "Calling all cars. Calling all cars." Quickly huddling himself on the floor, Jordan picked it up to listen in. He strained to hear. The voice returned, "We have Vespers on site. Requesting Esper support."

Jordan wrestled with the request in his mind. Then sirens began to echo in the distance. He didn't take their wails as a warning but as a cry for help. Moving with an urgency that seemed born within him, Jordan began throwing on his vigilante garb.

Bounding across the Houston rooftops, Jordan was like a gymnast, and every roof was his springboard. After about two years of on and off practice, he had trained his muscles and plasma to time the gravity burst and charge at the point of impact. As his toe hit the roof, plasma gathered together and shook the gravitons under the soles of his feet. By the time his heel came down, those gravitons exploded in a series of golden dots of plasma that sent him vaulting into another graceful leap. When he first attempted this, he accidentally launched himself up and over a series of rooftops. Thankfully, practice makes perfect.

As Jordan sprung across the rooftops, his body moved with muscle memory and created adequate room in his head to dissect the situation.

Sounded like a robbery. If I can get there before the police do, that'll be much easier to deal with. Then another thought entered his mind that gave him a bit of a chill. *And if I can get back home before Khadija comes back, that'll be much easier to deal with too.*

The police radio made a garbled noise, before coming through again. "Alarms activated at the Contemporary Arts Museum. Esper backup is inbound."

Inbound? Jordan shivered. *A real hero. A real Esper is on the way. Let's get to work.*

Jordan felt his precious gloves slip a bit, but he yanked them back down over his hands, took a glance at "Be Your Own Hero," and decided to follow the advice of that great hero that came before him. Jordan spiraled in his eagerness to run, burst off the edge of a building, and glided into the night towards the sirens in the distance.

While the Contemporary Arts Museum of Houston housed a record number of art exhibits, the building itself was a work of art. The stout, rectangular building with its large silver face reflected the sun during the day and the moonlight at night. The building's design and appearance were a monument to contemporary metal works. A single slab of metal ran from the roof all the way down to the main entrance.

But Jordan wasn't concerned with the main entrance. He was focused on the rooftop entrance. In a trail of glittering plasma he landed on the roof. He took in a greedy breath to satiate his lungs, but he needed more. Jordan pulled his turtleneck collar down, took his hood off, and took deeper breaths.

I gotta work on my cardio game, Jordan whispered to himself, then rushed to the rooftop exit door and tried the handle. Locked. Jordan tapped into his Plasma Crystal and sent sun-gold plasma to his gloved hand. The plasma swam under his skin, filling his muscles and tendons with an added density. In one motion Jordan crushed the door lock while shouldering the metal door open. The lock crumbled in his palm, and the door popped open. Jordan recalled his plasma then crept inside.

The museum was a spacious one-floor facility that was built with a labyrinth of white walls. Seemingly an open-faced maze, each wall was adorned with art, and each of the art-laden walls hugged various sculptures and free-standing designs. However, Jordan didn't care about the art. His primary focus was on not getting trapped or caught inside the building once the police, or−worse−the professional hero showed up. Jordan took a staircase from the roof down to the main floor where he entered the museum proper. Gathering gravitons under his feet and keeping them steady, he was able to quiet his footfalls to keep his presence unknown. While he could pad the sound of his feet, Jordan struggled to will his heart from beating so loudly. He could feel the pressure through his chest and hear drumming in his ears. He was half-certain the police could pick it up on their radios. Jordan stalked down the aisles of art and paused as he rounded a corner and exhaled in a whisper.

There they were. Two hooded individuals in black robes. Both wore porcelain masks with gold accents. The taller of the two, certainly a man judging by the frame, wore a mask that featured a beard and an expression of anguish with streaks of gold tears running down its porcelain face. The smaller of the two−maybe a man, maybe a woman−wore a bird mask with gold designs sifting across its pale face as the moonlight drifted past their hood.

Jordan's heart stopped in his chest. While the smaller one acted as a lookout, the taller one used superheated plasma from his fingertips to burn through a metal statue of Titanus. The mighty hero's face was solemn as the thieves smelted through his chest where an opaque jewel sat in wait.

Okay, okay. Do I warn them? Do I just jump in? What do –?

Suddenly, the device in his ear jumped to life and called out, "Esper is inbound. I repeat. Esper is inbound." Jordan eeked and slapped his hand to his ear to muffle the sound. By the time he looked back up, the pair was gone. The statue was left relatively untouched except for the smoky tendril rising from its chest.

"Where?" Jordan whispered to himself. "Where did th–"

Jordan was unable to finish that thought as an authoritative male voice called out from the darkness, "Now."

Suddenly, from Jordan's blind spot, the smaller one with the Nightingale bird mask lunged at him. Startling olive green eyes flashed behind the ornate mask. Jordan saw the green light first, and then his mind dipped back to the horrors of the Green Night, but he rebounded to reality quickly this time and knew he was about to be clobbered.

Jordan threw his arms up making an X and sent plasma rippling into his crossed forearms. Just as he did, Nightingale's punch connected. The plasma-packed punch met a plasma-backed defense. Even though Jordan blocked it, he was still knocked off his feet. Jordan sent plasma to his back to pad the impact and landed hard. His muscles complained, but it was better than bruising his shoulder blades. Jordan used the momentum to carry himself into a roll, rolled up to one knee, and–

Nightingale was already on him, throwing a roundhouse kick.

Jordan ducked, and the kick whooshed over him. The very air vibrated from the plasma packed into the effort. Nightingale's direction and momentum carried them awkwardly into a wall where they slammed leg first. From under their black cloak a gold square clattered free and onto the floor. Jordan didn't think twice before he snatched it up in his loosely gloved hand. But, before he had a chance to inspect it, Goldtears rumbled, "Get down."

Jordan whipped around to see Goldtears' body and cloak being lifted by unseen energy currents of plasma. Red lights danced off his frame and reflected off his mask as his crimson plasma ignited and rushed to his gloved hands. Light-daggers of red plasma sparked in Goldtears' eyes before he clapped his hands, and Jordan's eyes went wide.

As Goldtears packed red plasma into his palms and slammed them together, it released visible cerise shockwaves that tore across the room. Jordan had heard of people seeing music and hearing environmental tremors, but he had never had this experience personally. Plaster cracked. Glass shattered. The ground was torn up as a wave of debris and a torrent of trembling light slammed into Jordan. Like being caught in the riptide of a river Jordan was swept up and hurled like a ragdoll right into a wall.

The next thing Jordan knew he could hear Goldtears barking orders, "We gotta go. He's coming." Jordan tried to shake the ringing from his ears. *Who? Who's coming?*

Nightingale's voice came through, muffled under the ringing in Jordan's ears, "But what about the...?!"

"Forget it," Goldtears shot back. "There will be more."

Suddenly, the room quaked and something shattered from above as a hulking figure stormed from the roof and plummeted into the museum. Jordan quelled the shock and cleared his eyes. He had to blink once, then twice, then a third time to grasp the situation.

Am I – am I seeing double? Jordan asked himself.

He rubbed his eyes in disbelief, but he was sure of it. There were two of Titanus standing before him.

It wasn't until his eyes readjusted to the gloom and moonlight, that it became clear. The real Titanus was standing before him, with Titanus' smoking statue hulking above him. Jordan felt his breath catch in his throat.

It was unmistakable, the blue bodysuit with silver accents compressed the bulky, large frame. Heavy chrome shoulder pads complete with the silver star in the middle complemented the entire ensemble.

The pads framed his shoulders, his neck, and then slid up into a silver wall over his mouth and nose. Only those beady laser-focused black eyes and that mane of unruly blue hair were visible, but that was all Jordan needed to see to know exactly who had just dropped in.

"Titanus," Jordan whispered.

"Freeze." Titanus' words thundered through the museum.

Jordan didn't move. He didn't blink. He didn't even breathe. He wasn't sure if Titanus was talking to him or had even seen him yet for that matter, but he wasn't going to chance it.

Goldtears whipped around to face Titanus, while ordering Nightingale, "Go." Red plasma flickered off his right shoulder, ran down his arm, and into his ample fist, which he drove into the ground. The plasma-packed punch hit the ground like a pile-driver. Chunks of concrete were blown into the air creating a temporary wall of debris, then it was carried by the augmented shockwaves right at Titanus – and Jordan who was cowering to his right. Blue light flared off Titanus' body, and Jordan knew what was coming even though he had never been eye witness to it. From the news, the trading card stats, and the video games, Jordan knew what Titanus would do, but it still shocked the daylights out of him to experience it.

Blue energy burst off of Titanus' massive frame and coated his body like a second skin. His aura ballooned into a massive humanoid shape that made Goliath look like David. Titanus' Esper ability wasn't just a force field but a mountain of power whose appearance was that of a demonic force. An exoskeleton with fanged teeth, a twisted face, wild blue hair, empty eyes, and the ability to block out the sun – Titanus' goliath force field materialized in an instant around him, and in the next instant he threw a punch from an arm the size of a California redwood tree. While Titanus' own arm was only two feet long, the exoskeleton that emanated from him had a reach of seven feet that sent its blue pillar forward, smashing through the wave of fragments. Jordan huddled down as the two energies met and debris flew. Clouds of pancaked concrete exploded around him.

Jordan coughed and closed his eyes, trying to keep the dust from interfering with his senses, but it was too much. He rolled back to his feet and stepped out of the cloud. As the dust settled, the pair of criminals disappeared. Titanus simmered and then allowed his goliath force field to disperse into light blue drops of light. His eyes scanned the area once more, not finding the thieves, but landing on Jordan.

Jordan froze. *Oh, no.* Titanus took two towering steps towards him, like Zeus stepping down from Mount Olympus. His stature was that of a God amongst men, an immortal amongst mortals, a professional hero amongst vigilantes. Jordan backed up as those hard, black eyes latched onto him.

"I'm not with them. I'm a vigilante," Jordan spat out quickly. He reached into his pocket to grab the gold square Nightingale had dropped. Titanus' eyes flashed blue as he studied the trembling kid. "Please, one of them dropped..."

"Freeze." There was another commotion from the museum entrance as the police officers filed in, guns drawn. Titanus raised his arm to them, projected only the arm of the blue creature that lived within him, and blocked the officers from himself and Jordan.

"Don't fire," Titanus commanded.

Jordan offered him the golden plate from his pocket. Only now in the moonlight – and not in the chaos of the fight – was he able to recognize it. The plate was adorned with a bull framed by a star on the front. Jordan tossed it to Titanus, who caught it with his own hand. His wise eyes looked down at the plaque, his expression unreadable but clearly keeping Jordan's movement in check while examining the new evidence. It all led to two words from behind his mask. "Arrest him."

At that command, a terrible sunken feeling punched Jordan in the gut. He felt dizzy and his legs nearly failed him. Titanus' goliath arm disappeared and allowed the officers to come running at him. Jordan froze for a beat. *What? No. I – I came here to help. I – No. No. No.*

"Stop. Wait. I'm on your side. I'm a vigilante," Jordan pleaded in a rush of words and emotion.

Titanus turned away from Jordan. "Exactly."

The cops mobbed Jordan. He backed away like a caged animal, then he spotted the shattered skylight that Titanus had plunged through earlier. It was high, but he was certain with a gravity burst that he could clear it.

No time for any calculations. Let's go. Jordan tapped into his crystal.

His body rippled with gold pulses before he commanded a torrent of gravitons under his feet, launching himself upward. He gripped his gloved hands into fists, making sure not to let the gloves fly off in his launch – the last thing Jordan wanted to do was leave more evidence.

I got this, Jordan thought as he gritted his teeth. *If I can just...*

Suddenly, a current of electricity ran through Jordan like a lightning rod, seemingly coming from nowhere and everywhere at the same time. Jordan felt his spine go rigid, his arms go soft, and a spike of energy punched the back of his skull. His body went limp, and he fell backwards. As he turned, he saw Titanus scowling at him with blue energy crackling behind his eyes.

What – what did he do? were Jordan's final thoughts as he fell back to the museum floor. At that moment, he fixated on the broken skylight above –the stars, the night, and his last chance at freedom.

He hit the ground, and the officers swarmed.

CLAYTON ASIMOV

Hero Alias: Titanus

Height: 6'3

Weight: 275

Birth Date: January 21

Plasma Color: Blue

Plasma Level: 100,000

Gift: Clayton possesses the ability to create a plasma based exoskeleton around himself. Its shape and face are conjured by his inner ID; a physical manifestation of his own interpersonal demons. The size and shape of his exoskeleton are only matched by his plasma level.

CHAPTER SIX

Lay Down the Law [The Blue Giant Remix]

Jordan slowly came back to reality, like a swimmer clawing to the surface from the depths of the ocean. The lights grew a bit brighter. His vision a bit sharper. The sounds became a bit clearer – and there was something familiar, as if someone was calling his name from inside a cave. Jordan could sense he was upright, so he must be in a chair of some sort.

He tried to move his arms. Couldn't.

He tried to tap into his plasma. Couldn't.

Then came that voice again, distant, but close to his heart. "J? J, can you hear me?" This time the voice came clearly and roused him from his slumber. He cracked one eye open, squinted under the lights. The room was lit by a pair of halogen bulbs that ran along the cracked grey plaster ceiling. The smell of the place carried with it a hint of mold and stale coffee.

Khadija sat across from him. Jordan pulled himself up with great effort from the scarred metal table. He blinked again as his sister's face came into focus. She rushed over and hugged him. Khadija held him close, but he could feel her trembling. Jordan knew this feeling well, it was the juxtaposition of her caring and her concern. It was the same type of hug she gave him the day after the Green Night. It was equal parts tranquility and anxiety. She held him as if he might slip away from her. She was afraid and hiding it behind a hug.

"Jordan, can you hear me?" From her tone, he could tell she had skipped anger and was in a different state. This tone was yet another reminder of that tragic night. It was only now that Jordan realized two things simultaneously: One, he was handcuffed to the table, and two, Khadija was wearing her officer's uniform. Jordan put them together and realized –

"We're at the police station," she whispered. "They called me in after they ran your ID."

Jordan could only utter one word, and it was a struggle to push it out, "What?"

"You really messed up this time," Khadija said, the words carrying anguish that caused his stomach to drop.

Jordan tried to adjust his cuffs, but they clinked against the table. It was only now that he realized his gloves were gone. His hands looked so much smaller than he recalled, as they were dwarfed by the size of the handcuffs.

"Adamant," she warned.

Jordan nodded. He had always heard of professional heroes using adamant cuffs on Vespers, but this was his first time in them. Adamant cuffs were made from a metal famous for negating the flow of plasma. Jordan tapped into his plasma and – nothing – then a sharp pain cut through the base of his skull! Jordan gagged and dropped his head to the table.

Khadija came around the table and grazed the back of his head.

"I know, I know, it hurts," she whispered. "You can't use your plasma in these cuffs."

"I'm sorry." Jordan shuddered, unable to look her in the eyes. "I'm sorry."

Khadija backed up from him and wiped her runny nose with the back of her hand. She trembled for a beat. This, this exact scene, had been her nightmare for years, and now that it was reality, she had little to no idea of how to handle it. "I told you, again and again, to cut this vigilante stuff out. I told you not to use your powers, and now look at you," Khadija pleaded wearily.

"I just," Jordan struggled to find the words. "I just wanted to help."

"Well, look where it got you," Khadija replied. "You're not a hero; you're a kid."

The words cut through him deeper than they had before. Jordan wasn't sure if it was the fact that he was cuffed in a police station or that he was unable to tap into his plasma, or a combination—but her words resonated with the emptiness that echoed from his powerlessness.

"I called your uncle," Khadija admitted.

"Darius?" Jordan said the name like a question since it had been so long since he had seen or even spoken of him.

"He's the only lawyer we know, so..." Khadija nodded and then followed up with, "He's on his way. He should be here any minute."

Jordan nodded, then picking over the other few facts he knew about Darius, he asked, "Wait, you still had his number after all this ti—"

Before Jordan could finish, the door gave an audible click at the release of the locking mechanism. Titanus stepped into the interview room and filled it with his intimidating mass. In the glaring light and close quarters, Jordan had the opportunity to scrutinize this legendary hero. His eyes were sunken pools that were tainted with too many long nights and too much knowledge. His face was a map of scars and lines that framed those tired eyes. In truth, seeing him walk and stand before them, Titanus gave the appearance of an old heavyweight boxer. The years had clearly done a number on him, and in the proximity of Jordan and behind closed doors, the hero's age and diminished posture showed.

"Sir, I'm sorry," Khadija pleaded.

He responded flatly, "This is your brother?" Titanus' voice was familiar to Jordan from video games, commercials, and various clips about Esper service. It was hoarse with age and war as if he had just left a battlefield where he had been shouting orders.

"Yes," she replied, "and I swear on my badge, he's never been in trouble."

Titanus took the moment to really examine Jordan; under that aged and scarred scowl were a pair of calculating eyes.

I – I should say something. Jordan's thoughts scrambled. *I should at least apologize.*

"Sir." He opened his mouth, but it was dry. "I'm only 14, I prom—"

"Did I ask you a question?" Titanus boomed from behind his face-plate.

Jordan closed his mouth, swallowed hard, and shrunk backward against the hard plastic yellow chair.

"Officer," Titanus ordered, "give us the room."

Khadija looked from Titanus to Jordan, then back to Titanus. She opened her mouth to reply, but Titanus' faceplate cracked down to reveal his full scarred visage, and it silenced her immediately.

"Give us *the room*," Titanus ordered.

She turned to him and said, "Jordan. I'll be back. Okay? I'll be right back." Khadija gave Titanus a once-over to communicate *We're not finished.* She stormed out and slammed the door behind her. Jordan jumped at the bang; Titanus did not.

While Jordan had seen Titanus' full face on TV numerous times, this was one of the first times he saw it up close. He was certainly built for combat. However, his face, with the deep underlying circles, the slight hunch in his shoulders, and the scar tissue decorating it told Jordan a story of just how he had aged over time. Some heroes let their faces and even their identities be known to the public, but those were few and far between. When you're Titanus and one of two surviving members of the Olympians, your identity was known world-wide – the face mask was purely for aesthetics.

"Who do you work for?" Titanus asked. He didn't sit; he just stood and towered over him.

"No-no one? I'm-I'm a student," Jordan answered with nervous energy.

"Where? Fort Olympus? Artemis High?"

"No. No. I don't go to a hero school. I-I-" Jordan's voice broke for a moment, and he hesitated, "My sister has me going to a public school-she-she wanted me to hide my Gift."

If this changed anything for Titanus, it was hard to tell. Though his face was mapped with marks and trails, it was unreadable. "What were you doing at the museum?"

The truth. Just keep giving him the truth, Jordan told himself.

"I heard they needed help," Jordan answered with more confidence harnessed.

"You heard about a robbery, and you came running?"

Jordan attempted to nod, but Titanus barked, "I need a verbal confirmation."

"Yes." Jordan's voice cracked mid-way, so he repeated it louder, "Yes, sir."

"Without a hero permit?"

Jordan paused. He knew where this was going.

"Without a hero permit?" Titanus asked the question like an accusation.

The truth. Just tell 'im the truth. Jordan shivered under his gaze, the chains rattling against the table.

"You know it's illegal to lie to a licensed hero in the midst of an investigation, correct?"

Jordan was about to nod. Instead, he answered with a soft "yes," his momentary rally of spirit crushed by Titanus' demands.

"And you know Espers aren't allowed to participate in hero activities without a permit?"

"I'm sorry, sir," Jordan mumbled. "I am, but—"

"But what? There is no but. That is the law, and it does not carry any substitutions."

Tell 'im the truth, J. Just tell him why you were there. Jordan steeled himself and fought against every urge to bury the truth. *Tell 'im why you wanted to be a hero – like him.*

"I–If–If –I," Jordan struggled to find the words. Then they spilled out, "Sir, if I have a Gift-If I have a Gift and I've got the power to save people, I'm not going to just sit by and let people get hurt. I can't. It just isn't in me to run from danger." If the words had reached him, Jordan was unsure. He felt like he was talking to a brick wall that simply recited the law and didn't bend from it.

Titanus reached into his pocket and pulled out the golden square Jordan gave him earlier. "Do you know what this is?" he asked.

He placed it on the table, and Jordan was able to see it clearly. Indeed, there was a bull embossed on the front, as if was some sort of art or jewelry. Before Jordan could answer, the door opened, and Darius joined them.

It had been years since Jordan had seen Darius, though Jordan had not forgotten how tall he was. He looked more like a bouncer or professional wrestler than a lawyer. In fact, the last time Jordan saw him was at his parents' funeral over 10 years ago. Darius looked like he had been chiseled out of stone, then draped with fine linen. He was as broad as he was tall, and it made it difficult for him to blend in, so he embraced it and dressed in fine suits. Tonight's suit was a burnt yellow, double-breasted, three-piece suit tailored perfectly.

"Uncle Darius?" Jordan asked.

"By Odin's beard..." Titanus, for the first time all night, faltered. "What are you doing here?"

Jordan caught the tone of Titanus' voice. *Wait? Do they know each other?*

Darius was bald, yet his chin and neck were home to a finely sculpted full beard. "He's my nephew," Darius declared.

This news reached Titanus, who absorbed it like a tremor. His expression faltered, and he smirked, which was unnatural on his hardened face. Titanus glanced back at Jordan, then to Darius, putting two and two together. Darius turned to Jordan. "Long time no see, kid."

"Yeah...Hi," was all Jordan could offer, but inside his head, his mind was flooded with questions.

How do they know each other? Is this Titanus' lawyer? Have they seen each other in a trial? Were they working together? Oh... Or were they working against each other?

"It was just basic vigilante work," Darius stated. "No one got hurt."

"The kid just told me that he's been practicing vigilante work for a while," then Titanus emphasized, "without a permit."

Darius countered, "Must be genetic."

"I can't just overlook this." Titanus shrugged.

Jordan's mind was swimming. *How do they know each other? My uncle is just a lawyer and Titanus is, well – he's Titanus.* Jordan attempted to speak up to get a word in between the two men. "Hey, hey, what's going on?" Jordan was ignored like a call swallowed in a storm.

"I talked to the DA. We've got a deal on the table," Darius announced as he picked up the golden plate. "We'll help him find whoever dropped this so that he can catch the thieves. In exchange, the DA will drop the charges."

What? I don't even know what that is. What type of deal did he get me? Jordan pulled at his cuffs. He cleared his throat and pushed his way into the argument between the giants. "Can someone tell me what's—"

Darius shut him up with a smoldering look and a barrage of words, "I'm trying to keep you out of jail and the scarlet V off your face, so I'd appreciate it if you kept your mouth shut!"

Jordan felt the blow before he heard it. He sunk back in his seat, shut out of the conversation about his own future. *To think – he's on my side.*

Darius returned the golden charm to Jordan, so he could see it under the light again. "This is a badge. You follow?" Jordan swallowed hard and nodded. "This badge," Darius continued, "is the badge of a hero cadet at Fort Olympus—"

"Impossible." This time Titanus tried to interrupt Darius. "Fort Olympus is the premier hero training institute in the country—"

"What are you the God of Justice?"

"No, but he is a distant relative."

"Well, unless your forefather has any other leads, then I suggest you back off."

Titanus, the great and scarred hero, was silenced.

Darius pressed his advantage. "The DA's office will give Jordan a deal if, and only if, he works with me."

"Work with you?" Jordan asked.

"You'll be sent undercover to Fort Olympus to catch the thieves before they strike again." Darius dropped the golden badge on the table. "Whoever dropped this is a student at that school, and you're gonna help us catch 'em."

"Or . . . ?" Jordan whispered.

"Jail," Titanus said with a sense of finality.

Oh my God. This is really happening. Oh my God. They want me to help them. I can't – I can't end up in jail. I can – I can't – do this, but – I don't have much of a choice. Jordan's thoughts fluttered as he looked between both men.

"Please, please I'll – I'll do anything to help," Jordan replied. "I'll go undercover. I'll go to Fort Olympus...I'll catch them. I can do it. I promise. Just give me this chance."

Darius nodded at him, then turned to Titanus. "He's got a deal."

Something clicked in Titanus' skull. An invisible switch went on in his head that he didn't turn on often. A sign that read: You lost. Strangely enough, that tapped into the same hemisphere of his brain that made him smirk again. He regarded both of them with a nod. That was gracious as he could be in defeat.

"Don't get too comfortable, Darius," Titanus warned. "He messes up once, and he's out of that school and locked up with the rest of the Vespers." He turned to Jordan. "And if I were you, I'd start thinking where you want the scarlet V tattooed on your face."

"Good night, Clayton," Darius said to the tune of *Leave now.*

Jordan blinked once, twice, then blurted out, "Clayton – Is that – You two know each other?"

Then something truly frightening happened: Titanus laughed. A hearty scoff, like sandpaper over metal, escaped Titanus' belly.

"You've got no idea who your uncle is, do you?" Titanus teased.

Jordan blinked. *What. Is. He. Talking. About?*

"Good night," Titanus paused for emphasis, "Kinetic." Titanus then flashed him a humorless smile, full of teeth. Titanus' half-face mask snapped back up to cover his mouth and he marched out of the room, leaving them in silence. What began as a dozen questions when Jordan woke up exploded into a million. Darius turned back to face him and, as his bald head hit the lights, Jordan glimpsed a scar right above the big man's ear.

The same scar he saw on the Kinetic action figure --

The same scar that Kinetic received from the Battle of Detroit --

His uncle and Kinetic were one and the same.

CHAPTER SEVEN

Bullies in Orbit

Honestly, Jordan didn't have much to say. He sat in the back of his sister's mid-size black sedan in silence as they drove home. His hero gear, which included his hoodie and gloves – signed by Kinetic, aka his uncle– were in a plastic bag marked EVIDENCE in the seat next to him.

As Jordan stewed with his face pressed against the cool glass, he felt the arms of his anxiety reach out en masse and grab him, pulling at the tendrils of his mind. Even alone in the back of his sister's car, under her watchful eye, it pushed its way in. He always felt it return when he least expected it. His anxiety would hide behind a memory, then lunge off the back of a triggering thought to ensnare him.

Darius said he would meet them at home, and he was true to his word. He stood waiting for them in the hallway of the apartment complex. Jordan was unsure how he got past the front door, but if he truly was who Titanus said he was, then he had more important questions to ask. Khadija and Darius greeted each other with a narrowed glare that was definitely genetic. Khadija's look said, *Go easy.* Darius' expression said, *Not a chance.* Jordan refused to look at either of them, head down, shoulders slumped as he sulked into the living room of their apartment.

Keep your head down. Get to your room. Sleep it off. His sister and uncle followed him inside.

"I told you. I told you…" Darius grumbled, his voice loud and robust even at a grumble.

"And I told him," Khadija stopped. "Nuh-uh. Jordan, where are you going?"

C'mon, I'm so tired. Jordan stopped and turned on his heel. "Uh, to my room."

"No. You stay here," she snapped. "How many times? How many times did I tell you not to use your powers?"

Jordan was silent. He kept his eyes on the floor. *I just want to go to sleep.* "A lot," Jordan mumbled. "A lot, okay?"

"Okay? You do not 'okay' me." Khadija's tone hardened.

Please, just stop yelling at me, Jordan pleaded, silently. He felt his anxiety grip him from all sides.

Darius roused from his brief looming silence in the corner. "Show your sister some respect. She's raised you and – "

"And where have you been?" The words were out of Jordan's mouth before he had time to think.

Darius' eyes narrowed. Right now Jordan didn't see him as Kinetic. Maybe it was the lack of sleep. Maybe it was the lack of Kinetic's costume or just lack of basic communication, but Jordan didn't see him as a hero right now – he barely saw him as family.

"You don't know anything about us," Jordan snapped back. "We haven't seen you in – in ten years."

"And we survived," Khadija stated. "I made sure of it."

Darius simmered at the retort. "I left because I had a job to do," he said. "After the Green Night and most of the Olympians died, crime rates skyrocketed. I was needed in DC, New York, London. The world needed heroes and –"

"And we needed you," Jordan shouted.

The words hung in the air, like the thunder that rumbled through the night. Darius didn't feel pain like most people. He rarely felt anything like most people. His Gift allowed him to absorb the kinetic impact out of any object in motion. He often feared his Gift was affecting him emotionally, and because he had shut people out for so long, he no longer felt anything. While he was used to numbness in the face of bullets, plasma-packed punches, and long falls, these rare humanizing moments awoke a feeling in him that was easy to forget. And now he felt pain for the first time–since when? A decade, he guessed.

"You didn't even tell us who you really were." Jordan looked down; his fist was clenched so hard, the evidence bag carrying the signed gloves shook. Darius glanced at the gloves with a sense of recognition. Then for a moment, his face softened.

"I did that to keep my identity safe," Darius replied. "To keep you safe."

"But alone – "

"No. No." Darius' body bristled, his patience running thin. His eyes flashed purple, and the lights in the room flickered. Jordan's body buzzed like it had with Titanus earlier as something unseen whirled through the room. He nearly dropped to his knees but caught himself against the wall. Darius boomed from the corner and marched toward him, his eyes alight with raw violet plasma.

"You have no idea how close you were to going to jail tonight. Jail. Your old life is over. Your school, your friends, everything you've known is about to change drastically. And if you had just kept your behind inside and listened to your sister, this wouldn't be happening."

Jordan finally fell back against the wall and let it fully support him. *What – what was that?*

"Tomorrow," Darius fumed, "you go to school. You clear out your locker, and next Monday – you start at Fort Olympus. This isn't a gift. This isn't freedom. It's a mercy operation. You do this operation, and maybe, just maybe, they'll show you mercy."

"Darius, go easy on him," Khadija chided.

"No," he shot back. "Apparently that doesn't work. Tonight is the last night anyone will go easy on you. You are being sent to Fort Olympus – boot camp for Espers in hero training. Fifty percent of their students do not graduate. If you get kicked out, if you screw up even once before the mission is over and those two thieves aren't caught, if you fail like the abject failure you were tonight – you go to jail. Jail, where they'll tattoo a scarlet V on your face for Vesper, and you'll wear that reminder of your crime for the rest of your life."

Failure. Kinetic thinks I'm a failure. Jordan nodded from the wall, barely able to lift his head.

"Look at me," Darius growled.

No, not just Kinetic. Jordan could barely pick up his head; it even hurt to breathe. It felt like the world was slowing down from orbit. *My uncle thinks I'm a failure.*

"Look. At. Me. Jordan," Darius' voice bellowed around the small, dank apartment.

Jordan blinked tears from his eyes, yanked his head back up and wiped snot from his nose with his t-shirt.

"Here, right now, I am not Kinetic. I am not Darius or your uncle. I am the last thing standing between you and jail. Do you understand?"

"Yes," Jordan gasped. "Yes, sir."

"Go to bed. You've got a long day tomorrow."

Jordan nodded, risked a glance at Khadija, whose face was equally as stoic as her uncle's. Jordan didn't waste another second and limped off down the hall.

As soon as he was sure the kid was out of earshot Darius turned to Khadija. "He could have been killed," Darius spat.

"I know. I've been dealing with it," Khadija returned fire.

The two held eye contact for a stiff moment, before Darius concluded, "Straighten him up – or the world will do it for you."

Jordan entered his bedroom, and as he shut the door he shut out the world. He closed his eyes for a beat, letting the tension and anguish of the last few hours break through. It felt like his lungs had gone rigid as miniature lightning storms ignited within him. Jordan sighed, gripped his chest, fought against the pain of the storm, and swallowed it. He looked up and nearly jumped out of his skin.

Darius was looking right at him.

Jordan took a shaky breath and realized it was only a poster of Darius, one of many Kinetic posters, trading cards, and figurines in his room. Those same beady eyes bore down on him from behind the mask. It was as if he couldn't escape the outside world. Even in the safety of his room they were everywhere. No place felt safe; no place felt like home. Not wanting to see the many pairs of Darius' eyes judging him, Jordan turned the lights off. There was a swelling in his chest that he tried to will away, but it stayed – even in the dark.

He slumped to the ground and leaned his head back against the door. Jordan reached inside the evidence bag and pulled out the signed gloves. He felt them in his hand and gently touched the black synthetic leather. He slowly rubbed his thumb over the armor-plated palm of one glove then flipped it over to the back where his uncle's message was written in gold.

Be your own hero, huh? Jordan scoffed at the message. *What a cape-drag...* He sat in the silence of the dark with the lights of the Regulus constellation beaming over him, yet only one word came back to him: *failure.*

Jordan was conflicted.

It was only now as the bus pulled up to his high school for the final time, that he appreciated the sights. The drive, every bump in the road, the way the cheap leather seats hugged him as he got in a few extra minutes of sleep and the multitude of conversations he picked up on while traveling–he was going to miss it and his high school all the same.

He was about to transfer into one of the most prestigious hero training schools in the world. He wanted to rejoice, but every time that joy rose within him he felt it plummet back to the pit of his stomach. His life, so far, had been normal by the standards of many high schoolers – Esper and human alike – yet that was all about to change.

Because of his mistakes, he was going to his dream school.

As Jordan walked down the halls, he absorbed it all. The slam of closed lockers. The illustrations of various heroes on the walls. The way sneakers skipped and skidded across the chipped, green linoleum floors. He marinated in it while no one sent him a second glance. Jordan opened his locker, heard its familiar click as the locking mechanism settled. Jordan surveyed the Kinetic and other professional hero merchandise in the locker. Then he heard a squeak. It wasn't sneakers on linoleum, but it was familiar. It was Nathan's crutch as he shuffled across the hall to meet him. Jordan avoided eye contact and began to pull his posters off the door and into his backpack.

"Hey, what's up?" Nathan asked.

"I'm leaving," Jordan replied.

"Like switching lockers?" Nathan inquired with a smirk.

"No…" Jordan tore a picture of Kinetic down. "Like schools."

Nathan blinked. Though he understood the words, he couldn't comprehend them. Nathan paused, looked over his locker, and realized he was telling the truth. "Wait – what?" Nathan gasped.

"Sorry, but I can't talk about it," Jordan stalled.

"J, what's going on? The school year, like, just started."

Jordan didn't even have half the answers himself. He stuffed his explanation along with his belongings into his backpack. He reached back into the depths of their locker and glimpsed a photo – him, Nathan, and the Esper Hero Club. It was from last year sometime, before they all left for the summer. Jordan picked the photo up and stuffed that in his bag too.

"I have to go. I'm sorry," Jordan replied and then stalked off, well aware Nathan couldn't keep up to follow.

Nathan watched him go, then tried to follow. "No, wait."

Man, please just turn around, Jordan whispered to himself. *Don't make this harder than it has to be.* Jordan pressed on and rounded the corner with Nathan still trailing behind him.

Jordan pushed through a knot of students entering the school and rushed down the stairs. He glimpsed behind himself and saw Nathan was still on his tail.

Oh, come on. "Nathan." Jordan stopped and whirled around. Nathan went down the service ramp and caught up to Jordan.

"What happened?" Nathan asked.

Jordan bit his tongue, fought against the truth. He wanted to tell him but – *I can't involve anyone else in my mistakes.* Jordan shook his head and walked faster, heading for the school's main entrance. Nathan cursed under his breath and walked down the stairs in pursuit. Jordan rounded the school and headed past the parking lot, away from large groups of the students filing through the front doors.

"Will you stop running from me?" Nathan shouted.

Jordan stopped, exhaled hard, and turned back to face him.

"I don't know what to say. Like – what – what happened? Where are you going?" Nathan asked.

"I'm going –" Jordan almost choked on his words, "away."

Nathan paused. He knew that tone because he knew Jordan. The truth of the matter struck him momentarily dumb. He opened his mouth to speak, but without warning a well-placed kick from behind knocked the crutch out from under him. Nathan flipped backward and landed hard on the pavement in time to see Trevor and his two friends circle them.

"Oh, what are you cape-draggers doing?" Trevor teased.

"Nothing," Jordan replied as he bent down to help Nathan up.

"Get off me," Nathan hissed under his breath.

Jordan ignored it, put Nathan's arm over his shoulder, and lifted when – Trevor stepped on Nathan's leg, pinning him down by his knee. Jordan felt Trevor's plasma broil forth, and Nathan's leg began to bend at a nasty angle. It wasn't near the breaking point, but with the amount of plasma Trevor was stomping down with it wouldn't be long till Nathan's leg snapped. Nathan hissed as waves of agony shot through his frame. Trevor's body glowed with that familiar, soft, seafoam green plasma that Jordan had grown to hate. "Nuh-uh. How about I just hurry up and break it? Actually, will he even feel it?" Trevor smirked.

"Please," Jordan spoke between gritted teeth, "let him up."

Trevor saw the glint in Jordan's eye, liked it, and leaned in to face him. His plasma-packed leg pushed down on Nathan's body, and Jordan felt his best friend flinch.

"Oh, sorry," Trevor teased. "You didn't sound like you meant it."

Jordan felt his own plasma stirring deep within him. His belly was full of fire, and his veins flooded with gold.

"Please. Let. Him. Up," Jordan stated clearly.

Trevor smirked. He liked where this was going. "Oh, that tone is something fierce," he said. "What are you gonna do about it...cape-dragger?"

Jordan felt his body chomping at the bit to be let loose, to finally show this Vesper what he was about. Right under the surface an ocean of energy swelled within him. Energy coiled off his skin, dancing along the length of his body.

"I'm gonna show you," Jordan seethed.

Jordan let loose, tapping into his network of energy and letting it flow. His body ignited and flared like a torch. An instant later Jordan's fist smashed into Trevor's jaw and sent him tumbling end over end. Jordan flexed his hand. His knuckles throbbed a bit, but otherwise, *Whoa, that felt good.* Nathan gasped hard and slid back from Jordan, more stunned by the revelation than hurt by the concussive force washing off of Jordan's body.

"J – Jordan, you're an Esper?" The words tumbled out of Nathan's mouth.

"Sorry," Jordan whispered, choking out the words. "I told you, I can't talk about it."

Nathan's eyes widened, absorbing his best friend's secrets. Despite the sense of betrayal Nathan could only utter, "That's so cool." Nathan was filled with child-like glee. He turned around to smile at Trevor and his cronies before announcing, "My best friend has superpowers."

"And you better keep it a secret."

"Oh yeah," Nathan chimed. "I will, scout's honor. I mean, I wasn't in the scouts, but it's our secret, and I never reveal secrets – like that my mom cheats on her taxes, but – "

"Nathan," Jordan said plainly, "shut up."

Nathan calmed, then nodded. "Yeah, sure."

Jordan gave him a confident nod and then turned to Trevor and his friends, who were stirring from the ground. Jordan eyed them hard from behind a golden hue. *Okay, just like you've done before. Make yourself sound big.* "That goes for you too," Jordan shouted, and then he cleared his throat and pulled it back some "You all better keep this a secret, or I will come down on you like Kinetic."

What would Darius say? Jordan took an encouraging breath, then last night came back to haunt him. He put on his best angry face and repeated what Darius said last night when he was looming down on him. "Here, right now – I am not Jordan – I am the last thing standing between you three and jail. Do you cape-draggers understand?"

The three bullies nodded and cowered back from Jordan, who locked the scowl on his face. It felt unnatural, but he gritted through it, putting on his best Darius impression.

"We understand," Trevor shouted through a blood-filled mouth.

Nathan climbed to his feet, using his crutch, and shook it at them. "That's right. Now get out of here."

"Go," Jordan bellowed and sent a flux of energy through the gravitons in the area that tossed Trevor and his friends backwards. They righted themselves like bowling pins and hurried back to the refuge of the school building. Nathan watched them retreat, then he turned back to Jordan, and despite all that happened, smiled.

"That was awesome," Nathan exclaimed.

Jordan dropped the light show, recalling his plasma and the energies back into his tiny frame. "Oh, that felt good," Jordan replied.

Then it all hit Nathan at once as he realized, "Why – why didn't you tell me? You're my best friend."

"Sorry. I just couldn't...My sister forbid me, and I just –"

Nathan nodded, and then another idea hit him: "Wait, were you cheating every time we went bowling?"

Jordan smirked. "Didn't have to."

They both laughed simultaneously. The stress of the past few moments had built up into this tiny moment of release between them. A laugh, much like the many they had shared over the years, yet this one carried the weight of finality. As the laughter subsided, Jordan picked up his backpack off the ground. It flopped open, and inside he spotted the photo of the two of them with the Esper Hero Club. He picked it out and handed it to Nathan. Nathan didn't take it.

"No, keep it," he said. "Something to remember the club by. Something to remember what being normal was like."

Jordan smirked; it was all he could do to not let his real emotions flood out. "I'll be around." Jordan nodded at Nathan, then turned away. He left Nathan in his wake, the Esper Hero Club in his past, and ardently wished he could pack all of it in the bag and take it with him.

DARIUS RHODES

Hero Alias: Kinetic

Height: 6'3

Weight: 280

Birth Date: December 10

Plasma Color: Purple

Plasma Level: 90,000

Gift: Darius possesses the ability to absorb, store, and redirect kinetic energy through his body. He can decelerate most, if not all, physical attacks, store that energy within himself and expel it at will.

CHAPTER EIGHT

H-Town Crown

Darius found himself alone in a familiar – yet foreign – place. He had stopped by Khadija's apartment about ten years ago after the death of his brother and sister-in-law. It was a brief stop, a brief conversation, and a brief hug that he wished could have lasted longer, but duty called. This apartment had once belonged to his brother, but now it was just Khadija's.

The door was the same pale blue, now chipped, but there were fewer shoes cluttering the doormat. The windows were all in the same place, but the blackout curtains remained drawn, closed off from the world. The pictures on the wall and all across the living room featured the same people he knew and loved, but as they aged, so had those memories.

While Khadija was at work, Darius remained at her place waiting for Jordan to return home. If he was open to admitting it, Darius felt rather awkward about this upcoming meeting with his nephew. He had spent time pacing the room and then searched, rather awkwardly for a man his size, for a cup in which to make tea. He chose jasmine tea with exactly two drops of honey, much like his mother used to make for him and his brother, Johnathan, when they were small.

It brought him back to Saturday afternoons on the farm in Dallas. It brought him back to Friday nights where they'd wrestle and end up bumping one another too hard, making their mom break it up. It brought him back to that first family conversation about being black and Gifted in America. It brought him back to Christmas mornings and July cookouts.

It brought him home, which was something he had been missing for a while.

There was a thump and a click behind him. Darius turned and stared at his brother walking through the door. Darius blinked and shook his head; it wasn't his brother – but his brother's son. *Oof, those genes are strong,* Darius mused.

Jordan removed his shoes, then looked over at Darius – the hero he had long admired – standing in his living room, drinking tea. "Sooooo," Jordan crooned, "I guess you're not a lawyer."

"It's my cover job," Darius admitted, then added, "I even had to change my legal last name."

There was a moment of awkward silence as they both wondered what to say next.

"I thought you'd be bigger in person," Jordan admitted.

Darius paused, studied Jordan, then replied, "Aren't you like five foot five?"

"I'm five-seven," Jordan shot back.

"And what are you, thirteen?"

"I'm fourteen."

"Don't worry," Darius smirked, "your father was a late bloomer too."

Jordan paused, absorbed those words, saw his own father's face reflected in pieces of Darius', and softened. "Do you miss him?"

Darius looked down, not wanting to show weakness, but his eyes landed right on a photo of Khadija, Jordan, and their parents. "Every day," Darius replied. "He may have been human, but his work ethic was superhuman. That's something I really admired in him."

Jordan smirked. He had heard the stories from Khadija, but hearing them from Darius was something else.

Darius fixed his face and then got down to business. There was much to do and not much time in which to do it. "Tell me, what color is your Plasma Crystal?" Darius asked as he sipped tea.

"Gold." Jordan tapped into his crystal, felt the familiar tingle in the base of his neck, and gold light flashed off his body and illuminated his eyes.

Darius nodded, then continued, "Which means your hair should also be gold?"

"Yeah," Jordan nodded. His black locks didn't show a glimmer of gold. "She makes me dye it every month."

"I know. I told her to. God, she's just as headstrong as your mother," Darius mused.

An Esper's hair color is often spliced with the root color of their crystal. Red plasma crystals will give you red hair, gold plasma crystals will give you gold hair. Purple crystals will give you – wait – Jordan stopped mid-thought. "D, isn't your hair supposed to be purple?"

Darius froze as if he was trying to shrink his giant size away from Jordan's prying imagination. Jordan bit his cheek and suppressed a chuckle at the thought of a giant man with a purple afro.

"It was once purple. It was a hit in the 80s."

Now Jordan laughed, unable to contain it.

"It was a weird time," Darius said. "You wouldn't get it."

"So that's why you shaved your head?" Jordan cackled.

"Yeah, yeah, yeah," Darius chanted. "Don't get me wrong, I look good in every color, but a guy my size and age with purple hair is gonna draw eyes."

Jordan exhaled the rest of his amusement and replied, "So you shave your head to protect your identity?"

Darius lumbered over to him and replied, "Yes, and we're going to shave yours to show off your identity." Darius laid one of his massive paws on Jordan's head and manipulated it around like a bobblehead on the car dash while inspecting it.

"Hmmm, looks like we'll start with a three on the clippers, then a one – your scalp is pretty dry kid, you oiling it?"

"Not as – much as – I should. Can you – stop? I'm getting nauseous."

Darius released him, then surveyed the back of his head. "I got a scalp conditioner for you. That'll clear that right up."

Jordan paused as a second realization hit him. "Hold up, does that mean you dye your beard?"

Fed up with the questions, Darius snapped, "Boy, if you don't get in there."

Darius led Jordan to the bathroom where a chair was set up in front of the mirror. A yellow towel on the right side of the sink and a set of clippers on the left side. Jordan took a seat on the stool, then Darius wrapped the towel around his neck, firm but gentle. Though the memory was faint, Jordan recalled that his father used to cut his hair the same way. Darius picked up a comb and began picking through Jordan's hair, untangling knots and twists.

"You're going to a school with people who have been training for this their whole lives. They've never had to hide," Darius began. "I can't have my nephew going around looking like a cape-dragger. I want you to walk in there like you own the place. Like you're the number one hero, Kurikara."

Kinetic is really my uncle. I can't believe it. Jordan smirked as he felt his hair begin to untangle and free itself. "Do you know Kurikara?" Jordan asked.

"I do. He even taught me the Impact Knee I use. He's a bit of a loner and spends most of his time in Japan, but we've worked together a few times. He's quiet, but he's the best for a reason."

"Can you tell me about his Gift?" Jordan buzzed.

"Now, that info is classified, youngblood." Darius picked up the clippers and slipped the plastic guard on the end.

"Hmmm, can you tell me about the Battle of Detroit? And how you beat Typhon?" Jordan asked.

Something cold washed over Darius, and for a second Jordan saw his uncle seemingly shrink and shiver.

Darius replied with a stern, "No." Darius busied himself with his clippers for a beat before continuing, "A three would be a good start to clear away some of this off."

"My – my dad used to cut my hair," Jordan said. "He called it the – the H-Town Crown." Jordan smirked over the fond memory.

"I bet." Darius continued, "He used to cut mine too. The first time he messed up my hairline so bad that your grandmother whopped both our butts."

The two shared a laugh, then Darius began to shovel the clippers through Jordan's hair. The dyed black locks fell to the floor in clumps. As Jordan watched Darius move and shift around him, he couldn't help but recognize how he even moved like his father. The way he shaved the sides, the way he held his head steady, the way his elbow was bent at just the right angle to graze the hair behind his ears. It brought back those memories but also a lump in his throat. Jordan fought it. He swallowed that lumpy memory like medicine.

"I'm sorry I snapped at you yesterday." Darius said the words so plainly that Jordan wasn't sure if he was talking to him. Jordan didn't have a quick reply. His uncle busied himself by switching the guard from a three to a one. Now that the heavy lifting had been done, it was time to polish.

"You had a right to be mad," Jordan replied, not wanting to continue the conversation.

Darius ran the clippers along the back of Jordan's head, burning his scalp as they raked down. "Darn right," Darius murmured. As Darius clipped away another layer of hair, he finally saw Jordan's roots. They were gold. Like all Espers, lines of their genetic plasma color framed the base of their neck. For Jordan, he had had four lines of gold trailing down the back of his neck and wrapping around his temple forming two parallel lines. For the first time in ten years, Jordan saw the familiar lines of gold that cupped his head – like a crown. This too brought back memories of his father.

"But you're important to me," Darius continued. "You know that, right? I don't have a family. Kinetic can't have a family. Darius Harris can't exist. Darius Rhodes, the lawyer, has to exist. If Vespers find out –"

"I know," Jordan blurted.

Jordan didn't mean to interrupt, but this conversation was not one he wanted to have right now. *This is the last thing I want to talk about.* The memories and the emotions associated with them brought back that lump in his throat that caused his eyes to water.

Darius registered Jordan's interruption. The kid was looking down, crestfallen. Darius changed the subject, hoping to pry just a bit more from him. "How did your last day go?"

Oof, okay, that's the second to last thing I want to talk about. Jordan coughed, trying to find a way to clear the lump from his throat.

"It was fine. It was – I – I said goodbye to my best friend," Jordan admitted, softly.

Huh, okay...That wasn't the reaction I was hoping for, Darius reflected as he continued trimming. The sound of buzzing clippers continued as Darius cut away the last few clumps of hair on Jordan's scalp. Darius read Jordan's face; his jaw and neck were tense from the effort of keeping silent. He wished his nephew would just say it.

Then Jordan's voice returned to fill the silence. "I messed up."

Darius let that hang in the air for a moment, choosing his next words carefully. "And you're going to make it right. Sometimes, to be a hero, you have to do the hard thing – and sometimes that includes keeping people at bay." Jordan didn't have a reply, but he felt the lump in his throat swelling. "I know it doesn't mean much after ten years, but I'm sorry. I'm sorry I left you and your sister for so long. I know what you're going through."

Jordan nodded and looked down at the hair in his lap, the hair that for so long had hidden who he really was. He shifted his hands under the towel and sent the hair fluttering to the floor.

"Your father and I would sneak out to do vigilante work when I was your age," Darius continued. "Even if he couldn't do much he wanted to lead the charge. So I guess you can say it's genetic. And if you thought our grandma beat our butts before..." Darius ended with a heavy laugh. Jordan followed with a soft cry that morphed into a shuttered chuckle.

For an instant, Jordan saw his father cutting his hair. Then he saw himself as a kid in the mirror, floating up, only for his father to guide him back down to the seat to stay still. At that memory and at that moment Jordan felt something break inside. It didn't hurt; it felt like a release behind his eyes.

Darius finished up the back of Jordan's hairline. Jordan appreciated the legendary hero's voice softly droning in the small space. "But your father was the reason I wanted to be a hero – to use my powers for good, and I see it in you." Jordan couldn't fight it anymore. He reached up and gripped the towel with both hands.

"I think – I think I got some hair on my face," Jordan lied through wet eyes. Jordan buried his face into the towel and let the truth free. It took Darius a few seconds to realize that Jordan wasn't just wiping the hair from his face and that Jordan had no intention of revealing his emotion. His nephew shuddered under his hand and a cry rattled through him. Darius heard the strain of emotion through the towel.

Gently, Darius brought Jordan's head, covered by the towel, into the crook of his shoulder and patted his back. Darius was often used to calming people he rescued by holding them, but this was the first time the cries really affected him.

"You're gonna be just like him," Darius whispered. "You're gonna be just like me. I'll make sure of it. I'm not leaving ever again."

And for a long, somber moment, nephew and uncle sat in silence while Jordan let ten years of pent-up despair rumble forth.

After Jordan stopped the charade of wiping hair from his face, and Darius finished lining up his hairline, the two went to Jordan's room, where Jordan immediately tried to place himself in front of all the Kinetic merchandise on the walls. "This is awkward," Jordan admitted.

"Not as awkward as it is for me," Darius replied.

"At least you don't have purple hair," Jordan added.

Darius chuckled, then glanced up at the Regulus constellation on the ceiling. "Aww, Regulus."

"Yeah," Jordan began, "it was the constellation I was born under. I–I couldn't pronounce it when I was a kid, so I just called it StarLion."

Darius smirked, then followed Jordan's gaze to the signed gloves on the dresser. "I take it Khadija didn't really win these off eBay?" Jordan challenged.

"No, they were a gift," Darius mused.

"What you wrote on there, did you mean it?" Jordan asked. "Be your own hero?"

Darius' scarred visage scrunched for a moment as he thought on his words. "As heroes, we all have a creed we live by. It's that– it's that lever that gets us out of bed in the morning, that thing that allows us to run into danger. We all have a view of what a hero is and what that person should be. Our own hero. And if you want to be in this business, you need to know it with your whole heart. What's your definition of a hero? We all got different answers, but they all exist, and you'll need to find your own."

Jordan paused, taking this into account. *My own definition of a hero...*

"But if you got the gloves," Darius walked over to the closet, "you're gonna need the suit too." Darius slid it open and revealed a metallic black suit. It was form-fitting, with gold traced along the body. Atop the suit sat a hefty pair of gold shoulder pads that stretched down to the torso and framed the neck and collar bone with a slanted defense. Jordan found his reflection in the gold star affixed to the chest.

Even though Jordan knew what it was, he couldn't help but ask, "Wha – what?"

"A standard-issue hero suit," Darius explained. "Titanium weave micromesh over poly rubber fabric with chrome-plated golden shoulder pads fit for a cadet of Fort Olympus."

Jordan gawked. He couldn't believe this suit was sitting right in his closet, waiting for him. He reached out tentatively as if he was afraid it might be a mirage, like something precious in a dream.

"Thank you," Jordan said. He pinched the fabric between his fingers. It barely budged; it had the texture of a tire but shifted with ease in his grasp. Darius leaned in and pointed to the shoulder pads and, more importantly, a golden plate locked into each shoulder. This plate was similar to the one he found in the museum, except there was a lion on this one, canines bared, eyes narrowed to slits, and mane flaring outward.

"A lion?" Jordan asked.

"Leo. Your birthday is..." Darius trailed off.

"July 24ᵗʰ," Jordan answered.

"Cadet uniforms are adorned with badges representing their astrological signs. It gives everyone a bit of an identity."

"So the bull badge I found..." It was Jordan's turn to trail off.

And Darius' turn to answer, "...belongs to someone who is a Taurus. Or someone in the Taurus regiment of cadets."

Jordan nodded, realizing. "Good, that's my first lead."

"You're gonna need more," Darius began. "This isn't a vacation – or a gift for that matter – it's a job. If you mess up, you'll go to jail, get marked as a Vesper, and innocent people will get hurt." Darius held his gaze, and Jordan nodded back at him. "Tomorrow you start a whole new life."

Jordan took a minute to think it over–to look at the figures of heroes in his room, to examine the life he was about to leave behind. There was a hint of that familiar pain again, yet he drowned it out. He had cried enough; he had hidden enough, and now wasn't the time for either.

"I always thought it was best to just be normal, you know? Go to school, get a job, run from crime, but – but that wasn't me," Jordan said. "I'm not going to fail. I'm going to be a hero."

Darius smirked, liking what he heard. "Well, if you're going to be a hero, we'll need a hero alias for you too." Jordan looked at the lion emblazoned on his shoulder pad. It was only now that he realized that the lion was superimposed on a star.

"Yeah," Jordan mused, "I think I got one."

JORDAN HARRIS

Hero Alias: StarLion

Height: 5'6

Weight: 115

Birth Date: July 24

Plasma Color: Gold

Plasma Level: 30,000

Gift: Jordan possesses the ability to mentally manipulate gravitons to collect them, reverse their pull, and even vibrate them until they explode.

CHAPTER NINE

Fort Olympus

Vast was the first word that came to mind as Fort Olympus came into view. Historic was the second that often followed. As the sun rose over the massive campus of Fort Olympus and bounced off of its 300 year old brick and mortar façade, the facility seemed to be illuminated. Midnight grey blocks and vanilla mortar made up the bulk of the establishments that had stood solid since the 1700's when George Washington and the Spanish Crown's royalty commissioned the base as a symbol of cooperation between the rebels and the Spaniards. Its location as a fort was chosen as a strategic high ground atop the Buffalo Bayou, which flowed through the campus. It allowed for the construction of ports and quick delivery of supplies.

As time changed, so did the need for Fort Olympus. Rechristened as a school after World War II, the aged brick and monolithic structures of impasse fortress walls remained unchanged – yet the occupants were younger and more astute than those who first took residence.

The military uniforms and marching cadets were replaced with teenage students walking about in black and gold uniforms.

The barracks became dorm rooms.

The mess hall became…Well, that remained the mess hall.

Fort Olympus no longer produced soldiers to fight wars against British Espers; it produced heroes to fight against Vespers worldwide. The school's insignia flew proudly at the top of the flagpole and graced the students' lapels as well as the stout gate outside the mighty, high, brick walls. That insignia featured an eagle with a thunderbolt clutched in its claws and red, white, and blue striped wings. It was distinctly American while also honoring its namesake, Zeus, with the words *Astra Inclinant* underneath the eagle's talons.

Today was a special day for "The Fort" as the students liked to call it. As the sun rose over Fort Olympus, it didn't just shine on the historic buildings, the various statues of famous hero alumni, and the mighty gate that surrounded it. The sun also struck a banner that read: "WELCOME NEW AND RETURNING STUDENTS."

Jordan was up a few beats after sunrise. Not only was it his first day at a new school, but it was also the first official day of his investigation. After having hours to pack, wash up, eat, and prepare, somehow he was already running late. He stood in front of the mirror in his new school uniform: black pants, white button-down shirt, a black dress blazer with gold trim along the edge and a thunderbolt eagle crest over the heart and, to his dismay, a black and gold tie that he was struggling to fix in the mirror.

"Jordan..." Khadija's voice echoed from down the hall.

"I know," he called out.

Jordan tried to loop it around again. *No, no, that's not it. Oh, come on. Why couldn't this be a clip-on?* Khadija appeared around the doorway. Her mane of black curls was the first thing he saw before her face materialized next to him. "We're going to be late."

"I know." Jordan struggled with the tie once more, but it still wasn't cooperating.

"Come here." Khadija waved him over.

Jordan sighed, accepted his fate, and walked over to her.

"Watch my hands as I do this. I won't be on campus with you to do this every day."

"I know, I know. I'm watching."

Khadija's hands went to work as she peppered him with questions.

"You packed enough clothes?"

"Yes."

"Not just action figures, right?"

"I packed some *collectibles*."

"Well, good, maybe you can trade some for the clothes you didn't pack," she joked. "Clean socks?"

"Yes," Jordan said, annoyed.

"Clean drawers?"

"Yes," Jordan exclaimed, now annoyed and embarrassed.

"Good. You better have packed enough for a few weeks." She finished with his tie. "It looks good on you."

Jordan smirked. Then Khadija, like Darius, palmed his head and swiveled it around to get a look at the gold streaks in his hairline. The two lines of gold in his black hair framed the sides of his head and matched the black and gold of his uniform. "Looking good, Goldie Locks."

Jordan simmered. It was a name he had tried to live down since he was born, and Khadija had teased him endlessly. "Please, don't call me that."

"I'm your sister, I'll call you whatever I want."

"Well, you can call me late if we stay here any longer," Jordan snapped.

As if on cue, an alarm beeped from Khadija's phone. "Ohhh, that's the GPS. We should have been gone. C'mon." Khadija rushed out and down the hall. Jordan stopped and studied himself in the mirror for a beat. Then beyond himself, he took in his bedroom and committed it to memory, the way the sunlight hit the blue tint of the walls, the way his bed was positioned just right under the window so the morning light wouldn't wake him, the posters of Kinetic and other heroes on the wall and their figures cluttering his dresser. Jordan turned and took it in for what he hoped was not the last time.

Jordan had read tirelessly about Fort Olympus for years. He had visited the website, seen their pictures, and even passed the campus on some occasions. But he had never stepped foot on the campus.

That changed today.

After parking in the campus parking garage, Jordan and Khadija joined a throng of people streaming through the garage and out towards the main entrance. Fort Olympus lived up to its name as the first glimpse of the campus was often blocked by the twenty-foot retaining wall that wrapped around the campus.

Jordan, backpack slung over one shoulder and duffel bag on the other, joined the other students and parents gathered at the main gate. The gate split open to reveal the "Fort Olympus" lettering that hung overhead. Just past it was a full-scale statue of Zeus standing before them. Enshrined in bronze, like all the statues on the campus, he stood at six feet with rippling muscles and clouds of hair with a thunderbolt latched in his hand, ready to hurl it into the heavens. The gate and Zeus welcomed visitors and students.

Khadija called out to Jordan as he rushed ahead of her, juggling both bags. "Careful J don't wrinkle your suit or mess up your tie," Khadija said as she dropped her car keys back into her purse. "I'm not driving two hours back out here to fix it."

"Okay," Jordan called back. He stopped at the gate, feverishly ready to meet the students and their parents. They were Espers of all shapes and sizes. Something fluttered above him, and Jordan paused.

Hybrids, Jordan gasped. From the sky, a mother and father with oak brown wings soared down from above, while their daughter with her own oak colored wings glided down behind them. She landed, and immediately her parents both began to smooth the wrinkles from her blazer. She fluttered her wings at them in protest, then the parents ushered her forward.

While Jordan's school had a few Hybrid students, he didn't see them often. Historical figures like Anubis, Pan, and the Yeti were well known throughout time, while the various Hybrid populations of today such as the elves and the minotaurs mostly kept to themselves and their native lands. They were still sparse in the Americas. As a parade of Hybrids marched past Jordan, he gazed with wonder.

It took Jordan a second to recognize the girl's mother. She looked like a bodybuilder with rounded shoulders, fruitful arms, and blonde hair streaked with blue. That build, those wings, that hair, and of course, those massive arms...*Valkyrie...That's – that's Valkyrie. I've never* *seen her without a mask...*Jordan realized, *and that must be her daughter.* Jordan fought the urge to run after her to ask for her autograph. Khadija caught up to him and nudged him forward.

"Oh, don't tell me that you're getting cold feet now," Khadija chided.

"It's Valkyrie," Jordan pointed out.

"Oh, yeah. And I think I see Buster Blazer over there. I recognize that limp and his height." Khadija gestured towards a bald man walking up with an older teenage boy who was wearing a "Buster Blazer" t-shirt.

Jordan blinked. *Oh, that is him. I didn't know he had a son. He's gonna be a hero too?* Behind them was another set of Hybrids, a small girl with bushy white bunny ears, and a bushy tail that poked out the back of her uniform slacks. She and another student arrived of their own accord, no wings required. Other students arrived with their dads through a portal that opened in the sidewalk. Families hustled to and fro, some with boxes levitating in their wake or above their heads.

Jordan was wide-eyed with awe. *So many Espers.*

Khadija looked down at her brother and mused. Yet there was a tinge of pain behind it. *I kept him from this for so long.* She fixed her face, grabbed his shoulder. *Maybe being with his own kind would do him some good.*

Before the pair made their way in, they both spotted–well, he was hard to miss since he was the tallest figure in the crowd–Darius. He wore a black suit with gold stripes, the colors of Fort Olympus. He stopped as a rather small woman approached him. The two shared a smile and handshake. It was only after the woman scaled over everyone that Jordan realized that was the professional hero Hopper. Jordan secretly hoped for a sighting of MegaTon, the most famous hero in the U.S.

"Took you long enough," Darius chimed.

"Sorry, check-in was crazy," Khadija explained. "I had to show my ID three times just to get to the garage."

"Yeah, security is tight for days like today. The public is not allowed anywhere near here, so it can allow heroes to drop their kids off without wearing masks. Hence, why I'm not wearing my mask today." Darius spotted another group of winged parents gliding in with their kids. "Then again, not all of us can hide our identities."

The new arrivals landed, and, to Jordan's surprise, their faces were those of owls and their bodies were humanoid. Large eyes, seemingly elastic necks, thin beaks, and wingspans larger than any seen so far made them beautiful and mysterious. The Father Owl used his beak to pick something out of his kid's hair. The teenaged owl and human Hybrid shook him off with a very typical teen gesture.

"Come on, not in front of everyone," the teen grimaced. The parents chuckled at him, picked something else out of his hair, then marched him forward.

Man, maybe I don't belong here. Jordan gawked. "There are so many –"

"Hybrids?" Darius chimed. "Yeah, the school upped their quota on Hybrid freshmen this year, so you'll see a lot. Incoming Hybrids are mainly from outside the U.S., which helps foster ties between nations training their heroes."

"No," Jordan replied, "I – I was going to say there are so many families." The word unsettled Darius for a moment, then he saw it. The multitude of teens with their parents coming in was certainly a sight to see. Jordan watched them with a flash of envy in his eyes.

"Well," Khadija began, "you've got family here too."

Jordan smiled. *She's right. I've got Kinetic and my sister with me. That's family.*

"Come on." Darius put a hand on his shoulder. "Let's get you registered."

Darius and Khadija led Jordan through the main gates, and they joined the leagues of families entering Fort Olympus. As they ventured forth, Jordan could feel the pressure from so many famous figures, names, and faces that had been enshrined on the campus.

"Hey, you probably have a statue around here, right, D?" Khadija asked.

"No statue yet. Maybe in time," Darius replied.

"Would be pretty cool, though. Right?"

Jordan was quiet; he could barely hear them over the sound of his own beating heart. *So many people. I just never thought I'd see so many Espers in one place. There are all these pros here and their kids who worked hard to get in.* Jordan stressed, *Then, there's me who is only here because I was arrested.* There was a sudden tightness in his chest. *Okay, almost arrested.* The tightness loosened a bit. *But I'm – I'm no hero. I've got one foot in jail and the other...*

His thoughts were curbed when Khadija put her hand on his shoulder. Like a wave, calmness washed over him. He relaxed, and his breath came easy again. Even from behind him, Jordan felt her presence buoy him. *And the other foot is at the most prestigious hero school in America.*

Jordan and his family reached the check-in desk where new and returning students were checking in and receiving their dorm assignments. A row of tables wrapped in Fort Olympus tablecloths formed a makeshift barrier across the main courtyard. Behind each table was an administrator who was checking students' names against a list on a laptop screen. *I'm standing at Fort Olympus, where the greatest Espers become heroes. Like Kinetic, like Lion Force, like the Olympians – and now me.*

The fabric of time and space snapped when the family ahead of him teleported away. It was his turn.

"We're next," Khadija pointed out and ushered them forward.

Cassandra, the administrator behind the desk, was a bald woman with lines of red pigment swirling around her scalp. Her green eyes, tan skin, and red pigments made for a striking look that betrayed her soft side but complemented her soft voice.

"Oh, Darius, welcome back," Cassandra purred coyly.

"It's been a long time, Cassandra." Darius walked up and gently shook her hand.

"Brings back memories, huh?" she asked.

Darius studied the school with old eyes. "Not much has changed, though."

Cassandra perked when her gaze fell to Jordan, "Oh and is this your –"

"Nephew," Darius explained, "and this is my niece. We came to drop him off."

At the word "nephew," Jordan buzzed as a burst of pride within him smothered the doubt he had been holding. *My uncle is one of the greatest heroes in the world. I've got his blood in me, I've got his blessing, and – even though it's new – I've got his trust.* Then, Darius' words during his haircut came rushing back to him.

"You're gonna be just like him." Jordan tensed at the thought of his father.

"You're gonna be just like me." Jordan gripped his fist at the recent memory of Darius. Then at the thought of Darius' promise Jordan felt something akin to tapping into his plasma: a power, a hope, a fire that stirred in his heart in remembrance of Darius promising, *"I'll make sure of it."*

Khadija and Cassandra shook hands.

"Well, welcome, young man," Cassandra said. "Can I have your name or your registered hero alias?"

I belong here. Jordan took in a fiery breath that filled him with confidence. He looked out at all the Espers, then at the bronze statue of a hero pointing to the sky–he felt great. Khadija reached out, patted the back of his head, and he straightened up. *I'm a hero, and my name is –*

"StarLion."

What felt like a wave of energy to Jordan was simply another in a long line of names for Cassandra, who paused, thought about it, and replied, "Is there is a space in between 'Star' and 'Lion'?"

"No," Jordan replied flatly, "all one word."

"Great." Cassandra began typing. Then with a flourish of her fingers, she punched the enter key and replied, "Oh, there you are: Jordan Harris. Welcome to Fort Olympus, StarLion. *Astra Inclinant.*"

Cassandra handed him a thicket of papers that she retrieved from the printer whirring behind her.

Astra Inclinant? Jordan repeated in his head.

"Latin," Cassandra read the confusion on his face. "The stars incline us."

Jordan accepted the paperwork. It included his name and information printed on Fort Olympus letterhead. He couldn't help but smile and reply, "*Astra Inclinant.*"

"All you need is right here," she explained. "Your dorm badge, your map, your schedule, and your meal plans. This packet includes everything you'll need for your first year at Fort Olympus."

Jordan opened the packet and pulled out a black and gold plastic badge with the Fort Olympus logo on it, which Cassandra explained was his key card to enter buildings, including his dorm and other facilities.

"In my day," Darius groaned, "we had real keys."

"How long ago was that?" Jordan asked.

Darius nearly blurted out the answer, but simply replied, "Back when I had purple hair."

Jordan chuckled, stepped past the table, then stopped as Cassandra motioned to Khadija and Darius to halt.

"Sorry," Cassandra explained, "only students are allowed past this point."

Darius and Khadija took the news in stride, then turned back to Jordan. Darius laid one of his massive hands on Jordan's shoulder. Jordan had to push plasma into his knees to stop himself from collapsing under the force.

"You know what this is? I don't have to tell you the stakes, right?" Darius asked.

Jordan nodded. "I understand."

"You better. I'll be around, kid."

Darius patted his head, and Jordan resisted the force. Then Khadija stepped in, and her hands found their way to his tie, fixing it for him again.

"I love you. You know that, right?" she asked.

"I love you too," Jordan said.

"And I'm hard on you only because you don't know how to listen."
They both chuckled, and she continued, "You know what you have to
do. This isn't summer camp or one of your late-night outings. It's the
real deal."

Jordan nodded again. "I understand."

Khadija finished fiddling with his tie and let go. Jordan tucked the
tie's tail into his blazer. She gave him a hug, and he hugged her back.

"Okay." Khadija offered him a smile, then added, "Go get 'em,
Goldie Locks."

Jordan laughed it off, then replied, "I love you too."

With that, Jordan turned with his belongings and entered Fort
Olympus mission-bound and ready.

COOPER GREENE

Hero Alias:	Ailurus
Height:	5'4
Weight:	155
Birth Date:	November 23
Plasma Color:	Red
Plasma Level:	42,000
Gift:	Cooper's biology is shared with that of red pandas. His overall speed, strength, and agility are higher than most teens his age. His tail also provides a useful tool in an assortment of techniques.

CHAPTER TEN

Meet, But Don't Greet

Jordan marched into Fort Olympus without a plan. By the time he realized he needed a map, he wasn't able to tell exactly where he was or even where to start. He found himself crossing the courtyard where a stone pathway led through a field of green pastures on each side and a bronze statue of notable hero alumni in each pasture. As he made his way through, Jordan mused that he could hopscotch through Houston across whole city blocks but somehow found himself lost inside the school of his dreams.

Jordan stopped when he spotted a young woman posing with a statue and taking a selfie with it. She was Jordan's age and just a bit taller. She had a runner's build with long springy limbs. She had mahogany skin, and her neon purple hair phased from pink to violet. She was currently striking a pose to take a selfie with a statue of Polaris.

Jordan marveled at the statue. Polaris' clothes were clearly from an earlier century with a scarf wrapped around his face, forever frozen in time behind him. *The Hero of the Underground Railroad*, Jordan mused. Polaris was one of the first black heroes who, in 1913, often led slaves up north using the star of his namesake – Polaris.

The young woman clicked her selfie and then paused when she realized someone was watching her. "Can I help you?" Alicia called out, shoving her phone back in her blazer pocket.

"Nope, I'm good," Jordan squeaked out.

Alicia rolled her eyes. *I've been here for all of five minutes and –*

"Actually..." Jordan began.

Ugh, what now? Alicia sighed to herself.

"I'm lost," Jordan admitted.

Alicia stopped, looked him up and down, and read his expression. *Yeah, I'll say.*

"Do you know where the Apollo Barracks are?" he asked.

She gave him a second look, then determined that maybe he was lost and not just a guy trying to creep on her. *Fine, fine, just be nice to the guy.*

"You're on the right path," Alicia explained. "Just keep going on down through this courtyard. Then it'll be on your left."

"Thanks." Jordan nodded. "And...uh, sorry about earlier. I just – I'm a big fan of Polaris. One of the first black heroes in the US – part Abolitionist, part Esper, all hero."

Okay, maybe it was just a mistake, Alicia mused. "You don't know how to tie a tie, but you know your history."

Jordan jammed his hands in his pants pockets, and then he looked down and saw that somehow his tie had come loose again. "Yeah, I gotta fix it later. Uh...Thanks," Jordan said a little too loud, and then added, "I'm Jordan."

"Alicia," she said with a nod.

Then – silence.

"Well, I gotta go. Thanks again," Jordan said, then rushed away.

Alicia smiled as he walked off. *Good luck, Jordan.*

Jordan took Alicia's advice and made his way through the courtyard and turned left where he found a building that towered in front of him. It was impossible to tell if this building was built in the 1700s or yesterday. Polished grey brick like the other buildings was built up into a mammoth structure that wrapped around the courtyard.

Jordan swiped his student ID to release the door lock; the building was modernized, even if it was old. There was a beep and a click when the door bolt pulled back. Jordan entered into a swath of bustling freshman boys. Jordan worked his way past a gathering of passing students, not all fully human, and made his way to the elevator that would take him to the eighth floor. He exited into a hallway adorned with photos that varied in timeframe, exposure, and subject matter, although most featured former residents. He arrived at his dorm room – 845.

Jordan swiped his keycard to enter. The dorm was about twice the size of his own room. A door to his right led to the shared bathroom while directly in front of him was a window that looked out onto the courtyard where he stood only moments ago.

Jordan took inventory of the dorm and found two of everything.

Two red oak chests of drawers.

Two red oak wooden wardrobe closets.

Two beds on opposite sides of the room.

Where is my roommate? Jordan thought. Then he paused as he noticed a pair of figures on the dresser. His eyes went wide. *A limited-edition Kinetic. And is that –no way – a first edition Lion Force.* While Jordan had a number of Kinetic toys, his Lion Force collection was pretty light. Lion Force was known as one of the Olympians who passed on during the Green Night, but before that he was one of the most popular Hybrid heroes. He was a stunning lion on two legs, with 300 pounds of muscle packed into his six foot four frame and a mane of lush hair that wrapped around his stern visage. He was a striking figure in real life – and as a figurine.

Jordan knelt beside the dresser and marveled at the Lion Force toy. In his excitement, he didn't notice something scrambling silently on the ceiling above him.

Look at the attention to detail, that hair, those clothes, those claws. When the thought of claws entered his mind, Jordan glanced up as a hand full of claws came into view.

"What the –" Jordan shouted and activated his plasma, mentally flooding the room with unstable gravitons. His roommate joined the shouting, and the gravitons threw them both backward. Jordan hit the ground hard and heard a thump as the other person hit the ground – softly.

What was that? Jordan's mind spun, and he pulled himself upright. The first thing he saw was a tail. His roommate was a Hybrid.

"Hey, are you okay?" Cooper asked. "I didn't mean to scare you." A soft voice came from the slight kid leaning over him. Cooper was small for his age, especially for a hero in training. Soft, pale skin clashed with his autumn red hair parted in two sections atop his head, to allow the tiny fluffy ears to poke through. He had a button nose and soft features but none so soft as his four-foot tail that waved behind him. His tail was the same burgundy as his hair but with brown stripes through it. His tail was hefty, and he used it for support, climbing, gesturing, and swatting.

"You're – You're –" Jordan couldn't find his words. "You're –"

"Cooper," he introduced himself with a handshake. "Your roommate. I hope you're okay; I just wanted to surprise you."

As Jordan shook his hand, he was further shocked to feel how rough his palms – or paws – were. The grasp was firm, and Jordan felt soft fingers, leather-like palms, and pin-point sharp nails. *Claws,* Jordan realized. *Red fur. Tiny ears.* Jordan took a moment to adjust to the idea of Cooper, and Cooper's eyes locked onto something else.

"You've got a Lion Force too," Cooper exclaimed and pointed to a Lion Force collectible that had fallen out of Jordan's duffel bag. Luckily it was still in its box, so it wasn't damaged. "I've got him and a few Kurikara's at home and a ton of MegaTons too."

"Oh. Oh, yeah." Jordan snapped out of it, then bent down to pick it up, but Cooper was faster.

Actually, Cooper didn't just move with speed; he moved with haste too. One second, he was behind Jordan. The next, he bounded across the wall, then dropped in front of him to grab the box. He moved just like –

A squirrel, Jordan realized as he looked Cooper over again. That flat bushy tail, those claws, the rough hands, those teeny-tiny ears on his head, and even the way Cooper held the toy in both hands was like a squirrel with an acorn.

"I've got a Lion Force too," Cooper chimed.

Jordan turned back to the Hybrid toy he was looking at on the dresser earlier. *Oh, of course.*

Cooper rotated the box in his hands. "Ohhh, this is the memorial edition, forty-five points of detail, and a bronze coating. I'll trade you."

Jordan didn't know if he wanted to, so he blurted out, "Lemme think on it."

"Okay, you do that," Cooper said with ease as he put the figure down on Jordan's bed. "As you can tell I'm a big fan of Hybrids." Then, in a burst of amazing dexterity, Cooper backflipped and landed atop his red oak wardrobe, and then from his new vantage point he opened the doors. "I hope you don't mind, but I already picked my closet. I had to put all my shirts up before they got wrinkled."

Jordan saw the shirts inside were a mix of Fort Olympus issued uniforms and a number of shirts that simply read "Hybrid Pride" along with a picture of various Hybrid heroes and icons.

"Oh, and you are – half..." Jordan said, unsure of how to ask this and respectfully trailed off.

Cooper, in yet another display of squirrelly dexterity, leapt off the wardrobe, landed on both feet, and posed dramatically. "Half man, half red panda, all hero."

"Whoa," Jordan exclaimed, "I see it. The ears, the fur –"

"The tail." Without turning around, Cooper used his tail to close the wardrobe behind him. "So, when I say I'm willing to trade for your Lion Force toy, I mean it."

"I know. I still gotta think on it," Jordan replied.

"Yours is limited edition, you know the price went up after – you know – the Green Night."

"Yeah," Jordan sighed, "but trust me. I got a lot more figures where that came from and signed gloves from Kinetic." As the words left Jordan's mouth, Cooper's eyes went wide. He blitzed behind Jordan, scaled the wall, and tried frantically to peer into Jordan's bag.

"Ohhh, show me, show me, show me." Cooper cheered.

Jordan clamped his bag closed. "Dude, chill, I've got my boxers in there."

"Ugh, you sure do." Cooper's nose perked up, and he recoiled from the bag with enough force that he stumbled backward. "My senses are turned up to eleven, so I'm really sensitive to smells and sounds," Cooper explained and stood up. "Like, I can tell the intercoms are on and –"

"Intercoms?" Jordan asked.

Cooper slapped his hands over his ears in response to the soft chime that echoed through the room followed by the sounds of a woman's soft voice. "Attention, students: this is Headmaster Patel. We'll be meeting for First Assembly in Roosevelt Yard in fifteen minutes."

It was accompanied by another soft chime. Cooper shook his head back and forth. "Oof, does she have to yell?"

Jordan studied Cooper for a bit. *Wow, he really does sense these things.*

Using his tail like a spring, Cooper propped himself off the ground. Then using a hand and tail combo, he smoothed out his blazer and tie. "Fifteen minutes," Cooper said. "I'm gonna head out to the assembly. I'll save you a seat."

"Thanks. I'm gonna finish unpacking, then head over," Jordan said.

Cooper scurried along the walls to the door, opened it from upside down, and crawled out. He called back, "Oh, your tie is undone." Cooper's tail left last, and Jordan was alone with his thoughts and awe.

I know. Jordan sighed. He turned to a mirror situated on the back of the door and saw that his tie was now dangling from his neck. *Why couldn't I just have a clip-on?*

Jordan fiddled with his tie. As he descended in the barracks elevator, he used the reflective surface of the doors to tie his tie–or at least attempt to.

Okay, a loop here, bring it around, then –Jordan fretted. *I swear one of the challenges of Hercules was learning how to tie a tie.* Jordan squinted at his reflection then leaned into the door trying to get a better look when – TING.

The door opened, and Jordan was face to face with a student quite surprised to find himself an inch from Jordan. Neither of them moved for a moment before Jordan shuffled back and offered, "My bad."

Reuben Alvarez stepped cautiously into the elevator. When the door opened on Jordan, Reuben stifled the flight or fight response, and flight was not his go-to. Reuben eyed Jordan again, but Jordan had gone back to fighting his tie.

Well, that was awkward, Jordan said to himself.

Reuben was a bit taller than Jordan with sunbaked skin over sharp features. He had the eyes of a kid who had been left alone in the desert. They had a quiet intensity with dark circles marring the skin beneath them. Though he was a kid, his face carried the weight of a person twice his age. His hair was black with red tips that were brushed up and to the side. Even while wearing the Fort Olympus formal outfit – complete with a straight and tied tie – he looked not only bored to be here but ready to fall asleep at any moment.

While Jordan first noticed Reuben's tie, it wasn't until Reuben raised his right arm to tap the "close door" button that Jordan saw that Reuben's right hand was wrapped in a series of tight bandages. Although Reuben's blazer sleeve covered much of his arm and hand, the bandages were unmistakable.

"Hey," Jordan quipped up, "I noticed your arm and –" At the word "arm" Reuben reflexively hid it behind his back. "And your tie," Jordan recovered. "And I was wondering if you knew how to tie one of these. I've been trying all day and –"

TING.

The door opened behind Reuben. He looked at Jordan for a moment and then decided, "Sorry, I'm running late too." Reuben made a move to leave but threw out one piece of advice. "Just... just hide it from them. You don't wanna get written up."

With that Reuben walked off, and Jordan was left with only his thoughts once more. *Wait. Written up?* Jordan stopped the door from closing and rushed into the lobby. Frustrated, he tied it into a strange knot and made his way to the door. *Okay, maybe they won't care. But he said "written up." Are there rules for clothing here?*

Jordan tried to calm himself. He walked while trying to tuck the knot away but somehow ended up choking himself. *Okay, that's not the way. All right, all right. I'll just hide it. No one will see it, and I'll try and get back here quickly before someone does.* Jordan's progress was thwarted by a wall of a man.

"Sorry," Jordan blurted out, "I was just –"

Jordan's breath caught in his throat. He recognized the face immediately. Those piercing eyes, that scarred flesh, and that wild storm of electric blue hair. Titanus smiled behind his crooked face. "Mr. Harris."

CHAPTER ELEVEN

Astra Inclinant

Cooper had to smile.

For years, everyone had told him he would never be a hero or even a sidekick, but after almost literally working his tail off, here he sat in the opening ceremonies of Fort Olympus. Most students got in by recommendation or completing hero prep course requirements, but he had applied and been accepted on the merits of his own words. When he heard the school was leading a new initiative for Hybrid students, he applied secretly. His parents were quite surprised when he was accepted. It took a long conversation and many promises to get them to agree for him to take this opportunity. Even his father had told him that he wouldn't be a hero – that their kind wasn't meant to be heroes – but he had this chance to prove him wrong. Despite his efforts and desperation to get to Fort Olympus, this sea of teenage prizefighters made doubts creep in, and he felt himself shrink. Maybe his father was right. Maybe his friends were right. Maybe his bullies were right. Maybe deep down inside, Cooper knew that he was wrong.

Cooper's smile faded.

Titanus was wearing a navy blue three-piece suit that seemed ill-fitting for a man of his stature. He looked like a Viking stuffed into a tuxedo. Titanus smiled, and Jordan shivered. It was a real smile, not the toothy threat from the other night.

"Clayton," Jordan said, trying to match the tone Darius used in their last meeting.

Titanus raised an eyebrow. "I see you made it to Fort Olympus."

"Well yeah, it was either that or – "

"Jail," Titanus interrupted. "Any leads so far?"

"Honestly, sir, I'm just trying to figure out how to tie my tie right now," Jordan said flatly.

A rough chuckle, like sandpaper, echoed from somewhere behind Titanus' façade. "Well, I just thought that with the stakes so high, you'd have found something by now. You don't want a scarlet V on your face, do you?"

"I just got here."

"Well, I see that. I also see that your tie is out of order, and your shoes are against regulation."

Jordan glanced down at his beat-up Zeuz Airwalkers and replied, "My shoes are on the way."

"And your jacket looks like you just fell down a flight of stairs. That's three infractions right there. Don't you know if you get three strikes, you're booted out?"

Jordan froze. *Crap. Written up. Of course.*

"Please, please, don't write me up. I'll do whatever I need to –"

"You got a problem with rules, Mr. Harris," Titanus declared, "and I–"

Suddenly, a voice cracked like a whip from behind them, strong, lean, and lethal. "Dad, can we go?"

Titanus froze, and Jordan saw a range of emotions play across his face before the pair of them turned to see Sydney Asimov marching their way. Tall, with the long legs and arms of a gymnast, a bundle of electric blue hair flaring behind her, and her father's beady black eyes, it was none other than Titanus' daughter; she moved like a fury in heels. While Jordan was rattled by her stature and presence, he felt Titanus seemingly deflating as his daughter shut them both down. She was wearing the Fort Olympus uniform punctuated by a skirt with the same black and gold color scheme.

Titanus greeted her with a one-arm hug. She didn't return it; she shuffled next to him, almost begrudgingly. "Sydney, I was just talking to your classmate, Jordan Harris."

"Hey," Jordan spat the word with haste, wanting nothing more than to use his powers to fling himself out of Titanus' gaze.

Sydney gave him a once-over, then replied, "Can we go?"

Jordan blinked. It was as if he didn't even exist to her.

"Fine, Sydney. Today is your day after all." Titanus turned to Jordan. "I'll let you go with a warning this time, because – "

"Dad," Sydney cut him off again, "we don't have time for your cape-dragging monologues."

After all Jordan had been through, he now suddenly found himself suppressing a laugh. Titanus' face twitched, and the giant simmered as his daughter humbled him.

Is he laughing at me? The realization hit Titanus like one of his own giant, spectral fists. Titanus fought the urge to monologue. He pulled Sydney closer and challenged, "Fine. Don't be late, Mr. Harris. That'll be another infraction."

Sydney rolled her eyes, spun out of her father's grasp, and walked off. Titanus gave Jordan a nod. *This was your last warning.* Titanus turned on his heel and followed his daughter.

Well, Jordan thought, *that apple doesn't fall far from the tree...* While Jordan was unsure of where the Roosevelt Courtyard was on the map, he decided to follow the sound of chattering voices and other late students that were streaming towards an area two blocks west of the barracks.

Jordan and a dozen other tardy students made their way through a gate and into a courtyard that was a whole city block wide. A grassy field, surrounded by stone columns enshrined in vines, welcomed them. At the back of the field was a makeshift stage that had been set up under a cloudy Texas afternoon sky. On stage was a set of chairs and a podium with a microphone. The stage and the area immediately surrounding it were set with wooden chairs.

Jordan couldn't count them all, but he estimated there were at least 360 students. All of various breeds – human and Hybrid. Plus, of all various nationalities – some had even adorned their Fort Olympus blazers with flag pins or national tribe sashes. Jordan walked down an aisle, trying simultaneously to find an open seat and absorb all the new faces.

Wow, it seems like everyone knows each other here, Jordan thought, shrinking a little on the inside. He spotted Reuben sitting by an empty seat, and Jordan paused. *I'd rather not.* Reuben shot a glance his way. *Yeah, he'd rather not too.* Jordan felt the warning from his narrow eyes. Jordan turned and continued walking down the aisles of chairs when he heard Cooper call out to him.

"Jordan. Jordan over here." Cooper's voice reached him despite the cacophony. Jordan spotted Cooper's tail before he spotted him. Cooper was waving it like a fur-coated flag.

"I saved you a seat." Cooper patted the saved seat with his tail.

"Thanks." Jordan smiled softly, then made his way down the aisle to a chorus of "Excuse me."

As Jordan made his way over to the seat, Cooper swiveled his tail under himself and used it as a cushion.

The pink-haired girl next to Jordan suddenly came to life and called out across the aisle to another girl who had brown and white wings tucked against her back. "Hey, I thought you were going to sit over here."

"No," the winged girl called out. "I was saving you a seat over here. Hold on. Let me see if she'll switch."

Jordan tried his best to ignore the side-bar conversation next to him, but the pink-haired girl to his right suddenly stood up and crossed the aisle to sit with her friend. The seat wasn't empty long, and his new neighbor was a girl with long black hair and sharp green eyes.

Jordan glanced her way and dread filled every fiber of his being.

It was Rhea, the girl he met at the Olympian memorial, the one with the sharp eyes, the one who guessed he was a vigilante from one look. *Wait, wait. What is she doing here?* Jordan screamed internally. *Out of everyone who knows I was a vigilante, why did she have to show up?* Jordan flinched, and Rhea glanced his way. Her look went from curiosity to recognition.

"Hey, do I know you?" Rhea asked.

"No. Uh –not at all," Jordan snapped and then turned his eyes forward.

"Wait," Rhea pressed, "you look really familiar."

"Nope," Jordan chirped. "I get that a lot."

Cooper leaned in. "Hey, J, who's your friend?"

"She's not my friend," Jordan snapped.

Confused by the outburst, both Rhea and Cooper leaned back in their seats. Just in time too. A series of horns echoed from the stage, pulling the student's attention to the sight of Richa Patel. The headmaster walked with a simple elegance onto the stage. She was in her late thirties, tall with deep brown skin–common in the South Asian community. Her skin glowed, her olive green dress was flowing around her body, and her hair floated behind her in a long black ponytail with stripes of green glowing inside the depths of her bundle. Richa's clothes and her hair rippled as if underwater, pushed by some invisible current. Richa reached the microphone and smiled at the crowd, obviously waiting for the chatter to silence. Even under the afternoon Texas heat, she stood patiently, radiating a welcoming warmth.

"Good afternoon," Richa beamed, "and welcome, students, to a new year at Fort Olympus."

The older students were the first to applaud, followed by those in their first year. Jordan, Rhea, and Cooper also joined in the applause.

Richa continued. "I am Headmaster Patel. Some of you may know me as the hero Saraswati."

Cooper leaned over and whispered to Jordan, "I got her action figure at home."

Jordan nodded. "I have her card. Ultra-rare."

"Oh, we're definitely gonna get along," Cooper chirped.

"But now I've begun to look forward to a new future, and I'm not alone. Let me introduce your professors for this semester." Richa waved to the sidelines. Suddenly, the stage began to fill as four dozen people made their own way to the stage. Some walked. Some flew. A few teleported. Richa was quickly surrounded by a fleet of humans and Hybrids. Jordan and Cooper mimicked each other, and both stared wide-eyed and gobsmacked by the fifty pros that overwhelmed the stage.

Cooper pointed out the half-man, half-tiger Hybrid who was widely seen as the successor to Lion Force. "That's Tigris," Cooper exclaimed over the welcoming applause of the crowd. Tigris was a bipedal man with orange and black striped fur that coated his body. His face was that of a tiger with large, wet, black eyes. And his body rippled with muscle that was barely contained by his teal blue XXL suit. He wore leather gloves that kept his claws at bay.

Jordan had fought the fanboy urge when Titanus had arrested him; he even felt the urge to shout when he realized Darius was Kinetic, but when four dozen superheroes were on stage in front of him pronouncing themselves as his teachers, Jordan went wild and yelled.

In particular, he picked out the hero Red Wing. He and Titanus were two of the surviving members of the Olympians. He was there on the Green Night, survived to tell the tale, and now he stood on stage before Jordan. Alexander "Red Wing" Robinson looked more cowboy than hero. Sandy-blonde hair that looked like hay hung from his head in a ponytail. His face, though handsome, was roguish and unshaven. He was all lean muscle like a runner. He didn't exude a threatening aura, unlike Titanus, but rather a gentle, carefree attitude.

His most telling attribute was that his right arm was missing just below the elbow. While the story of it was never publicized, it was well-known that he had lost his arm before the Green Night and even before he became a pro. Red Wing's name was a holdover from before his fame, but he was an Olympian, a survivor in more than one war, and an icon to the hero community.

Jordan cheered louder, hoping his voice just might pass the chorus of others to reach the heroes on stage. He swore if Kurikara or MegaTon stepped out on stage, he would lose it. Jordan flinched as Rhea called out, "Vermillion." He had almost forgotten about her in the rush of adrenaline he felt in the epic moment.

Vermillion is here too? Jordan asked himself, recognizing the professional's name as a mid-level hero, known for his work across the United States. Jordan studied the stage and spotted him. A well-built man in his thirties with crimson hair and sharp sideburns that ran down his face and framed it with an electric red goatee. His muscular form was comically squared against the thin reading glasses he wore, accompanied by a pair of aged brown leather suspenders. He looked like a bodybuilder disguised as a librarian.

Mrs. Patel raised an arm and added, "And due to recent events, I've taken a sabbatical from hero work to work with kids – most notably my own." Richa gestured to her stomach and finally turned to the crowd to show that there was indeed a baby bump. Her glow made more sense – she was pregnant. The crowd that had been cheering for the teachers applauded and cheered along with those same heroes in celebration of the news.

"Thank you, thank you," Richa said to quiet them. "Saraswati is my hero name, but Saraswati, my ancestor, was first known as the Goddess of Learning. So naturally, when I needed to take some time off from active combat, I decided to find a job – supervising the next generation of heroes." There was a break for light applause, and she continued. "The words engraved in our crest state, *'Astra Inclinant'*. 'The stars incline us.' And indeed the stardust that flows through our bodies and gives us these Gifts incline us to do better, to aspire for greatness. This is my first year as headmaster, and I'm sure I will learn a lot from you as you will learn from me and the heroes behind me. Now, I'd like to turn it over to a special guest this afternoon who agreed to join us for this special ceremony – the one, the only, Titanus."

The crowd applauded and welcomed Titanus. Jordan felt dread run cold in his gut, already worried he might be singled out again. Titanus shook hands with Red Wing, a mutual respect between the two surviving Olympians. Under a wave of even more applause, Titanus approached the microphone.

"Thank you for having me," he began dryly. "I'll keep this short. While this is a day for a certain celebration, we are living in dark times."

The crowd nodded with a somber realization of the reality he was addressing. "Ten years ago, this proud city of Houston, our home–and the world, for that matter–lost the Olympians. Seven of us went in, and only two came out. Since the Green Night and the Green Titan's defeat, crime has spiked all across the world. We are in need of heroes...We're in need of you."

Titanus stopped and looked out at the crowd expectantly, and the crowd looked back at him in anticipation. "Thank you," the man-mountain added and then nodded back to Richa, who fought to contain her grimace behind a blank face. Jordan, along with the other 359 students, clapped politely to not only fill the awkward silence but to alleviate the sense of dread that had befallen them. As Titanus returned to the lineup of teachers, he gave Alexander a thumbs up. Alexander bit his cheek and returned it through a strained smile.

"Well, that was certainly hmmm – uplifting," Richa commented. "In that spirit, we'll be hosting a small moment of silence for those we lost on the Green Night." The spotlights dimmed, and the heroes lowered their heads on stage. Jordan was the first among the people in the audience to dip his head and let the silence drown the moment.

*Seeing Titanus and Red Wing together was cool but knowing what they must have gone through on that night...*Jordan's thoughts were interrupted by the strangest noise – snickering. Jordan turned in his seat towards the absurd sound of laughter during the moment of silence. He twisted farther in his seat and spotted a tan fourteen-year-old boy with silver hair that was clipped short into a military buzz cut. Jordan's eyes jumped from his hair to the boy's sharp ears. They rose up into little spikes that framed the side of his chrome cut.

An elf? Jordan realized, his anger suddenly replaced with wonder. As the elven teen chuckled at something with a group of other elves who were heavyset with black and brown hair, Jordan's momentary wonder snapped back to anger. Before he could form the words, the lead elf looked up and met Jordan's stare. Those eyes were prismatic with an array of colors when they narrowed.

"Got a problem?" Lucas whispered at Jordan.

"It's the moment of silence, you dragger," Jordan shot back.

Rhea and Cooper turned back to see what was going on at the harsh whisper from Jordan. Rhea sized up the situation then, without a word, raised a single finger and sent a beam of green energy from her fingertip right through Lucas' phone, burning it out of his hand.

"Don't be rude," she challenged with authority, then turned back around.

Lucas and Jordan shared a surprised glance. Then Jordan's eyes followed the smoke trail to the burning hole in Lucas' phone. Jordan hesitated – Lucas' phone case was a mock imitation of the Taurus badge. If the burning plastic had not given it away as fake gold, Jordan would have thought it was the same badge. *He's part of the Taurus Regiment,* Jordan realized. *Could it be him?* Jordan studied Lucas for another beat before Lucas flinched under his gaze. Jordan continued looking directly at Lucas and didn't break his stare.

"You got what you deserve," Jordan snapped.

Lucas' eyes flashed green before a sudden rumbling got their attention. It sounded like the echoing of a monster truck's diesel engine, but it was impossibly coming from a barrel-chested man at the end of the aisle. He nodded at both of them, *quiet.* His appearance was striking: a pale face, spiky black hair, a muscle-bound body and most notably a scarlet V tattooed on his face that ran like a dividing line from his hairline to his jaw then back up his cheek and into his hairline.

*A Vesper...*Jordan recognized.

Cooper voiced the realization. "I didn't know the school hired Vespers."

The Vesper nodded at them to keep their heads down, and the group did just that. Jordan's mind raced. *We've got Vespers with a scarlet V on their faces just walking around here. An elf that's part of Team Taurus, and if I play my cards right I won't get written up by Titanus or any other teacher for my outfit, and I can maybe–just maybe–survive the first day.*

"May we all seek to join the ranks of those heroes before us," Richa said in closing for a moment of silence. Then she made an "all rise" motion with her hands. "Will the incoming freshman class please stand?"

Jordan looked around and saw a series of heads pop up. He spotted Sydney standing first, then he saw Alicia in the distance. In his peripheral he found Reuben rising. Jordan followed their lead and stood alongside Cooper, Rhea, and then he heard Lucas and his elven horde rise noisily behind them.

"It is my duty and my honor to swear you into the Esper Hero Services," Richa spoke with reverence. "Dedicating your Gift, your light, and yourself to public safety is the highest honor an Esper can hope to achieve. The Esper program is a five-year course program that culminates with one year of service as a sidekick with an active professional hero before graduating."

Richa pulled an aged leather-bound book from her pocket, flipped gently to a page, and began to read aloud. "Today you are no longer civilians. You are cadets in the United States Esper Hero Program. You are following in the footsteps of soldiers, generals, Presidents, and Olympians. Not many are born as Espers. Fewer are chosen to be heroes. Today you sixty students from around the world join the ranks of the other students seated around you and the leagues of Espers who have gone on to serve through the ages. It is we who must take the charge against those who seek to do wrong. Though the stars themselves flow through our veins and power our Gifts, it is the intent and action that matter. We do this not because it comes easy to us or even that it may be hard but because it is necessary, because justice demands it – because someone must uphold the banner of righteousness. Because the stars incline us." She took a firm breath and gazed out at the students. "Welcome to Fort Olympus, where…" Richa paused once more, then like the swelling of a great mouth bursting open the other cadets joined in with her in a chorus of voices all crying out the same phrase.

"Astra Inclinant!"

CHAPTER TWELVE

The Battalia

Khadija Harris couldn't remember the last time she had a drink. Between her long patrol hours, Jordan, cooking and cleaning, Jordan's vigilante shenanigans, and office work at the police station, she never had time for herself–let alone a drink in the middle of the day. Of course she knew Jordan would move out one day, but that day came much sooner than she anticipated. Even now, when she knew he wasn't home, the silence felt off.

Where was the heavy footfall of him running down the hall? Where was the occasional thump as he fell back to Earth? What was she was going to cook for dinner tonight? Jordan usually ate enough for two since he was a growing boy, but when was the last time she made a meal just for herself? When was the last time she slept in past nine in the morning? These questions and more ran through her head before the distinct sizzle and pop of a beer bottle being popped open snapped her out of it.

Darius lumbered over and sat down next to her. His hands were big enough that he could have held two beers in each hand, but he handed one to her and kept the second for himself. "Here," he offered, "you deserve it."

Khadija exhaled, felt a weight leave her shoulders, and then clinked bottlenecks with Darius. *Yes, I do.* Khadija took a hearty sip and beamed, feeling a familiar joy rush back to her. "It's so quiet already," Khadija mused.

"You miss him already?"

Khadija searched her thoughts and decided to be honest. "He's my brother."

Darius nodded. It wasn't the answer he expected, but it was an answer.

"Thank you for calling me," Darius began. "I – I know it's been a while since I've been back here, but thank you for calling. I wouldn't be able to forgive myself if something happened to him."

Khadija nodded. She hadn't expected the conversation to drift that way, but it was somehow good. "Thank you for coming." Khadija took another hearty sip. "I wasn't sure if you were even gonna pick up to be honest. But thank you..."

Darius replied, honestly, "He's my nephew."

Something stirred within Khadija. It could have been the effects of the beer, but no. This wasn't a physical or chemical reaction; this was raw emotion.

"I lied to him for so long." Khadija blurted the words out, and they hung in the air, judging.

"No one is saying what you did was wrong," Darius replied.

"I was afraid, Darius. I was just so afraid," Khadija began. "We had just lost both of our parents and...I panicked. It was just the two of us and – I was just 20 years old, barely an adult. So I hid him. I told him to hide his powers. I – I thought about putting him in a hero school. I thought about telling him the truth. I thought about all these things, but God it was just so much easier to hide. I told him to hide who he was. I – I hid myself and – " Khadija stopped. She was out of breath. She sunk back in her seat, a decade of lies weighing on her. "He's going to start asking questions, Darius. Questions about the Green Night. Things I don't want to face."

Darius nodded and replied, "You did what you had to do. You had just been through something tragic, and you didn't want it to happen again. You were suddenly taking care of this kid, and you didn't want him to become a target. You did what you had to."

Khadija shook her head. "If he finds out who our parents really were and – what I did to protect him. If he knew–if he really knew who our parents were...and Zeus forbid–if the wrong person found out, if a Vesper or any criminal knew just who we are, they'd come for revenge...and I've been trying to prevent that for years."

Darius, working from his trauma training and experience as a hero, realized the next step to calming someone was closing the physical distance, then it was touching. "He deserves the truth, but it's something he has to realize for himself." Khadija nodded, and Darius put a hand on hers. "Plus, the only person at the school who knows the truth about your parents is Red Wing since he worked with them. As long as he and Jordan don't get chummy, he'll be fine...We'll be fine."

Khadija nodded. *He's right. As long they stay apart, we can keep this secret. What are the odds they'll run into each other on the first day?*

After Richa's moving speech, a screen rolled down behind her to show students their Squad Leader assignments. To Jordan's elation, not only was Cooper on his team, but Alexander was going to be leading them. Soon after the screen dropped, Jordan found himself huddled around Alexander with Alicia, Cooper, and Reuben.

"Afternoon, Cadets, my name is Alexander, aka Red Wing, and I'm gonna be your Squad Leader," he announced in a weathered voice. "Meaning for the next five years I'll be your mentor, coach, and professional hero liaison. If all goes well, and I'm still in business, you all might even be my sidekicks in your sixth year."

Up close, Jordan couldn't help but notice that Alexander was shorter in person than he anticipated. While Alexander was usually framed in photos with the gigantic Titanus, Jordan realized Alexander was quite average in height – and a bit older in the face than he expected too. But those aspects, including his stumped arm, just made him more human and thus more alluring. This average-looking man was one of the most famous heroes in the world.

While Jordan's voice had been reduced to a harsh whisper because of all the shouting, Alicia was still in good form and gave a yelp when Alexander was announced as her Squad Leader. She leaped up, threw her fist in the air, and let off a burst of neon purple and pink lights from her fist.

Whoa. Did she just glow? Jordan's mind reeled.

Jordan glanced at Reuben. If he was excited, his hands in his pockets, shoulders slumped, and a thin lazy scowl was his way of showing it. Jordan glanced at Cooper, who was practically vibrating with pent-up excitement. Alicia did a one-two punch "Yes."

"Alicia," Alexander mused. "Bright as ever."

Wait, they know each other? Jordan asked himself.

"I talked to your parents before they left today," Alex said. "I was hoping you'd be on my team. Don't expect me to go easy on you."

"Easy on me?" Alicia cracked her knuckles. "I'm not gonna go easy on you, old man."

Alexander smiled and beamed with pride behind his sunbaked skin.

Oh, yeah. They definitely know each other somehow, Jordan mused.

Alexander nodded to her, then took in the rest of the class. "From here on out, we'll be known at Team 8-1, also known as the Freshman Leo Regiment." Alexander motioned across the field toward the other students meeting their teammates and Squad Leaders. "As you can see, there are eleven other regiments that freshmen are sorted into. You will also receive two of these." He reached into a bag and pulled out ten identical golden badges. Jordan recognized them from the museum encounter, and then again in the interrogation room. That badge had a bull and his own had a lion, but this one represented his team. Alexander handed two to Reuben first, who took it into his unwrapped hand. "Some of you may already have them if you purchased them with your suit that correlates to your birthday. But now that you are part of the Leo regiment, you are to install these Leo badges into your shoulder pads. Be careful, though as these things get lost all the time."

Yeah, tell me about it, Jordan mused to himself.

As Jordan received his pair, another thought hit him. *So my target had one of these. And if they're handing them out right now –* Jordan realized: *My target is here about to get a Taurus badge to replace the one they lost.* Jordan scanned the crowd, searching the unfamiliar faces of students and teachers until a second thought came back to him. *The elf,* Jordan recalled. *He had a Taurus badge phone case, so he's gotta be in that group, right?*

"What if I like the one I have now?" Cooper asked. "I'm a Sagittarius."

Silver hair. Silver hair, Jordan chanted to himself before his eyes found Lucas only a few yards away huddled with Rhea, her black locks unmistakable. They were members of the team led by Vermillion.

"Well, unfortunately, you're not in the Sagittarius Regiment, so you'll have to switch them out," Alex commented dryly. "On that note let's introduce ourselves. Sound off. Jordan?" Jordan's eyes focused not on what was in front of him but on Lucas, who was now examining his new Taurus badges. The elf's prismatic eyes were entranced with the gold plate. *Well, I think I got my first lead.*

"Ay yo, over here. Jordan?" Alexander's voice landed in his ear and brought him back to the huddle.

"Oh," Jordan exclaimed. "Sorry, my name is Jordan Harris, and, uh – my alias is StarLion."

"Well, welcome back to Earth, StarLion." Alexander nodded for Cooper to go next.

"Cooper Greene and my hero alias is Ailurus."

Alexander nodded politely then turned to Alicia. She was eager, but not ready.

"Alicia Jackson," she said proudly, then trailed off, "and I haven't decided on an alias yet."

"That's fine. Your brother took a while to figure out his," Red Wing replied softly. "Your hero alias should reflect your personality and likes, so we'll work on that. Next."

Who is her brother? Jordan studied Alicia's face for an answer.

All eyes went to Reuben next, who shrugged out, "I'm Reuben and...yeah. That's about it." Alexander paused, waiting for a bit more out of him, but after a moment of silence, the group quickly realized that was indeed all he intended to say.

"Okay, and rounding out the last of us is – aww, there she is." Alexander cheered sarcastically as Sydney strolled over to them, arms crossed and lips pouting.

"Sorry, I'm late." Her voice was dry and direct. "I got held up with my father." Sydney's eyes, much like her dad's, scanned the team and absorbed the situation rapidly. Jordan could almost hear her mind clicking. Then as her gaze landed on Reuben, there was a flash of curiosity, then recognition.

"You mind introducing yourself?" Alexander offered.

"Sydney Asimov." She said it as if it was obvious. "My father is Titanus. My alias is Battalia. I look forward to leaving you all in the dust."

"Well, you certainly have his disposition," Alexander chimed.

"I shouldn't even be here with these cape-dragging freshmen," she groaned. "I should have transferred in as an upperclassman."

"Well, we all have to start somewhere," Alicia pointed out.

Battalia made eye contact with Alicia and then made a point of rolling her eyes, dismissing her.

"Do you have a problem?" Alicia said, stepping forward.

"No." Sydney paused for emphasis. "I've got problems."

"More like issues," Alicia quipped.

Jordan and Cooper chuckled. Sydney noticed, then grimaced almost by instinct. She took stock once more of her teammates and felt her cheeks pull back into the scowl her mother swore she was born with.

"Hey, hey," Alexander broke in. His voice was subtle, yet powerful, like a cowhide glove around an iron fist. "Let's not start sparring already."

Sydney didn't miss a beat. She looked them all up and down again, then rattled off, "My father is the best hero in the world, and saddling me with you is an insult." She turned to Alicia. "A sidekick," then to Jordan, "A kid who can't even tie a tie," then to Cooper, "A squirrel."

"I'm a panda," Cooper corrected her under his breath.

Then Sydney's eyes fell on Reuben. His lackluster attitude seemed to quickly mutate into something primal. His eyes narrowed and his chest inflated, almost daring her to look.

"And you," Sydney spat the words out like spoiled food, "A dem –"

"Don't finish that," Reuben challenged her.

*Wait...*Jordan took another glance at Reuben, then at his arm, and his eyes. *No way. Is he one of them?*

Battalia sized him up and decided it wasn't worth it. "You know what you are, and it ain't a hero. This is the B-team, where they stashed all the Esper rejects."

They were angry, but Alexander continued as if he had rehearsed this conversation before – or maybe at least expected it. "And do you think maybe the reason you were paired with them, and me, is because I know your father better than anyone else?" Sydney was silent. Alexander continued, "Or that he'd tell me to make sure to look after his daughter because she can be a handful?"

Jordan studied her reaction and, like her father, Sydney was adept at hiding her emotions behind gritted teeth. "Humph. Whatever," she scowled.

Aw, Zeus, help us. Alexander's general good nature returned. "Well, welcome to Team 8-1, also known as the Freshman Leo Regiment. We'll meet in an hour at Coliseum Seven for our first exercise." Alexander clapped his hands to signal the end of the meeting, and no one moved except Sydney. Reuben was second to go, making sure to leave right after Sydney and go the opposite way.

Jordan heard Alicia whisper under her breath, "What a dragger."

Alicia nodded thanks to Alexander, who nodded back before Alicia walked off.

Jordan watched her go, then his eyes fell back to Lucas, who shuffled his Taurus badges into his pocket. Vermillion was just finishing his speech to his team when Cooper's voice lured Jordan back from his thoughts.

"Yo, Jordan? Earth to J," Cooper called out.

"Yeah, what's up?" Jordan blinked.

"We gotta get changed, c'mon."

"Yeah." Jordan took another look at Rhea and faltered – her eyes were searing right into him. Jordan quickly looked the other way and ran off. *She knows. She knows I'm a vigilante,* Jordan's mind screamed. Jordan followed Cooper into the crowd. Even though he didn't look back, and there were now a dozen people between them, he could still feel Rhea's eyes on him.

SYDNEY ASIMOV

Hero Alias: Battalia

Height: 5'5

Weight: 110

Birth Date: November 19

Plasma Color: Blue

Plasma Level: 27,000

Gift: Sydney possesses the ability to project her plasma into a repulsive force field. The size and shape of her force field are only limited by her plasma level.

CHAPTER THIRTEEN

The Hierarchy

It was a quick jog back to the dorms where Jordan and Cooper grabbed their battle suits. Cooper replaced the Sagittarius plates, featuring an archer, with the Leo plates from Alexander.

Jordan followed Cooper from their dorm room and across a courtyard towards the training centers. He had only ever seen them online and in the maps, but they were truly something to behold. In the back of the campus sat the Fort Olympus Coliseums. Eight rotund coliseums, built for training and mock battle exercises in the 1700s, still served the same purpose today – just for a younger generation.

As Jordan reached Coliseum Seven, the first waves of admiration hit him. *I'm about to train on the same grounds as Polaris and Kinetic...This is so cool.*

"This is so cool," Cooper exploded with delight.

Jordan smirked. His roommate was easily excited, but they always seemed to be on the same page. Jordan and Cooper rounded the corner of the last courtyard and came face to face with Coliseum Seven. The structure looked like it had been plucked from the ages, copied many times over, and placed in a row before them. Marble columns ran down from the lip of the building and cascaded to form the outer structure that greeted them. At the top of the coliseum was a series of recently installed statues of the Olympians. While Jordan beamed up at Red Wing, Cooper focused on Lion Force. When they passed by the columns to enter, both of them reached out to feel the warm rocks bleached white by the Texas sun.

Jordan followed Cooper's lead into the coliseum and through a pair of metal doors that clashed with the aged-rock walls of the exterior. Inside, it was pristine and lit by halogen bulbs. It felt like being transported from Rome to a state-of-the-art gym. What remained historic and grandiose outside gave way to a sleek and modern interior that betrayed the true age of the building.

The boys filed down to the locker rooms to change clothes. Well, Cooper changed. Jordan began, but he was a bit self-conscious. Jordan found this was where they differed. Cooper didn't seem to care; he was too busy rattling on about Sydney, or *Battalia* as she liked to be called.

"Can you believe her? She called me a squirrel. A draggin' squirrel." In fewer than three sentences Cooper was down to his underclothes. He balled his clothes up, and like a rodent packing for winter, stuffed them into his locker with both hands.

Jordan yelped and ducked away from Cooper's tail as it swiped right over him. Cooper, oblivious, continued. "My alias is Ailurus. Ailurus. That's literally the scientific name for the red panda. Okay, but it also translates into raccoon or raccoon bear. Do I look like a raccoon?"

Cooper yanked his suit out of the locker and unzipped it. The suit was a single piece of fabric that covered from head to thumbnail with a zipper down the back that ran on a magnetic track to be operated with little assistance. Jordan removed his shirt and again was assaulted by Cooper's tail. He punched gravity under his feet and hopped over it.

"Oh, sorry," Cooper called back to him, still fretting.

"It's cool. It's cool," Jordan reassured.

"No, it's not cool. She insulted you too."

Jordan nodded. He was right.

"I mean," Cooper continued, "who cares if you don't know how to tie a tie."

Jordan frowned. The concern had suddenly mutated into a subtle jab. Before he could reply, Cooper's tail came back around and walloped Jordan in the back of the head. Jordan flinched and stepped farther back.

"Oh, sorry, man," Cooper chimed. "This thing has a mind of its own sometimes." Cooper then dove into his suit, one foot at a time. Then he rolled it up over his legs, his torso, and chest. Using the magnets in the zipper, he pulled it tight and closed. Jordan stared perplexed at his own suit. If he was being honest, he only wanted Darius' gloves – but they were too big for him – and the suit literally had gloves stitched into it. *Whatever. My gloves are cooler. I'll just wear two.*

"And then she nearly called that other guy the D-word," Cooper exclaimed. As if on cue, Reuben appeared from around the corner carrying his outfit over his shoulder. He glanced them up and down for a beat, the silence emphasizing Cooper's last sentence.

Bye, Reuben's face said, and he ushered off to change somewhere else in the locker room.

"Guess, he's self-conscious," Cooper said as – WHOOSH, THUMP – his tail popped out the back of a pre-made hole in the backside of his suit.

Jordan double-checked his suit, then sighed in relief.

It didn't have the same hole. *Phew, okay, that had to be custom-made.*

"Hurry up and change. We're gonna be late," Cooper urged him.

Jordan stepped gently into the suit. It was form-fitting. His feet felt sheathed when he jammed them into the toe of the suit. He rolled the suit up his body and felt the leather fabric grip him. It felt like being in a plastic bag. At every joint and turn of his frame he felt pockets of air moving and shifting inside. Though the material was heavy, he still felt surprisingly light inside of it. He flexed his fingers in the suit's gloves. They felt lighter than the signed gloves he usually wore. Jordan's toes were sheathed in the suit's mesh, and while most heroes usually wore boots, Jordan shoved his feet into his beat-up black and gold Zeuz Airwalkers.

Cooper grunted and pulled the golden shoulder pads down over his head. The armor traditionally had been based on knights and their chainmail but had undergone some revamping through time. The improved armor was composed of chrome plates that were painted gold for cadets and interlocked between nylon straps. The chrome plates linked together as they were tightened, and the straps eventually hugged the chrome plates snugly to the body in a metallic embrace. All the straps were fed into a locking mechanism behind the star in the middle of the suit. With one pull everything constricted towards the center.

"Okay, I get the suit, but not the armor," Jordan chimed.

"Well, yeah, this is important. Watch me." Cooper pulled down on a strap under his armpit and –SHINK–the armor tightened down across his shoulder, chest, and back. He then yanked on the strap under his other armpit, and the plates closed in on that side too. "You're gonna wanna pull these tight, or the armor will be too loose, and it'll move while you're running. I put it on too loose one time and broke my nose while running up a tree."

Jordan gulped. He could feel the weight of the star hugging against his chest. Cooper gave an extra hard pull on the strap, and Jordan felt it smother him.

"Make sure they are all pulled tight." Cooper continued pulling on the straps on his torso. "Also, the plates are made to shift as you move. But if they are loose, and they shift, and you get hit just right...CRUNCH."

". . .This is supposed to protect me, right?" Jordan asked blankly.

"Okay, c'mon. I'll do it," Cooper offered.

Before Jordan could refuse, Cooper, with a light-hearted lunge, scampered over his shoulders and yanked on the straps. Jordan coughed out a mouthful of tail hair.

"Blah." Jordan gagged.

Cooper's hands found the straps. "Inhale," Cooper instructed.

Jordan inhaled sharply, taking in the same fur he had just spit out before Cooper pulled back on the straps. Jordan felt his chest crush against the force of the plates. It was a tight fit. Not even his anxiety gripped him this tight. He exhaled and only felt a bit better. Both of them froze when Reuben came back around the corner to see the pair in an awkward situation. If Reuben was fazed, he barely reacted. Reuben's suit hugged his body, the shoulder pads only moving in sync with his movements. He gently placed his clothes, which were neatly strung from a hanger, into a locker.

"You missed a strap under the armpit," he said dryly, then walked off.

"Oh, he's right," Cooper affirmed, then pulled the remaining strap. "Phew – J, you know Right Guard is used for the left armpit too?"

"Will you let me do this?" Jordan snapped, embarrassed.

Cooper sprung off Jordan's shoulder and waved his hands furiously over his button nose. Jordan grabbed the strap under the armpit and gave a pull. He felt the plates lock into place, then snap flush against his body. Jordan flexed in the suit and admired the feel.

My fingers still feel a bit light, Jordan thought. He searched his locker, found his signed gloves, then pulled them on as snugly as possible. *There.* Jordan then checked himself out in the mirror...He looked like a hero.

Cooper did the same. Then in the mirror he looked down at the Leo badge on his shoulder. Jordan mirrored him.

Cooper offered his fist for a fist pound. "Leo Regiment."

Jordan bumped his fist. "Leo Regiment."

The pair followed the hallway, headed up an exit ramp, and felt the heat stifle them. They exited from the ramp into the light of the Texas sun. The interior of the coliseum was much like its ancestor's. Rows of seating surrounded a sandpit that sparkled gold in the heat.

Alexander was waiting for them with Alicia, Reuben, and Sydney. The group was dressed and ready. The light of the Texas sun bounced off the stars on their chests.

Alexander welcomed them upon Cooper's and Jordan's approach, "Welcome, Freshmen Leo Regiment to Coliseum Seven, one of the many training grounds for Espers. Does anyone know where the word 'coliseum' comes from?"

Alicia's hand shot up, and before Alexander could call on her, she began, "It comes from the ancient Greek word *kolossós* or giant statue. From when giants used to exist and helped build it."

Alexander cooed, "Very good. I see at least someone has done her homework." He turned an eye to the rest of the cadets, who avoided his gaze. "And Alicia, do you mind telling the class what the Coliseum was used for when it was first constructed?"

Alicia launched into an explanation. "It was a place for Espers to engage in mock battles from the retelling of the Olympians fighting the Titans, to the Olympians fighting the giants. Then it went from mock battles to actual battles. The Romans believed if one could face an opponent in a sandpit then they could win in any setting."

"Correct again," Alexander mused. "It's where the Espers first showed their prowess in battle, and it's where we'll be training to learn how to use our Gifts in the real world. So with that in mind – let's do it like the Romans and fight."

Cooper squeaked, "Wait, like fighting – fighting?"

"No," Alexander quipped, and then he thought on it. "Well, maybe." To clarify, he added, "Well, yeah, there will be fighting."

Cooper suppressed a squeal, but his tail went upright.

Jordan felt himself shrink backward. *We're going to be fighting on the first day?* Jordan's mind was already swimming, then drowning with possibilities.

Alexander reached into his pocket and removed six red plastic stripes. "Each of these plastic stripes has a magnetic tag on the end," Alexander pointed to a magnet on the end of each strip, "that you all will attach to your suit. Your goal will be to take it from your opponent by any means necessary."

"So there will be fighting," Sydney perked up.

"Only if you want, Syd," Alexander emphasized dryly.

"Good," Sydney smirked, her hero alias, Battalia, becoming more evident by the moment.

"Very good," Reuben growled from the back of the group.

Jordan cringed. *Great, I'm on a team of psychopaths.*

"Okay, first off," Alexander held up his wrist and a thin screen beeped to life along his forearm, "can anyone tell –"

"Ohhh, it's where your vitals are displayed," Alicia chimed.

Jordan turned his wrist over, made a fist, and suddenly his vitals appeared on his forearm. There were color-coded lines for heart rate, plasma levels, oxygen levels, and brain activity. *That's cool.*

"This is new, right?" Cooper asked, doing that creepy thing where he said exactly what was in Jordan's head. "It's cool."

"It's necessary," Sydney lamented. "With crime rates rising, we have to keep track of our bodies. The more we know about ourselves, the better we can handle our enemies."

Alicia and Sydney shared a look, then a nod. *Finally, something we could agree on,* Alicia thought.

"Alicia," Alexander gave her a thin smile, "mind telling us what we're looking at here?"

Alicia did a fist pump that let loose a neon spark, then continued. "Yeah, so basically there are four states of matter: air, water, solids and...anyone..." Her voice trailed off for someone to answer.

"Plasma," Alexander mused.

"Yes. Good job," Alicia replied.

"Okay, but remember I am the teacher here," he said.

"Espers naturally generate plasma from our Plasma Crystal in our necks," Alicia said. "We can use this for various abilities like enhanced strength, plasma beams, and whatever mutation or Gift we've received. The best way to read the strength of an Esper is to measure..." Alicia trailed off again.

Cooper sheepishly raised his hand and she pointed to him. "How much electricity is resting in that person's body?"

"Exactly. That's why you can see the monitor labeled 'plasma level' on your screen," she explained. "It's a new feature that's been integrated into the suit. While we've had the tech for a while, they've miniaturized it so we can assess enemies before going into battle." She summarized it with a clap of her hands. "So in short, the more plasma you generate, the stronger your power level."

"Okay, thank you, Professor Jackson. I'll take it from here," Alexander said, and then replaced her in front of the class. "So we'll be pairing off based on power levels. Since there are five of you, the strongest person will face me."

This revelation rattled the teens.

"So who wants to go first?" Alexander asked to a reply of silence. "Oh, now you guys are quiet?"

Alexander raised his arm, gripped it twice to imitate touching the pad, since he only had one arm, and the screen jumped through options until it displayed 85,000 volts on his screen. The group swallowed hard. Suddenly, everyone was more interested in looking at the sand than at him. "85,000 volts is my current output. Not my best, but I'm old now and not as strong as I used to be. For scale, I used to be part of the Olympians–the strongest in the world. Titanus clocks in at 100,000, MegaTon clocks in at 150,000 and Kurikara, the current strongest hero in the world, clocks in at 300,000, but the Green Titan was 500,000. Don't be afraid to fight someone above your level. If you're smart, you can find ways to make even the most lopsided fight worth it."

"Fine," Battalia spat, "I'll go first. I'm the strongest here, anyway." She stepped forward and tapped her screen to reveal 27,000 volts.

"Not bad." Alexander explained, "You're way above most everyday Espers. Your power level–like any muscle in the body–is based on how often you use your Gift and how long you've been training. The longer you train, the higher your level. Next."

Reuben stepped forward and used his bandaged fingers to tap the screen, found his number, and showed it off with a sigh–25,000.

"Hmmm, I thought someone like you would be higher," Sydney said.

"Wanna clarify what you mean by someone like me?" Reuben snapped back.

"Oh, you're dumb too? The other D-word."

Alexander cut between them, "StarLion, you're next. Remember we'll be paired up by levels, so everyone will fight their equals." Sydney and Reuben glared at each other; they were currently paired to fight one another.

Oh boy, Jordan thought. *C'mon, don't be embarrassing. Just be higher than, like, ten.* Jordan pulled his gloves tight on his hand to make sure his fingers could accurately tap the screen. He tapped his arm, flicked through a number of options under Plasma Level, Scan Plasma Levels, Scan Singular Level. He tapped again, closed his eyes, and looked away. There was an audible gasp. *It's ten. It's gotta be like ten or something.* Jordan tensed. He opened his eyes, looked at his team's faces, then down to his arm. It read 30,000.

That's higher than Sydney. That's really high, Jordan said to himself. *It's got to be a draggin' mistake.*

"30,000?" Jordan gasped.

"Oh, you've been hiding something from us, huh?" Alexander teased.

"I – uh – I – had a lot of extracurriculars that kept me fit."

"All right, Jordan is currently the highest and will face me. Who's next?"

"Me," Alicia declared as she stepped forward. *I've got to face Red Wing. I gotta show him what I can do. Let's see them top this.* Alicia slapped the command key on her arm and her plasma display came to life. "Yes," Alicia squealed with bursts of neon fireworks popping off her hand.

Does she just explode when she's happy? Jordan wondered.

Alicia turned her arm to face them and the group gasped. Her power level was 32,000.

"Wow, impressive," Alexander said. "I don't think I was even 30,000 when I was your age. Okay, we got one more."

Darn, I was hoping they'd forget about me. Cooper sighed and then toed the sand with his boot.

"Ugh, the trash panda?" Sydney groaned. "He'll be the lowest, so take it easy on him, Reuben."

"Do you have to insult everyone?" Jordan snapped at her.

"Me, on this team, is an insult," Sydney replied flatly.

Jordan gave her a once-over. *Okay, maybe fighting won't be too bad.*

"Okay," Alex ordered, "Ailurus, let's get a reading."

Cooper with trembling fingers tapped the screen. *I hate this. I hate this.*

"Hey, man, we won't laugh," Jordan offered.

Cooper's finger hesitated over the final button before he heard Jordan's promise.

"No promises," Battalia quipped.

Okay...here goes literally nothing. Cooper tapped his screen and looked away. Laughter. Hard, chuckling laughter assaulted his sensitive ears. *Oh no. No. No.* Cooper cringed.

"I'm sorry," Jordan gasped. "I'm sorry, I just didn't expect it."

Now everyone's laughing at me. Cooper deflated, refusing to look at his number.

"That's got to be a mistake," Sydney steamed through gritted teeth.

Cooper paused. Their responses sounded vaguely positive.

"No mistake," Alexander chimed. "He's the strongest here."

Cooper's eyes snapped open, and he whipped down to see that his plasma level was 42,000.

"What?" His tail shot up behind him as he gawked at the number. "How?"

"Yeah. I got questions," Sydney sneered.

Sydney's blood burned at the sight. Her father was Titanus. Their lineage went all the way back to Forseti, the God of Justice, to his father Baldur, the God of Light, all the way back to the All-Father, Odin. Power ran through her veins and her family tree, and here she was nearly at the bottom of the hierarchy surrounded by "sidekicks."

Alexander smirked as if he had been expecting this, and in some ways he had.

"Hmmm, how often do you work out?" the Squad Leader asked.

"Like, three times a week," Cooper replied, then, "Okay, like, once a week."

"And would you say you're often in motion?"

"I guess," Cooper shrugged.

Jordan cut in, "Sir, I've known him for three hours, and he's never once stood still."

"Thanks...?" Cooper grumbled.

"You're always in motion," Alexander said as if it was obvious. "You're always using your inert plasma. Hybrids are constantly using their plasma in ways we human Espers just aren't. They often don't have a Gift such as telepathy or force fields, but they make up for it because their Gifts are genetic; it's always active. Hybrids with wings, Hybrids with gills, Hybrids with tails are constantly using their plasma. That's why most of them have a high base-power level."

"Oh, that makes sense. That's cool," Cooper chimed, absorbing this new knowledge.

Alexander concluded with, "So, you'll clearly be facing me."

"Oh..." Cooper gulped. "Not cool."

"Jordan will face Alicia," Alexander announced.

"Wait...what?" Jordan balked. "But I've never fought a girl before."

"I know you meant that as a quasi-compliment," Alicia cut in. "But rest assured, if you don't fight like you mean it, I'll give you a reason to."

Jordan felt his breath catch in his throat as Alicia's stare cut through him.

"Once again," the Squad Leader repeated with annoyance, "ladies and gentlemen, this is an exercise. There is no reason to go all out. Reuben will face Battalia."

"Just so you know," Reuben said, "unlike Jordan, I won't have a problem hitting you."

How am I the problem? Jordan screamed internally.

"Good, so long as we're clear," Sydney sneered.

"An EX – ER – CISE," Alexander emphasized again. "The goal is to simply remove the tag from your opponent's body. As much as I'd like to see it for some of you, your goal is not to beat your opponent sense-less. With that in mind, Sydney, Reuben, you're up." Alexander tossed tags to Reuben and Sydney and then led the other three to the sidelines.

Sydney pinned her tag to her shoulder and turned to face Reuben across the sand. "When do you want to start?"

"Ohhh, I'm ready whenever you are," Reuben replied, clipping the tag to his waist.

Across the sun-bleached sand, Reuben and Sydney stood six feet apart, hands at the ready to lay waste to each other.

Alexander led the other three students through a side door to a section of seating on the ground floor of the coliseum.

"Uncle Alex, I was really looking forward to facing you," Alicia groaned.

"Wait," Cooper insisted. "Can we switch?"

"Yeah, can we?" Alicia chimed.

"No," Alexander replied. "Rules are rules."

Jordan wasn't so much listening in but stuck on Alicia's phrasing. *Uncle Alex? Interesting.* Alexander and Cooper went to grab seats. Alicia grabbed Jordan's arm when he passed her.

Okay, be gentle. Lay your way into this conversation, Alicia told herself. "I really want to impress Squad Leader Robinson."

"You mean your uncle?" Jordan replied, unsure where this was going.

"He's a family friend, not like my uncle-uncle," she corrected him. *Okay, just be gentle,* Alicia reminded herself. "But either way, I really got to impress him."

Does she want me to throw the match? Jordan blinked, confused. Behind him was a gust of wind. Sydney and Reuben had blitzed each other behind their backs.

Okay, he's not getting it, Alicia realized. *Spell it out for him.* "I'm going to have to embarrass you." Jordan took a stiff breath, then took in her words, her direct stare, and then her follow-up, "I'm gonna wipe the coliseum sands with you." She patted him on the shoulder. "No hard feelings."

Alicia walked off, leaving Jordan in confused silence as – THOOM. A concussive blast of heat and sand erupted behind him, spraying the back of his neck as Reuben and Battalia clashed.

"It's a gift. No matter what anyone says, this power is a gift to be
used by me and only me."
- Reuben Alvarez

CHAPTER FOURTEEN

Coliseum 7: Repel // Demons

Sydney had not expected Reuben's first attack to be packed with so much plasma, but she was happy that she had packed enough plasma into her counterstrike to block it. After meeting in the middle of the sands, the two quickly separated and went back to defensive positions. Sydney studied him, feeling her own plasma turn and broil within her veins and under her skin, ready to lash out.

He's fast. I may be a fraction faster than him, but I can't let him sneak up on me. Blue sparks ignited in Battalia's eyes as the plasma moved across her body. She didn't move. She kept her eyes on Reuben, whose own body was crackling with red energy. *I can't risk getting too close. Let's see if I can get him to come to me.*

"That all you got?" Sydney teased.

"Just getting started," Reuben retorted.

"Oh, I hope so – " Sydney's words were cut off, and Reuben was suddenly in her face.

In an instant he closed the six feet between them.

Fast was the only word screaming through Sydney's mind as she struggled to focus. But, just as he blinked in front of her, Sydney pushed her plasma backward and, in another instant, Sydney leapt six feet backward.

"You can feel the electricity in the air," Alicia marveled in her seat next to Jordan.

"Like when you walk into a room, and the TV is on – you can feel the static," Cooper said.

Alicia nodded. "It's their plasma interacting with the air around us."

Alicia pointed to the hair on the back of her neck and showed them that the hair on her arms was sticking up.

"They're just getting started," Alexander announced. "They may have the lowest plasma levels, but don't be fooled, they're clearly experts at manipulating plasma." He leaned in with interested old eyes. "Watch and learn."

Reuben leaned in like a hawk. *She's goading me in.* His eyes focused. *Which means she doesn't want to take the fight to me.*

His shoulders pointed in Battalia's direction. *Then maybe...*

He felt his fiery plasma rush through his frame. *I should take the fight to her.*

He took off.

Jordan and Cooper both jumped. Reuben's body shifted forward with cannon force. Stranger yet, his feet weren't even moving; they were gliding across the ground as if some invisible force was pulling him in Sydney's direction.

"Shift step." Alicia marveled at the ability.

"What?" Jordan asked.

"It's a plasma technique where – wait – I'll tell you after."

"After what?" Jordan asked.

"After our fight," she replied as if it was obvious.

Jordan gulped and sunk back into his seat.

Eavesdropping, Alexander explained. "It's where you shift your plasma in one single direction."

"Oh, I've seen my unc – I mean, Kinetic do it before," Jordan said. "It looks something like teleportation."

"It's like jumping, but your feet never leave the ground. You're pushing your energy into one spot and directing it," Alexander explained.

"Pssh, you don't have to tell him everything," Alicia groaned.

"He's your opponent now, but he's going to be your teammate for the foreseeable future. Better start thinking ahead," Alexander said.

Alicia waged an internal dilemma. *Okay, the Squad Leader is right – but, like – I still need to beat Jordan's ass.*

Jordan leaned from his seat and watched the two fighters who moved like magnets with opposing force. Every time Reuben would shift right in front of Battalia, she shifted back. Their plasmas activated, and their bodies shifted, which created an accompanying WHOOSH that echoed around them.

"This ability allows you to sorta drift quickly across the ground." Alexander motioned to Cooper and Jordan to follow his line of sight. "See, look at the sands – their feet aren't even leaving traces behind."

Jordan focused, and Reuben shifted again in pursuit of Sydney. The bandaged teen simply disappeared, then reappeared in front of her. The only evidence in the sand was his starting and ending points.

Okay, so it is like jumping spot to spot, Jordan thought.

Sydney and Reuben sped across the face of the sands without disturbing it.

"If I'm being honest, you all are lucky not to be fighting them." Alexander added, "They may have the lowest power levels, but they clearly know how to wield it. You can have the biggest sword or the biggest army or the biggest gun, but if you don't know how to use those items strategically, you might as well not have them at all."

He's right, Alicia realized. *Power isn't everything.*

"Their levels are low, but their mastery of plasma powers is high. Pushing it into your limbs for amplified strikes –"

I'm getting closer. Reuben glided back into her flight path, sent plasma rushing into his bandaged fist, and threw a punch. Sydney spotted it coming and sent her plasma into her shoulder to block it.

"Plasma shifting," Alexander continued.

Gotta keep him moving. Sydney tapped into her crystal and released the plasma throughout her body. She relished the familiar hot tingle of her energies being recognized in the synapses of her brain. Like commanding eyes to move across the page, she commanded her plasma to the right. Her plasma went right and yanked her body with it. Battalia felt the world blur for a second. Then as she readjusted, she realized Reuben was already there. *He guessed where I was going.*

"Plasma blasts," Alexander continued.

He's getting too close. She was getting tired of shifting. Her vision whirled, and her breath came out in short, exhausted huffs. Sydney sent her plasma into her palm. An electric blue ball of energy crackled to life in her hands. She threw the blast up and shifted backward, anticipating the detonation. Reuben threw his bandaged arm up, packed it with plasma, and let the plasma ball hit him. It detonated with enough force to rattle his ears and blow up a cloud of sand around him. While lingering whispers of heat scorched past him, he held his position.

Reuben's mind raced to a conclusion: *This blast wasn't meant to hurt me.* He tried to spot her, but the cloud of sand covered his eyes and everything around him. *It was meant to blind me.*

Cooper's mind also found the end game. "Wait, they haven't even used their Gifts yet. Wait, am I expected to know all this for our fight?"

"Oh, I hope you do," Alexander mused.

Cooper took off his plastic tag and mockingly tried to hand it to Alexander. "Here just take this now, please."

Alicia, never one to miss a moment, bumped in, "Or you can just tag me in."

"Both of you watch. They're about to change their tactics," Alexander announced. "We're about to see their Gifts on full display." The trio turned to the dust cloud around Reuben, and there was a surge of energy in the air. The hair on the back of their arms perked with the current passing through their bodies.

Aw, now we're getting serious, Battalia mused; her energies brewed through her body.

The debris obscuring Reuben suddenly lit up with the crimson energy that flared off his body. But it wasn't light or energy that drew everyone's eyes to the cloud. It was pieces of fabric– his bandages were off.

With a wave of his hand, the sand cloud dissipated, and Reuben stood before them. The bandages had been blown off his right arm and revealed what he had been hiding. His arm was burnt and layered with red puffy skin – his fingernails black. Even as they watched, his arm evolved. Black scales slid out of his skin. The sleeve of his suit had been cut at the elbow in a custom suit allowing his arms to be bandaged at will. He grimaced with a familiar pain, and the scales slid through the top layers of his skin along his arm, hand, and fingers. Rows of spiked black plating popped up. The skin around his elbow parted with a spike of bone protruding, forming a type of blade.

"He's a – a dem – I mean the D-word," Cooper struggled over his words.

I thought…I thought they were nearly extinct. Jordan paused. Then his eyes went to Sydney. *Did she know?* Sydney couldn't help but smile. Jordan cringed. He had seen that devious smile on her father's face, and he knew the feeling of being on the receiving end. *Yeah, she definitely knew.*

Sydney brimmed with excitement. *About time he showed his true colors.*

Reuben flinched a bit as his skin settled under the new layer of black scales, and his elbow flexed with the new rigidity. Though the pain was familiar, it didn't make it easier to accept. *It's a gift. No matter what anyone says this power is a gift to be used by me and only me.* Reuben thought back to his mother's words and felt them calm his nerves.

Reuben glanced over at his other teammates. While Alexander and Alicia were passive, Cooper and Jordan were leaning over the barrier slack-jawed, stars practically in their eyes.

That's so cool, their expressions screamed.

Okay, Reuben realized. *Maybe not everyone hates me.*

Then he turned sharply to Battalia, who smiled like a cat with mice in her sight. *Let's go.*

Reuben snapped his right arm up, gripped his wrist with his left hand for stability, and then sent red plasma into his arm. His scales lit up with flashing red energy and converted plasma into methane, before combusting into a pillar of flames that spiraled from his hands and broiled across the field.

Despite the waves of flames rushing her way, Sydney smiled. She sent her plasma into her fingers and activated her Gift. While her father was descended from the All-Father, Odin, she considered her Gift as a gift from Baldur, the God of Light. Shimmering fluorescent blue sparks popped in front of her before forming an interlocking field of light-force and – WHOOSH. The flames of Reuben's Gift broke against the force field from Sydney's Gift. The heat waves crested around her field and coiled aside, but even under this immense heat, Sydney calmly kept her field intact.

Sydney flashed on her force field like flicking on a light switch. Electric blue lights protected her from Reuben's barrage. Battalia huddled under it like the world's toughest umbrella. There were many theories about how Gifts manifested, ranging from a psychic need to combat the world to genetics being passed down through generations. She was grateful for the Gift of shutting herself off from the world, especially in the face of flames.

"Her Gift is a force field," Alexander concluded.

Makes sense, Jordan thought. *If Titanus' power is a modified force field, then it checks out that she'd have something similar.*

"And his Gift," Alicia added, "is being a – a, well – a monster."

"He probably doesn't see it as a gift," Cooper admitted. "It's probably why he kept the bandages on – to hide it. He's a Hybrid – like me. But unlike me, he has to hide it."

Alicia nodded. "It's a shame what happened to his people. There aren't that many of his kind who sign up to be heroes or are still around for that matter."

"The Crusades took care of his people. To still want to be a hero in a world that fears his kind is admirable," Alexander explained. "His people were feared, persecuted, and hunted."

I got her. With a single mental command Reuben shut off his torrent of flames and blitzed across the field, appearing behind her. Sydney spied a flash of obsidian black in the clouds of hellfire swarming past her and pivoted quickly. She threw up her force field just as Reuben burst like a fiend from the depths and hurled a plasma-packed punch from his scaly hand. His fist struck her barrier with a thunderclap that echoed through the arena. He grimaced; at the wrong angle he would have broken his wrist, but he didn't care. Not now. The only thing he cared about now was tearing through Sydney's barrier and finishing this.

Almost. Reuben pressed against her barrier. He felt it fluctuate under his fist. *I'll make you pay. I'll make you all pay.* Despite his clawed fist a foot away and the flames that still crackled behind her, Sydney was smiling behind her field. She made eye contact with Reuben, his face turned up into a snarl as something deep and ancient within him howled to life.

"Come on." Battalia's scowl shifted into a calculated smile. "Show me what you got – demon."

Reuben's eyes widened. Her words sacked him like a migraine. He flinched at the very word, the very thought of what he'd been through and what his people had been through. And as he felt her voice split through his head, he felt something primal. His vision flared with light, and all he saw was red. He dragged up a well of plasma from the depths of his crystal and poured it into his arm.

Reuben caught his reflection in the broad gold star in the center of her chest. He couldn't tell if his reflection was distorted by the heat and the angle or the heat and the anger, but he pressed ahead.

You want to see a demon? The stretch of exposed bone from his elbow trembled for a second before punching into his flesh. It wasn't just a blade–it was a piston. *Well, here you go.* As the bone retracted it pushed an influx of air into his arm and fed right into his churning plasma. Sydney's eyes went wide. She felt a torrent of renewed flames surge through Reuben's arm, and a sea of hellfire blossomed between them. The last thing she saw was Reuben's eyes; they morphed from round brown circles to thin venomous black slits.

Both of them were suddenly replaced with an explosion; his flames and her field crashed against each other. A broiling, concussive blast swept out from their impact and sent hot sand across the field. The teens covered their faces as it rattled past them.

"It's over," Alexander said flatly. He stood up.

Before either teen could question him, there was a crack of energy, and Alexander shifted away to the sound of a thunderbolt. While Alicia was expecting it, Jordan and Cooper both jumped. Jordan's gravitons activated under his feet and flipped him over. Cooper's own red panda-like instincts took over, and he went tumbling to the side.

Alicia glanced at the two boys trying to get back up. For a moment she pondered the situation. *How are these two the strongest here?* Jordan and Cooper clambered back to a seated position and looked out onto the field.

"Wait, who won?" Jordan peered into the settling cloud.

"Isn't it obvious?" Alicia asked.

Jeez, why is she such a know-it-all? Jordan looked from her to Cooper, who was as confused as he was.

"He overwhelmed her with his firepower," Alicia explained. "But Battalia repelled it right back at him."

It was clear that Sydney was left standing with Reuben's tag in one hand and her force field up in a glowing C shape. Reuben lay on his back, exhausted, and with smoke rising off his scorched suit and face. Alexander stood between them to prevent any further interaction. *I'm just happy they're both alive.*

"Some things never change, huh?" Sydney quipped.

"That's messed up," Cooper grumbled.

Jordan turned to Cooper, but Alicia answered.

"Her father, Titanus, is from Europe, where the Crusades took place." She read Jordan's puzzled face, then answered, "Her ancestors hunted his." Jordan ruminated on this, then turned his attention back out to the field. Reuben was sneering up at Sydney with Alexander in between them.

"The fight is over. I don't care what happened between your ancestors. We're a team now, so shake hands."

Neither of them moved.

"Now," Alexander boomed with shards of red lightning sparking behind his hazel eyes. Jordan shivered for a beat then felt the familiar pulse of electrical energy ripping down his spine. He sneered then noticed everyone else except Alexander was grimacing too. It was the same thing that Titanus had done to him when he was escaping and when Darius was yelling at him. Then just as soon as it began, it ended. Jordan blinked tears out his eyes and took in the air while his body settled.

"You felt that too?" Jordan asked.

"It was Red Wing," Cooper answered before Alicia could. "It's called 'flexing your plasma,' where you send an electric pulse out. It moves like a current in the air, and anyone weaker than you will feel the shock." Alicia nodded in agreement then began to rub the back of her neck.

So that's what that was, Jordan thought, flinching from the residual shock.

Reuben rose from the ground but refused to meet Sydney's eyes.

"Good match," she said and offered her left hand so that he'd have to shake with his scaled one. Reuben hesitated and shook his head, *No.* The one-armed Squad Leader shut Battalia down with a glare.

"Do you think your father would approve of this?" Alexander's eyes bored into her.

She scoffed.

"Or your mother?" Alexander said sternly.

Sydney froze. Though she had just been essentially electrocuted, these words surged through her with a dull thudding pain. She fought the urge to argue her point with Alexander and switched hands. Sensing a change in her demeanor, Reuben took the opportunity and shook her hand.

"To the sidelines. Now. Alicia, Jordan, you're up," Alexander called out.

Jordan gulped and Alicia rose and slammed her fist into her palm. "Let's go."

With a whoosh from her plasma burst, she shifted out of the stands and into the sands, sending Cooper and Jordan falling over again. Alicia hit the sands hard and skidded to a stop, not totally in control of her abilities. She caught herself between Sydney and Reuben. She nodded at Reuben.

"Good match," she said as he sulked past her.

He gave her the briefest nod, then continued.

Alicia turned to Sydney. The two girls didn't have to say anything; their eyes said it all.

"Good match," Alicia remarked to the tone of *"better luck next time."*

Sydney smirked. "I'm still fresh if you wanna go."

Battalia walked away from her with arms open wide. *Anyplace. Any time.*

"Jordan, get out here before it's everyone versus Sydney, please," Alexander called out.

Cooper turned to Jordan and patted his back. "Good luck, J."

Jordan nodded, then rose to his feet. He felt a pit in his stomach churning. He prepared to leave when a massive shadow caught his eye. Jordan was the first to notice it. Then everyone else turned to see – Kinetic was walking over to them in his purple and gold hero gear.

"I'm not too late, am I?" Darius asked.

Da – Darius? Jordan's eyes went wide.

Alicia's eyes narrowed. *What is he doing here?*

Darius turned to Alexander and Alicia in the sands and waved heartily at them.

"Red Wing, old friend," Kinetic said, "I hope you don't mind if I evaluate the new recruits."

"Anytime." Alexander turned to Jordan. "You don't mind if Kinetic watches your match, huh, kid?"

Jordan felt that pit in his stomach burn away. "No. Not at all." He stood up straighter, squared his shoulders, and focused his eyes on Alicia. Jordan felt the sun hit the star in the center of his chest. It was as if he had absorbed its heat because he felt something swell within him. Alicia noticed the change in his stance and energy. Jordan seemed to evolve in front of her. Jordan pulled his gloves tight and glanced at Kinetic's message to him. "Be Your Own Hero."

"Let's get to work," Jordan whispered to himself.

Alicia tapped the magnetic tag to her waist where her calculations estimated was the best place to defend. *What's gotten into him?* Alicia asked herself, suddenly growing more serious.

"Alicia, what do you say?" Alexander asked.

She glanced between Jordan and Kinetic, then replied, "Sure."

"Well, then," Alexander chimed, "you're welcome to watch – " He was interrupted by an explosion of Jordan's gravitons under his feet; Jordan was suddenly airborne. As he had done so many times before, Jordan spun out of the arc and landed gracefully on one knee in a cloud of sand.

Sydney looked from Jordan to Kinetic. *Pity, he missed the main event already.*

Reuben's face was impassive, but inside he was raging. *What happened to Jordan?*

Cooper, who had flipped out as Jordan suddenly shot past him in the air, recovered and looked to the field. *A little warning next time–please.*

Kinetic took a seat and folded his arms. *Let's see what you got, kid.*

Jordan looked up from his kneeling position. His eyes sparked with gold plasma with his efforts to tap in and lock onto Alicia. *I'm not losing. Not in front of Darius. I refuse...* "I'm sorry Alicia, but the one who's going to lose," Jordan rose to his feet and slapped the red tag over his heart, "is you."

Alicia grinned and tapped into her energies, feeling the fusion of star-blessed plasma burn within her. She cultivated a torrent of firepower ready to let loose. *This may be easier than I thought...*

"She's on another level than all of us. Even me."
-Sydney Asimov

CHAPTER FIFTEEN

Coliseum 7: Double-Barrel Fireworks

Neither of them moved. They simply faced each other with dust wafting between them. Alicia's feet slid back in the sands as she took on a fighting pose–her arms forward, her waistline and the tag directly under shoulders just in case she needed to slam her arms tight and defend.

He's got some sort of gravity or energy-based power. I have to be cautious.

Jordan leaned back down to one knee and took on a three-point stance. Both gloved hands dug into the sand–one knee pointed forward, the other leg stretched backward where gravitons began to collect. *I'm not able to shift like her, but that doesn't mean she has the speed advantage.* Jordan studied her lean frame and his target – her tag. He could feel the gravitons collecting and vibrating behind his heel, gathering strength before...

"Let's get to work," Jordan taunted before launching himself. The gravitons burst under his heel and sent him flying at her like a missile.

He's faster than I thought, Alicia's mind shouted.

The next second Jordan was swinging into the space where, a moment ago, she was standing. Alicia pivoted hard on her back heel, then let Jordan rush by, a storm of light, sound, and flailing limbs. *He's too fast for his own good.* Alicia studied his every movement in those few seconds.

Jordan blinked past her and hit the sands hard in a tumble. He ate sand and scrambled hard to get back to his feet, trying to recover quickly.

Cooper's ears perked up to better hear the conversation between Alexander and Kinetic. Though Cooper was farther away from them than Sydney and Reuben, he could clearly hear them.

"I thought I recognized the last name," Alexander whispered. "He yours?"

"My nephew," Darius replied with a glimmer of pride.

At "nephew" Cooper's ears twitched hard. He fought the urge to exclaim out loud, though he did scream behind clenched teeth, causing them to vibrate. *He's related to Kinetic. What the Hades? He's his nephew.* Then he calmed himself with a realization. *He can autograph my collection.*

As Jordan hit the sands, he felt several things happen simultaneously: first, he felt his plasma fill his skin, and his muscles increased their density, which would cushion the blows. Second, he felt the armored plates on his shoulder shift and link together, also moving in sync to protect him. With dual-layered protection, what could have been a bruised or even a broken shoulder felt like a heavy thump instead. He rolled up off the ground, twisted in the sand, and aligned himself again with Alicia's path. He cringed when he felt sand had somehow gotten into his gloves.

He's not really that stupid, is he? Alicia asked herself. *It's the same draggin' move.*

Jordan exploded off the sands again with another burst of gravity.

It is the same move, she mused. *What an idiot.*

"You're wide open," Alicia shouted at him, then dived to the side as he whisked past. As Jordan fell towards the ground, mid-arc, he twisted around so that he landed on his feet instead of his shoulder. Before Alicia could turn around, he was already exploding gravitons under his feet and launching himself back at her – knee first.

Recognize this, Kinetic? Jordan said to himself. He leaned back and threw his knee forward the way he had seen his uncle do so many times before. He padded plasma into his leg and prepared to smash into her, mirroring the attack he had seen all his young life: the Impact Knee.

Darius smirked. Jordan's form was all wrong. *Good try, though.*

He twisted around to cut his reaction time in half. Alicia gasped when he came into her peripheral vision. Alicia tapped into her plasma and activated her Gift. Violet static energy pulses rushed down her body and compounded around her palms. Her hands buzzed with neon pink and purple lights that didn't fade or falter under the sunlight but expanded into flaring balls of neon plasma. She hurled them like fastballs right at Jordan.

What the Hades is that? Jordan's mind raced, running haphazardly into what could be best described as a cannon-blast of fireworks. He brought his leg back up, threw his arms over his face, packed them with plasma, and curled up just as the neon blasts concussed around him. They didn't explode with flames or heat but rather impact and force.

Darius cringed and then turned to Alexander. "What's my boy dealing with out there?"

"Oh, that's right," Alexander chimed, "you haven't met her yet. That Astro's little sister."

Darius thought he heard the words correctly, but they took a second to settle into realization. He was a bit distracted by Cooper's sudden yelp from ten feet away. Darius glanced at the Hybrid, who refused to look his way, then turned back to Alexander.

"Astro's sister, huh? Oof, then Jordan is in way over his head," Darius stated plainly. Then he whispered, privatizing his words, "And for that matter, these two should definitely not be on the same team."

"You know as well as I do that I didn't pick the teams. Only Battalia over there was added to my team. Everything was random, pre-determined – destined." Alexander let the last word hang in the air for a beat. He turned back around to see Jordan get suddenly blasted out of the air.

Jordan had been punched before. In fact, during his vigilante antics, he had been punched multiple times. But as his world blurred past him, and the impact tremors from Alicia's blast rattled through him, he found himself recalling every punch he had taken. This topped it. Even though he had flushed his arms with plasma, the impacts had detonated all across his body.

He stumbled out of the smoke cloud and shook the dull thudding out of his ears. When the smoke subsided and his vision cleared, he was greeted by Alicia blitzing across the sands. Raw hot pink plasma coated her hand; it appeared to be a sizzling blade. It was rough, fiery, and coming his way.

Jordan's knees nearly buckled from the first onslaught, so he gathered his strength and gravitons to blast himself backward to avoid Alicia's graceful slashing with her plasma-sheathed hand.

Sydney watched with interest as Alicia chased Jordan. *Those blasts from earlier were clearly plasma-filled globes. And even now, she's using her plasma to create a blade.* Next to her, she heard whispering between the two licensed heroes. She ignored them and focused on Alicia. *Her Gift is a form of plasma manipulation. My own force field is a form of plasma manipulation. But her scale and precision are on another level.* Battalia felt a chill run down her back as she came to a realization: *She's on another level than all of us. Even me.*

Darius frowned. While he had worked alongside Titanus before and through a dozen missions, he had never been particularly close with Alexander. The way Titanus and others spoke of him, he was like everyone's older brother, yet the two had never been closer than associates. And even sitting this close to him now, he found the man friendly – yet enigmatic.

Alexander gestured at his arm that was severed at the elbow, then explained, "Who am I to stand in the way of destiny? Who are any of us? I could have spent a decade doing healer treatments to get something like my arm repaired, but I haven't. Because this is how it was meant to be."

"But if they both start asking questions about that night..." Darius pondered.

"These kids deserve the truth," Alexander replied. "Not now. But in time they'll find out the truth, and we'll be better for it."

Cooper shivered. *They're talking about the Green Night.* Cooper then looked out to Jordan and Alicia's one-sided fight. *And they're connected to it somehow...*

Jordan lunged left as Alicia swung right, then dodged right as she swung left. He parried his body in time with her slashes. With every slash of Alicia's blade, Jordan pivoted away, his feet sliding backward in the sands. His vision was filled with her blade arcing and slashing past him. It was a shaft of neon purple, coarse and cutting, that broiled past him. *Too close.*

"You trained him well," Alexander remarked to Darius.

"That's the thing," Darius replied, "I didn't train him at all. He's self-taught."

Alexander smirked and turned back to Darius to read his face. The bearded man's expression didn't falter. Darius nodded to confirm. *He's not lying. Hmph, this kid really is something.*

Jordan backpedaled as quickly as his Zeuz Airwalkers would allow in the shifting sands. Alicia pressed her advantage with her broiling blade. He ducked and rolled away from her slash, then Alicia carved through the air above him. Jordan rolled back to one knee and did something he hated–but something that some situations called for.

He gathered gravitons under his hands. He had tried it years ago and broken his hand. It was a grim reminder of how volatile his powers were in terms of his fragile body, but it was a lesson he had learned nonetheless. *Just a tap. Just a tap. Just a draggin' tap,* Jordan repeated to himself.

He felt the warm glow of gravitons coil under his gloved palms. Then like pressing down on a trampoline, he felt the gravitons fold and pull like a fabric before – the gravitons snapped back into place and punched him upwards. Jordan tensed and felt the explosion burst under his palms. As he had trained himself to do with the explosion under his feet, he rode the wave and let it jettison himself upwards.

Alicia took in a sharp breath when Jordan receded from her. *He went up?* Jordan cringed and altered his flight path. He hadn't expected that much force to kick in automatically. He was higher – much higher than he had anticipated. He kicked into his gravitons and made them weightless to buoy himself in the sky. While he was already falling back down to Earth, he was now simply slowing his fall into a controlled descent.

Still twenty feet in the air, Jordan called down to her, "You can't catch me up here."

"Wanna bet?" Alicia sneered, and purple lights popped in her eyes. Without missing a beat, the neon blade around her arm shrunk down to a point, then elongated from both ends of her fists to form a spear. Alicia reared back, took Jordan's body in her sights, calculated his fall, and then hurled the javelin right at him.

"No. Way," were Jordan's last words as he dropped into the path of the spear. Again, two things happened at once: Jordan's chest filled with plasma to increase the density of his skin and bones underneath, and his suit's armor-plating linked together to form an interlocking barrier against the javelin. The efforts did little to help.

As the point of the neon weapon touched him, it didn't pierce his skin, his suit, or his armor. Rather, it detonated in a whirlwind of condensed air and shards of evaporating pink light. Jordan felt like he had taken a battering ram to the chest. The wind was knocked from his lungs, the consciousness was blown from his mind, and his body was punched out of the sky.

He felt the sky tilt – then the world went with it. He saw nothing but a great blur. Twisting and rolling wildly, all Jordan could make out was the ground racing to meet him. He reached out to the gravitons, pulling them close and curling them under him as he fought off a wave of dizziness. Then he saw the ground – closer this time. Jordan pulled on more gravitons, hoping to build enough that he could temper a fall from this height.

To fight the rising panic, Jordan closed his eyes. The last thing he saw was a wall of sand. Jordan tapped into every graviton he could, then willed them wordlessly. *Hold.* He felt himself slowly descend. His body stopped rolling, and then he felt the inertia of his body slacken before he felt his whole body finally come to rest. It was then, and only then, he felt safe enough to open his eyes. Jordan was face to face with the ground, the tip of his nose buried in the field of sand.

Jordan exhaled, released the gravitons, and dropped in a heap on the ground, exhausted. He took in a few deep, sand-encrusted breaths, and righted himself. Jordan came up tasting blood and sand. His chest had a dull ache radiating from the center, but that was the least of his worries. Alicia was holding his tag in her hand. Jordan looked down. Indeed, his tag was gone.

She threw the lance right at my chest for a reason, Jordan realized, *Not only was she able to attack, but she also dislodged my tag in the same move...Even after I had just surprised her by blasting myself above her.* Jordan marveled at Alicia, and her smile crushed him. Her words came rushing back to him: *"I'm gonna wipe the coliseum sands with you."*

Then she walked over and offered her hand. "No hard feelings?"

Jordan took a shaky breath, looked up at her, then over to Darius, feeling all eyes on him. *She's amazing.*

Jordan reached up and took her hand. Then with surprising strength, she helped lift him back to his feet.

Alexander shifted behind them with a crackle of energy that caused Jordan to flinch.

"That's game," Alexander declared.

Jordan nodded, accepting defeat.

"You leave yourself open when you throw yourself right at people," Alicia explained. "If you can find ways to use your powers in close quarters, you'd be great."

Jordan absorbed this. *She's right,* he thought. *Jeez, she pegged me in just those few minutes. Wow.* Then, despite the dual pains of the dull ache in his chest and the dubious feeling of defeat, Jordan nodded.

"Thanks. I'll keep it in mind."

As he walked back to the stands, Jordan shot a tentative glance at Darius, who was waiting for him. *I didn't even get to hit the Impact Knee.* His hands reflexively gripped into fists inside his oversized gloves.

Darius patted his shoulder. "Excellent work, Cadet."

"I –" Jordan began, "I didn't want to lose."

"I've lost a lot in my life," Darius replied. "Do you think that gets me down?"

Jordan nodded in reply.

"Look at me, Cadet," Darius ordered.

Jordan pulled his head up and swallowed the lump in his throat. Darius studied Jordan for a beat, knowing the next words were going to be important–not just as a mentor, but as an uncle and father figure. He looked his nephew over. Jordan was wearing the gloves with his signature and his star-blessed blood ran through Jordan's veins. Jordan had even tried, though unsuccessfully, to mirror his Impact Knee. Once Darius had the words, his face grew stern and honest.

"It's not the loss that affects you," Darius explained. "It's how you react to it. And right now, you've got a chance to learn from this. What did you learn from this loss?"

Jordan nodded, thought on it for a moment, then answered, "She – she said that I leave myself open when I throw myself."

"And she's right. You got to learn from your mistakes. That's how we grow," Darius remarked, and then patted his shoulder again. Jordan cringed. Even under the armor, Darius' heavy hands still crashed down on him. "That's how you become your own hero."

Alicia turned to Alexander. Behind him, she spotted Cooper, who was furiously stretching in preparation for their fight. Alicia beamed up at Red Wing. "Any pointers, Uncle Alex?"

"You did great," he answered. "If I'm being honest, I see a lot of your brother in you."

Alicia felt her smile stretch across her face.

"Maybe too much," he added. "Find ways to bring it down some. He too liked to go all out and impress folks, but sometimes less is more. You're smart. You're talented. It shows. Don't flaunt it; be about it."

Alexander then turned to the rest of the teens. "That goes for all of you," he said. "You've got Gifts. Find the best way to use them not for yourself but the sake of others." His eyes then found Reuben sulking in the stands, his arm huddled under his sleeve. "That goes double for you, kid. A Gift is a gift, no matter what the rest of the world says."

If the words reached Reuben, he did a good job of hiding it.

ALEXANDER ROBINSON

Hero Alias: Red Wing

Height: 5'10

Weight: 185

Birth Date: March 20

Plasma Color: Red

Plasma Level: 85,000

Gift: Alexander possesses the ability to manipulate the raw plasma in his body to create concussive and explosive bursts. His masterful control allows him to craft the shape and form of his plasma into complex shapes for various techniques.

CHAPTER SIXTEEN

Coliseum 7: Raise Your Head

Alexander turned around to search for Cooper, who was still busy stretching himself into contorted positions.

"Just a moment," Cooper said as he flipped himself into another stretch.

"Are you ready?" Alexander asked.

"If I say no, will that keep me safe?" Cooper asked.

Alexander smirked, then placed his tag over his chest.

Copper stood up and placed his tag on his shoulder. *No, too easy.*

He repositioned his tag on his other shoulder. *No, also too easy.*

Cooper then placed the tag on the center of his chest. *Okay, I think that can work.* Satisfied, Cooper focused on Alexander, who stood slumped about ten feet away, seemingly bored.

"Okay." Cooper sighed. "Okay. I'm rea–"

THOOM. There was a mighty crack as Alexander shifted from his spot and reappeared behind Cooper with Cooper's tag in his hand. With a delayed reaction, the force of Red Wing's speed finally caught up to Cooper and toppled him into the sands. His senses, which were all finely tuned to eleven, had barely registered Alexander's approach. Neither his ears, eyes, nor nose was able to keep tabs on him.

The teens, even Battalia, stared wide-eyed. *I – I didn't even see him.* Jordan gasped. *Is this what facing an Olympian is like?* Darius read the shock in their faces. "Alexander isn't just quick. He's lightning fast.

Trust me, he's far slower than when he was in his prime. If you know where to look, your eyes can follow."

Alexander tossed the tag back to Cooper. "Again."

Cooper was shaking. He wasn't sure if it was his nerves or the aftereffects of Red Wing blitzing by him, maybe both – actually, it was probably both – but his fingers trembled when he attached the tag to his waist this time.

"You're fast," Cooper admitted.

"And you're the strongest in the group," Alexander snapped.

Cooper opened his mouth to respond. He was about to speak when he stopped, swallowed his nerves, then ripped the tag off. He didn't place it anywhere, but he simply and formidably gripped it in his hand.

"I'm ready," Cooper said, between clenched teeth.

"Watch it now." Darius pointed his finger out across the field, and Jordan followed his gaze. Jordan squinted and forced his focus from Darius to Alexander as he blurred away then reappeared briefly. Alexander appeared in front of Cooper and ripped the tag from his hand, shoulder-bumped him in the chest, then reappeared behind him – all in a single breath.

"There," Darius pointed out.

Jordan nodded. Darius was right. By focusing just enough, he was able to spy Red Wing zip across the sands.

Cooper looked back at Alexander, then back at his empty hand. *What? How could I not see him?*

"Again," Alexander replied. He tossed the tag back to Cooper. Cooper reached and it slipped between his fingers. It hit the ground, but Cooper didn't reach for it. He just looked down at the tag sitting tauntingly in the sands

"I've already lost twice now," Cooper sighed.

"So?" Alexander asked.

"I can't beat you."

"Not with that attitude."

"I'm a sidekick, not a hero." Cooper said the words before he even realized it.

Alexander seethed behind closed teeth, tasting the words in his mouth like bitter grapes. "Who said that?" Cooper knew the answer, but he didn't want to admit it. *I'm no hero. I'm a panda. An animal, that's meant to be laughed at and –*

"Raise your head and tell me who said that," Alexander shouted accusingly.

"Everyone," Cooper snapped back. *Every day, everywhere, every moment of my life, people have said that I'm a joke.* Cooper felt the words building, then vomited them out. "Everyone said I wasn't good enough. Everyone said I was just an animal. A cape-dragging joke. A squirrel. A raccoon. That I couldn't save anyone."

Cooper felt his face flush with hot tears. He sniffled and blinked them away. *I'm not Kinetic's nephew or Astro's sister or the child of Titanus or born with powers like Reuben...I'm just a cape-dragger with big ears and a tail and –*

"Well, maybe they're right," Alexander replied.

The Squad Leader tore his tag off and held it out with one hand.

"Reach me," he said simply.

Cooper's ears were working perfectly, but at this moment he wasn't sure. "What?"

"Shift over here and take this tag from my hand," the Squad Leader ordered.

"I can't." Cooper panicked. "I don't know how..."

"Feel your plasma rushing through your veins. Feel every fiber of your Gift's being and visualize the direction you want to go."

Cooper stopped looking at the ground and pulled his head up to face him. Even so, he still repeated what he had been told for years, "I can't."

If Alexander heard him, he didn't react, he just continued barking, "Don't move your feet. Visualize what direction you want to go in and do it."

Cooper cringed under the assault of voices in his head. The same ones that had tormented him for years in grade school were the same ones coming back to him now. He fought them off, but then a single voice came out to him –

"Cooper," Jordan called out.

He stopped and turned back to face his roommate.

Jordan stared out at the field, *I know the feeling. He's got to be thinking the same thing I did. I know it.* "You can do it." Jordan cupped his hands to his mouth. "You never stay still. I meant it. You're always moving." Jordan looked back over at the rest of their group for help. Sydney and Reuben sulked, then looked away. Conversely, Alicia met his gaze. She ran the calculations in her head and decided...

"You can do it," Alicia shouted. "You're not a trash panda. I mean, technically, you are a panda, but you aren't trash. You're stronger than all of us."

They believe in me? They've got cool family members and powers, Cooper thought, *and they believe in me.*

Then Alexander's voice came roaring back to him. "If you can't reach me, then how do you plan on reaching people in need? How do you plan on saving people you can't reach? How do you plan on being a hero?"

Cooper nodded. *It wasn't a mistake. The plasma levels were right. I'm the strongest here.* Cooper remembered what the universe had gifted him and his fellow Espers at birth; he tapped into his plasma and activated it. He sent the scarlet red static energy pulses flowing from his head down to his toes. His body vibrated with pent-up energy that he could feel to the points of his teeth.

Jordan and Alicia tried a new strategy. "Shift. Shift. Shift."

Cooper thought back to what he had learned. *Direct the energy where you want to go. Your body will follow.*

"Visualize it," Alexander ordered.

As a sea of voices rang out in his head and chorused with the ones around him, Cooper's ears were suddenly tuned to a new voice.

"Cooper," Reuben called out.

Cooper stopped, leaving himself boiling in his own energies, and glanced over at Reuben. Reuben's usual resolve flickered at the eyes on him. He had found himself on his feet with no memory of standing. His lanky frame was standing in the shadow of a statue looming on the edge of the coliseum: Lion Force.

"Hybrid Pride," Reuben shouted.

Cooper nodded at him. His words and Lion Force's image reflected in his eye.

"Hybrid Pride," Cooper repeated. He focused on Alexander, who stood six feet away with arms open for his taking. Cooper took in a breath, felt the air fill his lungs, felt his plasma tremble within his body, down his back, in his legs, and his mind. He felt every ounce of his energy and shifted it forward.

Cooper felt like he had been yanked by something inside his core. One second, he was stationary. The next he was compelled right at Alexander as if riding an invisible trail.

Grab it. His eyes focused on Alexander's open hand.

Grab it. Even with the world blurring, he moved his hands as if they were pushing through water.

Grab. It. Cooper registered too late that his hands were too slow; he was going to miss him...

GRAB. IT. Cooper realized he'd have to improvise, and he twisted in mid-air. Then as he felt his body slowing, he lunged out and bit down.

There was a familiar whoosh sound as Cooper came out of his shift, and he appeared behind Alexander, with the tag clenched in his teeth. Cooper didn't stop but crashed head over heels into the sand.

Hmph, good job. Alexander smirked.

Cooper rose from the ground and grinned with the prize in his mouth. He could feel his stomach still settling and his world still stabilizing. One thing was clear: they were cheering. His teammates were cheering. Except for Sydney, who was at least clapping, but that was more than enough for him.

"Raise your head, kid." Alexander turned to him with honest hazel eyes and declared, "You won."

Cooper looked over to Reuben, who gave him a subtle nod. Above Reuben, Cooper saw the Lion Force statue beaming down on him too.

Cooper felt his knees buckle. *Phew, that took a lot out of me.* He dropped on his back, an exhausted panda, all four limbs pointing to the sky. Cooper exhaled and said between smiling breaths, "I'm 100% treating myself to bamboo cupcakes tonight."

CHAPTER SEVENTEEN

Ambrosia Cupcake Bomb

After the events at the coliseum, Jordan quickly showered, changed, and left to meet with Darius. Cooper was still behind. He explained that he had to dry his tail, which had been covered in sand. Jordan, with his suit slung over his shoulder, made his way down the hallway. He could feel sand crunching inside his Zeuz Airwalkers. He tried to shake it out earlier, to no avail.

Darius waited at the end of the hall with his arms folded.

"I just wanted to say good job, today," Darius began.

Jordan was silent for a moment. The dull ache in his chest was a heavy reminder of the beating he took from Alicia. "Thanks," he replied flatly.

"And," Darius moved his large frame to reveal he had a box sitting on the floor, "these came in the mail for you." Darius handed him the box, and Jordan took it gently. Darius gave him a nod. Jordan flipped the packaging off and lifted the lid to find a pair of black and gold tactical boots. "Military-grade pro hero tactical boots," Darius explained. "Made from the same material as your suit."

Jordan no longer felt the sand under his feet; he was enamored with the boots. They were a metallic black that reflected the lights, with gold accents around the heels, toes, and ankles: official hero apparel. They were sleek, stylish, and his.

Jordan felt the dull ache fade away, then he nodded. "Thanks."

"And they'll keep sand from between your toes," Darius said, with a hint of knowing.

Jordan nodded again, captivated by the gift, and the vision that his suit was finally complete. *At least I don't have to worry about being written up.*

"But don't get too comfortable, kid. You're playing student here. Your job is to find these thieves before they strike again," Darius warned.

Oh, yeah...that. Jordan cringed at the reminder.

"Just stay on mission. The thief is here somewhere, and you'll need everything you learned to escape," Darius reminded him. Suddenly, Darius' face scrunched, and he stood up straight. Jordan turned sharply as Cooper came out of the locker room and into the hall.

"Good job, Cadet Harris," Darius repeated, taking the softness out of his voice.

"Thanks, D– I mean, Kinetic." Jordan stumbled over his words.

"I know he's your uncle," Cooper retorted.

*Wha - What...*Jordan's own thoughts stuttered.

*Huh...*Darius paused.

Cooper continued, "My ears are super sensitive, so it's tough to hide things from me." His eyes narrowed to slits as he whispered, "But the only thing I wanna know is..." Cooper leaned in menacingly. "Can you autograph my limited edition sixth-scale Kinetic action figure?"

It took Kinetic a minute to realize Cooper wasn't joking. "Sure."

Cooper's eyes lit up, and his tail swayed wildly behind him like an excited puppy.

"How about I mail you a signed quarter-scale figure?" Darius upped the ante.

"Yes." A joyful shout escaped Cooper before he calmed. "That would be fine."

I'm buying people's silence with toys, ain't that something? Darius mused to himself. "Good job, Hybrid-kid." Darius added, "Consider it a gift for learning how to shift."

Cooper smirked and rubbed the back of his head, bashfully. *Not only did I learn to shift, but I got a compliment from Kinetic, and he's going to send me a gift.*

"Good job, J. I'll catch ya later." Darius patted Jordan on the shoulder. "Stay on mission."

While Jordan heard, "Stay on mission," he knew he meant, "Finish the mission soon before things get worse." To both of those he replied, "Yes, sir."

Darius walked off, and Cooper crept up next to Jordan.

"Oh, that's so cool," Cooper squealed.

"Thanks," Jordan said. "What does your family do?"

Cooper's eyes lit up, and he smiled wildly. "Funny you should ask."

Sydney Battalia Asimov found herself alone, but alone was how she liked it. After living in her father's home her whole life, she found that she appreciated being out from under his silence and his shadow. Even though he was often out on patrol and missions across the globe, she found that he still found time to somehow bug her about her regiment, ensuring that she kept up with her studies. It was almost as if he left only to live in her cellphone.

Now that she was on her own and living in the dorms of Fort Olympus, she found a freedom that she hadn't felt before. Her father had pulled some strings and secured a single room with a balcony for her in the upperclassmen dorms. After she had showered and unpacked, she found herself taking in the silence from her bed.

He hasn't called yet. Good. She blinked up at the ceiling, which she had decorated with a Fort Olympus banner. *I'm finally free of him.* Her eyes closed briefly, and her mind flashed to Reuben's attack on the sands. She recalled the venom in his eyes. While she regretted her words, she didn't regret her choices. *He was going to have to face someone like me soon enough.* Then her mind's eye went to Alicia.

Not only was she stronger than her, but she had total control of her Gift. *She's going to be a problem.* Sydney shivered at the thought. Problems weren't new to her – they were just uncommon. While Forseti, the Norse God of Justice, was long dead, Titanus being his ancestor had carried that title on his back just as he carried his blood in his veins. Her father had taken on the mantle with religious fervor. With most of the Olympians dead, Titanus took it upon himself to carry the world's problems on his tired back. Sydney had lived a life of privilege. Her father was rich after all, but that came with demands. Early wake-up calls, muscle straining drills, a constant eye on her development, and a dedication to heroism. Her father hadn't so much raised her but trained her. And for all her advantages...*Alicia is still stronger.*

Sydney shook those thoughts from her head, rose from bed, and decided to get some fresh air. She had a balcony; she might as well use it. Sydney opened the door and stepped outside, letting the cold wind from the Buffalo Bayou sweep over her. The campus grounds were sprawling, and each building that decorated it fought for space. Then as her eyes took in the sights of the campus from her balcony, she shuddered. *Well played, old man.*

Directly across from the dorm her father had hand-selected for her was a statue of her father – encased in bronze and guarding the courtyard. While she had physically escaped her father's sight, figuratively she was still sleeping in his shadow.

Upon getting back to their dorm, Cooper delicately removed a box from underneath his bed. He held it gently while presenting it to Jordan. The box was a soft yellow color with a trio of cartoon red pandas baking on the front of it.

"We own a bakery," Cooper explained.

He opened the box, and Jordan's senses were sent to Nirvana as the smell of sweets wafted out and caressed his tired face. Inside the box were a dozen cupcakes of varying designs and flavors that all looked tantalizing. Cooper handed Jordan a cupcake with pink frosting on top and decorated with soft sugar petals.

"It's cherry blossom," Cooper gleamed, "a mix of cherry extract with rose tea cream filling."

Jordan took a bite, and his eyes lit up. It was sweet one moment but tart the next. As the sugar petals crunched under his teeth, they dissolved back to pure sweetness.

"Yo," was all Jordan could say with his mouth full.

He took another bite and exclaimed, "Yoooooooo."

"I know, right? My parents gave me a bunch of these for move-in day."

Cooper moved to show there were more boxes stashed under his bed. Jordan was gleeful. Cooper searched the box and chose another cupcake. This one had an opaque sugar cover on top that looked much like a globe. Inside, sugar crystals reflected in the light. It almost looked solid as if it would chip a tooth upon the first bite.

Cooper gave one to Jordan, then picked up one for himself.

"These are another best seller." Cooper marveled at the cupcake. "It's our ambrosia flavor. It has a sugar crystal coating, then little sugar crystals inside."

"Ambrosia." Jordan tasted the word in his mouth. "The food of the gods."

"Exactly. It gives you a sugar rush. We designed it from the actual ambrosia from Mount Olympus that the gods used to eat. It gave them an insane power boost, then they'd flood down from Mount Olympus and slaughter the giants who didn't stand a chance – but this is just a cupcake."

Jordan bit into it, and as the sugar crystals crunched under his teeth and tongue, he felt his own body react to the sugar. It was sweet, energizing, and gone in three bites.

"Whoa," Jordan exhaled, "that was great. I feel like I just woke up." Jordan, buzzed off the sugar, jumped up and threw a few practice punches.

"See, those two are great, but this is my favorite." Cooper opened up another box, and inside there was not a variety of cupcakes, but a dozen identical cupcakes with forest green icing.

"Bamboo Cakes," Cooper said in reverence.

Jordan's eyes went wide – the smell, the look, the perfection before him was mesmerizing. It compelled him to reach out, but he stopped.

"Can I – can I have one?" Jordan asked softly as if in prayer.

"We got a whole box, man," Cooper replied.

Cooper took one and gently handed it to Jordan, who cupped it in his hand. Cooper took one for himself and held it up.

"To a good first day," Cooper offered.

"To a good first day," Jordan replied.

They toasted with the pastries, then took simultaneous bites. At the first bite, Jordan's mind was blown. He had never tasted something so sweet, yet it had earthy tones that crunched underneath, followed by a smooth aftertaste. It was a delicious hurricane upon his senses. Jordan paused, trying to contain the great well of hunger he felt in his belly, clamoring for more.

"Okay," Jordan exhaled. "Okay. I know I'm just hungry because we just worked out, but we have to be safe and eat these in moderation."

"Yes," Cooper replied mid-bite into his second Bamboo Cake.

The two looked at each other...deciding...

Reuben was tired. Not only had he lost to Sydney, but he had also almost been late to the first event and had to wake up early this morning to move in. While he wasn't sure what Cooper and Jordan thought about him, and people like him, he decided to keep to himself in the locker room as not to show off his scarred arm. He remembered how they marveled at his arm like he was an officially licensed superhero once he showed it off.

Maybe they aren't so bad.

His head was swimming, and his arm still ached as if he had been sunburned. He had never pushed himself that far for so long, yet Sydney had still beaten him – by using his own power against him. As he left the elevator, Reuben realized that Sydney wouldn't just be a one-time issue. There would be more. His roommate for one. While he hadn't gotten his name, Reuben recalled the guttural response to the glimpse he got of his arm. Maybe it was a one-time thing.

Maybe he isn't that bad either.

Reuben entered the dorm and could tell instantly that something was off. His roommate had gone. His bedding was gone from his side of the room. His clothes and suitcases were also gone as if he had simply never existed.

Then he saw it scribbled on the mirror in some sort of red ink: *Demons Ain't Heroes.*

Reuben felt something within him quiver, then deflate. Whatever damage Sydney had done to him earlier paled in comparison as he read the message and caught his reflection in the mirror. He searched his own face, his own despair, and despite his own pain coursing through his arm, he threw it right into the mirror.

Thirty minutes later, both boxes of cupcakes were empty, and both boys were in sugar-crash-induced naps. Each was passed out in his respective bed with icing crusted on his face and fingertips. Jordan slept noisily, one hand on his stomach and one leg hanging off the bed. As he snored, he rose an inch off the bed, then dropped back down – his gravity powers fluctuating as he slept. Cooper slept on his bed with his tail curled up around him, the way a ferret sleeps curled into a flat circle.

In the distance, outside the room, a soft thump echoed. Jordan stirred from his food coma, twisted in mid-air, and the gravitons under his subconscious control fled away – Jordan dropped on the floor with a thud.

"Ow," Jordan groaned.

He heaved himself back up and listened. There was another thump outside. Jordan crawled to his feet, stifled a yawn, then peered out the window. It was night already. The moonlight and campus streetlights illuminated sections of Fort Olympus down below. As Jordan peered at the sleepy campus, he spotted a single figure stirring – Lucas.

Alicia knew from experience that losses were something to learn from. Yes, it was best to dwell on them in that light, but wins were also meant to be examined and studied. And, in her case, even celebrated. While she didn't consider a win over Jordan something to celebrate, she knew exactly how she was going to congratulate herself.

Alicia stood examining her recently constructed bookcase and pondered how she was going to organize it. There were few things in life she considered more soothing than an organized bookcase. The choices that went into the selections of her library, the choices that went into how to organize each shelf–she found a thrill in the possibilities.

"By hero? By author? By year? By subject? Ohhh, or by color?" Alicia chimed, with giddy excitement that caused a few fireworks to pop off her hands. She fought to control herself, then sighed.

Okay, I got this. By subject, then by hero. She studied the five boxes of books at her feet. She had to use plasma to carry them from the car to the dorm, and she relished the thought of what her library would look like. Then her alarm went off – *ten minutes until bedtime.* She sighed at the thought of what tomorrow would bring. She shook off the dark cloud and picked up the first book. A History of Power: Olympians and Gifted Through the Ages. She weighed the book in hand, then shelved it.

Okay, forget my alarm. I deserve this. Alicia silenced her alarm and began celebrating one book at a time.

Though Lucas was wearing all black, he was impossible to miss as the moonlight hit his silver locks.

He's making his move, Jordan gasped.

Jordan watched the elf make his way through the dark spots in the courtyard and continue on.

No. No. No, Jordan repeated. *What is he doing? I gotta follow him.*

Jordan searched for his Zeuz Airwalkers. *C'mon. C'mon.*

In the darkness of the room, he was unsure where they were, but he caught sight of the box with his new tactical boots.

Okay, let's crack them in. Jordan stuffed his feet into the boots. They, like the suit, were form-fitting and snug. Jordan scrambled atop the dresser and opened the window. In the distance, he spotted Lucas' shadow receding.

I've done this before. I've followed people before – this is no different. Jordan, like he used to do at home, slipped on his gloves, then slipped out the window. He collected gravitons under his feet to stick to the walls, then with a soft running start, he crept after Lucas.

CHAPTER EIGHTEEN

The Dead Don't Hunt

Jordan felt himself shake. He hated that feeling. It never changed even after a year of vigilantism when he ran along the sides of buildings. The fear was always with him. This time, like many others, he swallowed it and pushed on.

In little gold bursts, Jordan stalked across the walls of Fort Olympus. Down below he followed little silver streaks of Lucas as he disappeared and reappeared in the moonlight. As Lucas dipped and hid between pillars and darkness, Jordan jogged along the brick face of the building and huddled behind corners. Jordan stopped when he passed a window. He didn't so much as look in at the sleeping students, but his reflection was impossible to ignore.

Yikes. Jordan cringed at his reflection. In his rush to leave, he had forgotten to check his face. He still had icing on his mouth. With a groan of disgust, he wiped his mouth and brushed the crumbs away with his gloved hands. He regained focus and saw Lucas round yet another corner.

Where are you going? Where is your partner? Jordan asked himself.

It was gold-cat and silver-mouse through the school's courtyard.

If Lucas ran, Jordan ran.

If Lucas hid, Jordan hid.

If Lucas stopped, Jordan stopped.

After about twelve minutes, Lucas stopped at a gothic marble gate that extended from a marble mausoleum. In the moonlight, a statue of

Hades stood in front of the mausoleum, forever a guardian of the Underworld.

Jordan exhaled, then greedily began taking in air. He could really go for another ambrosia cupcake to replenish himself. Jordan watched Lucas take out his Fort Olympus student card and scan it. BEEP and a flash of red: denied. Lucas swiped his badge again at the door to the mausoleum, and he was denied again.

"Okay, dragger, you've reached the gate, but it's closed," Jordan narrated from the shadows.

Lucas peered around as Jordan crouched in the shadows of a building, sinking into the dark. Lucas took a moment, exhaled deeply, then walked away from the gate.

"Okay, you're angry. You can't get in. So you're heading back to the dorm because we could both use some sleep and –" Lucas charged the gate, then with a graceful leap and plasma infused in his legs, he went up and over. "Ugh," Jordan sighed. "Can't I have a moment of peace?"

Jordan slipped out of the shadows, dropped softly to the cobblestone road, and waited. Nothing moved. Jordan listened for a change in the silence. Nothing came. He rushed out of the shadows and to the front gate, where Hades stood waiting. As Jordan crept closer to the statue, he could make out writing on the door of the mausoleum:

FORT OLYMPUS CEMETERY
From the Stars, to the Earth
Espers are born
Here lie the Espers who grew into heroes
Heroes that returned
From the Earth, to the Stars

He's meeting someone at a cemetery? Jordan gulped. He gathered gravitons under his feet, then in a golden arc, went up and over the gate. He landed in the grass and took in a hushed breath. It occurred to him that he had skipped this location online. He knew Fort Olympus had a cemetery but had never really thought about it when he thought of the rest of the campus. Being here was one thing, but being here at night felt eerie and a bit disrespectful. He glanced along the rows of tombstones and sought out Lucas.

C'mon. Where did you go? Jordan scanned for his silver locks, but he couldn't find them. Jordan crouched low, staying in the darkness, making his way through the tombstones. He stopped when a figure came into light.

Jordan paused as he realized the figure wasn't breathing.

It was a statue.

Jordan stepped into the moonlight cautiously until he faced the statue. It was Saint Lightning, one of the Olympians. Even made of bronze, she was adorned in her trademark suit with a nun's veil cloaked over her head and her mask covering her mouth and nose. Only her eyes poked out from under the veil. Jordan looked up at the eyes. As he did, he felt something deep within him pulled in her direction. Though he had often seen her face – or, rather, her eyes– in books, video games, figures, and memorial videos, it was only being this close to her physical presence that he felt something within him stir.

Before he could search himself for an answer, he heard Lucas' voice coming from the dark distance. Jordan went back to incognito mode, staying low and using gravitons to pad the sound of his steps. He made his way toward Lucas' voice.

Did you find your partner? Jordan asked himself. *Maybe if I catch both of them here and now, they'll also let me stay in the school. Not going to jail is good. Not being expelled is better.*

Jordan crept closer and could finally make out what Lucas was saying. It gave Jordan pause.

"Today was my first day. I really wish you had been here," Lucas whispered. Jordan crept low and studied the landscape. Lucas was alone, whispering to a tombstone. Jordan sighed. The tombstone had thin, wispy Elvish writing inscribed on it.

He's not meeting anyone, Jordan realized. *At least no one who is alive.* Jordan wanted to slap his forehead but realized he had to maintain silence.

Lucas continued speaking to the grave. "I thought you should know that I passed my first exercise today, and–" Crack. Jordan's foot came down on a twig and resonated through the night. Lucas paused and Jordan froze.

Oh boy, Jordan said to himself. He looked out and saw as Lucas' pointed ears twitched, listening to the noise of the night.

"I hear you over there," Lucas called out. "These ears aren't just for show, you know?" Lucas turned and his prismatic eyes reflected in the moonlight like the eyes of a cat in the darkness. Jordan cringed. It was still cat and mouse, but now he was the mouse.

"Why don't you come out of hiding?" Lucas demanded.

No. No. This isn't happening. Jordan's mind raced, and he felt a cold sliver of fear rising in his chest.

"Don't make me come to you," Lucas warned the night.

Run. Run right now. Jordan told himself, but his legs didn't move. Jordan glanced at the gate; it was only five yards away, if he could just leap over – Lucas shifted right in front of Jordan, his fist pulled back and eyes blazing with green plasma.

"Oh," Lucas purred, his eyes bearing down with serpent-green energy. "Hello again."

CHAPTER NINETEEN

The First Strike

Jordan lunged backward, but Lucas was faster. His hand snapped out and snatched Jordan by the throat. In one motion, Jordan felt his breath and a scream locked inside his lungs. Jordan grabbed at him, but Lucas wasn't just faster – he was stronger.

"What are you doing here?" Lucas shouted. Jordan gritted his teeth and refused to respond. He raised both arms and brought them down on the soft point of Lucas' elbow, breaking his grip.

"Why are you following me?" Lucas lunged for him once more. Jordan dipped past his plasma-packed punch and swiveled around to his back.

Gotta go. NOW. Jordan's eyes flashed gold as he tapped into his plasma and sent sun-gold plasma charges rushing down his frame. Then he sent gravitons into his heels and prepared to leap when Lucas' hand came back around and grabbed him again.

The two swatted at each other for a moment in a rush of hands before Jordan brought his feet up with golden gravitons still attached to the soles. He stomped forward, kicking the gravitons into Lucas' chest while activating them in the same instant. Jordan became a rocket, and Lucas became a launchpad. A sunburst of golden light ruptured between the two of them and sent both teens tumbling end over end.

Lucas hit the ground and put a hand to his chest. He was winded and in pain. Jordan slammed into the Earth and skidded to a stop right under a tombstone. He put a gloved hand up to stop himself because the last thing he wanted to do tonight was break a gravestone.

"Who are you?" Lucas roared as he clambered to his feet.

"What are you doing sneaking out here in the middle of the night?" Jordan shot back.

"It's none of your business." Lucas pointed with an accusatory finger.

"It was you that night at the museum," Jordan snapped.

Lucas paused like a deer in headlights, absorbing this. He blinked blindly searching for the context.

"I don't know what you're talking about," Lucas grumbled.

"You know, and you're gonna tell me everything." Jordan dropped into a three-point stance, gathered gravitons into his heel, and launched himself at Lucas.

Lucas' eyes went wide. *He's fast.*

Lucas readied himself, tapping into his forest green plasma and bringing it surging forth into his fist. Jordan tensed and pulled his own plasma-packed fist back. Two shadows suddenly appeared in between them. The taller one threw his arms out and caught both by the wrist. Jordan felt his own momentum slam to a halt under the sudden grasp. Lucas twisted hard to the right as he felt the larger man tear him from the ground and hurl him like he weighed nothing. Jordan's vision whirled, and he landed hard on the grass on his left shoulder.

Both cadets sprawled on the ground and moved quickly to scramble up as a voice thundered, "Enough."

Jordan and Lucas both found themselves looking up at Vermillion, the bearded, bespectacled, muscle-bound teacher Jordan saw earlier that day. Next to him stood Rhea, who looked pensively down on them.

I – I didn't even see them coming. Jordan groaned. *Where – where did they come from?* Jordan shook his head, then finally zoned back into the shouting match.

Lucas was pointing at Jordan. "That cape-dragger was following me."

"Because...you were sneaking around."

Vermillion's eyes flashed with red daggers of light, and both boys shouted until they were hit with an electric tap as the wise instructor flexed his plasma. Jordan groaned. Although he had taken three previous hits, he was no more acclimated to the punch.

"Shut it," Vermillion ordered.

"Squad Leader," Lucas begged from the ground. "I was on patrol –"

"This isn't your area to patrol," Vermillion interrupted.

"I was on patrol as ordered." Lucas took in a hoarse breath then admitted, "My grandfather is buried out here. I wanted to visit his grave earlier today but didn't have time."

Vermillion seemed to deflate before Jordan's eyes. Vermillion then looked over at the grave with the Elvish text. "Your grandfather was Oakenvale?" Vermillion asked.

Lucas nodded, his Elvish ears dropping along with his head.

"So you broke in?" Vermillion concluded. "To see his grave?"

Lucas nodded.

Jordan sighed. *I'm such an idiot.*

Rhea turned to Jordan. "And you?"

Even though Lucas was no longer strangling him, Jordan still felt his voice catch in his throat. "I – I caught him sneaking in," Jordan admitted. *Hopefully, the truth is the best way out of this.* Rhea's eyes studied Jordan for a long beat, searching his face against her memory.

"You have a penchant for getting in awkward situations, huh?" she asked. "I think I recognize you –"

She knows I'm a vigilante. Jordan froze, and his heart seized in his chest, eyes widening. *She remembers that night.* Jordan's legs couldn't seem to move fast enough against Lucas. They now trembled under him and even threatened to buckle. *I'm gonna get called out here and now. What will Darius say? What will Khadija say?* He couldn't feel anything except a cold swirl in his panicked chest. *I'm going to jail.*

"We sat next to each other earlier today." Rhea nodded at him.

*What – what? That's true, but...*Jordan took in a weary breath, sensing an invisible trap set in her words but seeing no other choice. He risked it all with a quick reply. "Yeah. At the assembly."

Rhea turned her gaze to Vermillion. "Squad Leader, permission to escort Cadet Harris back to his dorm?"

She knows. But she – she's covering for me? Jordan's mind raced, coming back from the depths of numb fear to engage in this new chain of events. He was confused but at least he wasn't being outed as a vigilante and thus dismissed from the school.

Vermillion looked between them, then gave a nod. "Granted. But I will be reporting this to your Squad Leader, Harris. This will be a mark on your record. Three strikes and you're out."

A strike? On my first day. Jordan felt a surge of anxiety. He clutched his hands into fists, then forced them to relax.

"Yes, sir," Jordan mumbled, numbly.

Jordan glanced over at Lucas, who shot him a nasty glare from between his spiked ears. Jordan cringed, and anxiety rippled through him. Suddenly, his head ached.

"That's a mark on your record too, Lucas. Breaking out of your patrol area is a violation, not to mention fighting on campus. You're lucky I don't record two strikes for each of you," Vermillion spat.

Lucas growled under his breath and shook his head.

Vermillion took Lucas by the shoulder. "C'mon. Let's go." He turned back to Rhea. "Report back to me and the others once Cadet Harris is back in his dorm."

"Yes, sir," she replied.

It took a full five minutes of walking before Jordan could finally feel his legs. Neither he nor Rhea said anything. Jordan wasn't sure where to begin. Ten minutes ago, he thought he was going to be halfway to accomplishing his mission, but five minutes ago he thought suspension and jail were his next stops. The shifts made him dizzy.

Jordan needed to break the silence. "What were you all doing out here?"

"Every regiment does campus security. We do the Monday rounds," Rhea explained. "You'll probably be doing it later this week too – provided you aren't expelled before then."

Jordan didn't reply. He didn't have much left after the day he'd had.

"Now, you want to tell me what you were doing there?" she pressed.

"I told you," Jordan replied. "I saw him sneak in."

"No, do you want to tell me what were you doing out interfering with police business the other night?"

Like someone had smacked him with plasma, Jordan felt a shock to his system that rattled his bones. *She knows.* Rhea's eyes pierced him, searching for answers.

"I was making rounds of my own," Jordan answered.

"You were breaking the law." As they reached the doors to Jordan's barracks, Rhea stopped.

"I was doing what I thought was right." Jordan felt something churn within him.

"There are rules." Rhea leaned in, pressing her point.

"And there are people that need to be stopped," Jordan pushed back. The day's events and lack of sleep were making him impatient.

"And what if people get hurt?" Rhea lingered near him. "Because you don't know what you're doing?" Rhea's stare dug into him, then softened. "My brother went here for a bit. He dropped out a few years later because of people like you."

"People like me?"

"People who don't know how to follow the rules, even when they think they're doing the right thing." She sat in silence for a somber moment, before adding sternly, "I covered for you tonight. I won't do it again. I catch you outside or breaking the rules again – I'm letting them know who you really are."

Jordan nodded. That was all he needed to hear. He scanned his key-card and opened the heavy oak door to his barracks.

"Vigilantes and heroes are on the same side," Jordan said without looking at her.

"Tell that to the law," Rhea replied quickly with anticipation.

Jordan stepped over the threshold, stopped, then turned back to face her. Both stared firmly, unblinking. Then Jordan said something that Rhea didn't expect. "Thanks."

Rhea recovered from her surprise, before replying sternly, "Don't mention it."

Then with a sense of finality, the door clicked between them. As it closed with a resounding thud, the words on Jordan's gloves looked up at him tauntingly: *Be your own hero...*

RHEA BROOKS

Hero Alias: N/A

Height: 5'4

Weight: 110

Birth Date: January 31

Plasma Color: Green

Plasma Level: 35,000

Gift: Rhea possesses the ability to manipulate light photons to create energy blasts, bend light, and release blinding flash attacks.

CHAPTER TWENTY

Astro Day I: Rose Dawn

The sun rose early the next day at Fort Olympus. The various statues of former alumni who became notable superheroes cast their shadows along the face of the school's dormitories. As the sun peeked up over the clouds for a new day, it was met by the soft beeping sound of an alarm clock.

Alicia had a routine long before she started at Fort Olympus, and she intended to keep it. She wasn't going to let something like school, moving thirty minutes away from home, homework, and the occasional bouts of exhaustion break any part of her regular schedule.

Her alarm was tied to the rising of the sun, and she felt her eyes crack open at the sun's rays peeking through her dorm window. Alicia stirred from bed, let the sun's warmth fill her and invigorate her tired frame, right as she hit snooze on the alarm.

Ten minutes later, the alarm beeped again, and this time Alicia turned it off without a second thought. She was tired physically, but that came with hero training. Yesterday's events and the new place were not to blame. Her inquisitive mind never gave her a full night's sleep – the downfall of being a genius.

Time to get up, she thought. *For real this time.*

Alicia perked up. Her roommate was still curled up in bed and asleep under the sun's light, in spite of her repeated alarms. Alicia fought the urge to go back to sleep. She sat up, stifled a yawn, and levered herself free from the bed. Her trick to getting up was wearing her workout clothes to sleep. She exited the bed, already dressed in black and gold Fort Olympus sweatpants and a grey t-shirt.

Alicia slipped on a pair of running shoes she had put by the bed the night before. Then she grabbed her water bottle, which she had also placed there the night before. She paused. Something was buzzing. She checked. It was her phone, but it wasn't her alarm. Her dad was calling. Alicia felt a storm of emotions brewing. She bottled the storm and canceled the call. Then with one final envious look at her bed, she pushed the idea of sleep out of her mind and got to work.

Her workout was simple; it was a jog mixed with plasma techniques. It was something her brother swore he invented, but she knew how big brothers exaggerated to make themselves look cool. To Alicia, her brother, Cedric, was always cool – no matter what he did.

Having a big brother who was an Olympian was pretty cool.

Alicia embraced this workout as the perfect combination of physical and plasma-based exercises. As she turned and veered off of Crawford Avenue to Texas Avenue, she made her way past the historic Rice Hotel, known as The Rice. This was her halfway point and where she changed up her routine. She flipped to a different song in her headphones, something with a bit more energy behind it. Then she tapped into her plasma. She felt a rush of furious fuchsia static pulses traveling up her body.

In the middle of running, she shifted forward, threw herself four feet, and landed softly mid-stride. She started another sprint, followed by another shift. As soon as her toes touched the ground, she was back to running. Each time the world seemed to shift into a fast-forward motion, Alicia used those moments to inhale and refill her lungs. She had to be careful doing this on public streets, though. One time she shifted in the middle of an intersection and nearly paid with her life. She would never make that mistake again.

Alicia rounded a corner, turning mid-shift, onto Caroline Street. This was her favorite section, which included the justified trinity of the Harris County Civil Courthouse, the Harris County Criminal Justice

Center, and the Harris County Family Law Center. Alicia found a reverence for the area. Even though it was always a few streets out of the way, she decided today of all days she'd visit it.

Today of all days was important to her and the city. While she and her family knew it as Cedric's birthday, the city of Houston recognized it as Astro Day.

Alicia took a break to settle and take in the sights. Cedric was one of the Olympians who passed away on the Green Night. While most heroes kept their identities a secret, Cedric wore his on his sleeve. He never revealed his face or his name to the world, but he wore a customized suit that had the Texas flag emblazoned upon the right arm. His hero name was also a nod to the city and his love for the stars – Astro.

Alicia embraced the moment and saw that all three law centers were flying Houston flags with Astro's face on them. The flag was a special edition made to commemorate him. She inhaled, then absorbed her brother's face looking down on her from each building.

Alicia suddenly returned to her route, rounded an apartment complex, and made her way, as she had done many times before, to a set of exterior metal stairs that climbed the side of the apartment complex – all twenty flights. She took in a deep breath, peered up the labyrinth of stairs, and climbed.

Legs pumping, music drumming, arms flexing in sync, and plasma burning in her calves, she made her way up the staircase and towards the rooftop that had become her safe space. As she climbed higher, she could see the tips of other buildings drifting into view. She pushed and finally made it to the rooftop where she exhaled with a giant breath, taking in the Houston morning. Her music cut out for a second, and she checked her phone – her mother – she canceled it.

Alicia stood triumphantly atop the apartment complex and looked out at the city coming to life before her. Even though she hated waking up early, she liked being up early. Cedric was always an early riser and would often take her on jogs with him in the mornings when he had time. She'd often studied him when he ran. On holiday mornings, or after late-night patrols, and even after nights when he came home with a noticeable limp, he always made sure to run in the mornings.

Alicia looked down at the city he saved and took in the sights. "We're still here, you know?" Alicia remarked. "...Because of you."

Alicia turned around to face her brother, who was staring down at her and the rest of Houston. His face and appearance had been immortalized by a mural painted on an adjacent building. Alicia stood twenty stories above the city. Her brother gazed down from an apartment building forty stories high. Even with spectacular views of Houston, her brother was the highlight.

Astro's mural beamed down on her. Despite his mask, he had a youthful black face with tight bundles of silver and black cornrowed hair. He was painted in his trademarked signature attack pose: Crescent Cutter. He had two fingers pointed up to the heavens and white plasma gathered into his fingertips. His other hand was bracing his wrist to stabilize the flowing energy. To most folks, it would appear as if he just generated a star on the point of his fingers, but to his enemies, it was often the last thing they saw.

His hero attire was the traditional bodysuit in white with gold accents, and his right arm was customized with the Texas flag wrapping his bicep. Underneath his likeness was the inscription: *In Memory of Astro, the Star of Houston.*

Alicia nodded at his picture, quelled the storm within her again, then got back to work. She shifted across the rooftop exactly one foot, aka twelve inches. The world blurred around her as she put her plasma to work. It was like skipping across water, before skidding to a stop.

"One," Alicia began.

She turned around and shifted again, this time projecting herself exactly two feet across.

During her exercises, she felt the moments of the Green Night coming back to her. Even though it was ten long years ago, she still recalled how dark and terrible the sky was that night. She had been sitting in her parents' apartment when Cedric entered, already dressed in his combat clothes. He spoke into a cellphone, "I'll be right there." Alicia had to tear herself away from the window, where she was watching the jade thunderstorm crackle above and around them. She turned her big eyes and pink locks back to her brother, and her parents intercepted him.

"What did they say?" her dad asked.

"They're calling us in," Cedric said with a hint of trepidation.

Her mother took her father's hand, worry written on her face. Alicia searched Cedric's face. It was pensive, but also curious. His eyes were searching for something. She knew exactly what he was after–his Texas flag sleeve. She held it close to her, willing him to stay.

Alicia came out of the shift, landed on the balls of her feet, and used her momentum to spin around.

"Two," she exhaled.

Then Alicia shifted once more, her body drifted across the roof, while her mind slipped back to that night.

Cedric had approached her with that smile he always employed before he went out on patrol. It was calming to Alicia at one time, but she had since realized it was only for her benefit. He meant to put her at ease. Cedric cajoled the sleeve from her, but she made one last attempt to hold it before he got his arm through.

"Please don't go," she remembered herself saying. "It's scary."

"That's exactly why I have to go," Cedric said with his smile.

Alicia wanted to hug him, pin him down with her love, and keep him safe. Somehow, she got used to this. He would always come back the next day. He would always find a way back home, no matter how scary it was.

Astro put his hand up and offered, "Sparkle Five?"

Alicia responded, "Sparkle Five."

Brother and sister generated little sparks of plasma in their hands. Hers pink and purple– his white, and they high-fived. The plasma orbs collided between their hands and resonated with a thunderclap in the room. It was their ritual. Since neither of their parents had Gifts, this had always been a way for them to connect.

"Gotta go," Astro smirked at her.

Those two words echoed in her mind often because they were the final words he uttered to her.

Alicia came out of that memory just as her feet touched down on the rooftop.

"Three."

Alicia turned back the way she came, aimed for a spot six feet away, and directed her plasma. She was airborne. Her thoughts swirled back to how Astro had leaped from their balcony on the eighth floor and flew out into the green torrent of lightning and thunder that boomed across the city.

The next time she saw him was on TV when the news covered the battle of the Olympians vs. the Green Titan. While the city shook with rattles of explosions and blockbuster firepower miles away from the main event on TV, the scenes played out up close and in real-time.

She remembered the way her mother held her tight when they saw Cedric get caught in a fire blast.

She remembered the way her father whispered to her, "Don't worry. Red Wing is there. He trained Cedric. He won't let anything happen to him." Alicia remembered seeing her brother skid backward in the flaming debris, putting the Green Titan in his sights.

Astro threw two fingers in the air.

Then he grabbed his wrist to stabilize it as —

Cedric gathered a white-hot star of energy into his fingertips —

It was almost too brilliant to look at. Even on TV, she had to squint because it was uncomfortable for her eyes.

Then Cedric brought the energy down in a clean arc of white light that carved, like a cleaver, a line of destruction the size of a city block. The Green Titan took the brunt of the slash as it bit into his diamond body before the two energies collided into a shockwave that Alicia felt, even though she was miles away and safe in her mom's arms.

She dropped out of the flashback and broke her shift, then skidded to a stop. Alicia had overshot her landing a bit, and the gravel under her feet protested.

"Four." Furious fuchsia flashed in her eyes as she set her sights on a spot eight feet away.

Her body groaned, and her plasma flexed under her command. She was there, then she was gone.

Alicia was back in her mom's arms at that moment when they watched what they hoped and prayed was the finale of the Green Night.

First, came the reports that there were only two survivors.

Second, came the reveal that Titanus was one of them.

The way her mother held onto her – as if she might be able to shield her from the reality of what came next – was something she never forgot. Alicia couldn't breathe, but she felt her mom's breath cold on the back of her neck. Alicia couldn't feel her heartbeat but felt her mom's heart beating against her ears.

Then her mom cried out in a way that she felt it before she heard it.

Red Wing was seen being pulled from the rubble and was announced as the second survivor. Instantly, Alicia felt her mother and father pile on her, embracing her, and she reached out for what she could and grabbed at them too.

Alicia's feet hit the gravel and once again, she felt herself skidding. She gritted her teeth, and the gravel bit into the rooftop. Alicia turned around and focused on a spot now 12 feet away.

"C'mon. C'mon," she willed herself, dug back into what was left of her plasma, and pushed it. "Six."

Alicia blinked and –

She opened her eyes the morning after the Green Night to see an angel approaching her. Or, at least, she thought so.

The figure had wings and was coming her way, following the same flight path that Astro had, but that's where the similarities ended. Their wings were red and made of flaming plasma, igniting along the tips to propel the man their way. Alicia stirred from under her parents when the angel came into the light.

It was Red Wing.

The one-armed man was bruised and covered in dried blood. There was a crust of pain on his face that she had never seen before. While she grew up calling him Uncle Alex, he was her brother's teacher. He was everything a teacher should be: knowledgeable, kind, patient, and seemingly never without worry. But as he stood on their balcony, he was none of those things. His red wings composed of plasma burnt the moisture in the air around him, creating tendrils of smoke around his thin frame.

Her parents stirred from their stupor and joined Alicia. They looked to Alexander for answers.

"What happened?" her mom asked.

He took a grim breath, then answered, "There's something you need to see."

Alicia opened her eyes and realized she had overshot her shift. She had landed two feet ahead of her goal, jumping fourteen feet instead of twelve. She huffed in disgust, then shot herself back across the way. She didn't call out a number this time. She hit the gravel, twisted, and shifted again. She was reckless in her eagerness to both embrace and escape her haunted past. Alicia couldn't tell where she was going; all she knew was that she wanted to move. She didn't want to stay within the grasps of this memory, on this day, at this time. But try as she might, she felt herself brought back to that defining time when Astro was no longer with them.

She didn't remember the drive to the hospital, but she vividly recalled the smoke clouds in the distance. The wrath of the Green Titan could be seen from miles away. The city had become a charred husk of itself, where fires still burned, and people still cried out for help. The morning had come for the mourners, and the light of sunrise would do little to alleviate the horrors still left to be uncovered.

She didn't remember how long they waited at the hospital, but it was a frenzy of activity.

The victims of the Green Titan were everywhere. For all she didn't remember, she remembered when she saw Cedric again.

He looked like he was sleeping in his hospital bed – and from what Red Wing explained to her – he was sleeping.

"They don't know when or if he'll wake up," Alexander had explained to her parents. "But they'll care for him as long as he is here."

Wake up. Alicia remembered saying the words in her head.

But Cedric lay in bed, unmoving.

"Cedric," Alicia whispered.

But he didn't move. All was silent, save for the machines breathing for him and beeping with every beat of his heart.

Alicia remembered walking over and taking his hand.

He didn't move.

In her mind's eye, Alicia spread her hand over his and released plasma orbs. "Sparkle Five."

She whispered it, but he didn't return it.

The sparks died upon his hand, and Alicia felt a switch flip within herself, a terrible encroaching fear that welled up behind her eyes. It was a blur from there, but she remembered sobbing. She remembered Alexander holding her. She remembered how her body shook because she cried so hard, and she remembered feeling weightless, despite her parents' best efforts to hold everything together.

As Alicia came out of her shift, she had to remember to stop. Her feet hit the barrier on the edge of the roof, and she felt herself slam to a halt and career over the edge of the twenty-story building. Alicia fought against the air, trying to make sure she didn't tip over. She made a pair of firework blasts in her hands, clapped her palms together, and used the concussive blasts to throw herself back the way she came.

Alicia hit the gravel and stayed there. Covered in sweat, crushed rock, and the morning dew of the city, she took in air. She had forgotten to breathe. She had forgotten to think before acting. She had forgotten where she was. Alicia sank into the ground and allowed herself a moment to breathe – a moment to be at peace, with nothing but the sky above her.

I gotta keep going, she urged herself. *I'll prove myself to Uncle Alex, to this city, to the world.* Alicia turned over to Astro's mural looking down on her from his attack pose, and she smiled at him. *To show you that your loss wasn't in vain.*

She took a moment to reflect on her near-death experience only moments before, and whispered to Cedric, "Good looking out."

Alicia took the elevator down. It was her only real break in her morning workout, and she was going to enjoy it. When she walked out the front of the building, she was greeted by people on the sidewalk toting various Astro merchandise. The first thing she saw was a tiny kid, dressed like her brother, with a white balloon in the shape of a star. The balloon read, "Happy Astro Day" in gold text.

She smirked.

The kid then did the Crescent Cutter motion, two fingers in the air, one hand on the wrist, then he brought the wrist down to slash through an invisible obstacle.

Alicia smiled.

And the kid's balloon slipped loose from his hands. The kid glanced up and saw it rising above him. He leaped up and – kept going up. Orange plasma flared around the kid's body when he used his plasma and drifted up with the balloon, rising about three feet off the ground.

Alicia reached out and grabbed the kid's ankle just as he drifted up to catch his balloon.

"Careful," Alicia chimed.

Startled, the kid looked back down at her. She gave him a gentle smile and brought him and his balloon back down to Earth. His mother rushed over and grabbed him immediately. His father turned to Alicia and nodded thanks.

"Thank you," the mother gushed. "His Gift is just coming in, and I swear he never stays on the ground."

"No worries," Alicia replied.

The family favored her with grateful smiles, and she returned it with a smile of her own. "Happy Astro Day."

ALICIA JACKSON

Hero Alias: Meteora

Height: 5'4

Weight: 110

Birth Date: April 20

Plasma Color: Purple

Plasma Level: 32,000

Gift: Alicia possesses the ability to mentally manipulate the raw plasma in her body to create concussive bursts. Her control allows her to craft the shape and form of her plasma into rudimentary shapes for various techniques.

CHAPTER TWENTY-ONE

Astro Day II: The World Today

Alicia checked her watch twice on the way back and realized if she didn't hurry, she was going to be late for class. And not just any class, but the first day of classes. She broke from a walk into a jog that her body protested against. Alicia wished she had the strength to just shift the final way across town, but alas, only a few experienced Espers were able to shift that far – especially without running right into a building along the way.

Alicia got back to the dorms quicker than she expected and found her roommate still blissfully asleep. Alicia quickly glanced at her roommate snuggled in bed and sarcastically wished her sweet dreams. She raced into the private shower designed for her and her roommate. A few minutes later, she sprinted out dressed in the formal Fort Olympus uniform, then rushed to class.

The first class for her and the Freshman Leo Regiment was in Washington Hall Room Five. It was an auditorium-style room with rows of descending seats that led to a small platform at the bottom. Vermillion was leading the class from the platform with a set of images playing on the board behind him.

Alicia found her teammates sitting together amid the other freshmen. She made her way to the seat between Jordan and Sydney.

Ugh, what a drag. Alicia groaned at the thought of sitting next to Sydney this early in the day. She fought the urge to spite her, gave her a toothless grin, and took the chair.

"Thanks for saving me a seat," Alicia said.

"No problem," Jordan replied.

Jordan's own eyes were on a pair of students sitting a row above them.

Rhea and Lucas were both seated and preparing for class. Their overly relaxed body language betrayed the trials and tribulations of last night.

"Welcome to Modern Heroism," Vermillion announced as his watch clicked to exactly 9 a.m.

The students still not settled immediately shuffled to their seats, opened their books, took out their pencils, and prepared for the day. All except for Cooper, who was still in the midst of a sugar crash. He blinked sleepily, then shook himself awake. Alicia leaned over past Jordan and shot him a look: *Don't embarrass us.*

"In today's society, Espers are needed more than ever. The rise of criminals and Vespers has sent crime to unprecedented levels," Vermillion began. Behind him, the screen showed pictures of other professional heroes: MegaTon, Titanus, Kurikara, Kinetic, and many others.

Cooper's head dropped, and Alicia sighed. She nodded to Jordan. *Do something.*

Jordan leaned over and kicked Cooper's foot. He jumped and snapped awake.

Vermillion paused and surveyed them for a moment. Jordan felt Vermillion's eyes focus on him once again, reminding him of the embarrassment of last night. *Already one strike down...*

Vermillion continued, "And it is in this class that we'll be discussing the rise of the modern hero and what that means in today's age."

Alicia leaned over past Jordan and hissed, "Stay awake."

"I know," Cooper whispered, his words muffled by exhaustion. "I'm trying."

Alicia leaned back in her seat, where she caught Battalia's gaze.

Sydney gave Alicia the tiniest of nods. "Stay on him," Sydney whispered.

Alicia's first instinct was to search for an insult, but after determining there was none, she replied, "Will do."

"Like a lot of you, I too lost family on the Green Night. I lost my brother...And as a hero, as someone whose job it is to save lives, that hurts more than I dare to say. And I have seen firsthand as..." Vermillion stopped himself as a wave of emotion rippled through his colossal frame.

Jordan's eyes suddenly felt heavy. He felt the weight of the past bear down on him and the students in the room. *Him too.* He glanced about his fellow classmates. *All of us, really.*

"I've seen firsthand how crime has skyrocketed after the Green Night. And I'm sure you've seen it too – so please listen with all your heart. This class will discuss modern heroism and why heroes are needed now more than ever."

While the first class was difficult for Cooper to stay awake in, he soon found himself energized and excited for the next one. The team had filed out into the courtyard to make their way to Kennedy Hall. Jordan spotted Rhea and Lucas in the crowd when they passed each other. He did a double-take as they walked past, yet they didn't turn his way.

It's like nothing happened last night. Jordan sighed.

When Jordan turned back, Alicia was on him. "What happened last night?"

"Wha – what do you mean?" he asked.

"What happened to Cooper? He's exhausted."

"Oh," Jordan nearly shouted in relief. "He's just tired. We had cupcakes for dinner."

Alicia blinked. *There's no way he said what I think he just said.*

"You had what?"

"Cupcakes. His family gave him a bunch for move-in day," Jordan said as if it was obvious.

Alicia exhaled deeply. *Cupcakes. For Dinner.* "Boys," she grumbled and rolled her eyes.

Jordan blinked. *Was it something I said?*

Cooper led the team into Kennedy Hall, much more energized than before. He had managed to get a bit of shut-eye in the Modern Heroism class, and he was quite ready for the next to begin. He already knew where he wanted to sit. In the middle row – in the middle seat. From experience, he knew that was the best seat in the house.

The class was Hybrid History, and it was being taught by the pro hero Tigris himself. As the students filed in, Cooper bounded down the stairs on all fours and scrambled to a seat in the middle.

He was so excited, he nearly shifted himself getting to the seat. Cooper kept his plasma in check, then waved his team to sit with him. Tigris was already in front of the screen at the bottom of the hall looking over his notes. He was much bigger up close. He had orange fur, green eyes, and black tiger stripes that flowed around his body. He was built like a heavyweight boxer, so regardless of his fur, he had to wear XXL suits. Cooper studied the legendary hero. *That's him. That's really Tigris.* Just the thought of his Tigris collection at home and in his dorm made his tail wag. He accidentally bumped Reuben, who sent him a glare. *Mental note: Don't do that again.* Reuben turned away from Cooper and pulled red fur out from behind his ear.

Ew, Reuben grimaced, then tossed the fur to the side.

Tigris began the class by clearing his throat. It was enough to rattle them into silence. As he began to speak, the screen behind him showed various images of Hybrids throughout history: from crude cave drawings, to hieroglyphics, to abstract paintings, to black and white photos, to color photos, then finally to video.

"Our world is a rich and complex one," Tigris said with images of the Minotaur and Cerberus projected behind him. "For generations, Hybrids and humans have lived in peace – mostly." The screen jumped to a drawing of knights fighting a dragon, and the cadets chuckled. "The Minotaur, the Centaur, the Faun, and of course, my early ancestor – the

Wolf Man," he rattled off as images of those Hybrids appeared in rapid succession behind him. "Here in Hybrid History, we'll be detailing the history of man, animal, and everything in between."

Cooper's tail squirmed behind him, and Jordan ducked it mid-swing.

C'mon, bro, Jordan's face said.

"Sorry," Cooper whispered.

Behind Tigris, the slideshow shifted through a number of Hybrids, including elves, dwarves, Medusa, leprechauns, and ended with a frightening illustration of a winged angel slaying a monster, a demon. Cooper spotted an alarmed Reuben rearing back in his seat. Cooper looked away from him, then back down to the screen, content not to make eye contact with him.

After their first two classes of the day, the students headed to lunch in Annapurna Hall. The mess hall was built from the previously established brick and mortar cafeteria dating back to the 1700s. Midnight grey blocks and vanilla mortar, compiled over a hundred years ago, were mixed with metal and red brick additions to accommodate more students – and more food. The entrance of the hall was adorned with a bronze statue of Annapurna, the Hindu Goddess of Food. She sat with her legs crossed, her head-dress on, a bowl in one hand, and a spoon in another.

Inside, the hall was split into two areas. A set of tables where a self-serve buffet was set ran parallel to a vast set of tables and seating to the right. The interior of the facility felt like a fort with brick walls and wooden supports that lined the oak ceiling. In the back of the room sat a mighty fireplace surrounded by individual oak and leather seats. The Fort Olympus crest was adorned high above the fireplace, and above the hall.

Sydney got in line before her other teammates, and soon she had stacked her plate with portions of vegan meat, grilled vegetables, a salad, and a side of brown rice. As she exited the lunch line, she heard a familiar voice echo behind her. Though she had not seen this person in a year, Sydney knew exactly whose voice it was.

"Well, well, look who it is," Kristen Michaels chimed behind her. "Battalia."

Sydney stiffened and turned on her heel to face her. Kristen was tall with long strawberry blonde hair that trailed down her back and perfectly framed her piercing green eyes. She was an intimidating force in her own young right, and she was rarely alone.

Kristen was flanked by her twin sisters, Torrie and Samantha. They were triplets, but it was only when they stood this close, that you could see the resemblance. Torrie was the tallest of the three with short black hair that was cut close to the scalp along the edges and spiked on top. It gave her a more masculine appearance. The tips of her hair had green spikes that matched her eyes. Torrie's arms were muscular and large, and her plate was adorned with lean meats and protein to maintain her physique. Samantha was the smallest of the trio, with a bubbly personality that matched her blue-streaked blonde hair. Her plate was mostly filled with grains, rice, bread, hummus, and topped with a candied apple.

"It's been a while since Hero Prep," Sydney said, referring to their middle school academy.

"I like what you did with your hair," Samantha mused.

"Yes, it's something, all right," Kristen said with a smirk.

Sydney's mouth went tight as she fought to ignore the jab.

"And how are things here?" Sydney asked.

Samantha's eyes lit up. "Not bad, we –"

"We're excelling," Kristen cut in. "We're second-year Libras now."

"Hmmm, I pegged you all as Cancers," Sydney joked.

Torrie snorted behind her sisters. "Hey, hey, our father was born in July. Cancers are all right with us."

"Yeah," Kristen sneered. "Don't get too full of yourself, Sydney. You get into trouble here, your daddy can't save you."

"Luckily, I'm not the type that needs saving," Sydney replied, matching Kristen's energy. "But if you all get into trouble – who is going to save you?"

The young women stood in silence for a long beat, before devolving into giggles.

"Oh boy, I thought you had gone soft while we were away, but you're still sharp, Syd," Kristen laughed. Kristen brought her in for a hug and embraced her with one arm while balancing her tray.

"I missed you all," Sydney admitted.

Sydney exchanged hugs with the other Michaels sisters. It had been nearly a year since they had graduated from Hero Prep Academy and left Sydney.

"Well, if you wanna join us for lunch," Kristen said, "it would be nice to catch up."

"Let's do it," Sydney said.

The four girls walked off into the sea of tables just as Reuben entered and watched them pass.

At least we don't have to sit together here, Reuben thought and rounded the corner. He turned and stopped when he spotted Lucas with a few other Taurus students. If he got in line now, he'd be in line with them. Lucas' prismatic eyes glanced his way, and Reuben went cold. *He knows.*

Reuben turned away from the line, walked over to the front of the self-serve buffet, and grabbed an apple with his bandaged hand. He took a bite out of it, and his stomach growled. Reuben took another hearty crunch of the apple, loud enough to mask the sound.

As Reuben left the cafeteria, he passed Alicia and Cooper, who had just finished their rotation and walked out with trays of food. Alicia had her usual salad, while Cooper had plates of grilled vegetables with packets of honey. Cooper watched Reuben head out with just an apple.

"Uh-oh," Alicia whispered.

"Yeah, he's definitely going to be starving later," Cooper said, shrugging.

"What?" Alicia said. "No, no, they're coming over."

"I think we're talking about two different things," Cooper admitted.

"Coop." Alicia cringed.

Cooper followed her gaze to two black teen boys walking their way. He began to recognize them as they got closer.

The taller one was Tobe, who was wearing a regal scarf with a chain pattern over his Fort Olympus formal wear. The shorter one was Osin, who had locks of braided red hair running down his scalp. He wore the casual Fort Olympus uniform with chains on his wrist as decoration. As they moved through the crowd, people parted for them with double-takes and the occasional glance that screamed, *Wait, is that who I think it is?*

Cooper gasped. "Is that who I think –"

"Yes," Alicia hissed, her words choked with stress.

"No. Way," Cooper replied. "I didn't know they wanted to be heroes."

"Well, when you're the last remaining descendants of the African god Ogun, and basically African royalty, you can do whatever you want," Alicia admonished.

"Including walk right over here. He looks nervous," Cooper said, his voice hushed. "Ohhh, maybe he wants to ask you out or something."

"What? Me?" Alicia gagged on the words, increasingly nervous.

"Yes, you," Cooper replied. "He's looking right at you. Play it cool, you got this."

"Right," Alicia breathed. *I got this. I'm cool. I'm calm. I'm collected. I got this.*

Tobe and Osin stopped at arm's length from them. Tobe, the older of the two, paused and surveyed them with a gentle smile. Osin sulked behind him, one hand in his pocket and his eye on the lunch line.

"Hello, I'm Tobe, Crown Prince of Ogun," he replied with a light accent that decorated his words.

"Alicia." She offered her hand to shake it.

Tobe took her hand gently in his and kissed her fingers. "A pleasure."

Alicia fought the urge to squeal and centered herself. *Don't be a cape-dragger. Don't be a drag. Be cool. Calm. Collected.*

"And I'm Cooper," Cooper chirped from beside her. "Big fan. Love your ancestors' work. God of Iron by day, God of War by night. Great lineage."

Tobe smiled delicately. "Well, I'm glad to meet you both – "

"Hurry up and ask," Osin spat, cutting off his brother.

Tobe winced and glared.

Oh, he's nervous, Alicia smirked. *That's cute.*

Tobe exhaled, took a breath, bounced on his toes for a beat, then began again. "Forgive my brother; he is brash. But I hope I am not being forward when I say that there is a party my diplomats are throwing, and..." His voice trailed off as he searched for the right words.

Alicia tensed. *Okay, say yes, but not too loud and not too sudden. He's a prince. And I'm sure he's done this many times. Just be yourself. Don't be a drag.* Alicia put on a patient smile. Tobe was a prince, but he was still a teen, which came with all the awkward pitfalls of life.

Finally, Tobe just spilled it all out. "I'm curious to know if your family could cater the party, Cooper. We have heard delightful things about your parents' pastries."

For a long second, neither of them moved. Alicia deflated, and Cooper felt his jaw go slack.

Another long second passed before they both realized they hadn't said anything.

"Oh." Cooper gaped. "Yes. For sure."

"Good," Tobe chimed. "I'll have our Minister of National Affairs and Correspondence reach out."

"And I'll..." Cooper thought for a moment, "talk to my mom."

"Good day, Cooper," Tobe replied with a generous nod. Then he smirked at Alicia. "Nice to meet you, Alicia."

"Yeah," she said, blankly. "You too."

Tobe signaled to Osin that they were done, and the pair walked off towards the lunch line. While Alicia was still searching for a response, she failed to notice that Osin had glanced back at her for a second look.

"Huh," Cooper's voice reached her. "So they wanted to ask me out."

"Ugh," Alicia snapped. "Technically, they asked out your mom."

"Ew," Cooper bristled. "Please don't say that."

Jordan was late for lunch because he got hopelessly lost on the expansive campus. As he made his way towards the hall, he paused at the sound of arguing. One voice he recognized immediately, the second not at all.

Red Wing Jordan could hear how angry his Squad Leader was.

Jordan spotted Alexander following a rather large man around the corner of the cafeteria hall. Jordan's eyes flicked between the door to the lunchroom and the space where the two men disappeared.

Oh man, let me check this out. Jordan rushed away from the crowd of students flowing in and out of the cafeteria, and he hurried into the shadows of the building. Once he was out of sight, he brought gravitons into his feet and climbed up the face of the building. He rounded the side one careful step at a time. He pulled the straps tight on his backpack and yanked it against his back to quiet its motion.

He made his way around the back and positioned himself on all fours facing down at Alexander and the large man, who Jordan recognized from the opening ceremony because he had scolded him and Lucas. He was barrel-chested, with spiked black and hellfire hair, and – most notably – he had a scarlet V tattooed on his face.

Alexander spoke with a sternness Jordan thought was only reserved for him and his team. "David, if I find out that you've gone back to your old ways –"

David cut Alexander off. "I haven't done a thing."

"There is something going on around here, and I am going to find out," Red Wing replied.

The larger man took in a simmering breath and absorbed the mysterious accusation. "Alex, I've changed. I know the scarlet V under my eye says different, but I'm turning over a new leaf."

Alexander studied his face for a moment, before replying, "I hope so because I'll be watching."

Jordan stayed pressed to the wall and watched Alexander stomp off. David was left to himself for a silent simmering beat. Then Jordan watched as the big man radiated with red plasma.

Red, Jordan realized. *That's the same red plasma I saw from the second thief at the museum.* Jordan felt something pounce on his back. He nearly screamed at the sudden movement.

What the–? Jordan looked around and saw that a tiny grey squirrel had pounced on top of his backpack.

"Shshshssh, scram," Jordan hissed.

The squirrel stared at him curiously, then scurried up his backpack and onto the back of his neck. The squirrel's little toes slipped, and it tumbled off of him.

No. Jordan lunged out and caught the critter in both hands right above David.

David "Carnage" Roberts paused at the tussle above him, then glanced up to see – nothing.

Jordan had scurried as fast as the creature in his palms to the roof and set catching his breath.

"Okay, little buddy, here you go." Jordan sat the squirrel down next to him, and the scared critter scrambled away. Jordan sat for a beat, putting two and two together. *Alexander thinks that Vesper is up to something. His red plasma matches the plasma of the bigger thief.* Jordan took in a sharp breath. "I've found 'em."

Jordan's next class was in Lincoln Hall, which meant several things. One: he'd had to scarf down lunch really fast. Two: he'd have to race across campus to get there, and three: he'd most likely be late. While he did manage to eat his food in a manner unbecoming of a hero, and while he did race as fast as he could – despite just eating and then cramping –

he was also certainly late for class. He reached Lincoln Hall and slipped through the aged doors of the ancient building. Then, double-checking the classroom number, he gravity-burst up the stairs. He found himself at the top landing and did his best to get inside without being noticed.

Jordan took a few deep, calming breaths and entered another auditorium-style classroom. The teacher's voice was already booming across the class. "Villains are not often villains by nature, they are turned into villains by circumstance. No one – no sane person, for that matter – sees themselves as the villain in their life. They often see themselves as the hero."

Jordan, head down, made his way down the aisle, trying to look as small as possible. He stopped in his tracks as he recognized the voice and the signature V on the teacher's face. It was David. Jordan went stiff, then hid his face as much as possible. He nearly slipped on the stairs but readjusted to hide his face and navigate the room.

David continued speaking as a series of historical images of various Vespers with V's tattooed on their faces screened behind him, "Napoleon, Genghis Khan, and Blackbeard were all Vespers. Villains in life and in history. But for many, and to themselves, they were heroes. Villains are people too. They are real. They are powerful, and I should know because I used to be one. "

Jordan spotted his team down the aisle and began the awkward motion of walking past people already sitting to get to them. "Excuse me. Excuse me," Jordan uttered under his breath.

He had to stop when he found a pair of legs blocking him.

"Excuse me," Jordan repeated.

The legs didn't move, and now he saw who they belonged to – Lucas.

"C'mon man," Jordan whispered, "just let me pass."

"Sorry, didn't see you there," Lucas replied under a smirk.

"Boy," Jordan spat, "with them big ol' elf ears, I know –"

Jordan's tirade was interrupted when David's voice thundered over them. "Excuse me, Cadet." Jordan froze, and he felt all eyes on him. Lucas dropped his legs and scooted back in his seat. Underneath the silence, he could hear Lucas snickering. Jordan turned and looked down at David. The large man's eyes narrowed at him from behind his scarlet V.

Wait...I hope he didn't spot me earlier. Jordan was suddenly convinced, with a fresh wave of fear, that not only had David spotted him eavesdropping, but he was about to call him out in front of the class.

"You're a first-year, correct?" David asked.

"Yes, sir," Jordan replied.

His eyes glanced at the empty seat next to Cooper. He wanted nothing more than to just dive into it and keep his head down–anything but getting grilled by this teacher in front of everyone.

"And are you often late for your classes?"

"No sir, I was busy at lunch and lost track of time," Jordan answered.

"Busy sneaking around?" David's face was impassive. Jordan could easily see him shaking down mobsters and heroes – not just teens who were late to class.

"No. No, sir. I just got lost getting here on the first day."

David let the silence hang in the air like a weight for a moment too long, before deciding, "Well, take a seat. Just a reminder to one and all – heroes can't be late. Tardiness costs lives."

Jordan sighed hard and passed Lucas. Then past Rhea, who gave him a sideways glance that said, *What are you doing?* Jordan shrunk down into his seat next to Cooper and felt the world drop for a beat. David glanced up at Lucas and gave him a simple nod.

*Wait...Lucas and David...*Jordan then recalled both of their plasma colors. *Red and green. It's them. They're the thieves.*

Cooper's voice suddenly cut in. "Dude, what happened?"

"Nothing, nothing," Jordan brushed him off. "I just – I found a lost squirrel and had to help him."

"Oh," Cooper whispered in delight. "What was his name?"

Before Jordan could even think of all the questions and ramifications that Cooper just unleashed, Alicia's foot kicked his. She nodded for him to focus on David. Jordan turned away from Cooper and back to the lecture.

"Villains wearing masks originated from not only wanting to hide their faces but to hide the V tattooed on them. I too wore a mask." David pressed a button, and the slide changed to an archival photo from a police investigation. It was a picture of a mask on a sterile white table with a series of ID numbers and tags with dates underneath. The mask itself was a bright red black-horned Oni Mask. The word "Carnage" was painted in Japanese Kanji script along the forehead just under the horns.

"In Japan, I was known as Gyakusatsu; in America, I was known as Carnage. I was a loan collector for the Yakuza before I moved into the Black Market and onto bigger and larger heists."

Carnage took a weighted pause that made the one he used with Jordan seemed featherweight in comparison before he nodded in confirmation.

Jordan felt a rush of adrenaline spike through him. There was no doubt. *It's him. Heists? Did he say heists? Alexander was right to suspect him.* Jordan sent a worried glance to Lucas, who was staring down at David with a hint of a smirk. *They're right here in front of me...*

"Yet, after my defeat and arrest by Kurikara, I have begun to turn my life around. I've now dedicated my life to teaching heroes and young Espers how to not only avoid becoming like me but also how the underground Vesper network operates. My name is David Roberts, I am a former Vesper, and this is Villains 101."

Jordan's eyes narrowed on David with his Carnage mask looming over him. *I found you.*

"It's one attack with everything you've got."
- Alicia Jackson

CHAPTER TWENTY-TWO

Astro Day III: Crescent Cutter

Thankfully, the class ended without any more stunning revelations for Jordan. He had enough revelations for one day. His mind was occupied with the possibilities. He couldn't wait to call Darius and tell him what he found out, but he and the team were headed to dress in their combat gear for their next session with Alexander in Coliseum 7. It was clear that that call would have to wait.

At their approach, Alexander met and informed them, "Sorry to disappoint, kids, but we won't be working here today."

"What? Why?" Cooper was the first to ask.

"We're going to the field house for some extra training."

This answer did little to assuage their curiosity, so Alexander offered, "Don't look to me for answers. Cadet Harris is the reason we're switching it up today."

For the second time that day, Jordan felt all eyes on him. By the way things were going, he was going to have to get used to it.

"Wait, is this over last night?" Jordan asked.

Alicia turned to him sharply. "What *else* happened last night?"

"I – I snuck out," Jordan admitted.

"Indeed," Alexander quipped. "And he received his first of three strikes on his first night. It would be impressive if it wasn't, you know, unbelievably stupid."

"What happened?" Alicia sneered.

"Nothing." Jordan scrambled for an answer. "I just –"

"Well, obviously something happened," Sydney snapped.

"C'mon now," Alexander teased. "You'll have plenty of time to insult Cadet Harris later on. Follow me."

Ugh. What a drag. Jordan grumbled and face-palmed. He risked a glance at Reuben, who was sporting his usual stoic face. Before Jordan could ask his opinion, Reuben replied with a simple, "You know."

Alexander led the team in their combat gear across campus, in the Texas heat, toward the field house. By the time they reached the field house, they were already covered in sheens of sweat that glistened off their foreheads and rolled down their necks. Alexander was, somehow, not even shiny. He led them into the facility like a duck marching with ducklings.

"Oh, you look so tired already," he chimed. "Come on, Jordan, share some of that energy you had last night with the team."

Jordan had a few choice words, but kept them to himself and instead focused on the floor. They entered with sweet relief as the air conditioning hit them, and their trek across campus was all but forgotten. The room they were in was shaped like a giant shoebox.

It had short walls and a wide floor and ceiling. It was a squat room that left a lot to be desired. The walls themselves were tiled and equipped with white padding. In the middle of the room, waiting for them, were six blocks of a ten by ten black rubber substance. Behind them, the door rolled into place like a vault, and a series of bolts and clamps audibly locked into place, securing them within.

"nitrile," Alexander simply stated as if everyone knew what it meant. "Does anyone want to elaborate?"

Alicia's hand shot up. Alexander did his best to ignore her. "Anyone else?"

Sydney raised her hand, and Alexander pointed to her. Alicia scoffed.

"C'mon, you got to give others a shot," Alexander said. "Battalia?"

"nitrile is the strongest rubber polymer in the world. Transmission belts, oil seals, hospital gloves – it's got a ton of uses because it's durable and easy to produce."

"Exactly. And these blocks are made of five-inch-thick nitrile." Alexander patted the substance. "Whatever physical attacks you give, it absorbs. It's oil resistant, tear-resistant, and is used in everything from cars to space ships...and you're going to put a hole through it."

A long beat of silence passed between the kids before Cooper spoke up. "Say what?"

"This is often a test used for upperclassmen," Alexander replied, "But because of Cadet Harris' actions last night, we'll be running this drill today."

"Sorry..." Jordan uttered.

I've heard of nitrile, Reuben said to himself. *There's no way we could punch through the wall. Not even a bullet could pierce it.*

"Nope, no time to apologize. Each of you has a chunk of nitrile in front of you, and your goal is to put a hole through it. Feel free to go all out." Alexander then gestured to the walls around him. "The walls of this training room are padded with nitrile behind these panels – all the way down to the door. Ironically, that spot over there was blown out by some student two years ago." He pointed to a spot in the wall where the paint was a different color.

"Wait," Cooper responded, "is it even possible to push through this much rub–"

Alexander raised his fist to a wall, then sent a bolt of crimson lightning through the nitrile wall. The teens went quiet, and the wall collapsed with a dull thud.

He went through it, Reuben gasped.

"Have fun," Alexander said. "I'll be back in an hour or so to – "

He burned through it, Reuben realized.

Reuben snapped his bandaged arm up, gathered plasma underneath his skin, and sent a blast of plasma smashing into and searing through the wall. The teens and Alexander went quiet as his wall collapsed with a dull thud too.

"I didn't say go," Alexander snapped. "Reuben, you come with me."

That was...easy. Reuben looked down at his bandaged hand. The flames he emitted had scorched today's bandages. He grimaced in annoyance. He'd have to be careful of how he moved all day now.

"Uh, sorry," Reuben said with a smirk.

"Don't apologize; just listen next time," the Squad Leader said. "It can be done. You've all seen it twice now. Good luck, and we'll see you all soon."

Alexander motioned Reuben to follow him, lamenting, "You got a cannon for an arm, kid. Be careful where you point that thing." Alexander swiped a badge by the door. The door rolled open to let Alexander and Reuben out.

"I'd say it's impossible, but you saw Reuben," Alicia pointed out.

"Well, good luck, everyone," Sydney quipped. Her eyes flashed blue—matching her hair and her plasma—as she tapped in and sent her energies rushing to her hands. The familiar rush of star-born energy felt good before she released it in a blast of rolling, broiling energy. It slammed into the wall, with the sound of a thunderclap that echoed throughout the field house and sent a chunk of nitrile the size of a peanut flying.

Battalia frowned. *What...*

"These things are designed to absorb impact," Alicia calculated. "So –"

Impact, huh? Jordan leaped back into a three-point stance, then gravity burst at the wall like a missile, with his knee out. *Impact Knee.* He hit the wall with the top of his knee and felt his body buckle and recoil. The next thing he knew, he was on the floor holding his leg with his gloved hands.

"I said 'absorb' impact," Alicia snapped at him. "Physical attacks aren't going to work."

"Yeah," Jordan groaned from the floor. "I'm just happy I didn't use my head."

"You never use your head," Alicia quipped.

"That's not what I meant," Jordan shot back.

"It's what I meant," she said with a sarcastic smirk.

"Honestly, Jordan," Sydney huffed. "How did you survive past the third grade?"

"Okay, maybe it's just impossible for us," Cooper grumbled, and his tail swayed behind him curiously.

Sydney flexed a force field around herself and shrunk it down to fit her body before she threw her arm forward and sent her force field out like a battering ram. The condensed field slammed into the wall, then rattled as it absorbed the impact. Sydney stood up to the impact and cringed. Before rotating her fist, a sharp pain shot up her arm.

Alicia studied her for a beat, then took mental notes. "Hmmm, we'll have to think smarter." Alicia looked at Alexander's wall, Reuben's wall, and then the tiny chunk Sydney had carved out.

"Fire," Sydney concluded.

Alicia nodded at Sydney *You're right.*

Sydney nodded back *Duh.*

Alicia spun around to face her wall, gathered her purple plasma into her fist, and then released it as a searing burst. It hit the wall and detonated with enough force to make their ears ring. The smoke cleared, and a piece of nitrile the size of a penny crumbled out.

"Well, it worked," Alicia announced while scanning the room. "Let's try again."

Jordan turned his gloved hand to the wall and felt the familiar energy churning within before sending forth a golden spike of plasma. A tiny piece of nitrile, half the size of the one Alicia budged out, dropped from his wall.

Sydney sent another blast at the wall and pared out another small chunk of rubber.

Cooper sent his attack into the wall and made a tiny scratch that fizzled with simmering energy.

"It's plasma," Alicia chimed. "That's how you tear through it. It's a Plasma Drill. We can do this. We can do this."

The team went back to it with a renewed frenzy, sending plasma bolts into their respective walls. They all began to use the same strategy of sending plasma from their bodies into their hands and then firing it into the wall. The room crackled and boomed like a prismatic thunderstorm while the team worked in unison to power through.

Thirty minutes of sustained plasma attacks later, all four were lying on the ground, exhausted. Smoking crumbs of nitrile lined the floor, and a haze of smoke wafted around them. After those thirty minutes, they had each only carved out a tablespoon of rubber.

"We can do it," Alicia whispered, her voice strained from exhaustion. "We – We can."

They each tried to tap into their Plasma Crystals but found little to nothing left.

Sydney sat up and pointed her hand at the wall, but the plasma fizzled from her hands.

"This a cape-drag," Jordan sighed.

"Yeah, and we wouldn't be here if it wasn't for you," Sydney accused.

"For once, I agree with Sydney," Alicia added.

"Get used to it," Sydney chimed to Alicia's annoyance.

"Hey, I apologized," Jordan clapped back from the floor.

"You run headfirst into problems without thinking. It's why I beat you," Alicia said.

"I just can't believe you'd be so stupid as to sneak out," Sydney continued.

"You wouldn't understand," Jordan snapped. "Neither of you would get it."

Cooper rolled on the floor. His nose was picking up something strange, yet familiar.

"Huh? Really?" Alicia asked. "Lay it on us. Because the two of us went to hero schools, we know who's who, and which cadets are the ones to look out for, and neither of us has heard about you, dragger."

Sydney raised her brows in agreement with Alicia. *You're right.*

Alicia nodded back. *Duh.*

Cooper froze when he recognized the smell. "Guys..."

"Who are you?" Alicia asked. "How did you get into this school?"

Jordan shook his head, tried to push the conversation away, but they continued.

"Jordan, tell us the truth. What's going on?" Sydney asked.

"Guys..." Cooper tried to speak up over their argument.

Battalia pressed him, sounding just like her father, Titanus. "You're hiding something, Harris, and it's going to get us all in trouble if you don't – "

"There's a fire," Cooper shouted.

Immediately, everyone paused and looked at the wall Cooper was pointing to. It was the one Alexander had blasted through. The thin smoke tendrils it had been issuing earlier had blossomed into a column of smoke that was now working to fill the room.

"No. No," Alicia repeated. "It must have been smoldering this whole time."

The squad, though exhausted, rushed to their feet and crowded around the smoldering wall. Indeed the fire had begun to spread to the rubber insulation, churning out more smoke and more haze that threatened to obscure the room. Cooper used his tail to pat the wall, to no avail.

"Hot. Hot. Hot," Cooper seethed, and then frantically brushed the embers from his tail.

"It's spreading." Sydney coughed, covering her mouth. "The fire must've been building this whole time."

"We gotta go," Cooper urged and ran on all fours to the door. He took out his badge and swiped it, but the door remained closed.

"Let me try." Alicia swept in and swiped her badge too. Nothing.

"Hold on. Hold on." Sydney pushed through. "My card has admin privileges."

She swiped her card. Again, nothing happened.

"It's not the badges. It's gotta be the door," Jordan realized. He regretted opening his mouth because as soon as he did, it filled with bitter smoke that blanketed his tongue. He coughed it out but still felt it clinging inside his throat.

Suddenly, a claxon alarm blared to life over them. Flashing red lights and a screaming siren filled the room. The thick smoke took on rotating hues of red dancing lights to a rising alarm. Like a fog, the smoke rose and morphed, obscuring their legs and encroaching quickly.

"Sydney," Alicia ordered, "use your force field."

"I can't contain that much smoke," Sydney retorted.

"No, put it on us," Alicia shot back.

The two girls shared a trusting nod. Then Sydney dug deep within her vacant well of plasma, tapped into what she had left. Sydney felt Baldur, the God of Light, breathe through her as his Gift to her, a force field of light, bloomed from her hands. She formed a C-shaped dome between the door and the floor, shielding them under it.

"I can't hold this for long," Sydney shot. "I've been using my powers all day."

The cadets shared a grim look, then dipped their heads in understanding.

"Wait – wait–" Cooper butted in. "Red Wing said everything in here was made of nitrile. From the walls to the door."

"So?" Jordan asked.

"So, if we can cut through the walls, we can cut through the door," Alicia gathered.

"Yes, but we've been trying for thirty minutes to cut through one wall."

"Whatever you all are doing, do it soon," Sydney shouted. "I'm getting light-headed."

Outside of her shimmering force field, the smoke had mutated from grey tendrils to a black haze that threatened to swallow them. Cooper appreciated the examination of Battalia's force field. From a distance, it appeared a spherical mist was draped over her, but upon closer inspection, he noticed that each droplet was ablaze with electric blue plasma that was weaved into a dome. *That much plasma has to be hard on her crystal.*

"We can cut through it," Alicia shouted. She put her hand to the door. *The metal, I know I can pierce. The nitrile underneath, though...*

Sydney tapped into more of her plasma. She felt like she had been punched in the base of her skull, and the fist was still in her cranium. Her force field blinked for a second, and smoke rushed in before she gritted her teeth and sparked it back up.

"Hurry," she shouted through the pain.

Jordan cringed. Battalia's usual cold and stoic demeanor morphing into a frantic cry sent a chill down his spine. Alicia sparked a small purple blowtorch of plasma on her fingertips and seared through the metal. She felt the metal push back for a moment before it slid apart–a hot knife through cold butter.

If I concentrate my plasma into a compact point, I can keep pushing through with a sustained burn. Alicia began pushing her fingers through the wall as fast as the metal would let her.

"I'm going. I'm going. I'm almost through the metal," Alicia called out.

Then her fingers torched their way through, and the superheated plasma touched the nitrile, making it smoke. As she began the first incision, black smoke issued like a geyser. Alicia coughed twice before she furiously blinked to clear her eyes and backed away.

"I can't." She coughed again and rubbed her eyes. "If I burn through the wall like this, we'll fill the force field with smoke before I'm even halfway through."

"We'd die before you even cut through the wall," Cooper realized.

Alicia nodded, grim-faced.

"Okay, if anyone is hiding any amazing fire extinguishing abilities, now is the time to say so," Jordan snapped. Sydney's jaw tensed. That fist in the back of her head seemed to twist, sending currents of pain down her body. She was running low on plasma, and her arms shook.

"I can't believe I'm gonna die on Astro Day," Cooper whined, defeated.

At the mention of her brother's name, Alicia's mind flashed back to her brother sending a cleaver of energy right into the Green Titan.

*Crescent Cutter...*Alicia gasped. "That's it...Astro."

"Astro?" Jordan snapped. "Has the smoke gone to your head?"

"Yes," Sydney shouted.

Alicia blinked in realization. She knew what to do.

"I got this. Battalia, give me all you got for thirty seconds," Alicia called out.

"No promises," Battalia retorted.

Sydney's body threatened to fail. The force field dimmed around them, now blocking out an ocean of black smoke bearing down. Her nose began to bleed, and Sydney tasted metal, but she had to keep her arms up. Jordan and Cooper swung under Sydney and grabbed her arms to support her.

Alicia threw her arms up into the air as she had seen her brother do so many times. She tapped into what was left of her plasma, pulling it deep from every inch of her body. She felt searing hot energy rise up and into her fingertips, and she pointed high at the ceiling.

Alicia's fingers lit up with a violent, violet star. She gripped her wrist with her other hand. *More. I need more. I'm only gonna have one shot at this.* She thought back to Reuben's and Alex's attacks. *Uncle Alex cut through the wall with plasma, in one blow. It's possible. It's not small sustained attacks. It's one attack with everything you've got.*

Jordan and Cooper held onto Sydney, and their hands quaked.

"Alicia," Jordan called back to her.

More. I need more. Alicia willed her energies from her body and sent them to the star resting on her fingers. She pulled at her grief. She scooped up her pain. She heaved up her agony. She pressed every memory–happy and sad–every pent-up, neon-purple fiber of her being, and sent it surging into her fingertips. *Cedric, this one is for you.*

Jordan cried out, "Do it." He glanced back at Alicia and stopped. Her eyes were closed, her hands upright, holding a glowing sphere of crackling neon energy above her. Her hair was floating, pulled at by unseen currents of energy. Her body radiated with a surge of energy, then –

Sydney slipped from Jordan's and Cooper's arms, and her force field went with it. In an instant, they were swept away in a sea of black smoke. Alicia made her move.

She ripped her fingers down and released that energy like a coiled spring. She felt that heatwave of plasma rippling and reshaping itself mid-swing, turning from a globe to a razor-thin line of energy that braced against the door and tore its way through in a burst of metal, nitrile, and torrents of smoke.

Crescent Cutter, Alicia's mind screamed as she felt the last of her energies leave her and cleave through the wall. There was a screeching sound of metal on metal, collapsing upon itself, before the door – and wall – cracked open like a melon, spilling the contents of the room into the hall.

Under a haze of black smoke, all four teens rolled out into the hallway of the field house, accompanied by chunks of burnt metal and rubber. They hit the ground and let the fresh air rush over them, cleansing their lungs, minds, and bodies.

As they hit the ground, the ceiling vents outside the room instantly switched on and began vacuuming the smoke. Even through the sound of the vents and the sound of the fire alarm, a single calm voice reached them.

"Impressive. Another five seconds and I was gonna have to step in," the Squad Leader remarked.

Jordan shook his head. There was no way he had heard that right. *Step in?*

"What you went through is a – oh, hold on – " The vents inside the room chimed when the last of the smoke cleared the hall and the room.

An automated voice sounded overhead, "Simulation over."

Sydney grimaced along the tiled floor. *That was a draggin' simulation?* She finally took in a breath that didn't smell of burnt rubber. Battalia felt her mind ease, now that she wasn't scraping it for plasma.

"It was a drill to inspire teamwork," Alexander revealed. "To see what you all can do when you're left to your own devices."

"A test?" Jordan gasped for air. He coughed out his words, raw and hoarse. "That was a test?" Jordan slapped the star on his chest, hoping to dislodge the smoke from his lungs underneath it.

Alexander nodded. "And you all passed," he said. "But usually people just go through the wall, not the door."

Cooper followed Alexander's eyes to the portion of the wall Alexander had mentioned before leaving, the one he had told them had been blown out before. *We – were supposed to go through there.*

"It's actually impressive because the door is – sorry – the door was reinforced to keep you inside."

None of them replied. They simply stared up at him in exhausted shock.

"Hey, hey, don't give me that look," he teased. "I could take all of you with just one hand."

Reuben stepped up. "If it's any consolation, I asked him to put me back in the room after he told me, but –"

"Hey, hey –" Alexander interrupted, "whose side are you on here?"

"Mine," Reuben replied bluntly.

Alexander shrugged. "Well, get some fresh air and come back here in thirty. We're doing rounds tonight. You're familiar with that, right, Cadet Harris?"

Jordan rolled his eyes. He didn't have the breath or the energy to argue with him. Jordan stood up, stumbled, and then righted himself. Reuben turned to Cooper and offered him his hand. Cooper took it and he helped him up.

"Thanks," Cooper huffed.

Alexander turned to Sydney, who was seated against the wall catching her breath. Sydney wiped her bloody nose with the back of her hand, then wiped the blood on the pants of her combat suit.

"You good, Asimov?" Alexander asked.

Sydney responded by standing and shaking off the exhaustion with a grunt.

"I'll be back in ten," she said as she walked off.

"I said thirty."

"I know."

Alexander saw her march off down the hall and shove the door open. He turned and saw Alicia still sitting on the floor. He was silent for a moment, collecting his thoughts.

"You did good," he said.

Alicia nodded.

"Your brother didn't even get this far when I put him and his team in there."

Again, Alicia nodded but still couldn't bring herself to meet his gaze. "I'm – I'm still shaking. Uncle Alex, I'm still shaking."

He put a hand on her shoulder and looked down. Her fingertips were burnt pink from the amount of plasma she wielded. *Poor girl,* he thought. *Maybe today was the wrong day for this.*

"Go walk it off. You did well," Alexander continued. "He'd be proud of you." He gestured to the smoldering slash left in the depth of the brick wall behind him. Her attack had cleaved clear through the door and into the brick wall face. "He'd also probably be a little scared of you," he joked.

Alicia felt a chuckle in her throat, then felt it settle. Alexander helped her to her feet, then patted her back again. "I mean it." Alicia gave him a somber smile, then walked outside.

Stepping out of the front doors, she was greeted by sunshine and a breeze that ruffled against her face. She felt her eyes watering, fought the storm within, and pushed it back down. She spotted Jordan and Cooper lying down in a patch of grass, still panting. Reuben stood over them. Jordan hung his head and let sweat and spittle drain from his face to the grass.

"You weren't in there for that long," Reuben said.

"You weren't in there at all," Jordan snapped breathlessly from the grass.

Alicia had no time for petty arguments, so she drifted along the backside of the building. Out of sight, she felt that storm threatening to break free, but she held back her tears. She walked away from the field house and was about to let it out when she heard vomiting. Alicia stopped and spotted Sydney.

Sydney had just finished depositing her lunch into the bushes when she whipped around. They said nothing. It was their first time seeing weakness in each other, and it seemed they were equally matched. Alicia wiped her eyes with her fingers. Sydney wiped her mouth with the back of her hand.

They circled each other like two tired boxers. Sydney fell back against the wall and slid down.

"That move you did...it was Astro's, right?" Sydney asked, staring at the ground.

Alicia bowed her head in recognition. It was the best she could do without releasing the cry that had been building in her throat.

Sydney looked her over, then replied, "You're related, huh?"

"He's my brother." Alicia choked the words out.

Sydney nodded then closed her eyes as if relishing an old memory. "My father still talks about him. He was something special."

Alicia put a hand to her mouth to physically stifle a sob, but she tamped the feelings down once more.

"Thanks for saving us back there," Sydney offered.

"Thanks to your force field."

"Hey, someone's got to save us, cause it ain't gonna be the boys."

Alicia let out a wet chuckle, a bit of a laugh, and then wiped a tear from her face.

"The smoke..." Alicia sniffed. "The smoke made my eyes water."

"Yeah, the smoke," Battalia repeated as she used a shaking hand to wipe something from her eyes too.

CHAPTER TWENTY-THREE

Astro Day IV: Sparkle Five

Alicia went through the rest of the day on auto-pilot, simply going through the motions in her drills and long after they were done. Even when the warm shower hit her face, she was not stirred from her stupor. When the ride-share she ordered picked her up, she didn't have the energy for small talk with her driver.

The sun had already set, and she'd need to be back on campus soon to go on patrol with the others. In the distance, she heard fireworks popping.

They're early, she thought. Alicia felt her mind relax when she pulled up to the hospital. She had been here many times; in fact, it was the central location in her dreams and, sometimes, her nightmares.

As she was lulled by the elevator carrying her up to the 9th floor, she felt the world slow. She knew what awaited behind this door. The elevator doors chimed open, and Alicia felt herself come back online. She made her way down the hall. After being numb for most of the day, she was suddenly aware of so much: how her shoes clacked against the tiled floor, *did I always walk this slowly?* How the hallway smelled of bleach and lemon. *Did they change their cleaning products?*

Alicia stopped when she reached door 919. It was a non-descript door that any passerby would assume was just the door for another patient. It was locked to the general public because the secret was better left kept. Alicia put her thumb to the keypad, felt the scanner glide underneath, then the door beeped and unlocked.

Alicia entered his room, and the cold made her skin prickle with gooseflesh. She shivered, even though it was August. The room was uncaring. The AC was always on here. It was one of many things about this room about which she was always puzzled.

How the AC was always on.

How good the view of the city was.

How it always seemed to have fresh flowers.

And how her brother always seemed to be asleep.

Cedric's chest rose up and down to the hum of the respirator. His eyes fluttered listlessly under his lids. Alicia stared at his body for a moment; he always seemed at peace, as if he would just turn over and wake up one day.

"Hey," Alicia muttered.

She heard a soft pop in the background–fireworks. *There they are.*

"I think I got here just in time."

Alicia pulled up a chair next to him. It was only now that she was this close, that she noticed a few circles under his eyes. *Oh, that's new.*

"You're getting old, bro." She brushed his hair and felt his body shift slightly under her.

"I'm here. I'm here." Alicia took one of his large, cold hands and cradled it in her own.

Right outside the window, a trio of fireworks went off and hovered over Houston. She smiled at them. This was always the highlight of Astro Day.

"You hear that? That's for you" Alicia smiled. "To let you know we're still here."

Then a thought came to her "Oh, Mom called. Dad too. Wanna hear?"

Alicia took out her headphones, put one in her ear and the other in his. She flicked through her phone and found her voicemails.

"Hey, honey," her mom's soft voice came in, "it's me. I hope all is fine. I know how hard this day is for us, but I wanted to make sure you're okay." Alicia looked up from her phone as more fireworks popped in the distance. They were becoming a steady stream of white bursts, matching the color of Astro's plasma. Alicia felt that familiar storm swelling up within her.

Her mom's voice continued, "Your dad and I stopped by earlier to drop off flowers for him. Oh, he looks so much like your father now. He's even started to grey." Her mom laughed the same laugh that Alicia remembered. It was heartfelt, with a hint of pain. Like a cry that was sprinkled with hope.

The storm grew in size and scale deep inside Alicia's chest. She felt the flood brace against her eyes, then the winds howled in the depths of her throat. She bit her cheek.

A steady chorus of fireworks exploded across the sky, like a hundred stars marching into the night.

"We hope your second day is going well – oh, who am I kidding? You're gonna do us proud." She could hear her mom smile warmly from behind the phone.

Alicia sniffled, feeling everything she had been bottling up spring free. She took a hold of Cedric's hand, attempting to will him to squeeze it back, to comfort her.

"You're gonna do us all proud," her mom repeated.

Alicia took Cedric's hand and held it up for a high-five. She held her hand a foot away from it, and thanks to the fireworks lighting up the night sky, it looked as if they were trading streaks of plasma.

"Sparkle Five," Alicia said in unison with her mother, who signed off with the same phrase.

With that, Alicia felt it all surge forth. The storm was set free, and Alicia let it carry her away. She buried her face on his chest and sobbed deep, heavy cries as white stars went streaking through the night.

CHAPTER TWENTY-FOUR

Astro Day V: HUSH MODE

More than anything, Alicia wanted to go back to her dorm and sleep. It had been an exhausting day starting with the early morning jog when she nearly died by almost shifting off the building, to when she nearly died at the thought of African royalty asking her out, to when she nearly died in the nitrile simulation, and now she was going to have to go on patrol where they weren't scheduled to be done until 4 a.m.

Happy Astro Day, she joked to herself.

Alicia joined the other members of her team in the front courtyard, dressed in combat gear. Alexander surveyed them as he walked past.

"Being on patrol is where we all start. It's a time-honored tradition of Fort Olympus," he announced. "Most of what you'll be doing in hero work is surveying sights, patrolling, and hoping things don't go wrong."

Cooper yawned, and Alexander turned sharply to him.

"Sorry," Cooper squeaked.

"But," Alexander continued, "when things do go wrong, you should be prepared for any eventuality. You'll work in pairs. Battalia is with me on the south side. Alicia and Jordan got the north side. Reuben and Cooper, you take east then loop through the west."

"Wait, why do we have to patrol two areas?" Cooper asked.

"Because you yawned."

Cooper sighed in mock defeat, and Reuben shot him a glare.

"What?" Cooper asked.

"You know," Reuben said flatly.

Jordan cringed. Reuben had hit him with the same line earlier.

"Check in on comms every fifteen minutes," Red Wing instructed, pointing to the ear mics within the collar of their suits. "We'll meet back here at four in the morning to break." The group nodded, then quickly went their separate ways.

Jordan was always curious about the fortress walls of Fort Olympus. They were the oldest facility structure and thus the most well-known. Despite all the pictures and videos online, he could never find the staircase to climb to the top. Luckily, Alicia knew where it was. They were flush against the side of the fortress walls. Every twenty feet, she explained, was another set of stairs, and it was Fort Olympus' policy not to show the stairs on social media for security purposes. Jordan and Alicia soon found themselves walking the outer wall of Fort Olympus. In the distance, fireworks still erupted in the night sky.

"Good work back there," Jordan offered.

"Thanks," Alicia replied. "It was my first time using that move."

"Crescent Cutter," Jordan replied.

Alicia took a momentary breath, though that was what she called the move. "No one's called it that for ages. Usually, people just say Astro-Slash or some equally corny thing."

"Yeah," Jordan chuckled. "Well, I – uh – I studied heroes for a while. I'm a bit of a nerd."

"And where did you study at?"

Jordan's mouth zipped shut, and he felt his body tense.

"Don't think just because we nearly died earlier that I forgot." Alicia's inquisitive eyes locked onto his. "Who are you, Jordan Harris, and where do you come from?"

Reuben and Cooper had yet to reach the stairs ascending the fortress wall on the east side. They had been walking and advancing to their destination for about ten minutes when Reuben reached his breaking point. Cooper had been talking non-stop and gave no sign of slowing or concluding his biographical monologue.

"Can you believe kids used to be afraid of me?" Cooper inquired. "Me? I look like a cape-dragging teddy bear. Well, maybe it's my claws – nails – talons? Whatever. They used to be afraid of me, then something changed. I don't know what. Maybe they realized I wasn't tough, so they began picking on me. Ganging up, really. *'Cape-dragger,' 'dragger,'* and *'ferret-cape'* were the usual insults. *'Trash Panda.'* That was their favorite one. They actually threw trash on me one time too. Can you believe that? I kept that name for years and – wait – I'm sorry, did you want to say something?"

Reuben replied flatly, "No."

"You're really quiet."

"We're on patrol," Reuben said, but what he wanted to say was *Because you haven't given me a chance to talk.*

"Doesn't mean we can't talk. We're Hybrids, you know? We got a lot in common."

"I guess."

"You guess? Your people are so cool –"

"We're basically extinct."

"So are my people," Cooper exclaimed, somehow seeing the bright side of extinction. "Well, not my people – I mean, red pandas are an endangered species and –"

"Cooper, shut up."

Cooper took the words to heart, then swallowed them. They continued their trek, and the sound of distant fireworks popped in the background. It was growing late, so the chorus of fireworks was lessening.

Two more pops in the distance sounded. Reuben noticed that Cooper's fluffy ears flinched at each distant explosion.

They hurt his ears. His ears must be super-sensitive, Reuben realized with growing guilt. *He's talking because it masks the explosions. How did I not see that? Okay, I'll let the ferret talk.*

"You remind me of my brother," Reuben admitted. "He's younger than me, lives with my parents in Mexico."

Cooper was quiet for a few steps, then softly replied, "I didn't know you had family down there."

"Yeah," Reuben replied. "We moved there after – after the Green Night." He paused to gather those memories before continuing. "Though they killed the Green Titan, they never released the identity. There were tons of conspiracy theories about who or what he was. Was he human, Hybrid, or a God who come back to Earth? But most thought he was a demon."

Cooper cringed at the word *demon*. He had rarely uttered it aloud, and even hearing Reuben say it made him uneasy.

"Of course that's what people wanted to assume," Reuben continued. "That my people had something to do with it." He took in a shaky breath as something horrible flashed in his mind's eye. "Some people, they – they burned our house down. With me and my little brother inside. I saved us, I guess. I don't know how. But no one cared I had saved him."

"That makes you a hero in my book," Cooper said.

"No one sees people like me as a hero," Reuben replied heavily. "They saw my arm. They knew my people's past. They burned the house down, and the police blamed me – a five-year-old who had a fire Gift– for starting it. So we left town – we ran – to Mexico. Started over."

It was Cooper's turn to pause and let Reuben's silence fill the void. After a moment, he replied, "I'm sorry to hear that, man."

Reuben nodded, still shaken up by the memory. *Ugh, maybe I shared too much.* "You can uh – you can keep talking if you want," Reuben said softly. "I prefer it to silence."

Cooper smirked, then like a lit fuse he went off. "Soooo, yeah – like – the worst thing that ever happened to me was being thrown in the trash."

Jordan felt that sliver of cold fear slide into his heart. He exhaled quietly and let the silence hover between him and Alicia. She continued her interrogation. "Sydney and I went to top hero training schools, and we would've heard of you. Did you go to Star Academy or Andromeda Prep?"

"Uh... Andromeda Prep?"

"That's funny," she replied coldly.

"Why?"

"Because I went there," Alicia said matter-of-factly.

Jordan felt that cold blade in his chest twist. *She's got me.*

"Now, who are you, and how did you get here? The only way in is a recommendation from a licensed hero or graduation from a hero-prep school."

Jordan paused, tried to stack his truths with his half-truths in order, then factored in some straight-up lies. His head throbbed and he told himself, *The truth, just give her the truth.* Jordan consoled himself, *Okay, but not the whole truth.*

"Kinetic is my uncle," Jordan admitted. He felt that frozen blade slip just a bit from his body.

Alicia took a moment to absorb this, and the reaction played clearly across her face. "Is that why he was at our match?"

"He recommended me for this school." Jordan showed her the gloves. "He even gave me his gloves for a birthday gift."

"Oh, okay. That's why they clearly don't fit," Alicia realized.

"They fit just fine," Jordan retorted, trying to hide his embarrassment.

"Wait, wait, wait." Alicia had one answer, but that had led to more questions. "But where did you train at? How do you know how to use your powers so –"

"So good?" Jordan offered.

"So *well,*" Alicia corrected. "Now I know you didn't go to Andromeda Prep."

"How many different ways are you gonna find to call me dumb?" Jordan snapped.

"I got an IQ of 160, so you better buckle up," Alicia replied.

Jordan sulked. *Oh, okay, I'm being interrogated by a literal genius. Great.*

Alicia leaned forward. "There's something else you aren't telling me."

Jordan's eyes went wide. *Just tell her. Just tell them all the truth, now.*

A series of fireworks exploded in the distance over the fortress, and they both noticed it at the same time: *A pair of cloaked figures were crossing the courtyard below.* Jordan went rigid. He recognized those cloaks, those figures, those masks. The thieves. *What are they doing here? They were robbing a museum last time. What is there to steal here?*

Alicia's eyes narrowed like a lioness on the hunt. *Who are they?*

First things first, Alicia turned back to Jordan. "We're not done talking about this."

"Bet on it," Jordan replied.

Alicia put a finger to her ear and called out, "Squad Leader, we've got a possible situation on the north side, we're gonna check it out."

Filling their legs with plasma, they jumped from the fortress wall, dropped down fifty feet, and landed. Alicia was graceful in her crouched position, but Jordan landed with a thud and hit the ground butt first.

"Get. It. Together," Alicia spat at him and stalked after the hooded figures. The pair rushed hurriedly, but stealthily, through the courtyards, hiding in the shadows. Alicia noticed Jordan had not only taken the lead, but he recognized all the best hiding spots for stalking someone.

Did Kinetic teach him this? If he didn't go to a hero school, then where did he learn it? Alicia shoved those thoughts from her mind. *Who are they? Why would someone sneak into a school in the dead of night?*

The two took up residence under an alcove by the barracks that looked out on the courtyard where they had first met.

"Hold," Alicia ordered.

Jordan froze where he was in the shadows but studied the hurried pair when they stopped at the Polaris statue. *There they are...*Jordan saw their masks hit the light and felt his blood run cold.

The taller one with the wide wingspan, he assumed, was a man. He was wearing the same mournful mask with gold tears running down his face. Then there was the smaller one, whose gender was harder to identify, but the bird mask showed a bit of the mouth underneath it.

Villains wear masks. Carnage's words came back to Jordan, who gritted his teeth at the thought of ripping that mask from him. *Carnage...Lucas...*

"They're here," Jordan seethed.

Alicia read the tone of his voice. "You know them?"

Jordan pulled his gloves tight around his fingers and made a fist. "We gotta stop them."

"Hold on," she cautioned.

Alicia turned her wrist over and tapped the screen on her arm. It scanned the plasma levels of the mystery visitors. Her breath caught in her throat. "We're way out of our league here."

Jordan looked back and saw her device had read their plasma levels:

The shorter one, with the bird mask, read 35,000.

The taller one, with the gold tears, scored 65,000.

35,000 and 65,000. The shorter one we could probably take, but the taller one is a monster. Jordan shivered, but bottled the fear and pushed it away.

Alexander's voice echoed in their ears. "Hey, we're on the way. Hold off. Wait for my signal, that's an order."

There's no time, Jordan's mind screamed. *It's now or never.* Jordan turned back to Alicia. "I think – I think I know who they are."

Alicia's eyes went wide in the darkness. "What?"

"Alicia, Jordan, do you copy?" Alexander's voice came back, worried. "You are to hold your positions."

Alicia kept her eyes trained on the two cloaked figures. They were clambering over the Polaris statue and reaching for the opaque jewel set in his hands that represented the star he was known for.

Alicia felt a different type of storm brewing inside of her. Not wet, or sad – but loud. It made her blood run hot and angry. "You know, yesterday, when we met here?" Alicia's voice came out sharp and cold.

"You were taking a selfie." Jordan nodded.

While the shorter bandit played lookout, Goldtears was examining how to remove the jewel from Polaris' hands.

"Yes," Alicia seethed, "because Polaris was my great-grandfather."

Jordan blinked, realizing the implications. *They're defacing her great-grandfather's statue. Wait – if Polaris is also related to Astro, then she's got to be related to both of them.* Jordan's thoughts were confirmed by the raw plasma steaming off her body. He pulled Kinetic's gloves tight against his knuckles. The words "Be Your Own Hero" reflected back at them.

Alicia whispered into the microphone on her wrist, "Squad Leader, we've got a robbery in progress in the Polaris Courtyard." Alicia turned to Jordan and saw the same steely resolve roaring in his eyes. Her eyes flashed hot purple as she tapped in and declared, "We're going in."

Alexander's voice boomed back at them, "No. You are to hold."

Alicia and Jordan both turned off their mics, then blitzed out of the darkness.

"Sup?!"
- Jordan Harris

CHAPTER TWENTY-FIVE

Astro Day VI: The Thieves Part 2

Alicia simmered as if a dark cloud had been summoned over her. In many respects, this cloud had been hanging over her the whole of Astro Day, but now it was ready to storm. All the pain she had endured this day, and throughout the last few years, was ready to swell up and smite these poor souls. As the pair emerged in the moonlight, the two masked thieves whipped around to face them.

"Freeze," Alicia shouted as she stormed onto the field.

The smaller one, Nightingale, wasted no time. As soon as the command was out of Alicia's mouth, the masked figure was bounding across the courtyard at them. Goldtears went back to the jewel in Polaris' hands. They flared a familiar red plasma around their finger tips and melted the bronze encasing it.

"Jordan," Alicia's eyes were hurricanes of violet plasma, "stop him."

Jordan didn't have to be told twice. He used a burst of golden gravity and arced over the incoming Nightingale, who watched as Jordan flipped over them. Nightingale spun back around, and Alicia was on them bringing a right hand up and over. Nightingale blocked the plasma punch and engaged Alicia in a series of strikes and blocks.

Jordan rushed the taller one, who quickly abandoned the statue and curled around to face the incoming StarLion. Jordan sent plasma surging through his gloved hands and exploded off the ground, hurling his fist forward. Goldtears threw an arm up and caught Jordan's punch.

The collision echoed with a thunderclap when plasma met plasma. Jordan peered down through the mask assessing the man's stunned eyes.

"Sup?" Jordan shouted.

While still in mid-air from his leap, Jordan used the man's fist and his own as a pivot point and exploded gravity under his feet. The explosion sent Jordan sideways and his legs sailing for the man's head. His shin connected with the side of the man's head and tore him from the ground. Jordan twisted out of mid-air and landed hard, this time in a poised crouch, like a glowing celestial figure – a protector – right in front of the Polaris statue. Jordan looked up with a smirk and gasped. Goldtears had shifted right in front of him with his fist pulled back.

Too fast. He threw up both arms in an X and packed plasma into his forearms. But it wasn't enough. He felt the strike smash his arms against his head and carry him off his feet. *Too strong.*

Jordan felt his body flip backward. He twisted gravitons around himself to lighten his own weight and decrease the torque. Jordan landed in a three-point stance, then sent those same gravitons to his heels with enough force to launch him right back into the fray.

"Don't run straight at him," Alicia called out, still mid-match with Nightingale.

I know, Jordan said to himself. *You taught me that.*

Jordan gathered gravitons into his palms and threw them at the ground. Like yesterday, he felt the ground and forces of gravity bounce back like a trampoline. He went from running straight to being sent straight up. Goldtears snapped up, and his porcelain face peered at Jordan in surprise.

It's not enough to just change directions once, Jordan grinned. *You gotta try new things.* In the apex of his flight, Jordan pointed himself back down and exploded gravity under his feet again. The force sent him down diagonally at Goldtears. The masked figure had no time to dodge as Jordan re-routed himself and came down with both feet, dropkicking the man in the chest with two plasma-packed feet stomping down.

The masked man took the cannon blow to the chest and was tossed backward. Jordan landed awkwardly on his side but watched as Goldtears landed awkwardly on his – well, on his everything.

He's learning, Alicia mused to herself mid-match. *Let's keep them guessing.*

Alicia flared plasma to her hand, coating her palm and fingers, then approached Nightingale swinging her shimmering plasma blade. Alicia, her plasma blade alight, rolled up and into Nightingale, slashing with a violet flourish. She slashed and jabbed in a pattern she had practiced hundreds of times, but Nightingale dipped and dodged as if they had practiced it with her. Nightingale saw an opening, then leaped backward from Alicia.

But Alicia had practiced for this too.

She spun around and, in her behind-the-back twist, transformed the blade into a spear. When she finished her twirl, she had a new weapon that she flung with precision. As soon as Nightingale's feet hit the ground, the spear was ready for action. Its tip burrowed deep into the cloak before the entire length of the neon javelin ignited into a series of concussive blasts. Shards of purple light glittered in the explosion that swallowed Nightingale.

Jordan and Alicia re-grouped, shoulder to shoulder, and looked at the smoke cloud that replaced Nightingale.

"Where did they go?" Alicia asked.

"I think the shorter one has a cloak Gift," Jordan theorized.

"An invisibility Gift?" Alicia asked in irritated disbelief.

Before either of them could push further, the thieves blinked back into existence a few feet away. The masked figures wavered into their vision as the taller one was helping the shorter one stand. For a moment, neither team moved. Then, the masked figures took up a fighting stance, prepared to continue.

"You take the high ground," Alicia ordered.

"And you take the low," Jordan confirmed.

Then Battalia's voice resonated not in their ears, but above the courtyard, "And we'll take the rest."

Both teams paused and looked up to see Sydney perched atop one of the barracks on the south side of the courtyard, like a gargoyle, and she wasn't alone. Reuben was posted on the east side of the courtyard, Cooper on the west side, and Alexander was directly above them on the north side.

They had them surrounded.

"Freshman Leo Regiment," Alexander's voice boomed, "on my mark, engage the enemy with suppressive attacks."

They all tensed.

Light-daggers of plasma flared in Jordan's eyes as he tapped in and sent sun-gold static pulses traveling up his body.

Sydney powered up her force field around her fists, like supernatural boxing gloves. While Sydney was not known as the God of Light, she felt Baldur's light filling her veins.

Cooper rose and prepared to leap from the ledge – safely. Very safely. He even considered taking the elevator down.

Alicia sent plasma rushing into her palms, and her body ignited like a violet flare.

Reuben tore his bandages from his burnt arm and groaned when black scales and red plasma sprung from his skin.

Alexander's plasma surged out from his body, radiating simmering hot energy. It rushed down from his neck and around his shoulders, before bursting from his back in a pair of red wings. Then from his arm, just as he had taught Alicia, he formed a crimson plasma blade. Alexander whipped his sword down and pointed the burning edge at the enemy.

"Go."

In one bright motion, the team rushed the thieves.

Alicia and Jordan were the first to reach them. Alicia created another lance of neon energy and hurled it at them. Before it could impact, Nightingale grabbed Goldtears, and they both went invisible.

Jordan was right, they can cloak. Alicia realized just as –THOOM. Her lance hit where the pair sat a second ago and detonated into a smoke cloud.

Where did those cape-draggers go? Jordan skidded to a stop. *They're using the smoke as a screen.*

Then, a familiar nightmare spilled from behind the cloud as the taller one punched a fist into the ground and sent a current of rippling, vibrating shockwaves at Jordan and Alicia. The courtyard was torn asunder by Earth rising up and rushing them.

Seeing his students go flying back, Alexander swooped in low and right above the wave. He tensed his body and spiraled up. Then with every ounce of his haggard, yet star-blessed plasma, he brought his sword crashing down on Goldtears. The taller man caught the blade in his red plasma-coated hand. Both energies sparked and fissured upon connection.

He's strong, Alexander lamented as the big man swung him up and over his head.

Alexander flew right over Reuben as he came sprinting low, arm pulled back to strike Goldtears, yet Nightingale blinked into view in front of him. *Was he invisible? Or did he shift in my path?*

Reuben got none of those answers; instead, he received a kick to the stomach that he wasn't prepared for. He felt his body fold and sail backward. Cooper cringed when Reuben bounced past him. Cooper scrambled along the face of the buildings looking for an opening, or at least an opportunity, to jump in.

"What do I do? What do I do?" Cooper screeched as he passed Sydney.

"Just find an opening, dragger," Sydney screamed at Cooper, who scurried up and away. Sydney raced them, but Nightingale sent a burst of green plasma arcing her way. Sydney formed a wall of energy, and her shield smashed to life against the attack and held.

Alicia glanced up from the destruction at Alexander's shining figure overhead. She sat hunched away from the explosions around her. Then, for only a second, she felt something within her call out for Cedric. To wish he was here by her side, to tell her what to do, to guide her hand. But she fought against that tide and willed the idea back into the pits of her mind.

Cedric isn't here. She hardened herself. *But I am.*

Cooper watched Battalia and Nightingale in a stalemate and glimpsed Alicia and Jordan racing across the courtyard to intercept Goldtears. Both teens met him halfway across the yard and, in an instant, both threw punches and kicks in tandem. Goldtears' eyes went wide behind the mask, and he went into a frenzy to block their blows. It was like watching a fight sped up. Neither Jordan nor Alicia gave pause between blows and counterblows.

In the chaos of the attacks, Jordan threw his fist forward and grabbed the man by the mask. Goldtears blinked in shock. Though Jordan's fingers couldn't grip it behind the extra fabric of the massive glove, he felt the tips of his fingers claw around it.

Gotcha, Jordan cheered as he tried to pull it back.

Goldtears grabbed Jordan by the wrist and hurled him into the air. Jordan was used to throwing himself into the air of his own volition, but he had rarely been tossed like this. Using gravitons, StarLion took flight above them for a long moment.

Quickly, Goldtears turned back to Alicia, eager to resolve this. But the girl was too quick for him, unloading more strikes. Now that Jordan wasn't shoulder to shoulder with her, she had a wider range of motion.

Not here. Not today. Not my ancestors. Not on Astro Day. Alicia clenched her jaw and pushed forward.

Let's go for the Impact Knee. When Jordan felt his arc complete, he twisted back around and, using a burst of gravity, shot back down at them. Mid-strike with Alicia, Goldtears heard the explosion of gravitons and anticipated Jordan sailing back down to join the fight.

Goldtears dove to the side. Suddenly, Jordan's knee wasn't aiming for his back but right at Alicia. Jordan hit her right in the star of her chest armor, knocking the wind from her lungs and extinguishing the lights from her eyes.

Both teens tumbled over one another and were left sprawled on the ground. Jordan tried to right himself, but his vision was still swirling, and his breath came out in short panicked bursts. Cooper watched the action erupt below him as he saw Jordan and Alicia go down. He realized no one was covering Goldtears. The tall figure was sprinting towards the statue again.

An opening, Cooper realized.

He spun off the sides of the barracks, where frightened and alarmed teens watched from their windows, and dropped down on Goldtears. When he closed the gap to about a foot, Cooper heard Reuben call out, "Get down."

Cooper turned and saw the flesh along with Reuben's arm ripple as the black scales flared to life. Reuben sent a torrent of fire pumping from his hand. A cascade of rumbling, rolling flames spilled across the courtyard, and everyone froze. Their world was suddenly blanketed in flames.

Nightingale saw the torrent coming and turned invisible as they shifted up and out of the courtyard. Sydney warped her force field into a dome that let the flames crash into it. Even behind her field, she could feel the heat of the fire when it washed past her.

"Reuben," she shouted.

Cooper, who had just seconds ago been dropping onto Goldtears, found himself diving into a pool of fire. *No. No. NO.*

An instant before he was toasted and roasted, Alexander swooped down and grabbed him by the collar. Cooper felt his collar yanked up around his neck, and suddenly he was airborne as Alexander's wings ignited, and they curved into a V formation, going down, then shooting back up.

Cooper glanced up at Alexander, gratefully. He looked down in dismay as the courtyard baked with hellfire and flashes of light.

Jordan and Alicia hid behind a column of marble while flames punched against it and flecked past them. They huddled down and took short breaths, watching Reuben's flames hurricane past them.

Then as soon as it began, it ended. Jordan peered from behind the column. The courtyard was scorched beyond belief, with many small fires still shaking in the wind. What worried Jordan the most was that Goldtears was back up. Though his cloak was frayed and smoking, he was still rushing towards the statue.

"No..." Jordan gasped.

He glanced down and saw Alicia was still recovering from her second heavy dose of smoke inhalation today. Jordan rushed from behind the pillar, detonated gravitons under his feet, and shot across the courtyard. He felt the heat sweep past him in waves as he closed in on Goldtears. Goldtears ignited scarlet plasma around their fingers and buried them into the statue, before tearing the opaque crystal from it. Goldtears turned around, and Jordan burst out of the cloud of flames with his fist pulled back.

"Stop," Jordan screamed.

One instant he was poised to blast Goldtears into oblivion –

The next instant he felt a burning bolt of serpentine plasma punching into his side –

By the time he knew what hit him, Jordan was smashed against the wall, stunned. Nightingale stepped out of the darkness, fingers still burning with green plasma. Nightingale limped over to Goldtears, who clutched the crystal to himself.

"Stop," Jordan pined from the ground. He tried to pull himself up, but couldn't find the energy. He was still struggling to stop his world from spinning while catching the air that had been blasted out of his lungs.

He glanced up as the pair stood side by side, victorious. Without warning, Alexander, wings flaming, soared down from the heavens and smashed his sword down in the spot the thieves occupied only a moment ago. The dust cleared. They were gone, stone in hand.

"You can't apologize when someone loses something precious…something irreplaceable. You have to live with it and so do they."
- *Alexander Robinson*

CHAPTER TWENTY-SIX

Astro Day VII: The Second Strike

"Where – where are they?" Sydney asked, stumbling through the burnt courtyard.

"No." Jordan punched the ground. "No."

Cooper crawled down to them, then spoke to life what they all feared. "They got away."

Jordan looked up to movement coming from all around. The students began to file out of their dorms. The bravest among them had come down to the courtyard, while others huddled in their windows watching from above.

Jordan felt all eyes on him, and a sudden pain in his chest hurt worse than the damage he had taken from this fight. Then he heard a shout and felt the masses shift their attention from him to Reuben.

Reuben cried out while the flesh on his arm warped back to normal. He dropped to his knees and clutched his wrist to contain the pain and stifle his cry. The scales slid back under his baked flesh. Though the flames had stopped spilling from his hand, the skin around it was hot pink and still simmering. Reuben tried to stand, but the jolting pain in his arm was too much.

This is bad, he realized. *It hurts. It hurts so much worse than before. I went too far.* Reuben flinched under the splintering pain of his bones realigning and skin rapidly cooling. As he looked around at the baked courtyard, a new pain struck him – everyone was staring. Then began the whispering: distant, airy, accusatory. "Demon. He's a demon."

He tried to curl inward, to hide, to revert into the nothingness, but all their eyes were on him. This new pain came from their words. *They see me –*

"He destroyed the courtyard." *They saw what I did to the courtyard.*

"Did you see that? He's trying to hide it." *They saw me transform –*

"He's a monster. How did he get in here?" *There's no going back. There's no hiding this. There is no more hiding who I am. To them, I'm the monster. Now – and forever.* The words seemed to come from everywhere, even as Reuben fought to push them out. However, one voice came charging through.

"You cape-dragger," Battalia spat, marching over to him. "I had them."

"Shut up," Reuben snapped behind gritted teeth.

"I had – "

"Shut up," Reuben screamed in her face; the force of the outburst was enough to scare himself. Battalia stepped back but didn't blink. She was ready to fight again at any moment. Reuben looked from her to the faces in the crowd, all staring at him and the thing he wished to hide the most.

Jordan crossed to Alicia and offered her his hand, but she slapped it away with enough force to almost knock the glove from it.

"Get off me," she ordered. "I told you not to go at him directly."

"I went for his back," Jordan snapped.

"And he read your movements, just like I did," Alicia shouted. "Just like any novice could."

"I was trying to h –" Jordan was cut off.

"You're a fraud." Alicia sneered. "I don't know what you're hiding, but you're not a hero. Your gloves don't even fit. You're a kid playing hero. A cape-dragger."

Jordan opened his mouth to reply, but nothing came out as –
THOOM.

Alexander shifted in between them like a bolt of red lightning.

*Uncle Alex...*Alicia gasped.

Alexander looked between both of them, his eyes brimming with energy, but not plasma... Rage. He spoke with a calmness that threatened to crumble his words.

"Inside. Now."

Jordan stepped back and took a few calming breaths. Now that the adrenaline was wearing off, he felt the rush of small injuries and bruises begin to weigh on his body. He stopped and scanned the crowd under the smoky moonlight for an easy exit. Lucas was in the crowd dressed in shorts and a t-shirt. Obviously, he had just gotten out of bed, like most of the students here.

*Lucas...*Jordan studied him for a moment...*If he was asleep, then who were we fighting?*

The Fort Olympus Infirmary had always served the same purpose in the same location since the Fort was opened lifetimes ago. Located in the back of the school, it was a quick walk – or frantic run – from the training coliseums or other training centers on campus. The infirmary itself was two floors of a long, rectangular room. It felt like a hallway from an old castle that was still in the process of being updated. Clean white tiles on the floor matched the grey stone columns that held up the ceiling. The wooden beams and carved stone ceiling clashed against the luminescent bulbs that hung over the hospital beds. There were twelve beds on each side of the room, and above each bed was a stained glass window looking out over the campus.

The head doctor of Fort Olympus was Heather Wilson, a charming forty-year-old. Her lips were always pursed as if she was about to one-up a joke. It served her well because people always assumed that after she explained their ailments, she would drop a remedy as easily as she would a punch line. She had a wild bundle of orange curls framing her face and sharp cheekbones highlighting a pair of green eyes that studied people incessantly.

Doctor Wilson was always a light sleeper, so she was wide awake around midnight when Sydney and Reuben were escorted in. The pair of students were sent to separate beds, and Doctor Wilson set her healer students to begin preliminary assessments.

The infirmary was also home to the class of incoming healers. While the Healing courses ran parallel to the Hero courses, and they shared the same campus, the two schools often did not meet unless, of course, in the infirmary or common areas. Healers, as the course suggested, were for those Espers with various healing abilities. While heroes were often the first-responders to emergencies, healers were just as important. Heroes often studied combat and rescue operations, but healers studied medical textbooks and how to properly fix a wound. If the Hero Esper course was the brawn, the Healer Esper course was the brain, which is why Sydney shivered as a half-dozen glasses-wearing teens hovered around her.

Nerds, Sydney hissed.

The uniforms for the healers were the same across the discipline. A red bodysuit with a white flourish, and a thick white cross in the middle. They looked like walking first-aid kits. They wore white protective body armor over their shoulders, though far less bulky than the hero suit. While heroes had their corresponding Zodiac sign on their shoulders, healers had the Caduceus symbol on their shoulders – a short staff entwined by two serpents. Doctor Wilson wore a white lab coat over her outfit. She strutted past her students, went to Sydney first, and looked at Sydney's vitals displayed on a scanner. The nodes attached to Sydney's arm read her biometric data and reported it for Doctor Wilson to see, much like how their combat suits did.

Sydney's vitals came back, and Doctor Wilson whistled. "Oh, you've had quite a day, huh?"

Though like the suits, this machine showed their plasma level output, it also gave a reading of how much a patient was capable of outputting at any given moment. Regularly, Sydney could output 27,000 volts of energy, but currently, she only registered 1,700. Doctor Wilson had seen this before and knew plasma exhaustion when she saw it.

"I'm fine," Sydney groaned.

Doctor Wilson looked her over again. Sydney was grey in the face with bruises forming along her parched face. She was far from fine.

"Your plasma levels say otherwise." Doctor Wilson nodded to the vitals, then to her students, who all looked as tired as it was past midnight "Notice how low her numbers are. She's in clear danger of plasma fatigue."

Sydney glanced at the numbers, then at the students, and rolled her eyes. *There is literally no one in this room I don't hate right now.*

"I don't have time for this." Sydney sat up with a groan.

"You need rest. Nothing a good night's sleep won't fix," Doctor Wilson chimed.

Sydney grumbled like her father, "I told you – "

Doctor Wilson tapped into her Gift, then tapped Sydney on the forehead. The effect was instantaneous. Battalia collapsed like a puppet whose strings had been cut. A feeling of intense drowsiness prickled across her brain, and before she hit the pillow, she was already dreaming of turtles and spicy ramen.

Doctor Wilson sighed pleasantly, then turned to the nearest student. "Keep her under for a bit, until her vitals return to normal."

"Yes, ma'am," the young healer replied.

Doctor Wilson strolled over to Reuben, who was lying in bed across from Sydney. Her healer students followed her the way baby ducks follow their mother. She evaluated his vitals. They were in moderate need of rest, but the more pressing issue was his right arm, which was in a protective sling.

"And how are you doing, Cadet?" she asked.

"I'm fine," Reuben replied.

"A lot of that going around, huh?" she smirked. "But you're in the infirmary. My infirmary, in fact. And trust me, as much as my sunny disposition would like me to believe, no one comes to my infirmary, especially in the middle of the night, if they're fine."

Reuben shuddered. He was hurting, but it would hurt even worse to admit it.

Doctor Wilson turned back to her students. "Out there, the heroes think they are all big and bad, but in the infirmary, you're the hero. You're the boss. I've fixed broken arms, lost arms, and even pulled a splinter out of a giant who was too afraid to pull it out himself."

"I don't have a splinter," Reuben grunted.

"Duh, but you do have first-degree burns all along your arm."

"It happens," Reuben let slip, not looking at her.

"Every time you transform?"

Reuben was quiet. With a wave of her arm, she sent her students back, then turned to whisper to him in private.

"Not every hero I treat is MegaTon or Kurikara, you know?" She leaned in. "I'm here to help."

Reuben grunted, "It only hurts when I lose control."

"Hmmm, I see." Doctor Wilson nodded. "I don't have much expertise in your kind..."

"For good reason," Reuben spat.

"There is a reason – " she paused for empathetic emphasis, "but, it sure isn't good."

Reuben turned to her and saw the sincerity in her soft face.

"Your people deserved better. And as a doctor, I'm here to make sure of it," she remarked with a smile.

Doctor Wilson reached out and grazed his arm with her fingers. Orange tinted plasma cased her hand, and Reuben exhaled gently as a warm comfort spread over his arm. From the layer of burnt skin to the stressed muscles underneath, to the very bones at their core, he could feel her energies numbing and healing his body.

"That should numb it for a while and also speed up the healing ointments in the sleeve. Get some rest. I'll have you out of here in no time."

Reuben nodded at her. She smiled back. Then, he sunk back into the bed and found merciful rest.

Jordan had never been to the principal's office. He knew kids who went a lot and the reputations it got them. Due to Khadija's strict teachings, he had maintained a low profile in school. Finding himself in

Alexander's office felt foreign and terrifying. It was a sliver of a room, which barely had enough space for the single window that looked out on the campus. Both walls were adorned with books. There was an expanse of ten feet between the bookshelves. Nestled directly in the middle was a five-foot desk with two chairs sitting opposite. Jordan and Alicia tried to be still, but those chairs were not built for comfort.

Alexander paced as he talked. "I gave you both a specific order to stand down and wait."

Alicia stuttered, "Uncle Alex –"

"Don't call me that here," he shot back. "I'm not your uncle. I'm your Squad Leader. So you will sit, wait, and listen."

Behind Alexander, a column of smoke still churned as a taunting reminder for Alicia of the events in the courtyard only hours ago. She bit her lip and looked down.

Alexander pointed a finger at her and said, "I know you of all people have had a long day, but that does not excuse what you did out there." He pointed to Jordan. "And you? Are you – are you trying to get kicked out? Last night you accumulated one strike, and now I'm thinking I'll give you two more and kick you out before this night is over."

"I'm sorry," Jordan muttered.

"Oh, now you're sorry. Now you two wanna listen. When you're on the field and you're taking orders with people's lives on the line, apologies don't cut it. You can't apologize to a dead person. You can't apologize to a city that...You can't apologize when they lose an arm –"

Jordan held his gloves in his hands, while Alicia's words played in his mind: *Maybe I am just playing hero. Maybe...maybe I'm not meant for this.*

Alexander took a calming breath, feeling the weight of his words echoing profoundly off the walls. His anger had gotten the better of him. He paused, centered himself, then tried again. "When – You can't – You can't apologize when someone loses something precious – something irreplaceable. You have to live with it, and so do they."

The students looked down, steadying themselves against their teacher's barrage. There was a knock at the door.

"Come in," Alexander boomed, without turning around. He continued, "And because of your actions –" He stopped when he realized they weren't looking at him, but rather, the new arrival. Alexander turned to see Richa Patel standing in the doorway. He deflated at the sight of her. "Headmaster..."

Richa wore an olive green nightgown with an electric green and gold robe over it. Her hair swayed behind her, coiled together and held by green fabric. She moved belly first at an ethereal pace, as if she were walking underwater and pressing the very reality of space-time away from her as she strutted towards them.

"I was just talking to them," Alexander reported.

"Ohhh," Richa said softly. "I heard you talking to them when I came down the hall. If you want to teach kids, you have to be gentle, even when they make mistakes." Richa glanced over at both teens with her kind, warm eyes.

"Headmaster Patel," Alicia began, "we're sorry, but we couldn't wait. That statue was –"

"Your great-grandfather," Richa interrupted her gently, like the calm in the storm. "I understand. And, it being your brother's birthday, your emotions were heightened."

Richa turned to Jordan. "And you, you're the most curious of the students I've seen in a while. How do you factor into this?"

Jordan paused and tried to gather his thoughts. "I – I wanted to make up for my mistake last night."

Richa smiled. "Oh yes, you were the reason I was awake last night too. Two nights in a row. You're certainly headstrong."

"That's one way to put it," Alexander grumbled.

"Alex..." Richa admonished him, then turned back to Jordan. "You got your first of three strikes last night, and tonight..." She trailed off and turned back to Alex.

"A second strike," Alexander spat. "You're lucky it's not two."

Jordan felt his heart sink and glanced back down to the floor.

"And that's a strike for you too, Alicia," Alexander added. "You both disobeyed a direct order and nearly got your whole team hurt. Not to mention, the thieves got away with the stone. This was a failure on every level."

Alicia took it like a gut punch, but she held her breath and her tongue.

"Sir," Jordan struggled to speak, but Alexander was having none of it.

"Keep talking, and I'll add an extra point. I hope you're not already unpacked. This time next week, you'll be going home."

Alicia glanced at Jordan, and her eyes screamed, *Don't push it.*

Richa found the silence and quickly filled it. "That'll be all, Cadets. Rest, reflect, sleep."

Being adequately scolded, Jordan and Alicia stood up and walked out. Alicia stopped at the door, looked back at Red Wing and his bristling frame, then closed the door. With the kids gone, Alexander exhaled deeply and let the stress of the night melt away. He plopped in his chair, exhausted.

"You can't be too hard on them," Richa cautioned.

"They're my students."

"Aren't they mine too?" She gave a gentle nod to Alexander's confused face. "We need to talk about the other thing too."

Alexander nodded. As much as he had dreaded having to lecture them, the smoke still rising from the courtyard reminded him of the other pressing issue at hand. "I've got two other kids in the infirmary. Can we talk later?"

"Yes," she answered warmly. "But tell me. Did you get a look at them? Their masks? Their power skills?"

"The shorter one was 5'6, maybe 5'5. Male or female, it was hard to tell. They had green plasma and a cloaking Gift. The other one was a real heavyweight. I clocked his red plasma at 65,000. He's 6'2 or 6'3, well-built. I couldn't determine his Gift though," Alexander rattled off the facts.

"65,000, hmm," Richa mused. "We're certainly not dealing with amateurs here."

"The way he threw me," Alexander slumped, "I talked to Carnage already. I think –"

"I think we should save all suspicions until we know for sure," Richa interrupted him the same gentle way she had with Alicia.

"Rest," she ordered. "Check on your kids. We'll talk later."

"Thank you."

Richa turned on her heel and drifted out of the room. As she went, her thick braid drifted up, grabbed the handle, and closed the door behind her.

Alexander, now alone, allowed his body to melt into his seat for a moment. He turned in his chair to a photo on his desk. It featured himself, Titanus, Saint Lightning, Lion Force, and the other two Olympians he once called friends.

"Oh, how far..." Alexander cast a pensive look out the window. "Oh how far we have fallen." Then he heard the clock strike midnight, chiming the end of Astro Day. Alexander cursed under his breath. He had missed the fireworks.

REUBEN ALVAREZ

Hero Alias: N/A

Height: 5'8

Weight: 135

Birth Date: August 24

Plasma Color: Red

Plasma Level: 25,000

Gift: Reuben possesses the ability to regulate his body temperature to convert plasma into flames. Secondly, to protect his body from the flames, his body mutates into a protective scaled form that boosts his offense and defense.

CHAPTER TWENTY-SEVEN

Alone Across the Rubicon

Jordan took the elevator to the 8th floor but felt as if he had taken the stairs. His body was complaining, and his mind was strained. He wasn't sure if it was the mental or the physical taxations from the past two days, but he felt in dire need of sleep. He swayed as he walked, and a wave of dull aches and pains crested over his body. With a swipe of his badge, Jordan opened the door to his dorm and stopped. Cooper's side of the room was bare, except for a suitcase that he was furiously packing.

"Coop?" Jordan asked softly.

Jordan wasn't sure if he was seeing things or if he had stepped into some new reality. He gripped Kinetic's gloves in his hand.

"What?" Cooper asked, not bothering to turn around.

Cooper's dexterity, which Jordan was getting used to seeing crawling around the room, was put to use packing with blinding speed.

"What are you doing?" Jordan asked, his mind's gears turning to catch up.

"I'm going home," Cooper mumbled.

Jordan paused to take this in. He shut the door and crossed the room. As he passed by the wardrobe, he saw that half of Cooper's Hybrid pride shirts had already been taken down.

"I couldn't do anything." Cooper spoke so quietly Jordan thought he was talking to himself. Cooper's tail rose, then dropped morosely to the floor. He stepped back from the suitcase on the bed, then dropped down on his tail by the dresser. Jordan avoided his eyes. He didn't want to cement this moment with his feelings.

"I couldn't..." Cooper repeated, "I couldn't do anything in the fight. I couldn't even do anything when we were trapped in the field house."

Jordan walked over to him. As Cooper looked up, Jordan froze. He knew that look; he had seen it many times after losing during a bad night of vigilantism. He empathized completely.

"Maybe they were right. Maybe I'm a dragger. Maybe I'm just meant to be a sidekick or not even..." He stopped for a moment, almost afraid to say the words aloud. "Or maybe I'm not even a hero at all."

Jordan stopped to think what he would tell himself. "You – you did what you could."

"I couldn't do anything!" Cooper exploded, and then immediately calmed. "I was – I – When Reuben attacked, I saw nothing but fire – nothing but fire heading my way, and I froze. If it hadn't been for Red Wing – I –I couldn't even save myself."

He slammed his head back against the dresser. Jordan crossed over to him, knelt, and placed a hand on his shoulder.

"But you're here. You're still here, and you got time to learn how to build – how to build courage. Heroes aren't born; they're made."

Cooper nodded, glanced down at the ground, and bit his lip. His gaze fell on the words on Jordan's gloves.

"Be your own hero..." Cooper mused, quietly.

"Yeah. Your own hero, you know." Jordan looked from them to Cooper. "Like, you're half-man, half-animal. No one looks like you. No one. But you go out into the world every day and face it. That in itself is courage." Jordan gripped Cooper's shoulder and looked up at him. "That in itself is being a hero."

From the ground, Cooper's tail snaked up and grabbed the Lion Force action figure from the top of the dresser. He brought it down into his hands. Cooper examined the figure in his hand – a golden mane, a roaring mouth full of fangs, and talons that would make one's skin crawl just by looking at them. Cooper found it inspiring. Lion Force's appearance wasn't something to fear, but something to aspire to. Cooper ran his thumb over the toy's star on his chest.

"Lion Force...He saved me, ya know? On the Green Night. I was five, maybe four, I guess." Though Cooper was here physically with Jordan, mentally he was back in that night. "Nothing but fire, nothing but chaos. I had gotten split from my family and – he found me. He could have run. He could've gone to save some of the other heroes, but he came for me. He saved me that night. He didn't run from the danger." Cooper blinked, and something churned within him, an invisible switch that had suddenly been flicked. "And that's...that's the hero I want to be."

Jordan gave him an encouraging nod. "We've had a long day. Unpack and get some sleep. We almost died, like, twice today."

Cooper scoffed out a laugh. "You almost died twice. I almost died, like, a hundred times." The two chuckled, and Jordan helped Cooper up.

"I tell you what, though," Jordan chimed, "I could use one of those ambrosia cupcakes. My body is wrecked."

"You and me both," Cooper chimed. "I'll talk to my parents and see if we can get some for this weekend."

"I'd like that." Jordan offered him a thin smile that said, *I'm happy you're still here.*

"Me too," Cooper replied to both of Jordan's spoken and unspoken sentiments.

It was late when Alexander returned to the faculty dorms across campus. He had spent a few moments reminiscing about the past in his office after Richa left. Then he spent the next thirty minutes visiting Reuben and Sydney in the infirmary. They were both asleep, and he decided not to wake them. Doctor Wilson had also given him a stern warning not to disturb her patients. And though he didn't know what her Gift was, he didn't plan on finding out.

He felt as if he had simply sleepwalked to his on-campus apartment. It was smaller, much smaller, than his home in Dallas, but staying here saved time on travel. It also reminded him of his younger teaching days and student experiences. All in all, he had spent a dozen years on this campus, and he hoped to give back all that he had received from Fort Olympus.

He had spent his first tour of Fort Olympus in the five-year student program, with the licensed hero: Fomalhaut as his teacher. Alexander made tea in his room and reminisced about how Fomalhaut loved Earl Grey. She always smelled of it. Even in passing, she often left a cloud behind. Calming, ethereal, and with a depth that always left him yearning for more. He spent his sixth year as a licensed sidekick for Fomalhaut. Once he graduated, he found himself settling in Houston.

After a decade away from Texas, traveling the globe as a rising professional hero, he hoped he had done Fomalhaut and Fort Olympus proud. While the true story was still wrapped in classified material, he had lost his arm in combat. For him, it was a sign to slow down, come back to basics, and rebuild himself. And when he found no place to go – he went home.

He began his second tour of Fort Olympus as a teacher. In his early 30s, he found himself inspecting the crop of incoming heroes in their teens. He saw his eyes in their faces. He heard Fomalhaut's honesty in their voices. During reminiscing moments in his room, he brewed her same brand of Earl Grey.

While he was rebuilding himself, he was also building up the heroes of tomorrow. His squad, the Ares Regiment, included a young man named Cedric Jackson, who would change his life. Cedric was like him in many respects; he had come from a Texas family and was raised with a serious work ethic that kept him pushing, no matter how hot and high the sun was. As he found himself teaching Cedric the basics of Plasma Techniques, Alexander realized he was re-learning how to do it on his own. As he taught Cedric the principles of evacuation and public safety, Alexander realized he didn't need a book or a reminder; he knew it. As Alexander established the principles of being a hero in these young teens, he recalled what drove him to put on the suit and serve his country.

Alexander thought he had lost a part of himself, but he soon realized he was whole and had a lot to offer. His injury wasn't a loss but something that helped define him. He could still be a hero; he could still be the man Fomalhaut promised him he would be. For all his despair, he realized that not only was Cedric the future, but he was part of that too. This school had given him purpose when he was just a boy. Then, when he lost his arm and his drive, it rekindled that purpose again as a man.

Now, as he stood on his balcony at the age of fifty-five, he hoped the school would do it once again. Alexander sipped his Earl Grey and felt the gentle, somber warmth fill him.

"That was your team out there tonight?" a voice called out.

Alexander turned to find Vermillion on his neighboring balcony, beer in hand.

"Yeah." Alexander paused, sipped his tea, pressed his lips into silence, then continued, "I – I nearly lost them tonight."

"I'm sorry," Vermillion began, but Alexander interrupted.

"Don't apologize. It's not your fault." Alexander struggled, and then admitted, "It's mine."

Vermillion looked down on the campus; smoke still rose in the distance. He ran a large hand over his beard and stopped to think for a moment, suddenly regretting this conversation. "You – You probably don't remember me." Vermillion's line rekindled Alexander's interest. "I was a student here in the Taurus Regiment when Cedric was here...the first time you taught here." Alexander's hazel eyes looked him up and down. He had heard bits and pieces about the hero Vermillion, but they had never crossed paths professionally. He searched his mind for a past recollection of Vermillion–nothing. "Cedric and I fought in the Olympiad in our junior year," Vermillion added.

"Ah...William Holt." Something clicked inside Alexander's mind, and suddenly the image of Billy Holt came flooding back to him with a vivid recollection of Cedric and Billy wielding their Gifts against each other. "I do remember your match. I got to apologize; I didn't commit your face to memory. I'm glad to see you're still serving."

"Oh, I don't blame you for forgetting, Cedric beat me before I even got my footing. My brother, bless his soul, was human. He never let me live that whooping down. He even said he could take me. Cedric was – Cedric was really the best."

Alexander nodded, then raised his glass. "To Cedric."

"To Cedric," William responded and lifted his drink in response. "Happy Astro Day." They both drank and took in the night for a long second.

Alexander's old eyes scanned the landscape of Fort Olympus. "I missed this place. I almost didn't come back here. I almost said no."

"What changed your mind?"

"Cedric."

Alexander let the word hang in the air, then he read the confusion in Vermillion's face. "His sister was accepted here. I've known her since she could walk. Cedric was so proud of her. He lit up anytime she walked into the room, and she glowed anytime she saw him. I raised him from a boy into an Olympian. I don't have any kids. Never had the time, but him – Cedric was like my son." He paused for a moment, recalling some terrible memory, then spoke it aloud. "...Then after the Green Night...After we lost Cedric...I was lost for a bit. I didn't know where to go."

"But you came back here?"

"Yeah..." Alexander smiled at something distant. "I – I – I met a genie."

Vermillion nearly choked on his beer. "What?"

"At least, she said she was descended from genies. She – she was in the back of this bar in Dallas, somewhere on the forgotten side of town. She had plasma, I asked her what her Gift was, and she said, 'It wasn't free.' I asked her again, and she said, 'For one gold coin, I'll grant you a wish.' I thought what the hell, I – I had a gold coin." He stopped as if he had just realized he was on the wrong page of a book and changed course. "You believe in destiny, right?"

"I do, sir."

"Drop the sir. We're both teachers here."

"Okay Alex," Vermillion said with a chuckle. "Then, yes, I do believe in destiny."

"Well, that morning I had found a coin in my driveway. A gold coin. Hand to Zeus, how often does that happen, huh? So, I gave her that coin and made a wish. I told her, 'Give me a second chance to save Cedric.' Then, uh – the next day I was visiting the campus to talk to Patel about a job. I didn't want it. A job I didn't think I needed. I didn't think I had anything left to offer. Then when I left, I ran right into Alicia and her family. She had just been accepted and was visiting the campus. What are the odds of that, huh? A gold coin. A genie. A wish. And – her on this campus?"

"I'd say that's destiny."

"Me too," Alexander agreed. "Long ago, Cedric was my second chance to get back to the man I used to be. Now – now she's my third...and I nearly lost her tonight."

Vermillion examined Alexander for what he was–an old hero. Vermillion idolized legends like Alexander, imperfections notwithstanding.

"I don't know what it's like to lose a child, but I know what it's like to lose a student," Alexander admitted. "I had to tell Alicia and her parents what happened to Cedric. I didn't know their pain, not fully, but I felt something close to it. And I swore – I *swore*– I'd never feel that again. That I'd never let anything else happen to that family, to her, to the man who had given me so much." Then something cold and violent took hold of him. "I'm not sure who that was on this campus tonight, and I don't care. But if I find them again," daggers of red plasma flashed in Alexander's eyes, "I'm gonna kill them."

Sydney stirred to life, feeling a rush of light assault her eyes. The first thing she was aware of was how comfortable she was. The infirmary bed had seemingly swallowed her. She silently hoped she hadn't been snoring. The next thing she was aware of was a movement in the room. Sydney rose out of bed and stopped.

It was Reuben.

He was gingerly moving out of his bed with a grunt punctuating every effort. She looked him over: the arm delicately in a sling, his eyes heavy with sleep, and his hair tousled every which way. Sydney was confident she didn't look much better. She examined her hands and the sleeves of her combat suit. They were still covered in soot from the attack earlier that night.

Reuben made it to his feet and began straightening his bed with one hand. The infirmary was down to a skeleton crew of a single nurse and a trio of sleepy healer interns, who were busying themselves in books.

"You nearly killed Cooper," Sydney began, her voice still raspy with dream sleep.

"Yeah," he replied softly.

"And me," Sydney pressed.

Reuben didn't reply. He simply pulled the bedsheets into their rightful positions. Sydney rolled her legs out of bed; she was shocked at how heavy they felt. Reuben fluffed the pillow, then smoothed it out. If he hadn't just almost cost Sydney her life, she would have been a bit impressed with his attention to detail.

"I see why my ancestors feared y'all." Sydney paused for emphasis. "They called your people the boogeymen."

"I'm not my ancestors." Reuben still didn't look her way. He used his free hand to unlock his arm sling, then removed his hand delicately from the sleeve. When he arrived earlier that night, his hand was hot pink. Thanks to the ointments in the sleeve and Doctor Wilson's touch, it was now several shades lighter and returning to its normal sunbaked hue – and not baked.

"Neither am I," Sydney declared as she stood up.

"Yet, they still wiped my people out." Reuben gently folded the arm sleeve and placed it atop the bed.

"You need to learn to control it." Sydney found her boots next to her bed and began to stuff them on. "The reason I beat you is because I baited you with a single word. That's why you lost. The reason you're in here is because you couldn't control your anger."

"Then I'm not sure why you wanna continue this conversation." Now Reuben looked at her, cutting her down with a glare.

Sydney didn't flinch. She was used to these conversations with a lot of men scarier than him. "You're quiet, but inside, you got a lot of demons just begging to get out."

"You're scared of me," Reuben jabbed.

"And you're scared of your Gift," she jousted back, then pressed the advantage with a combo of words. "Everyone is scared of your Gift because you don't know how to control it."

Reuben nodded. She had won that round, even if he wouldn't admit it. As he reached the door, he realized he had one parting shot. "Scared? That's funny coming from you." Reuben turned back and fired off, "Because, in *my history*, your people are the boogeymen."

He waited for a beat for her to return fire, but none came. Reuben left, and Battalia sat there alone with her thoughts, contemplating simply lying back down.

That night as Jordan slept, he tossed, turned, and floated. Within his dreams, he wasn't alone. He was back at Coliseum Seven. The stands were full of students now, much like how he felt when Carnage had called him out in front of the class. Except in the dream, it wasn't just a handful of students, it was every student and professor watching as he battled Nightingale and Goldtears across the sands. He was tossed in bed as he felt Goldtears toss him into the air. He felt himself come back to face them. He managed to get in two good hits, and their masks fell off to reveal – Carnage and Lucas.

"They're here," Jordan called out to the crowd.

No one moved.

"They're right here. Help me," Jordan screamed to the crowd.

Still, no one moved.

Jordan spotted Red Wing and his teammates sitting on the front row. He waved at them, frantically. "Help me."

No movement.

They just watched, stone-faced. Jordan sighed, then felt something coming. Jordan turned, and Carnage and Lucas rushed him, their cloaks billowing out behind them, like the wings of some great bat. And as the darkness enveloped him...

Jordan shot up and thumped his head on the ceiling. He groaned and pulled back to grab his forehead. In his restful sleep, he had floated high above his bed. And he wasn't alone. His blanket and pillows had floated up too. Then he saw something oddly shaped and fluffy coming his way. He double-checked that he had his pillow and blanket, then looked back as this alien thing rolled toward him in the dark. It hit the moonlight and Jordan sighed – it was Cooper, curled into a ball around his tail.

Jordan waited for him to get in arm's reach, before lightly shoving him, like a ball, across the room and over his bed. Then Jordan slowly reset the gravitons in the room, dropping everything gently back to the ground. It was a bit messy but done. Jordan drifted back down to the bed and felt himself settle along with the room. He glanced over at his clock. It had landed facedown. He picked it back up: 3 a.m.

He found his way to bed and got comfortable. Jordan finally found himself drifting mercifully to sleep when his phone buzzed. He checked it and found it was a short text from Darius: *Field House. 5 a.m.*

Jordan groaned so loud he felt the tremor of it in his chest.

Dressed in his purple and gold Kinetic combat suit, Darius met Jordan outside of the field house. Jordan contemplated just bringing his blanket with him. Despite his lack of sleep, he met his uncle out there in his combat suit. The blush of the morning sun reflected off the star on Darius' chest and somehow, someway, made its way right into Jordan's eyes.

"I talked to your Squad Leader last night," Darius began, sternly.

"Okay, and..." Jordan answered, squinting and stepping away to avoid the glare that reflected off his suit.

Darius opened the door to the field house and led him inside, where Darius continued, "You're already at two strikes."

"It's only been two days," Jordan replied.

"That's not an answer." Darius walked him past the wall that Jordan swore Alicia had carved through hours earlier. He examined it and the door to the simulation room. They had been repaired. The wall had a fresh coat of paint that was still tacky. The door itself shined like a new car – sleek metal, untarnished, and smelling of chemicals. Darius opened the newly installed door and waved Jordan inside.

"What are we doing here?" Jordan asked.

"I spoke to Headmaster Patel last night too."

Jordan cringed, then replied, imitating him, "That's not an answer."

Darius' eyebrow poked up at the imitation. "Are you trying to get kicked out?" he asked.

Jordan shook his head, not bothering to even address it, but Darius continued, "What's going on? Didn't I give you specific directions –"

"Yeah, to infiltrate the toughest military school in the country –"

"Or go to jail," Darius barked. "Where they will slap a red V on your face and scar you forever. Do you understand those are your only options?"

"It's way too early for this." Jordan made a move to go to the door.

"Don't. Don't run. Talk to me."

Jordan whirled around and snapped back, "Talk? You want to talk after all this time? You missed out on my whole life."

"And I apologized."

If Jordan heard him, he didn't respond. He continued, "You weren't there. You weren't there when my parents died. You weren't there when it was just me and Khadija."

"If I could have been there, I would have."

"But you show up now?" Jordan threw his hands in the air. "Now? All these years I had to do this on my own. No one believed in me. No one even wanted me to use my powers. No one wanted me to be a hero. They wanted me to be a cape-dragger."

"So what do you want to do?"

"I want to go back to the way things were," Jordan sighed. "I want my old life back. I want my old friends, my old school, and to go back into hiding where no one knew about my powers. Maybe Khadija was right. Maybe it was best being a nobody, hiding who I was – being a cape-dragger. I had to hide who I was from my best friend – my best friend. Do you know how messed up that is? But what is more messed up is that I would go back to that right now, if it meant I didn't have to deal with this." Jordan swallowed hard, then whispered as his voice was muffled by a hundred stress-born hands, "Because I'm not good enough...I'm not a hero. I'm nothing close to a hero."

Jordan took in a hot, shuddering breath and began to pace. Jordan wanted to grab Darius, shove him against the wall, and hurt his uncle as he was hurting.

Darius' words were slow and careful. "I know you're angry."

"You don't even know me!" Jordan exploded. "You don't know what it was like to be alone. To try to do the right thing and constantly be punished for it. Nothing I do is ever good enough. I try to be a vigilante, and I get arrested. I try and catch Lucas, and I get a strike. I try and stop the thieves and get another strike. Now I'm out here being talked down to by a man who couldn't care less about me." Jordan's voice cracked as something akin to a scream escaped from that broken place.

He really thinks I hate him. The thought hit Darius like a train – or, in his case – a train he didn't see coming and couldn't use his powers against.

Jordan rushed him, no longer able to speak, but only able to push against him. Jordan shoved against him with plasma-packed arms. Darius didn't move, didn't even budge, but Jordan fought against him all the same. Darius went quiet. He searched his thoughts calmly and knew what he said next was going to shape their relationship for years to come.

"You're my family," Darius declared, freezing Jordan mid-shove.

No, no. He's lying. Jordan stepped backward, and Darius caught him by the top of his head. *He lied. He doesn't care about me.* Darius palmed Jordan's head like he did earlier when he cut his hair.

"And I wish," Darius now stammered over his words, "I wish more than anything I could have been there, that you two didn't have to go through that alone."

He's – he's telling the truth, Jordan admitted to himself.

"You're my family." Darius tilted Jordan's head so that he would look up at him. "When you – when you look in the mirror, and you can't figure out who you are, you remember – you're my family. I may have changed my last name, but I'm still a Harris. I'm still here for you, always will be."

I'm all the family he's got left... For an instant, Jordan saw his face in Darius', then a second later he saw his father's face. *And he's all I have left.*

Jordan stepped back from under his hand, the vision all a little too overwhelming.

"But why did you come back now?" Jordan asked.

"Because I was tracking them, and it led me here."

"Here?" Jordan shouted. "Darius, you gotta tell me something, just anything to –"

"There is going to be another Green Night," Darius said, coldly.

Jordan stopped mid-sentence. He felt like he had taken a hundred punches to the face. His nose and eyes scrunched, and his ears rang. *What?* Jordan blinked, and Darius repeated himself, clearly. "I am tracking them because I fear there is going to be another Green Night."

For a long moment that felt like an eternity, Jordan didn't reply. The air had been expelled from his lungs, and his mind slipped through a decade's worth of green-tinted nightmares. A hundred anxious hands seemed to grab at him from all sides, punch through his back and out his chest. He grappled with his anxiety. After a long moment, he finally got enough air in his lungs to softly utter the word, "How?"

"The pattern of heists and crimes is the same," Darius explained. "The crystal they stole last night isn't just for show. It was put in the middle of a military academy to hide it in plain sight. To protect it."

Jordan paused, thinking back to the opaque crystal that had been in the Polaris statue. A hundred hands crawled along his body, tightening his chest and wringing cold fear from his lungs. A cold dread began to course numbly through his body.

"What – what is the crystal made of?" Jordan asked.

"Ambrosia," Darius answered. "It's the nectar of the gods in crystal form. This isn't available for the public, but before the Green Night happened there was a string of ambrosia robberies. We're seeing the same pattern now."

"And..." Jordan's mind was spinning, but paused long enough to ask, "And you're telling me that the Green Titan, they – they got their power from ambrosia?"

Darius nodded, and Jordan felt for the wall. He dropped back against it, then focused on controlling his breathing.

"It's not a myth. Not much in our history is," Darius explained. "Centuries ago, Zeus and our ancestors would use ambrosia to spike their powers before they fought and exterminated the giants – and before they fought and eventually defeated the Titans."

Jordan didn't have a reply. He simply wanted to breathe, shout, and run across the campus – to run across all of Houston and shout a warning, but not even his legs would obey him now.

Darius stood, watching him. "Any Esper who gets in contact with ambrosia could double or triple their plasma levels in an instant. They would be a walking catastrophe waiting to happen."

Jordan nodded.

"So you understand now, why it's imperative that you help us find them. There are four crystals hiding in plain sight, one was at the museum and –"

"And I stopped that one," Jordan blurted out.

"Yes," Darius explained. "You stumbled right into it and stopped them."

That also explains why Titanus was there to stop a simple robbery, Jordan realized. *He must have known what was there.*

"The second crystal was here. But we all know what happened last night." Jordan looked down to avoid Darius' stare and let his uncle continue, "So, they now have one crystal, and they'll be looking for the others."

"Others?" Jordan gulped.

"We decided not to collect the other ambrosia crystals. If we do, we'll never lure these two out of hiding. We need the gems as bait to catch them."

That's dangerous, but it makes sense. Jordan nodded.

"So you realize, it's not just me who needs your help," Darius put a hand on Jordan's shoulder, "but the city itself."

CHAPTER TWENTY-EIGHT

[Young Lions] X [Rubicon]

Jordan couldn't feel his feet, but he felt their weight. He couldn't feel his legs, but he could tell they were moving. His mind was a shell of itself, still recovering from what Darius had told him. While he had heard him continue speaking, he only recalled a few choice things: "...another Green Night," the way Darius' face flexed with concern when he said it, how the paint along the walls of the simulation room looked a bit off, "ambrosia," and as always how heavy Darius' hand felt on his shoulder.

It, like his own experience on the Green Night, was all a blur – a terrible blur. As he drifted across campus, alone with his thoughts, his mind was suddenly pricked by a distant and familiar voice.

"Hello, Earth to StarLion." Rhea's voice sprinkled his conscious mind like a light rain. He wasn't sure when it started, but he suddenly had awareness.

Jordan shook it off and wiped the concern from his face in time for Rhea to approach him. She had a water bottle in one hand and a towel over her shoulders. She was in Fort Olympus jogging sweats that were a bit damp from a morning run.

"What are you doing out here this early?" Rhea asked.

Jordan paused to regroup; he had to tell yet another lie. He shoved aside his good nature once more, and he replied with the best half-truth he could muster, "Uh – I had to meet a friend. I'm heading back to the dorms; I'm not trying to get a third strike."

"Oh, you're fine. Students are allowed to be out at this time." Rhea peered around. They were alone. "But only the people who truly care about their health are up at this time. I mean, it's not like you're up to vigilantism in broad daylight."

Jordan cringed, feeling a bit exposed. "Yeah," Jordan sighed, "about that...I'm done with that now."

Rhea smirked. She could read right through him. "What, too many strikes too fast?" she asked.

Jordan sighed. All he wanted to do was sleep – to shed his old burdens and carry the new ones without being interrogated. "You know, it wasn't so much the voice that I recognized," Rhea continued. "It was the shoes."

Rhea nodded down at the black and gold Zeuz Airwalkers currently on his feet. His first instinct was to kick them off – to hide them and any other evidence that may lead her to condemn him.

"Do you remember what I said, though?" Rhea inquired. "Heroes come in a lot of different shapes and sizes."

Jordan buzzed, not so much hearing the words, but feeling her meaning. *She knows who I am...but she doesn't care...because I'm doing the right thing.*

"In New York, I went to Citadel Rhodes Hero Academy. Now they have a very strict no-vigilantism policy, but that didn't stop a lot of us from going out for our own extra-curricular activities."

Because she used to do it too. Jordan nodded. Rhea turned to face the wind as the morning breeze swept a cold spread off the Buffalo Bayou and caressed them. Before she turned back to him, Jordan marveled at her shiny black hair with hints of green and flashes of light. Whatever she was mulling over, she had reached a decision.

"I got it from my brother, I guess. My father said our Gifts were useless," Rhea revealed. "Told us to hide them, not use them. Don't even think of being a hero with Gifts like that."

Jordan winced; the words sounded familiar. *I'm happy Khadija was never that strict.*

"He even made me dye my hair." Rhea sighed as if a great secret had been lifted from her shoulders"But you know what I realized when I got to that school?"

"What?"

"That he was wrong. That my Gift was special – that I too could be a hero. My brother, Griffin, dropped out of here, but not me. I'm gonna make the difference. I'm not gonna tell anyone, Jordan. In fact, it might even earn you some brownie points with some kids here."

"If the administration doesn't kick me out," he joked, and it felt good to let go of some of the burden weighing on him.

"There are different ways to be a hero, Jordan. The law may never agree with all of them, but it's on us to do the right thing, regardless. In other words..." Rhea's words trailed off.

"Heroes come in a lot of different shapes and sizes," Jordan replied.

Rhea gave him a thin smile and slapped his shoulder. "Exactly. And none of us can do it on our own."

"Thanks," Jordan replied, shyly.

"It'll be our secret." She winked at him, then jogged off into the rising sun. As Jordan watched her go, her words trailed back to him. *We all can't do it on our own.*

Alicia was just finishing the final sprint of her morning workout when she finally cured herself of last night's mistakes. She hadn't slept much. Cedric's birthday, nearly dying – three times – losing her fight against the masked thieves, Uncle Alex's tirade. And to top it all off, she had gotten her first strike. For most of those issues last night, Jordan was intertwined with half of them. So when her phone buzzed with a text from "Jordan Harris" she felt her heart rate rise again. *What now?*

Now what? Sydney asked herself as she stirred awake.

She was not one to sleep in late, but after last night's troubles – after she came back from the infirmary, she went immediately to bed and didn't set an alarm. She wasn't entirely sure what Doctor Wilson had done to her, but she slept like a brick throughout her time in the infirmary and again when she got to her dorm. She awoke from what she feared was her own snoring, but it was her phone vibrating on the dresser. She picked up her phone and was prepared to silence it and return to bed. When she saw who it was from and clicked the message, she knew sleep was not an option.

Reuben awoke with a start, to the sound of his phone buzzing, then he felt a tingle in his arm as he became increasingly aware that the skin was still tender. He gingerly lifted it from under the blanket and examined it. It was almost back to its "normal" hue of black and red splotches, but for that reason and more, he spent the next ten minutes carefully wrapping gauze around his arm. "*Coliseum Seven. Thirty minutes. I have a secret.*" Reuben had to read it twice to make sure he understood.

This was the first time he got a text from Jordan, and he wasn't sure if it was legit or a trick. Either way, Reuben felt the need to get up and investigate.

Reuben double-checked the time: *twenty minutes left.* He made his way to the elevator, and when it opened – *Are you freaking serious?*

Cooper was mid-yawn when the elevator doors opened, and Reuben was there, looking bedraggled. Cooper coughed mid-yawn and ended up choking out the rest of it, like a sputtering engine. Reuben looked him up and down. Though he had a lot of questions, he just asked the first one that came to mind.

"Jordan texted you too?"

"Yeah," was all Cooper could muster.

"I thought you would be with him," Reuben admitted as Cooper slipped inside the elevator and tapped the lobby button.

"No. I woke up, and he was gone."

"That's comforting."

The doors shut, and the two rode in silence for a moment.

"Are you – are you okay?" Reuben said.

"Yeah...I just – I kinda," Cooper stuttered before admitting, "I kind of had a panic attack."

Reuben stopped and faced him with mild concern.

"The whole uh –" Cooper paused to think. "You know – flamethrower you set off from your arm and the robbery, and nearly dying, I just...," he trailed off.

"Oh..." was all Reuben offered.

"Well, yeah." Cooper cringed. He didn't want to put it so bluntly. "It just left me rattled."

The doors to the elevator opened, and they exited into the lobby of the Apollo Barracks. Reuben took his time walking. He was in no hurry to fill the silence before responding, "Well, I'm sorry about – the whole fire thing. I...uh...I didn't mean to..."

"Nearly barbecue me?" Cooper offered as they reached the front door.

Now it was Reuben's turn to cringe. "Well...yeah." He paused to collect his thoughts, then blurted out, "My bad."

Cooper paused for emphasis and replied, mockingly, "I know."

Cooper opened the door, and they stumbled into the courtyard between the girls' and boys' dorms. Alicia and Sydney were huddled together comparing texts outside the doors to the Athena Barracks. They all shared a nervous glance and realized...

"Something's up," Alicia said.

The boys nodded, and then turned back to her, ready to meet Jordan at Coliseum Seven.

Jordan met them in the sandpits of Coliseum Seven. He was leaning up against the stands, his shoulders slumped, eyes heavy, and face twisted with concern. Cooper was the first to reach him and speak up. "J, what are we doing here? Do you need help?"

Jordan sized them up, then replied quietly, "I needed to talk to everyone in private."

"Is this about last night?" Alicia asked.

"It's about everything," Jordan replied. "Last night, the night before – I – I need your help."

The words hung in the air for a moment. Everyone exchanged curious glances, their minds running through the various scenarios. As Jordan spoke, he felt his burdens lift, his chest tighten, and his shoulders clench, before he handed them his first burden. "I'm a vigilante."

There was silence, then – Reuben exploded with laughter.

"Sorry, sorry," he gasped. "I can't handle surprises...You're serious?"

Jordan paused. That was not the reaction he was expecting.

Alicia folded her arms, then nodded at him to continue. That was the reaction he was expecting.

Jordan nodded back at her and got back on track. He laid down what he felt was his second burden, "And during a – a night of vigilantism, I was tracking two thieves in a museum when I was caught by Titanus."

Everyone glanced over at Sydney, who nodded. "I heard him mention something like that a while ago. He said some cape-dragger had gotten caught up in one of his ops."

"Okay, you don't have to say 'cape-dragger,'" Jordan said, defending himself.

"Well, it is the word he used," Sydney replied.

"Takes one to know one," Jordan whispered under his breath, before continuing ahead with a loud, "Anyways. That was me," Jordan admitted. "I was arrested, and my uncle, Kinetic –"

Reuben stifled another laugh, biting his cheek through it. The group glared at him to shut up.

"What?" Reuben shot back. "Are you telling me you all knew who his uncle was?"

Alicia nodded. "Yeah, Jordan told me."

Battalia nodded too. "My dad told me."

Cooper admitted bashfully, "He's buying my silence with toys."

Reuben shook his head; being the last one to know really sucked, and there was nothing to laugh at. Jordan, feeling lighter than he had felt in weeks, continued his truth mission–not a half-truth, not a partial truth, but the whole truth.

"My uncle...Darius, made a deal to get me out if I agreed to help them find the thieves. The only clue they had was a Taurus badge from Fort Olympus."

"So the thieves go here?" Alicia asked.

"At least one of them," Jordan confirmed.

Alicia nodded as if she had figured out the full story already. As smart as she was, maybe she had. "And that's who we lost to last night?"

Again, Jordan confirmed with a nod. He watched their body language as the team accepted this. Then Jordan took in one more breath and prepared to drop the final bomb on them.

"They're after ambrosia." He paused for emphasis. "From what Darius told me, if they get their hands on enough, there will be another Green Night."

The air was seemingly sucked out of the open-air coliseum. Sydney's face paled. Cooper bit his lip. Alicia inhaled sharply, and Reuben stifled a few curse words. For a moment, no one said anything. For that one brief, precious moment, Jordan felt weightless. All his burdens had been laid bare before them. Now he awaited their responses.

Alicia was first. She had a theory to confirm: "The stone they stole last night that was ambrosia?"

Reuben answered before Jordan. "It was crystallized ambrosia, right?"

"Yeah," Jordan answered. "They hid it in plain sight."

"Plain sight?" Alicia scoffed. "We've got nearly fifty pro heroes who work and live at this school; that's better protection than the President."

"And yet, those draggers still got away," Sydney spat.

"And we all know what happened last night cannot happen again," Jordan said. "So we need to be a team. A real team, if we're going to stop them. I – I called you all here because I need your help. Darius needs your help, and so does your father." He sent a glance at Sydney, who responded with a subtle nod. "I'm not sure who all I can trust here, but I know I can trust you guys. I'm – I'm a vigilante. I'm no hero, but I'm going to be one."

Jordan paused for a moment to let the words settle. He looked across their faces, waiting for them. He knew Cooper was waffling. *C'mon, Coop.*

As if on cue, Cooper stepped forward and admitted, "I'm just a Hybrid kid who got bullied at school – but I want to be a hero too."

Alicia looked the two over, then glanced at Reuben and Sydney. *Well, if we're all dropping secrets...*

"I lost my brother, Astro, to the Green Night," she said. "It tore me and my family apart. But I'm going to be a hero, just like him." Alicia glanced at Jordan with a tense smile. *I'm in.*

Reuben took stock in all their faces. *What a way to start the day. Here goes...*

"I'm a demon." Reuben stopped to let the word resonate. It felt gross on his tongue. "But that doesn't mean I can't be a hero too." Reuben stepped forward and offered Jordan his regular hand. Jordan didn't mind which hand Reuben offered him; he would have shaken it either way.

Battalia felt all eyes on her. She was used to the scrutiny after growing up with Titanus as her father, but here, in such an intimate space as everyone was spilling secrets, she found herself tongue-tied, so she deflected, "What? Oh come on, do you want some speech from me too?"

The teammates shared a look, and then nodded and shrugged back at her collectively. *Yes.*

"Fine." Sydney sighed so hard, they could feel it. "My father is the most famous hero in the country. But he's not the strongest. And – he's old, and he's tired, and he carried this country on his back for ten years. No one sees his pain like I do." Her usually stern voice went soft for a beat. Then Battalia continued, "I want him to retire peacefully; he's earned that. He's more than earned that – so I'm stepping up to take his place. I'm in because that's what heroes do."

Jordan looked at them with new interest. What began as a weight in his chest and on his shoulders was now a warm sensation that touched his heart. For the first time in a long time, he felt truly free. More importantly, he wasn't alone in this. He had found someone to help carry the burden.

"I didn't go to a hero prep school," Jordan explained. "I learned on my own, on the streets. There are a lot of things the streets can teach you that schools can't."

"And there are a lot of things we can teach you." Alicia glanced at her teammates. "There are a lot of things we can teach each other."

They shared a silent nod. Jordan was sure that this was the first time he felt close to a team. He saw his own raw emotions reflected at him in all their faces.

"All right," Jordan announced. "Let's get to work."

Alexander was quite confused when his students arrived that morning for training. After last night, he had half-expected them to be gnawing on each other's ankles. He had even arrived early to make sure cooler heads prevailed. When he arrived, though, he found his team quiet, but still friendly. It seemed last night's loss hadn't turned them against each other, but rather, towards each other. He was most surprised by Jordan and Alicia. From afar where he lightly sparred with Cooper, he spied Alicia and Jordan huddled on the side of the field.

"You have to imagine your whole body moving," Alicia explained patiently. "Feel every fiber of your being."

Jordan closed his eyes. He had long since tapped into his plasma and sent it spreading through his body, but as he searched his core, he had trouble finding where it specifically gathered.

"Search your body."

"Okay," Jordan said with eyes closed and a stern focus. He took a deep breath and felt the air invigorate his system down to his belly.

"Feel the very depths," Alicia instructed.

"I feel it," Jordan said, with a growing tightness in his abdomen.

"Now push," Alicia ordered.

Jordan clenched his body and – farted.

Alicia paused and looked him dead in the eye.

"Did you just...?" Alicia couldn't finish it.

"No. No." Jordan put his hands up. "It was my – just my stomach –"

"Yes, he farted," Cooper shouted from across the field.

"No, I didn't," Jordan shot back at Cooper.

"I can smell it from here," Cooper called back.

"Well, stay over there then."

"That doesn't help. My nose is really sensitive." Cooper paused to shake his head to rid his nose of the odor. "It's like everywhere."

Jordan slapped his forehead. *This is not happening.* "Okay, okay. Can we just try again?" he asked.

Alicia chuckled under a heavy sigh, trying not to lean into the embarrassment. "All right, I mean it this time. Search your entire body. Feel every ounce of plasma. Inhale."

Jordan inhaled on her command, and this time he doubled down on focusing. He cleared his head – and his stomach. He felt the air come into his body then down into his lungs once more.

"As you inhale, feel that air hitting your lungs. Feel it as it disperses through your body, lifting your heart. Imagine everywhere your blood goes, your plasma goes."

Jordan listened only to her words. He sought to visualize every avenue of his body. From his brain, to his heart, to his stomach, to his toes, to his fingers – all encased in gold plasma. In his plasma. In his energy. All in his mind's eye. All at once, he captured his full essence in one image. A tremor flowed through his body at the same pace as his heartbeat.

Then another, and another. He felt his heart beating all around him. He heard the monotonous thud in his ears.

"I - I feel like I'm vibrating," Jordan explained.

"Good," Alicia continued. "Now push that energy – all of it – in the direction you want to go."

Jordan tapped into it like a frequency, then projected himself forward. *Go.* He barely finished the thought when he felt his body being propelled off the ground. It felt like a magnet had locked on to him and pulled with all its might. Jordan felt himself shift across the sands. He was used to the free-flying sensation of exploding gravity under his feet, but this was a more controlled propulsion. Instead of being launched like a rocket, he simply felt himself moving and flowing –

"Open your eyes!" Alicia's voice called out as –

Jordan snapped his eyes open and saw nothing but the coliseum wall heading right at him. He thumped into the wall face first. He felt his whole body vibrate again as he collapsed on the ground. The team stopped to look his way and, after a long beat of silence, Jordan threw his gloved thumb up.

"I can shift," he declared.

The training concluded, and Jordan got two aspirin for his head. Afterward, he and Alicia walked along the courtyard. The sun was setting over Fort Olympus, casting the Houston skyline in shades of oranges and blues.

"I'm gonna watch tape tonight on my brother if you want to come over," Alicia said.

"Tape?" He wasn't sure if he heard her right, so he inquired again.

"Old footage," she explained. "News footage of him working in the field. I study it from time to time. Helps me learn by mimicking what he does."

Jordan's stomach growled. "Okay, that was my stomach this time."

"Clean up; bring some food; I'll start in thirty," Alicia said.

"Catch you then," Jordan replied.

Thirty minutes later, the two of them were on the floor watching her TV play old footage of Astro's heroic deeds throughout Houston – and eating Ramen noodles.

"You know, when you said food, I meant like real food," Alicia pointed out.

"I mean, if you don't want it..." Jordan reached over for her bowl, but she hugged it to herself.

"Nope. This is mine." She slurped the noodles up and paused. "It does need something, though."

Alicia got up and made her way to a mini-fridge in the corner of her room, where she retrieved a bottle of sriracha. She dropped three squirts into the ramen noodles and turned to offer some to Jordan, but – he had shifted over to her.

"Hit me," he said.

"Oh, now you know how to shift," Alicia teased. She dropped some sriracha into his bowl, and he nodded approvingly.

"You're not a bad teacher," he smirked.

Alicia rolled her eyes, took the bottle, and walked back over to the TV, where he joined her. They sat down just as the replay reached a critical point in the news coverage. It displayed a person climbing up the side of a building with a duffel bag flung over his shoulder, spilling random bills. Below him, Astro was running up the side of the building, using only his feet as if gravity didn't apply to him.

"The Vesper seems to have an adhesive Gift helping him stick to walls. We believe that's why they haven't dropped the money either," the news anchor's voice supplied.

Alicia pointed to the screen as Astro used a burst of plasma from his feet to jettison his way up.

"See how he avoids using his thrusters on the glass; he's protecting the building at the same time," she explained.

"Yeah," Jordan said softly as he realized. "I used to do the same thing when I was a vigilante. If you hit the glass, there's a chance you can go from running on the side of the building to suddenly being in it."

Jordan studied the screen. He felt a swell of relief as he settled into the idea that he finally had someone to chat with about his powers and his vigilantism. His first instinct was to tell her not to tell Khadija, but he calmed, realizing that this too was okay. It was finally okay to be himself. To be the hero he had hidden from the world.

The next day, Alexander took the team back to the field house. He suspected that yesterday might have been a fluke for his team's harmony, but he was pleasantly surprised to see Alicia and Sydney working together as they practiced shooting plasma at walls of nitrile. He could focus with Reuben on helping Jordan and Cooper.

Sydney's fist coiled and sent a wave of her force field at the wall. The energy twisted into a projection of her fist and connected with the wall of rubber. She cringed when she felt the recoil ripple and crush her wrist. Sydney seethed and shook her hand, waiting for the familiar pain to subside.

"You're gonna break your wrist before you get through that," Alicia cautioned.

Sydney spoke between gritted teeth, "Yeah."

"Don't use punches," Alicia suggested. "Using palm strikes will help disperse the recoil along your palm."

Sydney paused and listened. *That's not a half-bad idea.*

"You'll also be able to throw more strikes since you won't be worrying about the pain," Alicia added.

More strikes. Less pain, Battalia mused. *That might work.*

"Palm strikes?" Sydney confirmed.

Alicia nodded. "Lead with the heel of your hand. That's where all the force will come from."

Sydney raised her palm and crunched her fingers down until her fingertips touched the top of her palm. She felt her wrist flex, but this time with far less pain than what she was used to. It felt like she had turned her hand from a wrecking ball into a wall. Fingers tight, palm upright, and thumb tucked close, she threw a palm strike and sent her force field along with it. The strike hit the nitrile wall and sent a mighty shudder through it. This time the recoil came back and dispersed off her fingers and palm, and there was only a minimal ache in her wrist.

"Yeah, that's better," Battalia marveled. Then a devilish grin played across her face.

She launched another palm strike, and it too detonated against the nitrile wall. She sent another and another, building with intensity as one punch turned into two, then into four, then into eight. The mighty rubber wall bucked and rattled before she sent another pair of consecutive strikes into its core and tumbled over. The wall landed with a mighty thud that echoed smartly.

Alicia stepped over to her, and Sydney paused...Alicia had her fist out. *Respect.*

Sydney returned the fist bump. *Duh.*

That night Sydney joined Alicia and Jordan in Alicia's dorm to watch tape on Titanus. The trio watched the legendary fighter battle a lizard man through the busy streets of Houston. Crowds of people stood on the sidewalks, and others huddled in their cars as the two clashed.

Jordan put a squirt of sriracha into his noodles then passed it to Alicia, who put some into her honey chicken salad. She got her own food this time. She passed the bottle to Sydney, who took it without looking and doused her Tupperware container of steamed rice, vegetables, and vegan beef. As she ate, Sydney narrated for them.

"See." Battalia stopped to chew, then continued. "See how my dad waits for the Vesper to come to him, instead of going for them. He's doing it on purpose so he doesn't waste any movement and unintentionally hurt the crowd watching."

After watching footage on Titanus, they moved to footage of Darius, where Jordan focused on showing off how his uncle hit the Impact Knee. As usual, Jordan was the first to speak up, and Alicia was the first to correct him, followed by Sydney.

"See how that move comes out of nowhere when they least expect it?" Jordan exclaimed.

"It's not out of nowhere. It's focused and timed," Alicia corrected.

"Yuh–He–" Sydney stopped to chew her food, then followed up with, "Watch it again. He lines them up first."

Jordan rewound the video and watched as Darius grappled with a larger man. Then with a burst of kinetic energy from under his foot, Darius threw a knee up and into the man's jaw – flooring him.

"One more time," Alicia commanded.

Jordan rewound it again. This time, Alicia narrated as Jordan watched. "See how Darius takes a few steps back first?"

Jordan watched as Darius indeed slipped his foot back.

"He's making room," Jordan concluded.

"Yeah, he's lining up his body so it's exactly a straight diagonal line from his knee to the guy's face," Sydney confirmed.

"He lines them up," Alicia said, "sets his path, and then lets it rip."

As if on cue, Darius threw his knee up and let it rip once more into the man's jaw. Jordan watched, enamored. *Line 'em up, set the path, let it rip.*

"Also," Sydney began, "Jordan, can I just say that your fighting style makes no sense."

"What?" Jordan looked from Sydney to Alicia, hoping for some backup.

"Yeah, I gotta agree," Alicia added.

"Thanks..."

"It's not an insult." Alicia cautioned. "It's constructive criticism."

"Emphasis on criticism," Sydney quipped.

Jordan shot her a thin glare.

"She's right," Alicia added. "You running right at your opponent is ridiculous. Why run right at them, when you can run on walls and ceilings and go wherever you want?"

Jordan paused. *Okay, they have a point. Alicia did get on me about just going directly at people.*

"Plus, you're used to sneaking around," Sydney said. She took a second to wonder why Jordan was frowning at her, then added, "Oh, I didn't mean that as an insult. At least not this time. You're used to hiding from people, which means you know where their blind spots are. Why run right at them, when you can attack from the blind spot?"

"Hmm, you're right. If I'm good at anything, it's sneaking around," Jordan realized.

"Yeah," Alicia said. "If you can get in their blind spots or just out of their field of vision for a second, all you'd need is a second to get in close, then..." She trailed off and Jordan picked it up.

"Line 'em up, set my path, and let it rip," Jordan chanted. *That's amazing. I never would have thought of that.* He looked back at Darius' footage still playing on TV and saw his uncle's frame and movements in a new light.

After practice the next day, Jordan showed them the device he used to keep in his ear when he did vigilante work.

"I think you got some earwax on it," Cooper pointed out.

"No, it's just old," Jordan replied.

"No, it's pretty gross," Reuben insisted.

Jordan wiped off whatever it was. "It's gone, whatever it was."

"Okay, but what does it do?" Sydney asked.

"Darius said the last piece of ambrosia he knew of was at the Houston Museum of Natural Science. I was able to tune this device to pick up any outgoing alarms."

"So when the thieves strike again, we'll know?" Alicia queried.

Jordan nodded. "Exactly. We'll be ready."

"And the other one?" Cooper asked. "The other piece of ambrosia..."

"It's at the Olympian memorial," Jordan said. "If they hit that one, there probably won't be an alarm, just chaos. Cop cars, fire trucks...ambulances."

"I'll keep my ears tuned," Cooper smirked.

That night Jordan and Alicia went for a jog and made their way to the memorial for the Olympians. As Jordan stopped to catch his breath with his hands on his knees, he noticed Alicia was still upright.

"There's no air down there," Alicia panted.

"I'm going to find out though," Jordan heaved and stayed hunched over, struggling for air.

Alicia looked over the memorial for the seven Olympians. Her eyes lingered on Red Wing, who stood with wings encased in bronze – right next to Cedric. Behind them stood the wall of names that featured people who had passed away during the Green Night.

Jordan walked over to the wall. He knew where their names were. He had known for over ten years where their names were. Tonight, he looked on them with new eyes:

JOHNATHAN HARRIS & JULIA HARRIS

Jordan traced their names with his index finger. He felt a shiver run through him, then suppressed it. Across from him, when she thought he wasn't looking, Alicia ran her finger along another name: CEDRIC JACKSON.

"I'm uh – I'm sorry again, for what happened to your brother," Jordan said.

Alicia gave him a somber nod. "Yeah."

"You miss him?"

Alicia paused. She nearly spilled the truth but reconsidered. "I do. Every day." Though what she told him was true in her heart, it wasn't true in her reality.

"I – I miss my parents," Jordan admitted softly.

The words and the hurt lingered in the air for a beat. Then, simultaneously, they spotted the ambrosia crystal. It reflected the moonlight from its place in the middle of the marble wall.

"Say we just take it now?" Alicia teased.

"There would be a lot of angry villains out there," Jordan joked.

"I think your uncle would be mad too," Alicia added with a snicker. She peered back over the trees that framed the park and into the depths of the city itself. "Actually, if you're up for it, I wanna show you something," she offered.

"Yeah," Jordan said. "Lead the way."

Alicia took him to see Astro. Well, not her brother, per se. She took him to the apartment complex that was adjacent to the building with the Astro mural. From there, they could both look out at the city of Houston buzzing below them. No matter the time, it was always a stunning sight. The night is what Alicia preferred.

"He chose the name Astro after our forefathers," she explained.

"Polaris?" Jordan asked.

"Also known as the North Star," she said. "Back when my ancestors were using the Underground Railroad."

"So stars run in your family name?" Jordan nodded in understanding.

"Yeah," Alicia answered, then gazed up at the cascade of stars above them. "Do you know the difference between a shooting star and a meteor?"

"No," he replied.

Alicia leaned back and let the stars and ambient light of Houston fill her vision. "Sixty-two miles."

"What?" Jordan asked.

"A shooting star is a meteor that burns sixty-two miles above the Earth's atmosphere. A meteor is what makes it through the atmosphere and drops to Earth," Alicia explained.

"They're the same thing," Jordan concluded.

"Exactly, but for a moment, that meteor becomes something special. It becomes a wish, a light for the whole world to see." Alicia's eyes beamed up at the cosmos. "Then it becomes real."

Jordan stared at her for a bit, admiring her smile and the way she examined the sky.

"I'd like my hero name to be something like that, you know. Something tied into meteors and stars and...and wishes..." She stopped as she reached a certain word that spoke to her. "To hope."

"You'll figure it out," Jordan assured her. "You'll find it."

Somewhere between a meteor and a shooting star... Alicia took one last look at the stars and her brother's mural and smirked. *I'll find it. My own version of hope for the world.*

The next day, back on the sands of Coliseum Seven, Alexander switched partners to pair the strongest with the weakest. As Cooper narrowly avoided Reuben's attacks, it definitely didn't feel like much of a change. Cooper dipped and bolted away from Reuben's bandaged right hand as he threw plasma-packed punches rumbling past him.

Cooper dodged a punch, and then a kick came for him in the same instant. Cooper leaned back on his tail, twisted his body into a roll, and slipped between both attacks, landing in a sliding crouch and drifting away from his attacker.

Reuben paused, and Cooper assumed he was just formulating a new attack pattern, when Reuben blurted out, "Why don't you use your tail?"

"My tail? What? No. I only use it for defense," Cooper replied.

"That thing is like three feet long."

"Uh, four and a half," Cooper corrected him and silently commanded his plasma to cease.

"That's my point," Reuben bantered back at him. "Our legs are one of the strongest muscle groups since we use them every day, but your tail has got to be twice or three times as strong. It's all one giant muscle."

Cooper stopped to think. *He's right. But also it's, like, really sensitive. I'd rather fight with my funny bone.*

"C'mon," Reuben called out, "just try it. The same way you push plasma into your arms, try it on your tail."

"But what if – "

Mid-sentence, Reuben's arm erupted in black spikes and flames, and before Cooper could react, Reuben had shifted right into his face.

"Try it," Reuben hollered, his voice mutating along with his arm.

Cooper shouted and snapped into action to defend himself. He tapped in and sent a current of plasma into his tail. He felt his tail blossoming with warmth and weight as its density increased. He flicked his tail right into Reuben's path.

Reuben, mid-attack, turned and saw a wall of fur blocking his peripheral. *Wait, if his tail is heavier than his legs, then this is gonna feel like getting kicked by a wrecking ball.* Reuben sent as much plasma as he could to the side of his face, but he knew it was too late. *Oh, this is gonna be a drag...*

Cooper's tail came down on Reuben's head and slapped him out of mid-air with enough force to create a thunderclap. One second Reuben was in mid-air; the next second he felt himself twirling to the ground. Sand filled his mouth. His face throbbed. When his world stopped spinning and he could hear again, he coughed up sand and rose to all fours.

"I'm sorry. I'm sorry. I'm so sorry," Cooper chanted.

"Don't worry about it." Reuben heaved and wavered on his feet.

As he rose, he peered back across the sand and saw that he was at least six feet from where he had started. *How − how hard did he hit me?*

"Let's go again," Reuben coughed out.

"What? No. I nearly killed you," Cooper cautioned.

Reuben turned to face him and flashed a sinister grin. "You're gonna wish you did."

Cooper was startled as Reuben went back on the attack. Cooper sent another wave of plasma to his tail and defended himself against Reuben's incoming attacks. As Cooper began to use his tail as a weapon, he was also learning how to read attacks. Reuben had to catch up to his own advice and defend against five limbs, instead of four. He was quickly − and painfully − learning where his blind spots were and how to defend against them. They were learning how to use their Hybrid abilities in new ways. This was a new kind of opportunity. Under the shadow of Lion Force's statue at the apex of the coliseum, the two Hybrids continued their training.

That night, Cooper joined Alicia, Jordan, and Sydney to watch tape. The group had already assembled when Cooper entered with a box in hand. Jordan recognized the box immediately and resisted shifting across the room. Cooper had brought −

"Bamboo cupcakes for the group," he announced as his tail shut the door behind him. He winced; his tail was sore from using it all day.

"Yes," Jordan shouted and huddled around his roommate.

"Did he just say *bamboo cupcakes*?" Sydney asked.

Jordan took one and handed it to Alicia. As their fingers brushed against each other, they avoided eye contact. While no one else noticed the brief interaction, they each struggled with their composure.

Cooper handed one to Sydney. "They're made from bamboo shoots, with Vietnamese custard and candied rhubarb."

Battalia stopped, then replied blankly, "Is any of that actually edible?"

Jordan took a chomp and spoke through crumbs, "If you don't want it, Syd, I'll −"

"Nope," she cut him off, "I'll try it."

Sydney took a tiny bite with the tip of her teeth. As she swallowed it, her face lit up, and her force field blossomed, making her hair dance in the energy.

"Wow," she marveled with childlike enthusiasm. Sydney turned and went back to sit down. Her teammates were equally thrilled to see a break in her snobbish shell.

The break didn't last; she flipped it back on just as quickly. This was better showcased on the fields the next day when she and Reuben had a rematch on the sand. As Sydney formed a barrier between herself and Reuben's flames, she curled into a C shape, like a catcher's mitt, to thwart his attack. She felt her legs slide back in the sands before she leaned over and held the brunt of it back.

"More," she called out from behind her barrier.

Reuben gripped his scaled wrist with his normal hand for support, then sent a column of flame that punched out of his wrist and smashed into her barrier. *Don't focus on the pain.* He felt his scales flex through the slits in his flesh. *Don't focus on the heat.* Reuben turned away from the flames pouring from his hand, and sweat greased his face. *Just focus on pushing yourself.*

Sydney curled against her barrier while the flames threatened to engulf her. Sweat was already running down her face, neck, and back. She could feel the heat bursting and growing against her barrier. But it wasn't enough. *He's got more where that came from.*

At the spectacle, the students and Red Wing had taken to the sidelines to watch with caution. The space where the two energies met burned so hot that it hurt to even glance at it. Below the flames and Sydney's barrier, the sand was being superheated into glass. Flames danced, and heat rippled in waves around them.

"Uncle Alex..." Alicia whispered to encourage him to do something.

"No," the Squad Leader replied. "They need to do this."

Jordan glanced at Alexander, then back to Sydney and Reuben, or, better yet, Reuben and the fireball cresting over Sydney...

"Go." As if she heard them, Battalia's voice echoed from within the fireball. "You need to find your limit."

Reuben felt something within his plasma just begging to be released. A primal urge. Something he had kept locked up. He had once feared it as people had feared him...but no more. No longer would he keep what was natural to him hidden away. He let loose and felt his body embrace it. It pulsated behind his eyes, and he cringed as his pupils went from circles to serpentine slits. Then he felt the skin along his face slice open as scales pushed their way out, like dozens of paper cuts suddenly being lashed along his skin. For every scale that slipped free from his skin, he felt his plasma swelling and igniting with more fury.

It hurt, but it also fed his hunger.

The scales worked to absorb his plasma and convert it into fire. He felt the heat, not just in his arm, but now down his face and head. It rippled across his neck and shoulders before his protruding elbow bone retracted like a piston and sent an intake of air to re-kindle the flames and send a geyser of fire belching from his palms.

Alexander's eyes went wide when a surge of flaming waves rocketed across the field. *It's over.* He shifted across the field and had an instant to stop it before Sydney was swallowed. The Squad Leader blitzed in front of her, spawned a pair of red plasma wings over both of them, and braced for impact. He kept himself huddled over Sydney until the attack passed like the heat of a jet engine. The quaking hellfire came to an abrupt end. Suddenly, clean air found them, and Alexander stood with Sydney, smoke wafting off their bodies.

"You're good?" he asked.

She nodded, rattled, but trying her best to not show it. "Yeah. Yeah."

There was a shout from across the sand as an exhausted Reuben dropped to his knees. His arm was covered in scales—no longer a surprise—but the mutation reached his face and replaced it with an affair of scales with thin black slits for eyes; his skull was seemingly torn.

Reuben shouted when the scales flexed. *Focus. Focus. Lock it down.* The rage he had kept bottled for so long was still clearly hungry, but now was not the time. Reuben felt his body quake and simmer, trying greedily to tap into his own plasma and ignite it.

Stop. No more. No more, he pleaded with himself.

Sydney took a step towards him, but Alexander put an arm on her shoulder to stop her approach.

"Wait," he commanded.

Sydney looked back at Reuben shuddering on the ground. Gritting his teeth and pursing his lips in pain.

I did this...I pushed him, Sydney observed. *I did this.*

Alexander jumped as Sydney shifted right from under his touch, and she reappeared at Reuben's side. Reuben was momentarily startled when she materialized beside him.

"Don't," he warned. "Don't look at me."

Reuben turned away from her. He could feel his body warring with itself, wanting to lash out at her, wanting to purge her from his sight, but – Sydney put a hand on his mutated shoulder. She hissed at the burn from his smoking scales, but she held her hand in place.

"Reuben," Battalia whispered in his ear, "I'm sorry."

The words drifted through him like a cold wave, tempering his anger and settling his scales. Sydney then put her other hand on his shoulder and leaned down with him as if in prayer. She tapped her forehead against his, and Reuben felt his scales retracting under his skin. The soft underbelly of the scales acted as a soft massage for the slits that were punched into his skin.

"I pushed you. You needed to know your limits."

Reuben coughed out a response, then grimaced as his elbow bone cracked back into place, issuing a vibrating pain that ran along his whole right side. He gasped once more as everything settled back into place.

He didn't look up at Sydney but felt her touch, her closeness, and a calm that he didn't expect from her.

"You don't scare me anymore," she admitted, softly.

The words danced in his ears, and he sighed heavily as the last of the pain subsided. Sydney took his arm and gently pulled him to his feet.

A few nights later, Reuben finally joined the team to watch tape on various pro heroes. The group sat around Alicia's TV eating and listening while Sydney and Alicia narrated what was happening on screen.

Tonight's subject was the Olympian Saint Lightning. Behind her hood and her face mask, a pair of round honey-colored eyes surrounded by brown skin looked out at the world. Currently, she was in the midst of fighting three armed men.

"Watch what she does here," Sydney ordered. "She disarms them before engaging."

Indeed, and true to her name, Saint Lightning sent a burst of electric energy crackling into their weapons, superheating them and forcing the men to drop them.

Meanwhile, Reuben was superheating his Mexican Chili Gumbo with a generous stream of sriracha. He took a bite, realized it needed more, and added another squirt.

"Then," Alicia chimed, "she engages the Gifted one first to keep the situation in control."

The man in the middle of the three suddenly bulked up as extra muscle mass inflated his body. Even though he suddenly dwarfed her, Saint Lightning thundered forth and laid him out with a spin kick to the temple, which was left unprotected by the muscle mass.

Reuben took another bite, sighed, then simply poured the remainder of the bottle in. He stopped for a moment when all eyes turned to him.

"What? It wasn't hot enough," he said simply.

"Man," Jordan snapped, "you're the last person who should have issues with things being too hot."

The team burst out laughing, and Reuben, despite himself, joined in.

The next night, after finishing a–thankfully–peaceful patrol, Jordan and Cooper came back to their dorm exhausted. There were no team tape sessions tonight, so they took advantage of the downtime and headed for bed.

Jordan entered the dorm on foot, and Cooper lethargically crawled across the walls, devoid of his usual energy.

"I can't take too many more of these late nights," Jordan sighed.

"I feel ya," Cooper replied through a yawn. He wall-crawled directly over his bed, retracted his claws, and fell off the wall into it.

"You know," Jordan admitted, sitting on the edge of his bed and removing his boots, "I could go for one of those cupcakes."

"It's four in the morning," Cooper sighed.

"You're right," Jordan replied, "I should just sle–" His voice trailed off when he heard the buzzing. Jordan searched around the room, and Cooper's hyper-sensitive ears perked up.

"Is that what I think it is?" Cooper gasped, feeling a fresh surge of adrenaline rise within him.

Jordan reached under his bed, pulled out his old Zeuz shoebox. Inside, he kept the police scanner earpiece. He had made some minor modifications to the device, so it picked up alarms from the Houston Museum of Natural Science. Jordan plucked out the device and placed it in his palm for Cooper to see.

It was ringing.

"On the Green Night, 10 years ago, we all lost something, and this is our chance to make it right – to prove that we can be heroes."

- *Jordan Harris*

CHAPTER TWENTY-NINE

The Thieves Part 3

Jordan and Cooper had reassembled with their teammates on the north side of campus near the fortress wall. Jordan felt a surge of urgency well up inside of him. He shook the nervous energy from his hands inside of his extra-large gloves. He looked up at his teammates, his friends.

"Look," he began, "we faced them before and lost."

Alicia readjusted her shoulder pads and pulled them tight again against her frame; she had slipped them on so fast, but now she had to be ready. She assessed her teammates and realized that they too were ready.

"But we weren't a team before," Jordan continued.

Sydney calmed her breath. In the rush, she had nearly forgotten this meeting was supposed to be secret. She had kept a steady but quiet pace and made it to the meeting spot, just as the others arrived. Upon arriving, she too took stock of the team. She saw they were making efforts to breathe and stay calm. Battalia reveled in this unity.

"This time," Jordan continued, "we have the element of surprise."

Reuben fought his nervous ticks. He wavered on his toes and shifted his hips from side to side. He rolled his shoulders under the pads. Then he felt a breeze around the top of his right arm. His bandages were loose. He gripped the end of the fabric, yanked it tight, then tucked it within the wrap. He glanced about and saw Alicia tapping her foot on the ground, also nervous.

Cooper stood next to Jordan and stretched his arms over his head, feeling the sleep being squeezed from his frame. His whole body trembled from pent-up nerves; he hoped a stretch would get him feeling better and prepared for this fight. He glanced at the ground, and, despite his nerves, he smiled. Everyone was wearing their regulation boots, but, in keeping with tradition, Jordan wore his Zeuz Airwalkers.

"If we do this, we don't do it as pros, but as vigilantes," Jordan warned them, and let the silence hang for a moment while they weighed the choice. No one backed out, so he continued. "Even if we win, we might all get expelled."

"It's worth it," Sydney remarked, "if we can stop another Green Night."

The group sent around a series of nods, all in agreement.

"On the Green Night, ten years ago, we all lost something, and this is our chance to make it right – to prove that we can be heroes," Jordan declared.

Energized, the team was unified and ready to head out into the night.

"Now." Jordan leaned in and made eye contact with all of them as he reached the apex of his rousing speech and inquired, "Who can drive?"

A different type of silence hung in the air. They all shared surprised glances. This was not something that any of them had prepared for – well, except for one. Cooper slowly raised his hand, and they turned to him. "My parents let me borrow the company car."

The newly minted friends followed Cooper off-campus and into the depths of the parking garage, where on-campus students were allowed to park. As the group made their way to the car, something became increasingly clear – this was truly a company car.

It was a Volkswagen Beetle painted a glossy pale yellow, like the color of the box the pastries came in. The car was also decorated like a red panda. A faux red panda tail was suction-cupped to the trunk, and the front of the car was made to look like a red panda's face. A button nose was attached to the front bumper with eyelashes on the headlights and

284 - LEON LANGFORD

foam red ears attached to the roof. Cooper made his way to the driver's side door and stopped when he realized that his teammates were not following him.

"Sup?" Cooper asked.

"It's a uh –" Jordan searched for the words. "It's got a tail."

"Yeah," Cooper said as if it was obvious.

"And eyelashes," Alicia giggled, weakly.

"Oh, c'mon, guys. It's the company car," Cooper snapped. "We use it to deliver pastries, not justice."

"Hmm," Sydney hummed between flat lips. "Okay, well, we could run there."

"Really?" Cooper gaped.

"You know what?" Alicia added. "Me too. J talked about it so much and it seems...Fun...?"

"But what if you slip and fall to your death?" Cooper insisted.

Sydney whispered under her breath, "Worth it."

"I heard that," Cooper snapped, pointing to his ears.

Without another word, Sydney jogged off, and Alicia joined her. Jordan looked between Reuben and Cooper. Reuben glared at Jordan. *Don't you do it.*

Jordan shrugged his shoulders. "I should probably go with them to make sure they get there safely. Building parkour and all. See you there. Bye."

Jordan exploded gravity under his feet and went off after Sydney and Alicia. Reuben was left alone with Cooper.

"Yeah, yeah," Cooper mockingly imitated Reuben. "*You know.*"

Over the rooftops and lights of Houston, Jordan led Alicia and Sydney in a game of hopscotch along the buildings. While he had shown them in training how he used his Gift to throw himself from rooftop to rooftop, gliding sometimes hundreds of feet above sidewalks, using it for real was quite different. Alicia had studied her brother's technique of leaping with plasma, and she used what she learned from him and Jordan to do the same. She took her time with each jump, detonating the neon plasma under her heels at the right moment to send her up and over the streets.

Sydney had to modify her explosive steps because her Gift didn't explode. It repelled. She formed her force field under her feet at the apex of her jump and used it like a trampoline.

Jordan had to adjust his usual pathways. Even though he could still run parallel to the ground and on the faces of buildings, his two partners could not. He felt a familiar burst under him that sent him trailing to the sky with gold stars in his wake. Behind him, Alicia followed in a stream of hot purple fireworks. Bringing up the rear, Battalia left behind glowing blue plasma residue that added to the mosaic they painted across the rooftops and clouds above Houston.

As Jordan crested over another building, he pulled his gloves tight, then wondered aloud, "I wonder how far away Cooper and Reuben are."

"It's still late. There shouldn't be anyone on the roads," Alicia huffed. "I'm sure they're making good time."

"The light is green, dragger!" Cooper shouted as he punched the car's horn.

Though traffic was light, and the signal was indeed green, there was construction happening late that night that forced three lanes down to one. Cooper bridled and bit his cheek, which Reuben had not expected from his usually jovial friend.

"Come on." Cooper stuck his head out the window and slapped his door.

Reuben put a bandaged hand to his face and slid deep into his seat, wishing he had also followed the girls.

Jordan forced himself to stay put when Alicia landed next to him. She and Sydney were moving and evolving faster than he expected. Sydney landed right next to Alicia, and Jordan looked at them with appreciation. *Wow, they caught on so quickly.* He smiled and realized, *Good. Now I can let loose.*

Jordan's Zeuz Airwalkers burst with gravity underneath them and sent him soaring up and through the sky.

Alicia smirked. *Show-off.*

Battalia glanced at Alicia. *You ready?*

Alicia narrowed her eyes and shrugged. *Duh.*

Together, they generated their Gifts under their feet and launched themselves up and over the rooftops and towards the museum. As Alicia reached the peak of her jump, something familiar caught her eye.

In the distance, just peeking out behind the skyline, was the Astro mural. She smiled at it, felt a sense of pride within her heart, then dropped down after her friends. *I'm gonna make you proud.*

After several more colorful bursts across the Houston skyline, they finally made it to the Houston Museum of Natural Science. With only a few buildings in the distance, they had to dismount from a series of taller buildings to level with the museum, using a single-story bank to get them onto the museum parking roof.

The Houston Museum of Natural Science looked like separate buildings fused into one. A smaller two-story box-shaped building composed of black glass all around the exterior crashed into the hull of a towering white structure that branched off and rose into two separate globe-shaped buildings, which housed the Planetarium and Observatory, respectively.

"The police aren't here yet," Jordan stated plainly. "We probably have at least ten minutes."

The sound of a car-locking mechanism directed their attention to the left to see Cooper and Reuben exit the car. One of the eyelashes was crooked above the headlight. The tail in the back looked ratty and torn, and a pair of skid marks led to a crooked parking spot.

"Hey," Cooper followed their gaze back to the car, "I had a little road rage along the way, okay? You think Kurikara sits in traffic? Do you think MegaTon takes the bus?"

The team looked to Reuben for an explanation.

He shook his head and didn't meet their gazes. "And people say I'm a demon."

"Focus, guys," Battalia scolded. "Let's do what we came here to do."

The team shared a nod, then turned towards the front of the museum. When the door came into view, they realized it had been blown off its hinges. Cracked glass and torn metal decorated the lobby. They gave pause to assess the damage, and Jordan took the first step inside.

Within the museum, all was quiet, except for the sounds of glass crunching under their feet. The lobby was vast and stretched beyond the front doors to include an information desk that sat between two maps of the facility.

"Are they even still here?" Cooper asked, a glint of hope in his voice.

Jordan tapped the forearm of his suit. After clicking through a few screens, an image displayed two distant plasma levels: 35,000 & 65,000.

"Yeah," Jordan confirmed. "They're here."

Cooper cursed under his breath, then scanned the lobby, taking quick inventory.

Alicia made her way to a list of exhibitions and scanned it. "Where would they hide ambrosia?" she asked.

The team walked up behind her to read the list for themselves.

"Too bad it's not listed here," Jordan pointed out.

Sydney reached over him and pointed to the list "Maybe it is..." Her gloved finger landed on the Cullen Hall of Gems and Minerals.

"Wait, wait," Reuben cautioned. "The last gem was in a statue, so this one might be on display too." He pointed a bandaged finger to the Lester & Sue Smith Gem Vault.

Two options, Jordan grimaced. "Okay, so we split up..."

"No," Cooper called out.

They turned to him. He suddenly twisted his head to the right, and his ears twitched.

"I hear something," he confirmed.

"What?" Alicia asked, stepping up behind him.

Cooper put up a hand, and whatever he heard sent his tail upright. He gasped softly. Cooper put a hand to his chest and absorbed what he had just heard.

"Help," Cooper uttered softly. "Someone is calling for help."

The team resisted the urge to bolt but were bolstered by the fact that none of them ran. The cadets shared a nervous glance. *Now or never.* With a tap of their gloved hands, a signal was sent into the suits that triggered their face masks to shoot into place, obscuring their faces. Moving quickly and silently, the cadets followed Cooper's lead into the darkness of the stairwell.

After a few seconds, which seemed to stretch into hours, they reached the top of the stairs and found a darkened, carpeted hallway that fed into the entrance of the Gem Vault exhibit. Cooper sensed it first: the sounds of a man wailing, the scent of blood in the air, and, finally, the sight of an injured security guard lying prone on the floor. He had a terrible burn on his belly.

"There." Cooper pointed at the obvious.

The team jogged over to the injured man. He was wearing a grey uniform shirt and black pants, basic security guard garb. He was furiously trying to keep a hand on his burn. He froze when the cadets came into light. They all stopped, then slowly approached him to make sure they were not mistaken for the enemy.

"Sir, are you okay?" Jordan asked.

Upon closer look, it was clearly a plasma burn that had seared him. Even Reuben shuddered when he saw the melted flesh peeking out from his shirt. The guard was in pain, but he wasn't out of the fight. Even if he heard Jordan's question, he didn't bother to answer.

"They – they went that way." He pointed into the Gem Vault exhibit.

The cadets stopped and studied the darkness that lay behind the entranceway to the exhibit.

"Y'all are heroes, right?" the guard uttered, painfully.

Jordan glanced from him to his fellow cadets and nodded. "Let's get to work."

Jordan pulled Kinetic's gloves flush against his knuckles. The words "Be Your Own Hero" gave him strength. Then together, the cadets rushed into the gem vault. The guard grunted and leaned back against the wall. He watched with bated breath as the heroes ventured into the dark.

The Gem Vault was built like a cul-de-sac, with various exhibits placed along the circular walls and several smaller exhibits parked in the middle of the room on podiums for guests to examine. Though the main lights of the room were off, smaller auxiliary lights that were meant to illuminate the exhibits cast the room in just enough light for them to make their way around.

For an instant, Cooper thought he was seeing things because the darkness itself seemed to shift. Then as his eyes adjusted further, he realized it was the black cloaks of the two thieves.

He froze. *There...*

He stopped and felt his teammates creep to a slow pace to hold their ground. They found them. Goldtears was once again using red plasma-coated fingertips to burn through a metal grate that protected an opaque crystal the size of an apple.

Ambrosia. Reuben's eyes narrowed when he spotted the crystal glinting behind the gate. His eyes flicked to the two masked individuals. *Focus on the mission. Don't let your emotions get the better of you.* Despite his calming mantra, Reuben still felt the rage begging to be let out.

Jordan stepped forward and bellowed, "Lucas."

The two masked individuals stopped and turned in sync as they took in their assailants.

Sydney felt her body shake. *I'm ready this time. Last time we didn't know what to expect.* She felt her plasma flex almost instinctively, and her force field flashed around her body. Battalia steadied her body, already limber from running across the rooftops, and prepared to launch herself at them.

Lucas? Alicia caught the name.

Jordan had told them who he suspected the masked thieves were, but, in these close quarters she studied how the smaller person moved. A series of calculations ran through her head in her assessment: their walk, their stature, their movement. One thing was quite clear: the taller thief was indeed a man; the smaller one was not. Nightingale wordlessly stepped between Goldtears and the team. The two of them fashioned themselves into a human shield.

"We don't have to do this," Reuben called out, surprising even himself.

Goldtears spread his arms and generated more red plasma in his palms that began to vibrate between his fingers.

Cooper's ears twitched, and his mind began to replay the events of the previous fight. *I...I can hear his attack...I can feel it...Oh...Oh no.*

"Guys," Cooper warned, "I think I figured out his power."

The energy clusters in Goldtears' hands swelled to envelop his hands in cymbals of red, pulsating lights.

"Shockwaves," Cooper exclaimed.

As if on cue, Nightingale ducked, and Goldtears' hands clapped together. The resulting shockwaves visibly rippled from the pulsing red plasma that clung to his hands. The force of the energy tore across the room in a series of plasma-infused waves. The room vibrated and hummed before shaking violently and turning end over end.

"Battalia," Jordan called.

Sydney swept in front of the team, threw her hands up, and let her force field blanket them, just as the waves and the torrent of debris smashed against it. The team huddled as the room's contents and Goldtears' attack swept past them. Before the room settled, Goldtears launched another attack.

Sydney warped her force field from a C-shape that covered her friends into a wall-sized hammer. She had previously considered her power as an extension of her desire to shut herself away from the world, but at this moment, she realized that her mom was right: *Shields aren't built just for you.* Nightingale and Goldtears turned in curiosity as Sydney's field morphed into a bullet. Sydney aimed her plasma bullet at them, and her mom's words came back to her: *They're built to protect everyone.*

Sydney flexed her Gift and sent her force field whirling in the form of a bullet the size of a sedan. Nightingale and Goldtears dove to the side as Battalia's attack smashed into the wall. It was as if an invisible wrecking ball had just crashed between them.

"Let's go," Jordan shouted. "You know your marks."

In an instant, the team split in three directions. Jordan and Alicia bounded after Goldtears; Reuben and Sydney went for Nightingale, and Cooper went for the crystal. The thieves had little time to react because they were not just separated, but outnumbered.

Just as she had planned, Alicia met Goldtears first and threw a series of hot purple fireworks his way. They detonated off his body like a swarm of flash grenades. The concussive blows were amplified by blinding and disorienting lights. Goldtears was further assaulted by resulting smoke clouds. He snapped his fingers, and in an amplified burst of sound, swept the dust away, just as –

Jordan came twisting up and over the scarlet shockwaves and landed in front of him, throwing plasma-packed punches. The first one connected deep in the man's chest and sent him tumbling backward. The next two missed as the masked man read his attacks and dodged deftly.

Read this. Jordan gritted his teeth, then taking Alicia's advice, came at him from a different angle.

Jordan kicked off the wall, then off an exhibition podium, launching himself back to the wall. Then he rebounded to the ceiling and flipped wildly off the ceiling panels, like a buzz saw. He flipped forward and brought the heel of his Zeuz Airwalkers down in an arc, smashing the masked man on the crown of his head. It was a dizzying display that left Jordan's stomach churning. As he spun out of the attack, he felt secure because the big man now scrambled away.

"We got him on the run," Jordan declared.

Alicia raced after him and powered up a plasma blade in her hand as she got in close. Right under her nose, he snapped his fingers and detonated a number of shockwaves that stunned her and sent her flying backward. Mid-flight, she felt a loosely gloved hand latch onto her own.

Jordan, she realized.

Jordan swiveled on his heels. *I know she's gonna hate this, but she knows what I'm thinking.*

He's throwing me right at him. Alicia grimaced. *Smart...*

Jordan spun with Alicia's hand in his and sent her soaring back the way she came, like a purple missile zoned in on Goldtears. Behind his mask, the big man's eyes went wide at Alicia's sudden change in trajectory. Alicia skewered him in the shoulder with her plasma blade. Then, with an invisible fuse, she detonated the blade. It erupted from a sword into a concussive propelled plasma-torpedo that smashed the stunned man against the wall.

As the man blitzed past him and punched into the wall, Cooper had little time to celebrate or watch the clash. He scrambled to the gate. Thankfully, the man with the red plasma had partly destroyed the barrier. Cooper sparked red plasma around his hand and realized even though half the work was already done – judging by the sound of things – he'd still have to work fast. He pushed his hand to the gate and began to burn the rest of the way through it.

"I'm here," Cooper shouted.

"Congratulations," Sydney spat mid-fight with Nightingale. "Now get in and get out."

Nightingale's eyes darted behind the mask and locked onto Cooper. With a renewed fury, Nightingale burst into a series of kicks and punches from under the cloak. Reuben and Sydney fought hard to block the attack.

Oh, they know, Sydney mused. *We got these cape-draggers where we want them.*

Nightingale went invisible, blinking out of view right in front of them. While Battalia and Reuben paused to regroup, they were suddenly assaulted by a series of strikes that rippled through their bodies.

That's what I was waiting for. As he felt a punch connect with his gut, Reuben twisted and grabbed the wrist. Meanwhile, Sydney grabbed hold of another limb. They shared a glance and sent an invisible message: *Now.*

Reuben held onto the thrashing invisible limb and wrapped his bandages around it.

Gotcha, Reuben triumphed as he felt the invisible arm go taut in his bandages, essentially handcuffing them together. Just as Alicia had taught her, Sydney made a flat palm, ripped her arm back, gathered her force field around it, and drove a pile-driving flat fist into what she assumed was Nightingale's midsection. The physical attack drove into the assailant's abdomen, and the plasma field detonated like an internal battering ram, rattling through their ribs. The attack resounded with a thunderclap and had enough force to bring Nightingale back into their vision, huddled on the ground.

Reuben and Sydney couldn't give the culprit a chance to escape. Reuben yanked one arm, while Sydney dunked her force field on the top of Nightingale to secure a firm trap. The masked thief was now visible, shackled to Reuben, and imprisoned between the floor and the force field – exactly how Alicia had planned.

Sydney was descended from the Norse God of Light and the Norse God of Justice, and as she kept Nightingale pinned down under their Gifts to her, she couldn't help but think they'd be proud.

Reuben whipped around and shouted out to Alicia and Jordan, "They're neutralized."

The words peppered them like fresh rain as Jordan and Alicia tangled with Goldtears. Though he was taller, stronger, and more experienced, he was outnumbered. Jordan and Alicia threw plasma-packed punches at the man's defenses. While Goldtears blocked Jordan's punch, he ate a kick to the kidneys from Alicia that crumbled him. With Goldtears' head bent over, Jordan skidded back and took aim.

Jordan took a three-point stance. *Line 'em up.*

Jordan measured Goldtears in his tracks. *Set your path.*

Jordan gathered gravitons under his foot. *Let it rip.*

Jordan exploded gravity under his feet and launched himself like a torpedo. Visible golden shockwaves echoed behind him as he took off.

Just like he'd seen Darius do so many times, just like his friends had taught him, just like he had seen over the years, he was spearheading right at Goldtears knee first. As Jordan's plasma-packed knee blasted Goldtears' masked face, a voice in his mind cheered, *Impact Knee!* Though the mask didn't break, Jordan felt the mask slam flush against Goldtears' face, snapping his head back.

"Cooper, how's the ambrosia going?" Alicia shouted.

Cooper's small hands were frenzied in his efforts to burn through the gate. "Thirty seconds," he shot back.

Under Sydney's barrier, Nightingale came to life. Sydney glanced down, and her mind went to work. *What is happening?*

Reuben pulled on the arm again, and the fabric went taut when the arm thudded against the barrier.

Almost there, Reuben told himself...

From within the dome, Nightingale's arm shot up and grabbed onto the fabric, laying fingers directly across the length of the bandage and pointing their fingertips directly at the small space where the bandage punctured through Sydney's field. Reuben felt the heat before he saw it. Nightingale sent a bolt of superheated plasma right into the intersection of Sydney's plasma shield and the bandage. The shield popped like a balloon, and the fabric was burnt away, suddenly freeing the thief. Reuben took the blast in the shoulder. He grimaced as it seared across his suit and knocked him on the ground.

Sydney leaned back as her field disintegrated, and Nightingale threw a kick from the ground. The blow landed right into Sydney's unprotected stomach. It hit her like a cannon and toppled her. No sooner had Sydney hit the ground, than Nightingale had sprinted away.

Cooper shoved his hands through the molten gate. The heat of the plasma burned away some of his glove, which didn't register until he touched the crystal.

His bare skin came in contact with the ambrosia crystal, and he felt like he was plugged into a light socket. Every single hair on his body went upright an instant before he felt the current rush through him.

Energy snaked through his arm, surging up his shoulder and tapping into his plasma.

Both he and the ambrosia sparkled as crystallized red plasma glittered around him. His body was alive with energy like he had never felt before. He was all-powerful, all-knowing, and distracted.

Cooper's temporary power boost was put at bay when Nightingale sent a boot into Cooper's face. Cooper crumbled to the ground. His clawed hands went wide, and so did the crystal.

"Guys," Reuben shouted from the floor, recovering with short pained breaths.

Jordan and Alicia spun away from Goldtears' prone body as the ambrosia crystal spun above them. Before they could regain their stance, Goldtears shifted from between them and reappeared right underneath the falling crystal with gloves off and his bare hand raised to catch it.

"No!" Jordan screamed.

In unison, Jordan, Alicia, and Sydney used their respective Gifts and launched themselves at Goldtears. From behind his sorrowful, porcelain mask, his eyes were scrunched in a smile.

They were too late.

The crystal landed in his bare palm, and an instantaneous red light swelled around his body in a celestial storm of light and sound. His arms bulked with fresh multiplying plasma, and the room flashed blood red.

From the ground, Reuben checked his arm panel, and his plasma levels were dancing wildly across the screen: from 65,000 to 85,000, then peaked to a terrifying 103,000. Reuben opened his mouth to warn them. But he, also, was too late.

Goldtears snapped his fingers, and the world around them changed.

Jordan, Alicia, and Sydney were closest and felt the first change. It felt as if they had suddenly been grabbed by an invisible current. All three had launched themselves at him, but the powerful blast sent their bodies reeling backward. Then the second wave came stronger than the last and more violent. They were no longer being sent backward, they were being hurled away. The last thing Jordan remembered was the floor rippling...He thought it strange that the carpet was rushing against them. Then the plush red carpet split under the force of the third wave and shattered the concrete beneath it.

Jordan stopped trying to regain his footing because *the floor was gone.*

Everything exploded in a rush of the red tidal wave. The precious exhibits imploded, sending pieces sprawling around the building. The carpet was torn to shreds; concrete was reduced to chunks; the walls ballooned outward as if trying to contain a tornado, and the second floor plummeted into the first.

The security guard crawled backward as he saw the floor drop into clouds of dust. Despite the agonizing pain in his belly, he rolled up and over, crawling along the shattered ground attempting to stay ahead of it as it dropped in sheets below him. The guard, with one last grunt threatening to nearly tear himself in half, lunged from the floor and threw himself to the other end of the hall. As he landed, the place where he had been inch-worming seconds before was no longer there.

He hit hard and felt waves of screaming pain. He simmered and steadied himself. The attack, explosion, or whatever it was, had subsided. The gem vault on the second floor was vomited onto the first floor, and clouds of dust rose past him and into the moonless night.

He risked a glance over the crushed edge and into the darkness.

Then there was silence. A long, unsettling silence.

Then the screaming started.

A deep, hollow scream clawed out of Sydney's chest and vibrated through the darkness.

Battalia had come to only seconds after her body slapped the marble floor of the museum lobby. An instant later, the lobby was decorated with the second floor as an avalanche of debris crashed on top of her. Sydney figured her force field had gone up by instinct to protect her from the brunt of the attack. She wasn't sure where her friends were, or even if they were alive. As the rumbling subsiding and the rubble settled, she wasn't sure she was even alive.

Sydney couldn't breathe. She coughed, and nothing in her throat moved. She coughed again and attempted to run her tongue around her mouth, but it was full of dust. Sydney coughed harder and spit out the paste that had begun to congeal in her mouth.

Battalia tried to rise but felt a weight, unlike anything she had felt before, on top of her. She sent plasma into her arm, and with a couple of unladylike grunts, she heaved a pile off of herself. In moving, she felt something tear deep inside her.

Sydney screamed when she felt her leg burn with piercing intensity. She twisted to the side and grimaced. There was a piece of metal stabbing into her thigh. It had punctured her suit and skin. She could feel her muscles screaming as they pressed against the intruder.

Sydney shouted again.

No reply. Just her calls echoing back at her.

Sydney looked across the field of debris. The lobby and the second floor had melded; the museum was devastated.

"Help," she gasped through the dust. "Help."

The word was foreign to her, but she shouted it out into the destruction. She was about to scream again, but she heard someone–they had heard her. Cooper grunted and used his tail to push a sheet of metal and concrete chunks off himself. He rose unsteadily to his feet. Up felt like down; the ground felt as if it was shifting, and he had a throbbing headache in the back of his head. Despite the dizzying storm in his head, Cooper's vision cleared as he heard Sydney call his name.

"Cooper," Battalia pleaded.

"Yeah, I'm here," he gasped, coughing out dust.

"No. Cooper," Sydney called out, and this time her voice was different, alarmed, and shrill – as if she was warning him.

Cooper turned around just as Nightingale materialized next to him. The next thing he knew, he had a fist in his face, and he was back on the ground. Cooper hit the ground hard next to Alicia, who was lying prone and unconscious under debris. Neither moved.

"No," Sydney shouted. "No." She tried to move, but the metal in her leg sent volts of pain rippling through her body.

Battalia turned back to Nightingale, who readjusted the mask, slightly brushed the dusty cloak, and began moving about with an unrecognizable gait. *Injured?* Battalia wondered. Nightingale was not walking with the same ease and grace as before.

Nightingale moved towards Sydney on uneven terrain and uneven legs. Suddenly, Reuben's scaly arm shot out from under the debris and grabbed Nightingale's ankle. If Nightingale was scared, Sydney couldn't tell because Nightingale leaped back and yanked Reuben out from under the debris as if he was the monster from under the bed. He hit the ground, bounced to his feet, converted his plasma into a fireball, and sent it spiraling at Nightingale.

A moment before it connected, Goldtears shifted in the path of the blast and snapped his fingers. The shockwave hit the fireball with enough concentrated force to blow it into embers. The fire blast split into a million glimmering pieces before the rest of the shockwave rocked Reuben off his feet and flung him far. He felt the hit smash into the star emblazoned on his suit then plow his consciousness from his ravaged body.

The weary thieves turned toward the ruined entryway. Sydney studied them when they walked past. The taller one was holding the ambrosia crystal in a gloved hand. Whatever immense power they had moments ago had faded.

"Stop," Sydney hissed. "Stop."

They paused and stared blankly at the source of the sound. Sydney twitched on the ground, wanting more than anything to tear this blade from her leg and stop them, but the pain overwhelmed her and kept her pinned.

Battalia croaked, "No. No. Fight me. Fight me, dragger."

Goldtears looked down at her with what seemed to be pity, then gave a nod and retreated. Goldtears and Nightingale turned back to the door. Only a few feet from their great escape, the ground shifted under them. The pair stepped back, and Jordan rose from the ground, shedding debris from his ruined body. He was bleeding from the side of his head. His face was pale, and he was covered in dusty debris. His chrome armor had taken a real beating. It was cracked and sliding off of him, and his suit had tears all along it. The star in the middle was dented and askew.

Jordan stood on the brink of passing out, but he was standing.

"Where. Are. You. Going?" Jordan heaved.

The criminals didn't move. Jordan was the only thing standing between them and the door, but he struggled to stop himself from spinning, while also catching his breath. He felt like his stomach was left on the second floor.

"C'mon," Jordan seethed.

He tried to raise his arms, but they gave out halfway. *Move. Move.*

"C'mon," Jordan shouted.

Jordan stood upright and used his shoulders to help pull his arms back up to a boxing stance. He wobbled on his feet. His whole body swayed loosely, while his hands balled into fists. Jordan tucked his elbows into his ribs. His eyes flashed gold as he tapped in and commanded them to come at him.

"Come on," StarLion roared.

Jordan's body exploded with golden light, and he leaped at them, despite his whole body protesting in agony. He barely got a foot off the ground when Goldtears snapped his fingers at Jordan. The red shockwaves throttled Jordan in mid-air before hurling him like a rag doll in a corner of the lobby.

No. No. Sydney shuddered. *Get up. Get. Up.*

She lunged as best she could from the floor but felt a stinging well of pain spill from her leg. She hollered and collapsed back in the debris; she grabbed her leg with both hands and then looked around wildly for the thieves.

They were gone.

"Get back here," Sydney shouted. "Get back here."

In the distance, she heard sirens. Sydney rolled across the ground and flinched as another spike of pain threatened her leg.

"Stop. Stop it," Reuben spat as he clambered from out the darkness.

He stumbled towards Sydney then dropped down on all fours next to her. For a moment, they didn't say anything; they just held each other's gaze. They had survived, but at what cost? Sydney flinched again under the pain and the stress.

"I gotta pull it out," Reuben explained.

Battalia bit her lip, turned back to him, then nodded. "Do it."

"On three." Reuben crawled next to her, put his normal hand on her leg, and with the other one, he gripped the twisted metal growing from her leg.

"On three," Sydney repeated.

Reuben prepared himself, gave her a comforting nod, and redoubled his grip on the metal.

"One," they said in unison.

Sydney closed her eyes, bracing herself for what was coming next.

"Two," they echoed, and Reuben tore the metal from her leg. Sydney screamed and threw herself at him. Reuben wasn't sure if she was trying to punch him or hold him, but she fell limply over him. Reuben examined the metal shard. He decided it was best that Sydney didn't see it, and tossed it away.

Now the real hard part, Reuben told himself.

Sydney pushed herself off of him, and he held her gaze as he told her, "I have to close the wound or you're going to bleed out."

*Close it? He means cauterize...*Sydney glanced down at the hole in her leg and quickly calculated that –*He's right...*

"Do it," Battalia whispered, harshly.

Reuben nodded and raised his hand. It morphed into a series of cascading scales that poked out of his arm.

"This is gonna hurt you, a lot more than it hurts me." Reuben grimaced with the familiar pain.

"You don't scare me anymore," Sydney repeated.

Sydney shuddered and braced herself once more. This time she held onto him for support. They held each other's gaze, and her face went rigid. Reuben felt his palm heat up and begin to steam in the moist air.

This is gonna sting. Reuben stared at her. *You know.*

She nodded. *Duh.*

Reuben grasped her thigh with his searing hand and pushed his palm flat against her wound. He felt her skin ripple and pop. Sydney screamed in shock then passed out in his arms. He pulled his hand back and sent the plasma away. Sydney's chest was rising and falling, but she wasn't responding.

Reuben turned and saw he was the last cadet standing. He peered around the ruined room, and his mind was forced back to that terrible night. He was back in his house as it burned down. He wasn't holding Sydney; he was holding his brother. It wasn't police sirens coming around the corner, it was fire trucks.

Suddenly, he wasn't a soldier. He wasn't a cadet – he wasn't even a demon.

He was just a boy amid another tragedy.

So he did now, what he did then..."Help."

"Impact Knee!"
-Jordan Harris

CHAPTER THIRTY

The Third Strike

That night felt endless, yet it had ended with dust and blackness.

Jordan had lost consciousness, but he was able to recall flashes of events that felt like a nightmare. He remembered hands on his shoulders, pulling and dragging him out of the museum – or what was left of it. He remembered the lights of an ambulance and voices, distant and murky. Then back to darkness. He could recall that much entirely. There were other moments when he simply felt himself lying in the darkness, not even sure if his eyes worked.

And then pain. He acutely remembered a sharp pain in his ribs like he had swallowed a ball of needles. It hurt to breathe for a long, dark moment, before he felt a soft touch, then warmth. The warmth melted the needles, then dissolved them completely into the darkness.

The voices seemed to come from everywhere and everyone, but he couldn't identify any of them. He thought he heard Darius. He thought he heard Khadija. Then, for a brief moment, he thought he heard his parents. He recalled struggling to lift his head to find the sources but found he couldn't. It was too dark. It was too painful, and they were too far away.

Then, he found light. Or rather, light found him. Jordan pushed towards the surface of his mind's eye and saw a light welcoming him. He pushed towards it, then struggled to lift his eyelids. He thought he might even have to tap into his plasma to lift them, but thankfully, grudgingly, his eyes opened to the light.

Jordan's world came back into focus as sunlight through a stained glass window beamed down softly on his face. It hurt to see. He felt a sharp pain down the back of his head. He tried to turn his head, and his body protested with agony. It didn't just hurt to see, it hurt to move. Jordan coughed hard and felt the remnants of whatever had assaulted his ribs spike through him. He sighed, controlled his breathing to lessen the depth of the pain, and sank back into his bed.

From what he could tell, he was in the Fort Olympus Infirmary. He had seen photos online, but waking up here was certainly a bewildering experience. He peered down the hall as far as he could without reigniting the pain, then he turned the other way and stopped. Not out of pain or exhaustion, but surprise.

Khadija was sleeping on a chair right next to his bed. Her mane of bushy black curls caught the light and framed her face in a golden light. She looked at peace. Jordan studied her for a beat.

Khadija was wearing sandals and her pajama sweats, a familiar sight for Jordan.

She came here at night. She must have heard. Jordan felt a wave of despair wash over him as he realized, *She must know we lost.* Then another wave shot over him. *The others. Where is my team?*

Despite the pain, Jordan suddenly shot upright and looked around the infirmary. Though the other beds were empty, he suddenly realized they were not alone. Darius stood at an adjacent window, suddenly aware that Jordan was up. Darius turned to face him. From what Jordan spied in the man's eyes, he could tell – things were about to get worse.

"Morning," Darius said softly.

Jordan hadn't expected such a subdued start from Darius. *He's not mad...He's disappointed.*

"She's been here for the past two days." Darius nodded at Khadija. "We should let her sleep."

Two days...I've been out for two whole days?

"I'm sorry," Jordan replied hoarsely. He suddenly felt like his entire mouth was again filled with dust. He coughed, then swallowed the pain.

"No," Darius whispered. "No more apologies from you. You failed. This isn't just about you having three strikes now. You put the lives of other cadets on the line, and they're lucky to be alive too."

"I was trying to do the right thing."

Darius studied him, unsure.

I'd much rather he be shouting than whispering, Jordan realized. His uncle looked him over with his almond eyes, before looking away in disgust.

"I should never have involved you," he spoke to the floor. "The deal is off."

As Darius spoke those words, Jordan felt his world go fuzzy. For a second, he could swear he had been caught in another shockwave attack and sent spiraling. But no, he was seated in a hospital room as his uncle laid out his future.

"In a week, you'll report to the juvenile facility, and you'll spend the next five years in adamant cuffs; no powers, no friends, just time to learn from your mistakes."

"No. Please. Darius," Jordan called out.

At the raised sound of his shout, Khadija woke and blinked to life.

"J?" she said, her voice hushed.

Jordan reached for her, took her hand. She took his head in her arms, but Jordan kept looking back at Darius.

"Darius, wait," Jordan pleaded.

Khadija looked from Jordan to Darius' back as he retreated towards the doors. *He told him...*

Khadija wanted to pull her brother close, but he was still calling after their uncle.

Jordan pushed the pent-up pain into his voice. "What was I supposed to do?"

Darius stopped at the door.

"What happened to 'be your own hero'?" Jordan cried out. "What happened to not turning your back on your family?"

"You may be family," Darius looked them over for a long reflective moment, and then added, "but you're no hero."

With that, Kinetic nodded at them, then stepped out. The door shut softly behind Darius, but to Jordan, it felt as if a wall had suddenly been erected between them. He was gone, and Jordan was once again at the mercy of what he couldn't control. He felt his chest twist and his heart strain. Next, he felt Khadija wrap her arms around him. He closed his eyes, going back to the dark. He felt his heart thump wildly, and a new pain swept him. But the voice, the voice he heard was crystal clear.

"It'll be okay," Khadija whispered in his ear. "It'll be okay." She hugged him close, and despite her warmth, he could feel her arms tremble.

Jordan felt empty, as if he wasn't walking, but rather drifting, through the courtyards of Fort Olympus. He was sure he was moving but wasn't sure how or under what influence. Thankfully, Khadija kept a hand on his shoulder and guided him. He felt the world slip away much the same as when he shifted. One thought kept coming back to him out of everything Darius said.

They're alive, Jordan repeated to himself. *He said that, right? He said that we were all lucky to be alive. I gotta talk to Cooper and find out what happened.*

Jordan blinked, and somehow he was in the Apollo Barracks elevator with Khadija. How and when he had swiped them in, he couldn't recall, but the card was in his hand. He looked up at Khadija for a moment to ensure she was indeed still there. She smiled down on him, and he returned it weakly, feeling shell-shocked.

Jordan walked down the hall, and Khadija stopped to take a call. Jordan felt himself swim down the hall, reach their door, swipe through, and drift into his dorm.

Cooper was gone.

Wait...Wait...Darius said he was alive. Jordan felt his senses and equilibrium returning as he made his way across the dorm room. *But where is he?*

Then Jordan saw it.

A note.

A simple yellow piece of paper was left atop the dresser. It almost blended in with the pale yellow wood. Jordan stalked over to it and gently took the note in his hands. He almost feared reading it but was relieved when he saw it was only one sentence. But that one sentence was a gut check.

"I'm no hero."

Jordan gripped the letter in his hand, and he felt his world spinning once more. His chest heaved like the needles had returned with a vengeance. But there was no warmth to dissipate them this time. There was little he could do to stop it.

He dropped out. Jordan felt his legs buckle, but he caught himself on the dresser. *He dropped out because I nearly got him killed – again.*

There was a gentle knock on the door frame, and Jordan suddenly regretted leaving the door ajar for Khadija to just walk back in. He heard her enter then stop when she realized...

"Where's your roommate?" Khadija asked.

"He's gone." Jordan repeated, "He's gone."

That was all Jordan could say. He began to clean out his side of the room too.

Sardonically, most of Jordan's belongings had not been long removed from their bags. When all was said and done, his clothes and things had only been unpacked for two weeks. They easily found their way back into their bags. After shaking some feeling into his arms and the rest of his numb frame, Jordan carried them across the courtyard of Fort Olympus, passing the ruined Astro statue, the graveyard, and the courtyard where he and the other fifty-nine students were made cadets.

Jordan scoffed *Guess it's fifty-eight now.*

His macabre thoughts were interrupted by a familiar voice.

"Cadet," Vermillion's voice reached him.

Jordan and Khadija stopped at the large man's approach.

"Squad Leader Holt," Jordan greeted him.

"I heard what happened," he said softly. "I'm sorry."

"Yeah. I – I messed up."

Vermillion thought about his words for a moment. He looked from Jordan to Khadija, then back to Jordan. In this light, Jordan could see welts across his face. Sleepless nights and stress were written there for all to see.

"You did what you thought was right," he explained. "But – this world – this world abides by so many laws and so much red tape, it's hard to really know what's right and wrong."

"Modern heroes, right?" Jordan chimed.

"Well, I'm glad to see you learned something," Vermillion quipped.

There was an awkward silence, and at that moment, Jordan spotted Carnage's large frame walking across the courtyard. *He's limping...*

Vermillion put his hand on his shoulder. "Pay him no mind. I'll be sure to keep an eye on him."

Jordan peered up at him. *Does he know?*

"When you come back, find me," Vermillion urged. "Like I said during our first day, the world needs heroes now more than ever. We – we both lost people on the Green Night, so we know."

Vermillion softly nodded at him as if to confirm it without saying it. *We both know what it's like to lose people.* Jordan nodded back.

"You'll be back; the stars shall will it," Vermillion said. "Astra Inclinant."

"Astra Inclinant," Jordan repeated.

Vermillion nodded at Jordan, then patted him again on the shoulder. At that moment, Jordan realized Vermillion had a bandage on his palm. Vermillion nodded politely at Khadija, who returned the gesture. Khadija and Jordan made their way through the main courtyard toward the main gate. It felt like years had passed since walking through those gates for the first time. As they passed the Zeus statue, shining radiantly in the morning sun, Jordan noticed another figure in the gateway.

Alicia.

She's still here. Jordan, despite himself, smiled.

Khadija looked between the two of them, and sensing something unsaid, turned to Jordan.

"I'll leave you guys," she said. "I'll get the car."

Khadija and Alicia shook hands. Alicia was surprised at her grip.

"Khadija, I'm his sister."

"Alicia, his former teammate," she replied.

"Okay, Jordan, I'll be back in a second."

"Yeah," Jordan replied, and Khadija rushed off to get the car.

For a moment, neither Jordan nor Alicia said anything. He looked her over and noticed a bruise healing on her forehead.

"How are the others?" he asked.

"How are you?" Alicia pushed.

"Expelled."

Alicia snorted. She had expected a quip from Jordan, but not at this moment. She smirked and flinched. It still hurt to move 48 hours later.

"Well, we're – we're still here. Most of us, at least. Alexander put us all on two strikes, and Cooper–" She trailed off and gathered her words. "Cooper – Cooper didn't say much. You could tell he was pretty shaken up...We all were."

"Yeah, at least you guys are okay," Jordan replied.

Alicia looked down, shuffled on her toes. Not sure what else to say.

"I mean it," Jordan added. "I – I could never forgive myself if something happened to you guys."

"Yeah," Alicia agreed, then gave him a thin smile. "I'm happy you're still here too."

There was another long moment of silence between them, which was quickly shattered when a car horn blared behind them. They both jumped, then turned to see Khadija pulling the car around.

"I guess," Alicia remarked softly, "this is –"

"See you later," Jordan replied. "Not goodbye."

Alicia nodded; she went for a hug, while Jordan went for a handshake. They both blushed and switched tactics; he went for a handshake, and she went for a hug. They stopped, giggled, then finally hugged each other.

"Good luck, StarLion," she whispered in his ear.

"Good luck, Alicia," he replied.

They broke apart and shared a grin before Jordan made a slow walk toward the car. He glanced one last time back at Alicia, who gave him a pained smile. Jordan savored the moment: Alicia, the Zeus statue, and the Fort Olympus campus radiant in the morning sun.

Jordan turned away from it all, committing the vision to memory. Then he walked away without another glance.

The ride home was quiet, and if Jordan was being honest, it was the calmest he had felt in weeks. He sank back into his seat. He wasn't sure if it was because he had slept for forty-eight hours or that he finally had time to sit, but he felt a sense of calm course over him. He wanted nothing more than to just ride with his sister and marinate on his thoughts forever. The way things were looking – he had about five years coming to do that.

When Jordan was back in his old room, he felt that same calm follow him. *Home...For now.*

Jordan had planned on coming back home that first weekend he was at school, but because of the late nights with the team and their tape sessions, he found himself staying the weekend and not even missing this place. As he settled, he absorbed it all with a new appreciation.

He shut the door behind himself and found himself at peace. *Alone...for now.* As he looked up at the posters of Kinetic, he found the vise in his chest again; a pressure that twisted around his lungs and clawed deep into his despair. His breath became heavy and pained. He felt like he was submerged underwater. Jordan reached up, grabbed the poster by the face, and tore it down. He felt better. Then he tore it in half. Like a swimmer barreling to the surface, he clawed at every image of Darius around the room. He tore down another, then another, then another, refusing to look at his uncle's face any longer. With every tear came more relief. He tore them all down until his walls were bare like the prison walls would be.

Jordan collapsed back against the door and squeezed his eyes shut. He couldn't bear the world outside anymore. His breathing was too frantic, too pained, too short. Even as he closed his eyes, it only brought flashes from the last two weeks. Goldtears, Nightingale, his friends being wheeled out of the museum, his teammates who he learned to trust and vice versa, then Darius turning his back on him – it all hit him in a rush, and he snapped his eyes open. Nowhere was safe.

Make it stop, Jordan pleaded to his body. *Please.*

Then a revelation hit him. There was something else of Darius' he still owned. Jordan dug into his duffel bag and pulled out the signed Kinetic gloves. They were torn and frayed. Even the phrase on the back had been scratched horribly.

Be your own hero, Jordan thought. *What a drag.*

Jordan tossed the gloves into the trashcan, along with the rest of his Kinetic merchandise. As Jordan collapsed onto his bed, one final thought crossed his mind: *Free...for now.*

As he felt sleep carry him off, he once again drifted into the dark, distant place.

Jordan slumbered and felt his body rise and fall with the flux of gravity quaking. He was drifting; he could tell, but he didn't fight it. He imagined a few days from now wearing adamant handcuffs. They would stunt his Gift, and he was going to miss this. Jordan felt himself bump against the ceiling. He opened his eyes and found himself face to face with the Regulus constellation.

*Regulus. One of the brightest star clusters in the sky...*Jordan mused. It seemed so long ago when he had thought of the hero name he shared with Darius. It came to him while standing in this room, looking over the combat suit Darius gave him. It all seemed so long ago.

There was a knock at the door, and Jordan reversed the gravitons to send himself back down to his bed. He landed just as Khadija poked her head in, afro first. It was night now, and the starlight with the ambient streetlights reflected off her smile.

"You're up?" she asked.

"Yeah," Jordan replied with a yawn.

"Well," Khadija smiled, "you have a visitor."

Jordan looked up, and Khadija opened the door for Nathan to peek his head in. Jordan smiled at the sight of his old friend and climbed out of bed to meet him.

Jordan soon found out Nathan wasn't the only call Khadija had made. Pizza arrived soon after. The two friends sat at the table, enjoying pizza and catching up, while Khadija poured soda for them in the kitchen.

Nathan took his phone out and showed him grainy news footage of Jordan and the rest of the team being carried out of the museum. Jordan took the phone and studied the footage. *Oh, wow, so it wasn't just ambulance lights. There were news cameras too.* Jordan saw his own body being carried out on a stretcher; it was so surreal that he almost didn't hear Nathan's questions.

"This is you, right?" Nathan asked, leaning in to whisper.

"Uh–" Jordan paused. A lie was the first thing on his lips, but –

"C'mon, man," Nathan pushed. "I'd recognize those shoes anywhere."

Nathan paused the video right on footage of his black and gold Zeuz Airwalkers. Jordan smirked; there was no hiding it from him. He felt the urge to lie drift away, replaced by a sense of weightlessness that telling the truth brought him.

"Yeah, that was me," Jordan confirmed.

Nathan's eyes lit up. "Oh my God – Oh my Zeus, you're a hero."

"Was," Jordan corrected. "I got kicked out. I failed, and uh – I'm done."

Before Nathan could reply, Khadija returned to the table with their drinks. "Okay, cola for Nathan and orange soda for Jordan."

"Thanks," the boys chorused as she walked off.

"So...uh...what happened?" Nathan cautiously asked.

Jordan took a sip of his soda, enjoyed the silence for a moment, and then answered, "I was – I was trying to catch these two guys–these two thieves–and it didn't work out."

Nathan nodded, accepted this with growing curiosity, and leaned back in his chair. "Do you know who they were?"

"I guess." Jordan shrugged. "They were wearing masks most of the time."

"But they were Vespers? What were their powers?" Nathan asked.

"One was – a tall guy with shockwave powers and red plasma. The other was a girl or a guy. Hard to tell. But definitely a small person. "

"Hmm, like your height," Nathan joked.

"No, like your height," Jordan shot back with a laugh, "and – uh – they had green plasma and the Gift of invisibility."

"But you didn't know them?" Nathan asked.

"No. There was a teacher I suspected. A big guy. A Vesper who had been released from prison and Lucas, an elf."

"Get out. An elf. An actual elf?" Nathan marveled. "Tell me about him. What was his Gift?"

Jordan took another sip and paused to think. "He had green plasma, like the shorter masked one – but I don't think he had the Gift of invisibility. In fact, we got into a fight one night, but they caught us, and I got my first strike."

Vermillion and Rhea stopped Lucas and me that night. Jordan thought it over. *I didn't even hear them coming. Lucas didn't either. Like they had...*

"J?" Nathan pulled him away from his thoughts.

"Yeah, our fight, we got stopped by two Espers on patrol...They came out of nowhere as if they were...*invisible.*"

Jordan put his cup down, then felt that familiar twist in his chest. Something was brewing.

Could Rhea have been invisible? Jordan queried.

"J? What's wrong?" Nathan leaned back in to study his inquisitive face. "Who stopped you?"

What was Rhea's gift? Wait. What was Vermillion's gift? Jordan found blanks for each question, but answered Nathan's question. "A professor and his student...from the Taurus Regiment..."

"Oh, was it Vermillion? I heard of him." Nathan squealed with excitement. "He's got that red hair and is freakin' cool."

Red hair. Which means he's got red plasma, Jordan realized with increasing certainty. He placed Vermillion's mental image over the tall masked man...it was a rough match, but a match nonetheless. They were about the same size.

"But Rhea –" Jordan gasped out loud.

"Wait, wait, wait." Nathan put a hand up. "Who is Rhea?"

"She – she's another student. She uh – she –" Jordan stumbled over the words, before blurting out, "We met before – we met before I started."

"What? Where?"

*At the memorial. She was there, with me...*Jordan's mind flashed to that night the names on the wall – the way she snuck up on him – the way the ambrosia crystal in the wall reflected in her eye. *She was staking out the place.*

Jordan felt his world twist. *No. No. No. But she has black hair, so her plasma is* – Jordan thought back to when Rhea sent a green beam of plasma into Lucas' phone case. *Green.* Then he remembered their talk, days ago, when she said, *"He even made me dye my hair."* Jordan shot up from his seat, spilling his soda and scaring Nathan.

"Jordan," Nathan shouted, looking up at him.

A deep-seated panic seized Jordan's chest. He struggled to focus. He looked at Nathan and willed his world to stop spinning. He focused back on all he had learned about Vermillion and Rhea. *His face was bruised today, and his hand. His hand was* – Jordan reflected on the fight in the museum when the larger man grabbed the crystal...

It was the same hand Vermillion had bandaged this morning. Jordan finally looked back down at Nathan and the mess.

"Go home," Jordan warned, "as fast as you can."

Then Jordan bolted off down the hall. Nathan sat, fearful and confused, before grabbing his crutches and following down the hall.

"Jordan? Jordan, wait!" Nathan shouted.

Khadija poked her head out of her room to see Jordan and then Nathan walk by. "Hey, hey, what's going on?" she asked.

Jordan rushed into his room where he quickly dressed.

How could I be so dumb? How could I not see it? He stuffed his Zeuz Airwalkers on.

He paused. *I'm gonna need some protection.* He grabbed his ruined chrome-plated armor and shoved it over his shoulders, yanking it as tight as he could. It was crooked and loose in some areas, but it was going to have to do. By the time he was dressed, Khadija and Nathan were gathered in the doorway.

Jordan stopped as he realized his hands were bare. Jordan turned back to the trashcan and saw Kinetic's gloves looking back up at him. *Be your own hero,* Jordan mused. *Even if you get caught.* Jordan snatched them up and stuffed his hands into them.

They're going to the memorial. They got two pieces already...

Jordan ran to his window, threw it open, and Khadija's words stopped him.

"Jordan?" Khadija's voice snatched him from his thoughts. "What is going on?"

Jordan eyed Khadija and Nathan, the two people he cared most about in the world, and, though what he told them was simply the truth, it came out as a prophetic warning.

"There's gonna be another Green Night."

CHAPTER THIRTY-ONE

BAD MOON RISIN'

Alicia found herself back in Alexander's office. She thought it was cramped last time in the company of just Jordan and Alexander. It was now even more uncomfortable with Alexander, Reuben, Sydney, and Darius pushing the boundaries of personal space. Alicia sat in one chair – the same chair she sat in a few days ago when Alexander accosted them for failing to catch the thieves.

Currently, it was Darius who lectured them. Also, for failing to catch the thieves.

In the other seat, Sydney sat with her leg elevated on a futon. She had a white wrap binding her injured leg. Reuben had given her his seat when she joined them. After some awkwardness, she finally accepted it and elevated her leg. Alicia was fairly certain the leg wrap was the same material as the bandages Reuben used. Alicia sighed; she wished she had gotten some of that for her ribs. They were only bruised, but still buzzing...

Darius stood before them. "I just wanted to apologize on behalf of my nephew. I know he meant well, but –"

The big man stopped when his cell phone buzzed. He pawed his body, found it, and checked the caller ID: Jordan.

Speak of the devil. He grimaced, then declined it.

"Sorry," Darius said. "I know now I shouldn't have involved him. He wasn't ready for this, and now I'm not sure if he ever will be."

Even amid his turmoil, Jordan caught sight of the beauty that was the Houston skyline. It always simultaneously took his breath away and filled him with unbridled joy. Each of the lights represented a life. Thousands, if not millions, of lights illuminated the skyline, and he swore to protect them all. Even when he was just a vigilante, he had the same feeling. It wasn't just petty crime anymore; it was serious. A second Green Night was coming. All these lives and all these lights were in danger of being extinguished.

Jordan was mid-leap crossing a pair of high-rises when he heard the phone go to voicemail. His heart was pounding in his ears, while his feet pounded across rooftops. He checked his phone again and indeed the call had been ignored.

"Oh, c'mon," Jordan growled.

On his way to the park, he scanned for another number when his screen went black. Khadija was calling him again. Jordan glanced up; he was running across the face of a building and approaching a bridge. He sprung off the side of a high-rise, leaving gold lights in his wake.

Not now, sorry. Jordan canceled the call and went back to searching the contacts in his phone. The extra fabric of his gloves did little to help his scrolling. Jordan looked up, feeling the wind and seeing light speed toward him. Jordan twisted toward the bridge, and he suddenly realized it wasn't just a bridge. It was an elevated section of train tracks that traversed the city. He turned to the right, and his vision was overwhelmed by a rushing train coming his way. A wall of light and steel bore down on him.

Jordan landed on the train tracks. An instant after his toes made contact, he exploded a set of gravitons under his feet, sending him spinning wildly up and over the tonnage of steel that threatened him. Jordan landed on the train platform and sent patrons scattering.

"Sorry," Jordan chimed. His sneakers buzzed with energy before he burst off into the night.

*I can't believe they didn't tell me...*Alexander looked over his wards then to Darius. *Then again, Darius and Titanus didn't tell me, either. What else are they hiding?*

Alicia scanned the room and saw new worry lines in Alexander's aged face. *He's pensive. Something besides us clearly has him rattled, but what?*

Her thoughts were interrupted when her ribs reminded her of her own problems. This time it wasn't just a twinge from the fight, but her phone buzzing. Alicia reached down, grabbed it from her pocket, and answered.

"Jordan?" Alicia asked.

The room hushed. Everyone turned to face her, and she put the phone on speaker.

"I figured it out." Jordan's voice echoed through the room, reaching their concerned faces. "Rhea and Vermillion are the thieves."

Darius bristled, then placed his head in his hands. *What now...*

"Jordan, what are you talking about?" Alicia asked.

Jordan was out of breath, panting into the phone "The last ambrosia stone. It's at the memorial. Rhea and Vermillion are gonna steal it."

This sent ripples of thought throughout the room as everyone realized the depths of the situation.

"Ask Alex; he'll know. Ask him what Vermillion's powers are," Jordan snapped into the phone.

Alicia and the others turned to their Squad Leader.

"Shockwaves," Alexander and Jordan said in unison.

Wait a minute...Red plasma. Shockwaves, Alicia realized with growing certainty. Before Darius could push his way into the conversation, his phone rang too. He checked it again; it was Khadija. *Finally, some answers.*

"Khadija?" Darius picked up in a fury.

"Jordan ran away. I think he's headed to the memorial."

"What?" Darius growled. "Where is he?"

"I don't know right now," Khadija explained. "But he said something about another Green Night."

Darius felt his blood run cold and then turned back to Alicia as Jordan's voice practically screamed out of her phone.

"I was wrong." Jordan admitted. "Lucas wasn't the shorter one; it was Rhea. Rhea has green plasma, and I'm pretty sure her Gift is invisibility."

Darius glared at Alexander, who shared the same shocked expression.

"Khadija," Darius responded gravely, "we're on our way."

Jordan found out the hard way that there weren't many buildings around the memorial. As he leaped from atop an office building onto a high-rise, he had to surf down the face of it, before landing on the sidewalk. Then he trekked through the forest surrounding the park for a few heart-pounding minutes before he finally came to the clearing.

He stopped.

All was normal out here. It was a weeknight, so there weren't too many people. Just a few walking their dogs, some sharing a meal, and a handful of others somberly paying respects to the memorial.

They're not here yet, Jordan realized. *I need to get to that crystal first.*

Jordan bolted across the grass, passing some unsuspecting park-goers who glanced up in confusion. Jordan bounced past them, his heart racing away and leading him forward. Jordan skidded to a stop at the memorial. As the somber visitors noticed him, they quickly stepped back.

"Sorry," Jordan chimed nervously. "I'm in a rush."

Jordan reached for the ambrosia in the marble wall when a familiar voice echoed behind him.

"I got to say, I am impressed with your tenacity," Vermillion's voice slithered across his neck.

Jordan stopped his reach for the crystal and slowly turned around to see – nothing. But he could sense them. He had heard him, right? This wasn't just a fever dream he was experiencing? Vermillion was here and so was Rhea...

"Squad Leader Holt," Jordan called out.

Then as if Jordan had summoned them, the two thieves materialized standing only six feet away. Jordan took in their masked faces behind their hooded robes, and he felt his plasma flex on its own, ready to engage.

"Well, I guess the masks are of no use now," Vermillion said before he reached up and removed his mask and hood in one motion. Nightingale looked up at him for confirmation.

"It's fine" Vermillion nodded. "He knows."

Nightingale removed the intricate bird mask to reveal Rhea standing next to her Squad Leader. Both thieves were finally unmasked. Their plan was partially foiled, and his team had been informed, but this didn't make Jordan feel any safer.

"Please, stop this," Jordan pleaded.

"The world needs this," Vermillion replied.

"J, we're not going to hurt anyone," Rhea said softly.

"No. No. Do you know what these crystals are?" Jordan asked. "They're ambrosia."

"Yes, we know what they are," Rhea snapped back. "And we're collecting them for ourselves, so no one can have them. To keep the power in the right hands."

"You could have said that before," Jordan growled.

"I thought you of all people would understand." Vermillion stepped past Rhea. "I mean, we're all vigilantes, aren't we? We had to take justice into our own hands."

Jordan's eyes narrowed. "You can't just steal them."

"Yes, but we already have two." Vermillion parted his cloak to show that there were two crystals wrapped in a little hammock of thread at his waist. "No thanks to you."

"But the Green Night..." Jordan gasped, trying to put two and two together.

"We're trying to prevent it," Rhea said. "To save lives."

Jordan paused. *Wait...wait...Was I wrong? Was I wrong the whole time? Are they vigilantes just like me?*

"I'm sorry," Vermillion purred. "But I had to lie."

Jordan paled. *I was wrong this whole time.*

"I'm sorry, Rhea." Vermillion spun his hand around and pierced her with a bolt of blood-red plasma. "But a second Green Night is happening."

A sharp, wet gasp leaked from Rhea's mouth before she hit the ground in a heap. All around them, alarmed patrons ran in various directions. Everyone was running, except Jordan, who stood frozen between Vermillion and the final crystal.

He...he shot her. Jordan felt his stomach twist in knots. *He betrayed her.*

"What – what are you doing?" Rhea choked from the ground as her Squad Leader loomed over her.

"For too long, the world has been without heroes" Vermillion spoke as if he was in class on simply another lecture stage. "I needed to create another Green Titan. I needed someone with green plasma."

Vermillion blurred away. Then suddenly he was holding Rhea by the throat with one hand, while he cupped one of the ambrosia crystals in the other.

"To create the Green Night again, I needed you. I needed you and your green plasma."

He's going to turn her into the Titan. Jordan's mind spun to catch on. *But why?*

"Then with the other two crystals, I'll boost my own plasma and become the Red Titan to defeat you and save the city," Vermillion announced. Rhea's horror painted her face and contorted her features.

Stop, Jordan urged. *Stop him, Jordan. Stop standing here and –*

With one gloved hand, Vermillion leveled the crystal toward Rhea's face. It tapped against her forehead, and the effect was instantaneous just like before. Her green plasma lashed out and latched onto the ambrosia crystal, quickly pulling facets of ambrosia into her body. As the crystal was pulled into flesh, her flesh began to mutate into green crystals that sprouted from her body.

"I'm sorry it had to be like this, Rhea," Vermillion admitted. "But the world needs a new hero on top of the throne of the world. And for that, it also needs a villain."

"Stop," Jordan whispered, before exploding, "I said – STOP."

Jordan bundled as many gravitons as possible under his feet and launched himself, like the train he dodged earlier, right at them. Vermillion whipped around, just as Jordan blitzed right into both of them with a shoulder ram. Rhea and the crystal dropped to the right, while Vermillion and Jordan tumbled left.

Jordan hit the ground and rolled hard. His first instinct was to return to his feet and look for–

"Rhea," he called out.

She hit the ground and the ambrosia crystal rolled away from her mutated body. Like a fungus, jade crystals were creeping and multiplying on her body. Meanwhile, the ambrosia crystal, which was the size of an apple, shrank to the size of a walnut. It was disintegrating, leaving behind glittery dust.

Jordan and Vermillion spotted it at once, and both shifted in the crystal's direction. Jordan got there first, but a bolt of red plasma punched him backward. Vermillion appeared and grabbed the ambrosia crystal, right as –

Poof.

It evaporated like sugar in water, floating away in a cloud of stardust right past Vermillion. It was gone, but the second crystal was still attached to his waist. He reached down for it, but Jordan was back on him. Their gloved hands fought over the crystal and tumbled to the ground again.

"I will be the hero the world needs. I'll save millions." Vermillion spat in his face.

"By killing her?!" Jordan didn't mind the sweat on his brow or the spit in his face. All he cared about was taking this crystal from him.

"Someone needs to be the one to make the necessary sacrifices." Vermillion's breath came out hot in his eyes. "I told you – I told you – heroes have to make the hard choices. I am the only one who can make them. I'll be the strongest hero in the world, I will crush any villain who comes our way. I'm trying to protect – "

He's insane. He's insane. Jordan didn't bother to hear the rest; his point was clear. "You're not protecting anyone."

Jordan felt a knee plow into his ribs, but he refused to let go, even when the pain blossomed again. He dropped down but held on for dear life as he grappled with Vermillion in a losing battle.

"Or maybe I was wrong," Vermillion spoke between their arms. "Maybe we aren't alike at all."

"I won't let you hurt her," Jordan declared.

"Oh, Jordan." Vermillion leered down at him as his eyes reflected daggers of moonlight. "I think you should worry more about yourself right now."

Jordan let his adrenaline spike, then felt another knee driving into his injured midsection. He felt his fingers slip from the ambrosia crystal. While he was used to grappling mentally with a hundred anxious arms of his anxiety, he found himself applying that to this physical battle with Vermillion. He felt as if he was fighting – and losing – two battles. Metaphorical hands grabbed at his heart, while the gloved hands before him fought for his grip on the precious stone. *No. NO!* Jordan told himself. *Don't let go!*

Just as he felt both sets of hands winning and pulling away from him, a force stronger than both stormed across the clearing. Vermillion turned in time to see Darius plow into him; the contact was fist first in an explosion of purple plasma. Vermillion tucked his elbow into his side to block the hit, but it did little to cushion the almighty blast that came from the kinetic energy packed into Darius' punch. Vermillion felt himself go airborne, and he and Jordan were torn apart by the arrival of Kinetic.

Jordan hit the ground and rolled up to one knee, ready to fight, when he realized –

"Darius?!" Jordan shouted.

Kinetic, his mask down, turned to face his nephew. His brown eyes, which had refused to even look at Jordan earlier today, finally took him in.

"We got your call," Darius said.

We? Jordan flinched as he felt the echoing footfalls of many others heading his way. Instantly, he felt a hundred arms of his own demons retreat. Jordan breathed a heavy sigh of relief; he even felt his eyes well with tears. *They came...*

Jordan turned to see the entirety of the Freshman Leo Squad, minus Cooper, racing his way dressed in their combat suits, their stars over their hearts reflecting the starlight above. Alexander was in the lead. His plasma wings left twin arcs of flame as he swooped low over the field, rolled into a flip, and landed in a crouch next to Rhea. Battalia pulled up the tail end, the pain in her leg evident on her face.

Alicia and Reuben were running neck and neck. Jordan caught their eyes and gave them a nod. *Thanks.*

"Sup?" Jordan asked as they made their way over.

"Nothing much. You?" Alicia chimed.

"I'm glad you came."

"I'm glad you called," Reuben replied.

Jordan glanced over to Alexander, where Rhea's body was lying prone. The green crystals that had grown from her body faded into the wind, much like the ambrosia crystal only moments before.

This – this is just like back then. Alexander peered down in horror. *Just like that night.*

"Red Wing," Jordan called out. "He – he wanted to turn her into the Green Titan, then turn himself into one to defeat her. That's why he needed the crystals, so he could – so he could kill her and pretend to be the hero."

"He was gonna use her," Alicia realized in disgust.

Jordan nodded, somberly.

"Be the hero?" Vermillion's voice exploded from across the field. "I am the hero. I'm the only one willing to make the true sacrifice."

Darius approached him calmly. "Vermillion, please –"

"No," Vermillion interrupted. "You – you more than anyone, know what's happening out there. Crime is skyrocketing. People are dying. And you cape-draggers can't do anything to stop it. We all lost something during the Green Night, and it's only gotten worse. Not you, nor these – these kids are gonna be able to stop the tide of what's coming. But I can."

Oh no. Where did it go?! Jordan whipped around for –

The second ambrosia crystal was already in Vermillion's hand. He raised it high for everyone to see. It was the crystal from the museum. While it was still the size of an apple, it appeared as if someone had taken a bite out of it, and there was plenty of power left inside.

"I can," Vermillion repeated as he slipped his glove off. "I will be the hero."

"No." Jordan gasped.

Vermillion gripped the crystal in his full fist, and instantly his red plasma flowed into it. After a century of lying dormant, the ambrosia surged to life, giving up its body, converting from matter to energy in seconds as if it had been waiting for this moment for millennia to give birth to the horror that lay dormant in its host. Drawn to the flow of energy locked within the depths of its being, the crystal sent pulsing newborn celestial plasma rushing into the depths of Vermillion's being.

Suddenly, a bolt of crimson lightning erupted from his body and punched into the sky. The illuminated Vermillion swelled to a hot-white color that made it impossible to look at, then his whole frame disappeared behind waves of energy.

Up above, that single red bolt spider-webbed across the night sky, like a bloody aurora borealis. The sky began to twist into a haze of black and red energies coiling together over the city of Houston. Black pulsating clouds pushed against each other as if trying to smother one another, while the heavens began to bleed.

"Red...It's the..." Jordan gasped. "It's the Red Night."

CHAPTER THIRTY-TWO

The Red Night

A red thunderbolt tore across the sky.

Sydney shifted her weight from her injured leg to her good one, but even that wasn't enough to stabilize her against the winds rushing from the red core of energy surrounding Vermillion. She put her arm to her face to keep the wind and the dirt out of her eyes.

Something else caught her eyes. Her wrist panel was glowing and beeping as it calculated the rise in Vermillion's plasma levels: 95,000 –> 100,000 –> 120,000.

"Guys," Sydney screamed. "His power level is rising."

Vermillion cried out from behind his energy cluster, and the heavens groaned with him. Darius and Alexander glanced at their wrist panels, then at each other. This was growing exponentially worse.

"Cadets, get out of here," Darius shouted over the rising scarlet winds.

"No," Jordan shot back. "We're not leaving."

"This is our fight too," Alicia pressed.

Darius and Alexander exchanged glances. They were going to need the help. Darius nodded at the teens and turned back to Vermillion, who had been swallowed by energy whirling in orbit around him. Dirt, stone, and debris formed a vortex of carnage. As the red lights refracted in the tumbling vacuum of space and dirt, Vermillion had become the sun of his own blood-red solar system.

Across town, and only a few seconds before that conversation happened, Cooper was having a good night. He had moved back home, and his parents gave him a dozen bamboo cupcakes, so he could eat his feelings. For two days, he had focused on getting back into the swing of things.

He helped them open the pastry shop in the morning. He always enjoyed the smell of the sweets when he opened that door. He helped his parents mix, bake, and decorate. For most of the days, he found himself happy and content. He didn't have to worry about the hundred other things that came with being a hero.

As the workday came to an end, he helped his parents pack boxes of cupcakes into the company car. The car had been towed two nights ago on account of the connection with vigilante activity. His parents had to pay $400 to get it out of impound, which Cooper swore he was going to pay back by working at the bakery.

His mom handed him a box of cupcakes. He took it and slipped it into the back of the company car. He scoffed as he realized that his friends would never have appreciated it. Reuben did though; he had mentioned that the car smelled like sweets. Now that Cooper thought of it, maybe that had been an insult.

His thoughts were shattered by a red lightning bolt exploding in the sky with enough force to send a rippling thunderclap through the city. His ears felt it before he did. Cooper's parents were shocked. They threw up their arms and spun on their tails, before collapsing.

"Mom. Dad," Cooper exclaimed and helped them to their feet.

Cooper tried to steady himself. Windows had been shattered. Car alarms were going off, and the sky looked as if it had been stabbed, the heavens leaking red. Cooper made sure his parents were okay and peered up at the sky.

"What...What is this...?" Cooper followed his ears to the source of energy. *The memorial...*

For a long moment, Cooper couldn't move.

He simply stared up into the sky. Just like ten years ago – like the sweeping cold wave of a former terror, Cooper realized what he was looking at. The sky was as black as he remembered, impassible. Unread-able. The stars were smothered. The hair along Cooper's body rose, and it wasn't just from the static in the air. The energy in the air was the same sickly color he remembered. Except what once was green, was now red. What was once a distant turbulent memory, was now their stormy present. And who was once a child – was now a hero.

All at once, Cooper set off in motion.

Jordan glanced around and spotted the very last of the civilians running away. What must have started out as basic panic had turned into life-saving measures. People sprinted into the forest to save what and who they could. Just beyond the forest, the city loomed. Over the city was the daunting threat of the Red Night. His mind went back to Khadija and Nathan, who he had left in the city. Worry exploded in his mind.

"We have to keep the fight here," Jordan shouted. "We can't let it get to the city."

"I don't think that's going to be up to us to decide," Reuben replied.

"We have to contain him," Alicia said.

"That didn't work last time," Battalia fretted, with a sense of dread.

Alicia heard the anxiety in Sydney's voice and suddenly felt the same weight of defeat that had enveloped her two nights ago. Whether this was Vermillion's conscious doing or the ambrosia itself, Alicia didn't care. She'd push through if it meant getting a clean shot at Vermillion. She glanced at the city. She thought back to her parents, Astro, her friends, family, and all of them, now counting on her. *I...I won't get this chance again. I have to tell him, now.*

"Red Wing," Alicia shouted out to him.

Alexander turned to face her, with one eye on the energy core cocooning Vermillion as broiling windswept waves brushed past.

"I – I – I chose my hero name," Alicia declared.

"Now isn't the time."

"We may not get another chance."

She's right. Alexander smirked.

Alexander fully turned to face her, feeling the weight of the moment on him. He had felt this same weight on the Green Night when he lost his most prized student. Now he looked upon that pupil's sister, who had followed her brother's footsteps, hand over hand. She was standing before him on the Red Night. If this was the last moment the two of them were to share, he was going to hear her.

"My hero name is–" Alicia took a deep breath, then declared over the storm, "Meteora."

Alexander heard her declaration, rolled it around his mind like a fine wine. *It's original. It's not tied to Astro, or to me. She's found herself.*

"The world is gonna know your name, kid." Alexander nodded somberly. "I'll make sure of it."

Alicia nodded back at him. Her conscience was clear. If the worst happened, at least she got this one moment with her Uncle Alex. Above them, the Red Night unfolded like a flower with obsidian nimbus petals, cursed with rippling shades of red plasma. A field of storms blossomed in the heavens and threatened to swallow the city in their embrace.

He tried to kill his own student. Alexander seethed as he thought back to the promise he made to Vermillion back on their balconies only a few days ago. Alexander squinted as hot, billowing wind tossed dirt across his face. Before him, the supernova of man and the divine intersected. Alexander leaned into the hot wind and prepared to make good on that promise.

"How did you defeat him last time?" Darius asked him.

Alexander opened his mouth to reply, but a sudden thundering between them sent a renewed wave of dust and wind into the air as – Titanus shifted into place between them.

"We beat him," Titanus answered. "We threw everything we had at him till he cracked."

"Good." Darius grinned, seemingly unfazed by his arrival. "Ground and pound is my specialty."

Titanus glanced over at Alexander, and the two survivors shared a solemn nod, ready to once again fly into battle together. The big man flared his electric blue aura and felt his plasma kick into motion, churning within his aged body. Titanus turned around to the cadets and found Sydney standing at his side.

Sydney absorbed the sudden entrance of her father with bated breath. His skill with plasma-shifting was such that he seemingly teleported into the midst of the park. He arrived, took a hold of the situation, and joined seemingly mid-conversation. A revelation came to Battalia: *It's like he was here the whole time.*

She stood in the midst of the crimson storm watching his back. His back that she had seen with her own eyes long ago: scarred, sunken, bruised, but impossibly strong. While most saw him as a modern-day Olympian, she, more than anyone, knew that was just a title. When she saw him walk, she noticed the unsteady stride, the almost imperceptible stumble, and she realized something else:

It's going to be up to me. It's going to be up to me to protect him tonight.

"Dad," Battalia whispered.

"I'm right here." His usually solemn demeanor softened at seeing her. "And I always will be."

"Just don't embarrass me," Sydney smirked. "And don't go easy on me either, old man."

Titanus fought the urge to laugh. He knew her words' underlying meaning and took them to heart. *Don't go easy on me just because I'm your daughter. Don't go easy on me tonight just because you love me.*

Titanus glanced over at Jordan, and the kid met his gaze with golden light sparkling in his eyes.

"Your parents would be proud," Titanus remarked.

Jordan felt a sliver of cold silver run down his spine. *My parents? Did he know them?*

"His power level is slowing down," Alicia declared.

They checked their wrist panels and watched as the numbers rose, then dropped down to 120,000.

Kinetic cringed and thought back to Kurikara and his power level of 300,000. *It would be much easier if you were here, friend.*

Jordan froze. *120,000?! No way. No way. He's a monster. He's stronger than all of us.* Suddenly, Titanus' voice called out to them and calmed them.

"We're in luck. It's only a fraction of the Green Titan," he said. "Ambrosia can only multiply one's power by a certain amount. It's not half a million like the Green Titan was. It's less than half. We can win."

Well, at least something is going right, Jordan grumbled to himself.

All questions and time for talk were over when the energy surrounding Vermillion finally burst into red starlight that sparked around him in a fading wave of red lights. The rest of the lights cleared, and Vermillion stepped out before them. He was caked in crystal as if his body had been chiseled out of it. Vermillion no longer resembled anything human. He was a walking supernova of blood-red energy.

The team of seven stood ready in front of the monument for the seven Olympians. They were the last line of defense between the Red Titan and the last ambrosia crystal. The red crystals were so dazzling, it was hard to believe there was flesh and blood underneath them. "Team Leo, on my mark, engage the enemy with everything you've got," Titanus called out.

The cadets braced themselves, summoning up everything they had learned in the past two weeks. This included everything they had gleaned from each other and all they had lost on the Green Night. With that in mind, they tapped into their plasma and readied to face the Red Titan

"All-Fathers, guide us to victory," Titanus whispered, before crying out, "Go."

Titanus felt the flow of his Gift blaze through his body. The blood of the God of Justice, Foresti, the blood of the All-Father, Odin, their Gifts, and their actions had brought him this far. He was the new God of Justice, the new God of Light, the last of the All-Fathers, and he swore on their names that no one else would die tonight. He tapped in and felt the usual flicker of blue behind his eyes before he felt himself swell. Well, not himself, but his spectral self. A terrifying, ghoulish personification of his psyche materialized above him, towering to the heights of the nearby redwood trees. Titanus thought back to that night ten years ago when he was much younger and much less scarred. His thoughts at this moment mirrored those on that night: *Sydney, please stay safe. I'm not letting a loved one die in my arms again.* Then, with his spectral form roaring to life above him, he threw his hands out. Titanus hurled a fist the size and length of a redwood tree plummeting down right at Vermillion's new form.

Darius and Red Wing led the cadets, and they crisscrossed under Titanus' fist that rushed past them. Darius shifted, expending some of his pent-up kinetic energy to blitz past Alexander and reach Vermillion in the blink of an eye. He came down on him, and, up close, he realized Vermillion didn't have a face, merely a blank slate of red crystal that covered his head.

How does he see? Darius asked himself.

Darius skidded to a stop and changed plans to release a blast of violet plasma that soon joined Alexander's own blast of red plasma. Both attacks hit Vermillion and detonated against his body before the cadets followed suit. Just like they had trained mercilessly against the nitrile walls, they sent beams of their own plasma soaring into the smoke cloud that contained Vermillion. In an instant, he was hit with an artillery of plasma blasts that bombarded his body in a chorus of explosions. The attack was punctuated by the glowing projected fist of one of the strongest Espers in the world. It landed with enough force to quake the ground beneath them.

Titanus trembled. Though his fist had reached him, there was something wrong. There was no impact. The smoke evaporated to reveal that Vermillion was holding back the fist, the way one would block a train – both arms up, body at an angle, pushing against it with heels dug into the ground.

"Sydney," Titanus shouted.

Seconds later, Vermillion's body flickered with a pulse of red energy, and he sent a blast of scarlet plasma into the empty blue projection of

Titanus' arm. Like filling a balloon with fire, the projection swelled with rumbling clouds of flames, before bursting into a series of crushing explosions that littered the area. Titanus shut off his spectral form and leaped to the side, avoiding a rush of flames as it broiled past him, before devastating the nearby forest.

We can't let up, Jordan said to himself, and then shouted, "Go."

With a simmering burst of gravity from under his feet, Jordan jettisoned his way right at Vermillion. Sydney and Alicia, using their respective Gifts, launched themselves right behind Jordan. Alicia used a burst of neon purple plasma that sent her sailing up and over the clearing, while Sydney used her force field much like a trampoline to rebound from the Earth into the air.

Huh, where'd she learn that? Titanus wondered, watching his daughter take flight – with a hint of envy.

All three teens came down on Vermillion's crystal form, storming him with their attacks. Since his face was encased in red diamond, it was tough to see if he was surprised or even overwhelmed, but his body language said all they needed to know. As the trio came at him, slipping and flipping over each other and throwing strikes, he easily batted them away. It was like watching a fight on fast-forward, yet Vermillion knew every beat and hit before they even threw it.

He's blocking us. All of us. Battalia groaned and sent Jordan bouncing off her force field, sling-shotting him right back into Vermillion's defense. Alicia rolled away to avoid Jordan soaring over her and met Vermillion with a pair of plasma-packed punches.

They thudded against his frame, and Jordan paused. *Nothing. It's like hitting that nitrile wall.* An instant later, Vermillion's arm came around and smashed Jordan in the chest. Jordan had rushed to pad his body with plasma, but it did little to help. Jordan felt his body give way midair. He was weightless and not by choice. As he felt the wind surging past his ears, he realized he couldn't even breathe. First, he saw double, then nothing as the night blurred past. Finally, everything went black as Jordan slammed into the dirt, crumbling into the ground.

Jordan gasped back to life, greedily taking in air. He blinked away the darkness and realized he had been out for a few numb seconds. *He sent me flying, with one punch – with just one punch. I – I can't get hit like that again.* Jordan painfully and carefully unfolded himself from the Earth. He felt as if his lungs had erupted and were threatening to spill out of him. Unable to stop his vision from swimming, Jordan pressed both hands to the ground to steady himself and the world at large. His breath came out in ragged, hot gasps. He had often wondered what it would be like to face Kinetic or Titanus, but as the effects of a single punch kept him hunched over, he realized he wouldn't last a second with them. Then as he clawed back to his feet, a second and more terrible thought hit him: *I can't let anyone get hit like that. If Vermillion gets a serious blow on any of them...*He paled seeing Alicia racing at Vermillion...*They'll die.*

He's too fast. His senses must be off the charts. Alicia saw Jordan get swiped away before she blitzed into the fray, throwing a pair of punches. Vermillion caught her hand like a vise an inch from his face. Alicia sent plasma into her fingers and formed a broiling plasma blade that she forced into his head.

Dodge this. Her plasma blade touched his face and delivered a concussive blow. She was sure her wrist would have broken if Vermillion wasn't holding it so tight. She felt her arm twist, and she went with it. Vermillion's other hand was in front of her face now, brewing with swirling red starlight. She tried to move, but he had her arm locked in his grip.

Alicia's vision flashed red before a familiar voice called from above, "Get away from her."

Alexander swooped in on flaming wings with his own plasma blade, simmering like the beam of the sun itself. Vermillion tossed Alicia aside and reached to grab Alexander's blade in both hands. Alicia tumbled back. Sydney and Jordan were at her side in an instant.

"You good?" Sydney asked.

"He blocked," Alicia stammered. "He had to block his sword."

Battalia looked down on her in confusion. *What does that mean?*

"He's afraid – He's afraid of getting hit."

Alexander, wings aflame, hovered over Vermillion for a moment as both of their red plasmas clashed. Then, with a simple thought, Alexander morphed his wings into an assortment of energy tentacles that he shaped into spikes and quickly sent them spiraling down on Vermillion. As Vermillion felt the spikes punch against his crystal hide, he sprinted backward, but Alexander didn't let up.

"You betrayed her," Alexander raged. "You were going to kill your own student."

Alexander pointed an accusatory finger and sent a dozen spiked energy tentacles bulleting towards Vermillion. The Red Titan backpedaled to avoid the crimson weave of spikes. He slid backward but couldn't find a way through, so he did what came naturally: he destroyed them. Something deep within the Red Titan hollered before he snapped his fingers at Alexander. The very air seemed to ripple and quake. Then an assortment of blazing circles filled with plasma rushed forth, tearing apart Alexander's plasma spikes, then smashing into him.

"Uncle Alex," Alicia screamed into the smoke cloud that had enveloped her mentor.

Alexander flipped in mid-air, landed on both feet, and just as his feet hit the ground – Vermillion was on top of him.

My God. He's faster than –Alexander never got to finish that sentence because the Red Titan sent a clean right hand right into the star of his chest. He took it like a battering ram and heard something, or *somethings*, crack within him. He slipped out of sight and out of consciousness as he was launched back.

Before anyone could check on their mentor, Reuben soared in, his scaled arm ready to return fire.

"Get down." Reuben's voice came from behind them then he dropped down in front of them. *Keep your friends at your back and your enemies to the front.*

Reuben's arm exploded into scales that churned his plasma into flames and exploded from his palms.

Vermillion had barely dealt with Alexander when flames, bristling like jet fire, smashed into him. A blazing hurricane swept Vermillion away in a wash of orange and red clouds that smashed across the clearing. The teammates huddled behind Reuben as he unleashed another volley of hellfire into the inferno that held Vermillion.

Suddenly, there was a thunderclap, and rippling waves of plasma-induced shockwaves rushed out of the blaze, sending it all back the way it came.

No way. Reuben gasped as his own flames bore down on him.

Sydney grabbed his shoulder and yanked him under the umbrella of her Gift to save them all from the crashing flames. Alicia huddled next to Jordan. Then as the world burnt around them, her gaze found Astro's statue in the distance. Her brother's face and memory flooded back to her, followed by a plan.

"Battalia," she shouted up to her, "I got a plan."

The two girls shared a desperate look, then worked to get the plan in motion. Meanwhile, Titanus and Kinetic blitzed down the field, rushing through the flames to get in close to Vermillion. The red wind battered them as they battered Vermillion. The pair swung in with dual haymakers, and Vermillion caught them both in his hands. But they were ready and switched stances. Like boxers working the same heavy bag, the pair went at him with jabs and strikes that echoed in thunderclaps across the memorial. From a distance, it appeared like small explosions were going off in the memorial. Blow after blow, packed with plasma, detonated off each other, generating great shards of light.

He's just absorbing these attacks. There has to be some limit, Darius realized as he filled in a space Titanus missed with his own punch. Vermillion's hands were a blur as he matched their blows with equal defenses every time.

Let's see him block this, then. Titanus threw a punch with his right.

Vermillion caught the blow with his left hand but didn't see Titanus' left coming up for a body blow. Seconds before impact, the assault ballooned into his giant spectral fist that hit him like a rocket at point-blank range. Vermillion tried to block it, but it was the equivalent of trying to block a torpedo at launch. He was smashed off the ground and sent spinning into the air.

He hit hard and skidded backward. He righted himself, seemingly still impervious. His body flashed with a series of pent-up energy clusters before he fired a blast of red – THOOM. Sydney's force field dropped right around him in the same second the blast left his hand, trapping him in a tomb of his own broiling energies. A muted explosion detonated inside the field. Sydney quivered; she felt the limits of her Gift pushed to the breaking point.

Sydney's heart pumped the same blood as the Norse God of Light, Baldur. As her Gift weaved to life around the Red Titan, she felt his lifeblood surge within her. She hung onto her force field thinking back to her ancestors and gripping down on Vermillion as if she was trying to contain Ragnarök itself.

"I can't hold him for long." Sydney groaned.

"On it." Alicia threw her fingers in the air and sent as much of her plasma into her fingertips as possible–as her brother had done so many times before. Jordan and Reuben helped steady her against a whirl of energy as a violet star ignited in her fingers.

Titanus skidded to a stop. *What is she doing?*

Darius knew what she was doing. *Crescent Cutter.*

Alicia let it rip and tore the star down. She sent a buzz saw of vibrating fuchsia energy cleaving across the field right at Vermillion, who was currently trapped in an inferno of his own making.

Battalia felt her Gift tear open as she released her hold on Vermillion and the ballooning flames just as Alicia's attack slashed into him. Both attacks exploded simultaneously with Vermillion caught in the middle of the erupting force field and the incoming plasma cleaver.

The heroes ducked for cover to avoid the impact that rattled through the clearing; trees shook, eardrums thrummed, and the clearing rocked. The sheer force of Alicia's attack forced a pressure wave that sent the explosion up into the air diagonally.

Vermillion stumbled out of the flames, and the heroes were assaulted with two truths:

One, he was still standing.

Two, his chest had cracked.

"A crack," Jordan gasped. "We cracked him."

Alexander blinked himself back to consciousness, hearing his students talking. He rose and felt the weight of time and the many battles of hero service ripple through his bones. He shook it off and continued.

"But he's still standing," Reuben gasped.

"Not for long." Alexander, despite how his body screamed when he shifted across the clearing, was not going to let him stay standing.

Alexander met Vermillion just outside the smoke cloud and drove his blade into the heart of the spider-webbing cracks. Though both men were tiring rapidly, Alexander had a team to support him, while Vermillion had only himself.

"I promised to kill you and –" Alexander sneered. "I'm a man of my word." Suddenly his plasma blade evolved into a column of pure explosive plasma – *a cannon*. It launched into Vermillion's chest cavity with an explosion of simmering concussive force that blasted him and Alexander in opposing directions.

As Vermillion stumbled back to his feet, the spider-webbing cracks widened, getting closer to his body. Pure energy was leaking from him as if a spotlight was issuing from his chest.

"Stay on him," Titanus urged the tired heroes.

They blitzed across the field in a mosaic of multi-colored plasma trails, all orbiting around Vermillion.

"Enough!" Vermillion bellowed from within his suit.

Vermillion clapped his hands together, and the detonating shock-waves that followed exploded like cannon fire along their bodies. They were uplifted from their trajectories and sent smashing back the way they came, landing hard on plasma-packed backs and shoulders to cushion the blows. In an instant, in one single attack, Vermillion had turned them all back. Reuben curled into a ball and clenched tightly when he was sent rolling backward. As he hit the ground, he felt the armor shred as dozens of layers of Titanium mesh and military-grade rubber gave way to the grating force of the simmering plasma blasts and to the pulverizing friction of the Earth.

Darius was the first to rise. He paused and noted a couple of things: One, he had missed something due to being unconscious, and, two, Jordan was stirring next to him.

"You good?" Darius asked.

Jordan nodded, refusing to show weakness now. "Never. Better."

Darius could read the lie on his face, accepted it, and told his own. "Me too."

Uncle and nephew turned toward the Red Titan, who stood in the midst of the destroyed clearing, still looking stable, despite a crack in his chest.

"How dare you," Vermillion's voice echoed out.

He's out of breath, Alicia noted. *He's in pain.*

"I'm trying to save the world," Vermillion spat.

"By turning an innocent girl into a killing machine?!" Jordan shouted.

Reuben scanned the clearing. Rhea still lay prone on the ground several yards away. Miraculously, they had managed to keep the damage away from her.

"A necessary evil," Vermillion shouted.

"There's no such thing." Alexander rose to his feet, shaking off the pain in his bones.

"Hypocrites," the Red Titan declared. "All of you. How many rules have you broken to save a life, huh? How many rules?! You – you haven't even told the world the truth of that night."

Alexander and Titanus shared a nervous look.

"The number of lies you told about the Green Night pales in comparison to what I have done."

Alicia glanced up at the bruised-black clouds and bleeding skies. She matched them against her own developing wounds. *Girl, same,* she nonchalantly admitted.

The teens looked breathlessly over at the two Olympians. In the distance stood their own statues, proud as ever, but the slouched shoulders and pained faces of Titanus and Red Wing told a different story.

"How many rules did you break that night?" The Red Titan simmered. "How many people had to die? How many of your friends died to protect you?! Tell me – how many rules did you break?"

"I've got a lot of rules." Alexander's face twisted before he re-materialized his plasma blade.

"And you're gonna have to break them to stop me," Vermillion spat.

His body flashed with light before he threw his arm – not at them – but behind himself, where he sent a bolt of red plasma punching into the city. Something within Houston howled with terrible light and sound. An explosion burst forth, erupting deep within the metropolis. Whatever Vermillion had hit had released a chorus of shouts, and alarms rang from the depths of the city.

"No," Alexander shouted.

Now illuminated by the burning city behind him and the red and black storm clouds thundering above, Vermillion looked like the true nightmare they feared. The death bloom of the storm kicked up above them. Though they were in the eye of it, the rushing hot winds and crackling crimson thunder spiked all around them, all radiating from the forces at work within Vermillion.

"Help them or stop me," Vermillion sneered. "Heroes."

THE RED TITAN

Hero Alias: CLASSIFIED

Height: 7'2

Weight: 350

Birth Date: CLASSIFIED

Plasma Color: Red

Plasma Level: 120,000

Gift: The Red Titan's enhanced powers allow them to generate shockwaves of various destructive levels. Secondly, they can lace their shockwaves with plasma to amplify their explosive force.

CHAPTER THIRTY-THREE

Red Titan Rock

"Cadets," Darius shouted. "Get to the city."

"But you're going to need our help," Reuben shot back.

Before Darius could argue anymore, a voice came from their comm units in the collars of their combat suits.

"Stay where you are," Cooper shouted.

"Coop?!" Alicia asked.

Cooper, in the heart of the city, deftly zoomed through traffic in the company car. He zoomed past curious pedestrians and fellow drivers. After stopping at his house to change into his suit, he now found himself driving down the streets toward the chaos.

"I'm on my way there. I can handle the evacuations," Cooper shot back.

His eyes went wide, and he slammed the brake pedal to the floor as he reached a wall of traffic. The car skidded to a stop, and the tiny button nose on the hood tapped gently against the bumper of the car in front of him.

"The light's green," Cooper shouted.

Yet, the car in front of him didn't move and neither did the ones on either side of him. Cooper slapped the dashboard and sighed. They weren't going anywhere for a while, no matter what color the lights were. Cooper scrambled out of the car; a scent caught his nose. *Smoke.*

"Cooper, can you handle the evacuation yourself for a while? I'm sure other heroes will join you shortly," Alexander informed him.

"Yes, sir," Cooper said, then signed off.

He turned his nose down the block, and, sure enough, blocks away, he spotted the cloud of thick black smoke issuing from the side of a building. Leading the way were cars stuck in the bumper-to-bumper traffic. The only way he was going to make it was on foot – or, rather –paw. Then Cooper spotted several pedestrians who were also on foot but running away from the fire.

He'd be the only one running towards the danger.

Red lightning hurtled through the black skies, followed by a wind shear that swept over with enough force to nearly topple him. A red-wine ocean churned above them and cascading pillars of ruby light lanced through the shattered horizon. Waves of hot wind carried screams from the depths of the city while cymbals of detonating energies rang out in hollow shrieks. Cooper steadied himself, and his breath, and stared along the stretch of cars.

In the far distance, a column of twisting smoke rose from the impacted area, churning to the sky as if to touch the storm itself.

I'm the strongest. I had the highest plasma levels, Cooper said to himself. *I'm not much in a fight, but I can still be a hero.*

Cooper bounded across car tops, then rooftops. He flung himself into the air, taking leaps and bounds as if the city was his jungle gym. Cooper pushed through a wall of wind as another gust pushed against – then past – him. Cooper gained momentum and tossed himself into a streetlamp, which he used to swing on and hurl himself into another lunge.

"I'm the strongest," he called out.

He came down atop a car and then bounced off, flying into the air.

"I'm the strongest," Cooper shouted, making his way towards the flaming building.

Then, impossibly, a voice reached him mid-run, and he flinched.

"Coop," Alicia whispered, "you're still on the line."

Cooper wanted to scream in embarrassment, but he found himself scampering along the face of a building. He had to reorient himself first before he could reply. He scrambled to do both, then slipped back to them. "Oh, sorry. Over and out."

Cooper squeezed the right button on his combat suit and finally heard the line go dead. Cooper came down hard atop of a bank, then, after a galloping sprint on all fours, hurled himself up and over the city, heading towards the chaos in the distance.

Beyond the burning city and the rattled treetops, Vermillion stood before the heroes, his body cracking with crackling energies. As the storm hollered and shook above them, it cast red shadows against the bright lights. For a moment, he felt energy leaking out. He wasn't entirely sure when it started, but he had been reborn from the stars and could now feel himself returning to Earth, so to speak. Vermillion could feel it. The power contained within him and his crystal flesh was slowly dissipating.

Don't they get it? Don't they see that this is for the best? Vermillion thought. *One lost life would save millions. How –how am I the villain here? Didn't they also lose family that night? The world needs a new hero, and if these liars won't step up, then I will. I will stand upon their bodies if I have to.*

Behind rose-tinted armor, Vermillion's gaze fell upon the statue of the former Olympians.

Reuben simmered, feeling his plasma boil just below the surface of his scaled skin.

"Why?!" he called out, drawing their attention to him. "Why didn't you just take the ambrosia for yourself? Rhea didn't have to get hurt."

"Because heroes are born out of calamity," Vermillion replied. "The greater the calamity, the bigger the hero. And there is no bigger calamity than the Green Night. So, I needed her. I needed her green plasma. I needed to create a catastrophe."

"So you could sweep in and play hero," Alexander sneered.

"I had only planned on killing Rhea," Vermillion added. "I guess when all is said and done, I'll have to stop all of you. I'm relieved, actually. It's only right that the former survivors of the Green Night fall tonight."

"And your brother?" Alexander snapped. "What would he say about this?"

Vermillion paused. *My brother? How dare he – How dare –*

"You have no right to bring him up!" Vermillion exploded. "You – you and the Olympians failed him that night. "

"We all failed him," Alexander retorted. "And we have to live with that failure. All of us."

Jordan listened as Alexander's words from earlier came back to him: *"You can't apologize when someone loses something precious...something irreplaceable. You have to live with it and so do they."*

Vermillion paused, chewing on his tongue as he listened to Alexander, before replying mockingly, "It's destiny, huh?"

Alexander nodded, grimly.

"Forget destiny. I am in control now. I will make my own destiny." He raised one clawed red hand. "And I will be the hero that none of you were brave enough to be."

Titanus gritted his teeth. "You're insane."

Vermillion looked over the memorial, then over the seven before him. "I'll make sure they build memorials for you too."

Vermillion had felt impervious earlier tonight, as if his DNA was pure energy. As the battle raged, however, he felt tiny micro-cracks forming in his body. The team's incessant pile of attacks forced those cracks to break into fissures that he felt leak energy out of his frame. He was going to need more power to finish this and ensure humanity was saved. That no weapon formed against him—now or ever– would prosper.

"Power – I need more – power," he raged.

Alexander glanced at the panel on his arm: 120,000 – 110,000 – 90,000

"He's weakening," Darius observed.

"He's stalling," Sydney snapped loud enough to scare her father. "Let's go."

Vermillion sneered behind a cracked red face and saw them rushing his way. *Liars. Hypocrites. Villains. The entire lot of you.* Vermillion didn't just tap into his plasma, it tapped into him, filling him with a renewed wash of energy that swelled within his mind's eye, and spread like a horde through his body. He felt the cross-section of man and the divinity of the cosmos interlace within him anew.

"Come," Vermillion hissed. "I'll build the new monument upon your graves."

Darius took the lead, then shouted back, "Titanus, hit me."

Titanus heard Kinetic loud and clear. *You're as crazy as your nephew.*

Titanus reared back his fists, then sent both of his massive spectral fists launching forward. The teens looked up to see Titanus' colossal arms whoosh above them, then come crashing down into Kinetic's back. As they hit his shoulder blades, Kinetic's Gift blazed to life in a wash of purple flames. He absorbed the kinetic force of Titanus' titanic-sized fists into his body, like pushing two waterfalls into a straw. It filled him with a tidal wave of renewed kinetic energy.

The others shifted in front of Darius and met Vermillion first, engaging him for a beat. That beat was all they needed to give Darius an opening. He slipped in past them, lined up his leg, set his body aligned with Vermillion's, then let his attack rip. Darius drove his knee out and up, sending the compounded torrential force of Titanus' fists right into his knee, and that knee into a powerhouse blow that drilled right under Vermillion's jaw.

Jordan leaped backward while cheering on his uncle, who unleashed his signature move, *the Impact Knee.*

Vermillion felt the blow connect behind his mask, and he was certain that, if it wasn't for his renewed powers, he would have been killed. His brain rocked in his skull. His skull snapped back in his flesh, and a tremor whipped him off his feet, dragging him backward by his head.

Cooper landed on top of a police car with such force that the officers around it jumped. It was chaos outside of this burning apartment complex. There was an assortment of police cars and fire trucks, with echoing sirens and frightened patrons all trying to speak over the sounds of the red storm above.

Cooper let his half-mask obscure his face, hiding his identity as best he could. If it weren't for his tail, ears, and fingernails, he would pass as a normal human.

Okay, okay, speak with a hero's voice, Cooper told himself.

The officers turned to Cooper and looked him over. The lead officer was the first to speak up.

"What are you, some type of squirrel?"

"I'm a hero," Cooper said pointedly, doing his best to imitate Reuben's serious tone. "Is anyone left inside?"

A man wrapped in a medical blanket rushed over to Cooper. His face was covered in soot, and his voice was soaked in desperation. "My daughter is up there. Ninth floor."

The officer turned back to Cooper. "You got this?"

"I got this," Cooper said softly. He cleared his voice and repeated, louder, "I got this."

Cooper looked up the length of the burning building. For an instant, he was a kid again. A frightened kid on the Green Night waiting for a hero to come to get him.

Lion Force, be with me, Cooper prayed, then lunged from the car and onto the brick-face of the building. Catching his nails into the stone, he scaled up as fast as he could. Cooper peered below, where the first two floors were engulfed in flames. He scampered up the next floors: *Five – Six – Seven –*

He felt the entire structure sway and buck as it exhaled a plume of smoke that roared its way out of the sixth-floor windows below him. He felt the impressive heat lap at his tail, and he realized he had to climb faster. *Eight – Nine.*

Cooper tucked inside the window and rolled onto the floor. *Okay, here I go.*

He felt the heat surrounding the building. He landed in a roll and by the time he stood, that heat was smothering him. This building wasn't going to last long. This rescue mission needed to be fast. He searched his way through an apartment bathed in smoke. The heat came down in waves like he was walking through a pressure cooker.

"Hello?!" Cooper called out as he pushed his way into the hallway.

The ceiling was obscured with rolling clouds; so much so, that he almost thought he was looking into the sky for a moment. The paint was melting from the walls, exposing steaming wood and simmering metal piping. Cooper ducked low. *The oxygen is going to be closer to the ground. The smoke will rise, but the clean air will be pressed down.*

"Hello?!" Cooper cupped his hands to his mouth and shouted.

Then he heard a voice faintly call back, "Help. Help."

Cooper whipped around. He had just barely heard her. *Either she's far away or the smoke is getting to her,* Cooper reasoned as he scampered down the hall on all fours.

"Hey," Cooper shouted again.

"Help." Her voice echoed, closer now.

"I hear you." Cooper stopped outside of an apartment. "I hear you."

Cooper didn't bother testing the handle. It was already glowing hot; Cooper sent plasma into his arms and shoulder-rammed the door with enough force to send it cracking back on its hinges. Cooper slid into the room and skidded to a stop.

Part of the floor was gone.

The middle of the apartment had dropped away into a pit that led to nine floors of hungry flames and crushed debris. Cooper's claws bit into the edge and held him back. *This place is falling apart.*

"Help." The girl's voice came bounding from an adjacent room.

Cooper burst into the room. He spotted her hiding in the opposite corner of the room. Much of the floor here had already fallen away too. He studied the burning chasm and quickly developed a plan to get her.

"Hey," Cooper shouted. "Don't cry. I'm here. I'm here to save you."

Cooper peered down again. *This floor isn't going to last long.* He could feel it dip beneath his weight, ready to send him and this girl down into a blazing abyss. Cooper sent an encouraging glance to her. Then he saw her face – her button nose, round wet eyes, and little round cat ears.

She's a Hybrid. Cooper gasped.

Steeling himself, Cooper hopped from the floor and onto the walls. Using his claws as he had so many times before, he clambered across the wall and made his way to her. He dropped down next to her, and *crack* – the floor spider-webbed and dipped under his weight.

Gotta go, Cooper's mind screamed.

Cooper studied her frightened face, then thought to what Lion Force said to him. "You see my ears?" he asked. "I'm just like you. I'm not scared. Are you scared?"

The girl shook her head no, despite the obvious fears.

"I'm Ailurus. What's your name?" Cooper asked.

"Maggie," she purred, weakly.

"Okay, Maggie, I'm going to get you out of here." Cooper gave her a smile behind his mask. "Get on my back."

Cooper ushered the girl on his back, then turned to find an exit. He scaled back across the walls. He heard the room bend and crack as the flooring gave way, and the room they exited plummeted seconds later.

Yeah, time to go, Cooper's mind screamed.

Vermillion felt the Espers charge in with a mass of attacks.

Don't they get it?! He felt a sting as a pair of plasma bolts exploded off his body.

Vermillion swatted Titanus away with a single wave of his hand, sending the legendary Olympian cracking across the ground.

I'm trying to save them. I'm trying to save the world. Vermillion came back under fire, feeling another set of blasts that would have leveled a lesser Esper just pop off his crystal frame. *They'll see. I'll make them all see.*

Vermillion felt the rush of the heroes coming back around for him, but this time he was ready. He generated a densely packed blast of plasma in each palm, filling them with his essence, his rage, and his drive. Then he slammed them together into a thunderclap worthy of his vision. To Vermillion, it was simply a series of waves pulsing against his body. To the heroes, it was a tidal wave of thunder force.

The two energy blasts met in the middle, flowed out in ripples of light that tore apart the very fabric of the Earth. The pressure wave forced the trees to bow before snapping them like twigs. The wave crashed against the heroes in a tsunami of red lights and sound. An avalanche of plasma and crushed Earth swept the team. They were struck and sent airborne, like dolls tossed down a flight of stairs. The plasma wave hit the marble wall like a wrecking ball, shattering it and the names across the razed clearing. The wave didn't stop there. As it tore apart the clearing, then ravaged the forest, it rushed into the city, bringing destruction in its wake.

Cooper was a breath away from crossing the threshold of the apartment when the quake hit. He heard it coming but could do little to prepare for it. The building swayed left then right. Every beam and barrier in the building shivered. Right before he could cross, a pair of flaming beams crashed through the ceiling and cut off his exit.

Cooper felt the building settle, but the door was blocked. He was in trouble.

Jordan smashed into the ground, tossing up dirt with his landing. He tried to pad his body with as much plasma as he could but felt his neck and shoulders crunch hard, before bouncing him to a stop. He flipped hard and shook off the shock that was still rattling his bones. He had been lucky to be farther back when the blast detonated; the others were still skidding to a stop by the time he was standing.

He's still too strong, Jordan said to himself as he examined the blood-red sky. The red lightning hollered above them with enough force to make the stars tremble. Like a sentient being with crimson claws, the energies reached out as if to tear down the moon. Jordan pulled his gloves back on tighter and shoved himself back up.

Vermillion was finally visible. Half his face was visible through a V-shaped tear in his crystal mask. The armor was already sliding off his chest and shoulders in blocks, and the armor on his hands and forearms had been stripped away.

"Power," Vermillion groaned. "I need more power."

That's when they both saw it.

The third ambrosia crystal, which had been placed in the marble memorial, was now lying carelessly in the middle of the field.

"No," Jordan shuddered. "No."

Vermillion's eyes narrowed to slits, and he shifted away. Jordan scrambled to his feet, then raced as fast as he could. He gathered his plasma into his body and shifted himself in that direction, praying he'd make it in time.

THOOM. Vermillion appeared standing over the crystal.

THOOM. Alexander appeared in the air above Vermillion.

Alexander came down on him, sword arm blazing and aiming to sear through Vermillion's neck, but as fast as Alexander was, the Red Titan was faster. He powered a high-density plasma attack into his hand and backhanded Alexander. The blast erupted like a localized thunderstorm and sent Alex flying.

THOOM. Jordan appeared crouched over the crystal.

Got it. Jordan cheered, clutching the crystal.

He glanced up and saw Vermillion lunging down on him, fist pulled back to claw through Jordan's face.

Darius peered up from the ground in time to see Vermillion swing down on Jordan. *No!*

Jordan stared at the Red Titan's scorching hand coming down to meet him. He closed his eyes. Then, he heard a crunch and felt a warm splash on his face.

Am I – Am I dead? Jordan wondered.

"No," he heard Vermillion moan.

I'm alive. Jordan opened his eyes and found himself looking up at Vermillion bearing down on him. Something had trapped his hand, which was now slick with blood.

What – what is that?! Jordan asked.

He tapped his face. Indeed it was blood, but it wasn't his.

Rhea had materialized between Jordan and Vermillion. Her back was to Jordan, and her pale face loomed over Vermillion as his hand was buried in her chest and out her back.

"Rh – Rhea?" Jordan trembled.

She didn't reply, but from the depth of the wound and how Vermillion's crimson fingers were flexing out her back, he knew what had happened. Rhea spat blood, and it sprayed against Vermillion's shocked face.

"You – you," she gasped. "You told me we'd be heroes."

Vermillion's face trembled behind his cracked mask for a moment as something akin to sadness swelled within him. He felt a pit drop in his stomach. *I–I –I thought this would have been easier. That it wouldn't hurt this much.*

"I – I – I wanted to make things right," Vermillion whispered. "I wanted to be a hero, no matter the costs."

Vermillion yanked his arm back and let Rhea collapse into Jordan's arms. Jordan felt her body land on him, but it wasn't until he saw her dull face that Jordan realized how bad it was. He caught her right under the armpits and immediately felt blood slicking her frame and sinking through his tattered gloves.

"Rhea," was all Jordan could muster.

Vermillion stepped back and stared, wide-eyed and guilty, at his hand, now stained with blood.

"Heroes," Rhea whispered, "come in all shapes and sizes."

Jordan felt the weight of the world fall on him, crushing him to the ground as he let Rhea slip from his hands. Jordan laid her down gently, then shoved himself to his feet. His entire body trembled with a rising tide of renewed fury. Jordan looked down at his hand and saw the phrase, "Be Your Own Hero" looking back up at him.

It's time I stopped being a cape-dragger, Jordan realized, *and became my own hero.*

Jordan removed Kinetic's glove and let it fly off into the storm. The wind snatched the glove and sent it spiraling skyward. In his other hand, he felt the ambrosia crystal pulse with energy, seeking desperately to interact with his plasma.

Vermillion turned a pained eye back to Jordan. "I – I was going to give the world a hero."

Jordan dropped the ambrosia into his bare hand and instantly felt their powers interact. His renewed fury was joined by a brand new rush of plasma circulating through him. He felt his fist vibrating in response to the ambrosia crystal feeding into his system. Jordan raised his glowing fist for Vermillion to see.

"You want a hero?" Jordan growled. The ambrosia crystal ignited in his palms in an eruption of light and matter akin to a miniature sun. Like a shower of solar flares, golden light arced off the crystal and weaved into, through, and around Jordan. The newborn energy traced down his body, filled his muscles, and interlaced with his plasma. As it filled his being, Jordan felt the energy plunge deep into his Plasma Crystal and ignite his star-blessed blood –like the birth of a new sun.

"I'll give you one!" StarLion roared.

"You want a hero? I'll give you one!"
- *Jordan Harris*

CHAPTER THIRTY-FOUR

Regulus

Cooper's eyes squinted at the golden light just outside the window. He spun around and peered outside to see the flash ignite in the distance.

Jordan. Cooper gasped.

Cooper squeezed his eyes closed to steady the competing thunderclaps battering his ears. Even behind closed eyes, the skylight flashed ruby red, searing the images of the flaming city in his mind. When he opened them once more, a new shining figure stood in defiance of the red storm. It was in direct contrast to the Red Titan's light, standing aflame against the darkness of the night.

From the ground, Alicia covered her eyes to avoid a wave of dirt and debris that swept over her. She felt it all bounce off of her. Then she lowered her arms and peered out to see lights swarming around Jordan and pouring out of his thin frame. It looked as if he had just walked out of the cosmos and brought the stars with him from the gulf of infinity.

Jordan...What have you done? Alicia worried, then she glanced down at her arm panel and saw his plasma level skyrocketing.

Reuben brushed his black and red locks out of his face for what felt like the hundredth time that night, yet the wind kept gleefully playing with his hair. He didn't notice because he kept his eyes on Jordan.

"Jordan!" Darius shouted over gale-force winds and pounding flashes of light. "Let it go."

The space in front of Vermillion howled like a massive funnel. Ironically, Jordan felt like a funnel at that moment. A funnel for life, power, energy, and light; it was all of those things at once – and yet none of those words could fully describe what he felt. At best, he could describe it as plasma as it all surged within him. His body burned and so did the world outside.

This – this is how the Olympians felt, Jordan thought. *This is how they must have felt before defeating the Titans.*

At the word *Titans,* Jordan opened his glowing golden eyes and focused on the Red Titan standing before him.

He dropped the rest of the crystal. He hadn't felt the pain, but he had felt his skin searing along his fingers and palm. It made sense why Vermillion's hand had been bandaged this morning. Jordan paused, sensing this might just be enough. He felt his body settle as the last of the ambrosia he had absorbed ignited within him. Jordan felt like he was housing a cosmic storm in his small frame; as if the stars moved in currents through his veins, that his heart churned like a hurricane of fire, akin to the sun, and his Plasma Crystal felt like the void of space itself.

Jordan tapped into his plasma again and found not emptiness, but depth. *I – I – I've never felt this much power. I can't find the bottom.* Jordan stiffened as if he had just fallen into the deep end of the pool, with no clue or sight to the floor below.

Jordan peered down the length of his arm. It was sprouting clusters of gold crystals. He could feel them as if they were an extension of himself, like batteries of plasma. *That's it. The Plasma Crystal in my neck is a battery. And the body – my body – can only hold so much, so it adapts. It grows extra crystals to hold all this extra energy and –*

Vermillion appeared, hovering over him, fist pulled back to attack. Jordan willed himself away and felt his body shift away while Vermillion plowed into the ground where Jordan stood moments ago. Jordan's feet hit the Earth and slid backward.

That was fast. Jeez. He felt his bones shake when they took the impact from the skidding and stopping. *It's too much. I'm gonna break my legs before I ever get used to this.* Jordan simmered, feeling his body quake and tremble. *I have to end this soon.*

Jordan glanced up, and Vermillion was blitzing toward him already. At least he thought so. His vision was blurry; his bones were trembling, and a searing heat was building in the base of his neck and into his brain. *This is too much. I'm gonna explode.*

Jordan felt gravitons surge under him. With just a single thought, he had amassed more gravitons than he thought possible. *Just a tap. Just a tap.* Jordan gave them a light tap of his energies, and they exploded under him with enough force to send him spiraling in a corkscrew above Vermillion's swing. The burst of gravitons was enough to kick up a cloud of dust and even give Vermillion pause. Jordan hurtled into the red skies like a rocket. He was accustomed to using his powers to launch between buildings and as he crested from his explosion, he realized he was eye to eye with the Houston skyline. *That was just a tap!?* Jordan felt himself rising to the apex of his fall. *Focus. Focus.*

The city, flaming in the distance, reflected in his eyes. He heard their cries because for ten years they had been his cries. He felt their agony because for ten years that had been his pain. He felt the weight of every terrible moment from the past decade come rushing back to him.

"Not tonight," Jordan whispered. "Not again."

Jordan felt himself dropping and looked down. Vermillion gathered energy under himself then launched up at Jordan, ready to meet him in mid-air.

Focus, Jordan calmed. *One focused blow...*

The burning roof above Cooper creaked for a hot second, then cracked open the next as it spilled flaming wreckage into what was left of the room. Cooper curled Maggie to himself and realized he only had one move left...*My tail.*

Cooper thought back to his matches with Reuben where he used his tail to power through the flames. He sent his plasma into his tail and sent his tail whipping at the debris in front of the door. Currents of red plasma arced wildly around his tail as it smashed through the burnt wood like a hammer. Seconds later, Cooper and Maggie rolled into the hall.

"Hot. Hot." Cooper squealed and blew on his tail until the embers went out.

They made their way into the hallway, but now Cooper was certain it wasn't just the ceiling in the apartment that was coming down. The rest was quickly following.

There's only one way out, Cooper realized.

He turned to the window at the end of the hall and ran at full speed. He didn't risk a look back as a torrent of flaming debris crashed down behind him. He didn't slow when a door was blown open by issuing flames from a scorched apartment, and he didn't exactly know what he'd do once he was nine floors above the sidewalk, but that didn't stop him. He crashed shoulder-first through the glass and let the cold night air take them. He needed a plan, and quick.

Jordan dropped from the sky, like a fallen star, leaving glittering gold in his wake as he plummeted to meet Vermillion. He knew from experience just how much this might hurt since he had broken his arm doing it long ago, but he knew it was worth it. Even if his arm broke – even if every bone in his body shattered – even if he died, he was going to put it all into this one punch.

Jordan gathered gravitons under his fist. *More.* Jordan tapped into his newfound power and pulled as many gravitons as he could from the surrounding area. His mind searched further, and his senses dug deeper as he yanked the foundations of space and time toward him.

My head.

Jordan winced when he latched on to even more gravitons. He had never concentrated this much energy at once, or so quickly. Thanks to the power of the ambrosia crystal, every time he thought he had found his limit, he discovered he could dig deeper. Every time he thought he had picked the last cluster of gravitons, he found more–*more!*

Every inch of Vermillion's body stung: his flesh, his joints, his muscles, his entire body felt as if it had been superheated from the inside. But that didn't matter to him.

All that mattered was catching Jordan and ripping that power from his body. *That power – it's mine.* He needed to unleash that power upon the world to save it. *The throne atop the world, the savior of humanity, only I am brave enough to claim it – That title is mine.* Vermillion's body ached, yet he stretched one crimson-crystal clawed hand toward the sky and the power he craved. *IT'S MINE.*

Jordan braced himself against the pain roaring through his head. *Just bear the pain a little longer. Just a little more.*

Jordan didn't focus on the pain now, only on the pain of the last ten years. With his city burning again, he drew that pain inward. He drew on the pain Alicia felt from the loss of her brother. He drew on Cooper's fear of being a hero. He drew on Sydney's pain for her father and Reuben's pain of being an outcast – all this pain stemmed from that night. As their faces flashed in his mind, Jordan swore they'd never feel it again. All this agony eclipsed the pain of the ambrosia crystal, and he felt a fury swell within him.

From the ruined park below, Alicia stared up in terror as Jordan raced to meet Vermillion. She felt the world shift, and her body grow weightless. All around her, dirt, debris, and crumpled rock began to levitate past.

Gravity. Alicia gasped. *He's pulling at gravitons from everywhere.*

Alicia fought to weigh herself down and to not be pulled into his orbit as energy and debris began to rise past her and the team.

Vermillion felt the gravitons sweep by him, gathering en masse around them like the eye of a grand celestial storm. In an instant, Jordan was blocked from Vermillion's view, and a wall of golden light filled his field of vision. Gravitons, hundreds, if not thousands of them, were blanketing the heavens.

Never again and certainly not tonight. Jordan gritted his teeth, feeling them vibrate with pent-up energy.

Tonight, the heroes win.

Because tonight the stars will it.

Because tonight –

Jordan cannoned his arm down, and the hurricane of golden gravitons came roaring down.

"Astra Inclinant," Jordan roared.

With every fiber of Jordan's energized being, he tapped into the mass of gravitons and gave them one simple command: *explode*. What was once used to simply throw Jordan's tiny frame up and over several feet was magnified a hundred-fold and sent crashing down in a storm of condensed explosions.

Brother – was the last thought Vermillion had that night as the waves of light crashed down on him.

While Vermillion was sure Jordan's punch connected first with his face, the rest of the blows connected all at once, seconds later, in a pressure clap unleashed by the forces of the universe smashing atop one another – with him in the middle. As the strike connected and the gravitons exploded, they flashed from gold to a kaleidoscope of avalanching colors. The cumulative concussive force of a thousand explosions went raging through the night and crushing Vermillion's tattered frame underneath.

A flash of golden light burst across the park and city as it went from a red night to a gold night in the breath of a second. Jordan felt the pressure wave smack into him, then snap, crackle, and pop his arm every which way, before whipping him backward.

Vermillion, being driven down with the rush of renewed gravity, felt propelled like a comet, burning, crackling with embers of shattered rock, and on a collision course with the Earth. As he was pancaked back to Earth, he found himself leaving a trail of red and gold lights that ended with his meteoric landing into the clearing, which sent a dull eruption of torn-up ground and rock across the park.

Weighed down by the flood of gravitons coming back to life in the area, Darius felt himself drop back down to the ground. This was followed almost instantly by the quaking tremor that rattled the very ground he had just landed on as Vermillion smashed back down to Earth.

As Jordan felt his body arc backward through the night, he looked at his arm. It was in the shape of a K, with cracked bones protruding from the skin. However, there were no crystals. He had done it. He had sent every last bit of energy into that attack. *I – I just hope it was enough.*

Jordan dropped from the heavens and smiled when the sky above came into focus. The red clouds were gone. There wasn't a cloud in the sky, and the stars were beaming down on him.

Jordan recognized the constellation that hovered over his bed. *Regulus.*

As Cooper dropped out of the sky, he too noticed the constellation above them.

*The storm is over...*Cooper realized.

He twisted in mid-air to keep Maggie on his chest. There was nothing for him to grab; no adjacent roof, no streetlamp, nothing but air and racing concrete. He clutched Maggie to himself and felt the ground racing to meet him.

As he closed his eyes and tensed himself, something caught them.

What...What? Cooper opened one eye.

Maggie still had her eyes closed, hugging his chest, while the building they just escaped continued to burn. Cooper twisted and realized he was only an inch from the ground. Cooper looked up and saw that a police officer had her hand pointed right at them.

*An Esper...*Cooper realized...*Hiding as a police officer?*

The officer dropped her hand as if dropping a heavy weight. She exhaled heavily, her unruly brown hair shaking as she did.

Cooper plopped on the ground and curled around Maggie.

"You're okay?" he asked, and she nodded.

Cooper looked back at the officer. She raised a finger to her lips and whispered, "Sshhhh.*"*

Who was that? Cooper asked himself as the officer ran off.

Cooper caught a glimpse of her name tag before she rounded the corner.

"Harris..." Cooper muttered, with awe.

The memorial clearing had been utterly devastated by the battle. Where there once stood grass was now fire and turned up Earth. Where there once stood trees was now halfway to a new clearing. Where there once stood a memorial for the fallen Olympians and those they lost on the Green Night sat a crater.

Inside that crater sat the pulverized form of Vermillion.

Titanus and Alexander, survivors of yet another Night, crept to the edge of the crater and peered down at him. Vermillion was breathing, but harsh and heavy. He wouldn't be moving anytime soon, at least not without medical help.

"I think he's done," Titanus observed.

"Yeah," Alexander sighed. "His classes are definitely canceled tomorrow."

Titanus smirked, and then it evolved into a laugh as he pushed out all the stress he had been holding for the past few weeks. He smiled, then looked up into the skies. The moon was back, and the storm had been lifted.

Sydney looked at her father. His body trembled with the discharge of adrenaline and the surge of good humor. His suit and large frame were cut in several places. His head was split, and his limp was more pronounced. Yet as she studied his old and weary frame, she saw something akin to peace wash over him.

He's alive, she realized. *And I'm alive too.*

As she watched the peace rain down on him, she felt it pour on her too.

Reuben had collapsed next to Rhea. The strength left his body faster than he anticipated. His training had prepared him for an eventual fight with a Vesper, but no amount of training could have prepared him to face a Titan. *I stopped it. I was there. I fought a Titan and lived.* Reuben smiled behind a split lip, then flinched. He'd have to get that fixed. He glanced down at his arm and saw it was already back to normal. He hadn't even felt the pain this time.

My brother ain't gonna believe this. Reuben smiled.

Darius and Alicia were huddled next to Jordan. Darius had caught him, but Alicia was at Jordan's side before Darius could utter a word. He cradled his nephew in his arms and carefully laid him down. Jordan's arm was twisted terribly, and he avoided dropping him on it.

"J?" Alicia asked softly.

His eyes fluttered open. "Did I get him?"

Darius and Alicia glanced over at the smoking crater harboring Vermillion. Alexander flashed them a thumbs up.

"Yeah," Darius smiled. "You got 'em."

"And Rhea?" Jordan asked.

The duo looked to Reuben and Sydney, who were huddled with Rhea.

Sydney cast a weary look across the ruined field. Darius opened his mouth to respond when Reuben called out, "We've got a pulse – We've got a pulse."

"Rest," Darius urged. "You both need it."

Jordan took the words to heart and let himself sink back into the Earth and closed his eyes. The battle won and the Titan defeated, just as his ancestors, the Gods themselves, had done so many years ago.

"Tonight, the heroes win."
- Jordan Harris

CHAPTER THIRTY-FIVE

Kingdom Come

It took a day before Jordan finally regained his senses. He recalled blackness first. Then, of course, as seemed customary these days, pain. He flinched when his arm woke him up with a sharp reminder of the Red Night. He made a fist from under the blanket and was relieved that he could at least do that without much pain.

"Hey, Goldie Locks," Khadija's voice came from the doorway of the hospital room.

Jordan tried to shake off the haze he was in, then immediately sunk back into it. It was clear that he wasn't in the infirmary wing of Fort Olympus, but a hospital.

"They drugged you nice and well before they went to work on your arm," Khadija said as she walked in calmly. "Took the healing medics two whole hours to heal it correctly."

Jordan felt sunlight on his face and turned to the window. *The sun...the sun is out.* Jordan exhaled so hard, he was sure it would re-shatter his arm. *The storm is over?*

Sensing his sudden excitement, Khadija said, "It's over. You caught them."

Jordan closed his eyes again, settled back into his bed, and then remembered, "The team. What about the team?"

"They're fine. Waiting for you back at school." Khadija leaned over and wiped the cold sweat from his brow. "They sent you something. Well – a lot of people sent you stuff."

Jordan followed Khadija's gaze to a table sitting across from his bed. It was adorned with flowers, balloons, cards (professional and hand-drawn), and gifts. Jordan heaved himself up, pressing down with his good arm.

"Is that – is that for me?" he asked, feeling lopsided.

"Not for you," Khadija smirked. "They are for StarLion."

Khadija helped Jordan from the bed and led him over to the table of gifts waiting for him. He admired them gently. There were fruit baskets, flowers, get well balloons, and in the depths, he found a hand-drawn card.

"Get well soon," it read.

Jordan searched the card and found a photo of the Esper Hero Club from his old high school taped inside. *Nathan*...Jordan beamed.

Then he saw that the words "Esper Hero Club" were crossed out and written in tiny ink was a new inscription: The StarLion Hero Fan Club.

Jordan couldn't help but chuckle at it. "I've got a fan club now."

"Oh, you got more than that." Khadija smiled.

She reached into the back of the table and pulled out a shoebox. She handed it to him, and he gently took it with one hand, opening it with his recovering one. He felt a shiver of pain, but it quickly subsided when he saw what was inside.

A new pair of black and gold Zeuz Airwalkers.

Jordan absorbed the kind gifts for a moment. Then Khadija put a hand on his shoulder.

"I'm sorry," he blurted out. "I'm sorry for causing so much trouble. I nearly got hurt – got killed and I – I ran into danger without thinking and –"

"Jordan," Khadija stopped him. "I know. You don't have to apologize. Your heart was in the right place...It always has been."

Jordan nodded and felt the weight of the past few weeks leave him. "Yeah, I guess you can't be too surprised – I get it from you."

Khadija smirked, then laughed. *Boy, you have no idea.*

She hugged him close then kissed his forehead. Brother and sister, hero and heroine, stood still in the sunlight as the last of the stress from these past few weeks evaporated. He stood in her embrace, and neither of their arms trembled.

Then Khadija realized something and pulled back to tell Jordan, "There is someone you should see."

The Acheron Maximum Detention Block– aka "Acheron-MDX"– was the fifth oldest Esper prison block in the country. With twenty in the United States, the Acheron-MDX was known not just for its history, but for its formidable nature. It felt like a city that had been constructed underground. It ran twelve floors deep into the Earth's mantle and had only one entrance: a service elevator that descended for two whole minutes before reaching the first of four security checkpoints. It was a place that not even the sun could reach.

Prisoners were kept in adamant handcuffs twenty-four-seven, even to shower and eat, never giving them a chance to activate their Gifts. Even the concrete used for their cells, hallways, and common areas was mixed with ground adamant. Thus, even if a prisoner managed to slip from the cuffs, the surrounding area would neutralize his or her plasma. This place was not a place for Espers.

Understandably, Darius and Titanus felt strangely drained when they entered. Though the administrative hallways they took were not mixed with adamant, they could feel the distant effects of the metal already tapping against their plasma. The staff was a mix of humans and Espers. While the humans were truly unaffected, the Espers had a bit of a paler complexion.

A human staffer led them down an adjacent hall. The halls were tight, like a submarine, with blocky concrete painted an off-white with blue piping scaling the ceiling. This wasn't a place meant to invite warmth. As the name implied, it was a block of concrete hidden in the Earth and contained within were the scum of the Earth. Darius felt an extra depth in the pit of his stomach as he recalled the horrors unleashed during the Battle of Detroit and his victory over Typhon; Well, more his survival over Typhon, he would never call it a victory. As he walked the halls, he felt distinct fear. Below the layers of concrete and adamant, he knew that Typhon was imprisoned in the deepest, coldest cellblock of Acheron-MDX.

Darius and Titanus were led into a small room with a dividing glass set between them and the newest guest of Acheron-MDX: William "Vermillion" Holt. He was still bruised from last night and was sporting a fresh red V tattooed under his right eye. The only two choices prisoners were allowed here were how big they wanted the scarlet V and where they wanted it on their face. Vermillion's bloodshot eyes looked up at them lazily as they entered.

"Rough night?" Kinetic asked as the door shut behind them.

"You're the ones limping," Vermillion replied.

"William," Kinetic began, "we need to know if there are any other pieces of ambrosia out there."

"Oh, come on, guys, we used to be friends. At least drop the masks," Vermillion offered.

Kinetic turned to Titanus then turned to the guards in the room.

"Give us the room, please," Titanus ordered.

The guards paused for a moment before a voice in their comm mics approved it, and they stepped out. Kinetic turned to the security camera watching them and nodded, knowing the warden of Acheron-MDX was watching them. While Kinetic knew his cruelty as a warden and his escapades as a former hero were all subject to interpretation, he knew he could trust him.

Kinetic dropped his mask, and Titanus did soon after.

"How many people died last night?" William asked.

Titanus paused for a moment. While he was relieved there had been no casualties in the fight against the Red Titan, he could not say the same for the single blast the man had sent into the city.

"Fifteen," Titanus answered.

Vermillion accepted the answer like a gut punch and sulked against the bonds in his chair. *Fifteen...*

"I was trying to – " Vermillion was interrupted by Darius.

"We know. To be a hero. Think your brother would've been happy with all that?"

"My brother would have understood, knowing that crime is rising out there and you all can't handle the burden alone."

"We handled you," Titanus spat.

"You had help from kids," Vermillion snapped back. "Kids."

Vermillion let out a hollow, stretched laugh. "Imagine – imagine how hard the Vespers are laughing at you right now. Imagine how much the real threats out there are laughing at you all being saved by children."

Darius and Titanus were silent for a beat as Vermillion controlled himself.

"You all barely defeated me, so let me tell you something. The world is going to find out soon enough." He pressed against his bonds, to lean in and make his point clear. "The Green Titan was not defeated."

A cold chill ran through both Espers.

How – how did he figure that out? Titanus wished he had kept his mask on to hide the little gleam of shock he was sure his face revealed.

He knows more than he's letting on, Darius growled inside.

"He escaped," Vermillion continued. "He wasn't killed. He wasn't blown to dust – and even though he killed five of you, you couldn't stop him. Injured him, maybe. Killed him, not a chance. You all are hiding the truth. One day, he's going to come back and set the world on fire again."

The silence hung in the air like a guillotine before Clayton brought it back to what they came here for.

"The ambrosia – is there more?"

"No," he admitted. "No, there is no more."

Darius and Clayton shared a nod. *Good.*

"How is Rhea?" Vermillion asked hoarsely. "Is she – Is she one of the fifteen?"

"What do you care?" Darius asked.

"She was my student. She – She trusted me, and I – I knew what I was doing was wrong. If I had my way last night, it would only be her you were burying, and not fifteen others."

"She's alive," Darius revealed.

Vermillion gave the smallest of nods as he let the news sink in. "Good...She – she deserves better. She deserved better than me."

"Is that remorse I hear?" Clayton continued.

"I – I had the best of intentions."

"The road to hell is paved with good intentions," Darius replied.

"The road to hell?" Vermillion smirked with blood in his eye. "Hmph? The road to hell is leading right here."

Titanus leaned down to face him, his beady eyes drilling through him. "Anything else you'd like to share with us?"

Vermillion's face twitched, then shrank backward as he smiled. "Oh, I think I'll take my cues from you and keep the best secrets to myself."

Rhea woke up with a pain in her chest. For a moment she feared Vermillion still had his hand in her lungs. As she oriented herself, she felt a series of different pains assault her. There was one in her chest that she figured was going to yield a nasty scar; it was currently hidden under layers of bandages. Then there was the pain in her head from her own crystal, which was being blocked by the adamant cuffs that had her linked to the hospital bed frame. She had been in and out of consciousness all night. Even as she lay awake now, she still felt the terror and pain from last night clouding her mind.

She stirred once more from her slumber and heard the door open. A pair of pro heroes in combat suits opened it earlier to let the nurses in. This time, it wasn't a nurse, but Jordan being escorted by his sister.

"I'll give you two a minute," Khadija said and slipped out, closing the door behind her.

"Hey," Jordan offered softly.

His arm was in a sling, and he was dressed in street clothes Khadija had brought him from home.

"You're alive," Rhea gasped.

"Thanks to you." Jordan walked over to her bedside. "How are you feeling?"

"Under arrest," she replied, showing Jordan her cuffs.

Her ankles and wrist were looped with adamant cuffs. Even from here, Jordan could feel that teal blue metal tapping into and against his own crystal. "I can't even feel my plasma," she remarked.

"How is your wound?"

"Hurts to talk," Rhea coughed out, then added, "Ironically, the healers said that the ambrosia actually helped keep me alive. In some weird way, him trying to turn me into a monster ended up saving my life."

"I'm just happy you're still with us," Jordan said softly.

Rhea nodded, a lump caught in her throat.

"Thank you for saving me last night," Jordan replied.

"Are you an idiot?"

"What – ?" Jordan shook off the surprise insult.

"You were the one who saved me." Rhea turned to the window, where they both could still see smoke rising in the distance from last night's fight. "He was going to kill me. Use me to set the world ablaze, then put it out himself. I thought – I thought he was my friend."

Her eyes began to tear, and Jordan comforted her.

"You've still got friends," Jordan whispered.

"For all my talk about rules and being a hero – For all my talk about being better than my brother – than my father – I..." Rhea choked on her own tears.

Jordan took in a weary breath. He recognized the look on her face, the look of a person with a hundred hands on her throat, so he did what he could. He offered her a hand and put it on her shoulder. As he did, he felt the adamant rush through her and into him like a current. His Plasma Crystal thudded painfully in the base of his neck, but he didn't mind it. She was his friend, and she needed a hand.

"Hey," Jordan urged, and she turned to him. "You still got a friend. You didn't rat me out. You didn't give up on me, and I won't on you. Friends..."

Jordan trailed off, and Rhea finished the sentence for him, "...come in all shapes and sizes."

Much like the opening festivities at Fort Olympus on the first day, the students were gathered in the Roosevelt Courtyard to hear Headmaster Patel speak. Now there were only fifty-four freshmen in the crowd because the five members of the Freshman Leo Regiment were on stage behind her, and Rhea was still in the hospital.

"Ten years ago, this city suffered an unimaginable loss," Richa began. "One that you students grew up in the shadow of. Two weeks ago, that loss was nearly upon us again when a fellow teacher of ours tried to recreate it – it was only for the brave works of your fellow students that this was prevented."

She paused for applause. Jordan shrank a bit with the number of eyes on him, still not entirely used to it. He glanced at Reuben. Though he expected him to be sunk in his seat too, Jordan was surprised to see that he was sitting upright and tall for everyone to see.

Reuben wasn't wearing his arm bandages. He was fully exposed for who he was in front of the world. Reuben must have felt an extra pair of eyes on him because he turned to Jordan. The two shared a nod, then Jordan turned back to Richa. Behind her stood Darius, Titanus, and Red Wing.

Red Wing had concerns about why his own team, Alicia included, had kept secrets from him. However, he was more concerned that Titanus–his fellow survivor–and even Darius had kept the secrets of the ambrosia robberies from him. *It's fine,* he told himself. *I've got my own secrets to hold.*

"Ten years ago, we thought the world as we knew it was over," Richa's voice rang out, reaching the crescendo of her speech. "That heroes no longer existed – well, cadets, teachers, Espers, heroes, and more importantly those who wish to do wrong, let me state right here, right now – heroes still exist."

The students and teachers applauded. Then as the team had been informed earlier, they stood up at the end of the speech to be awarded their medals.

Titanus gifted a medal to Sydney.

"Your mother would be proud, Battalia," he acknowledged to her.

"Duh," was what she wanted to say. Instead, she allowed herself to be soft for just a moment and replied heartily, "I know. She'd be proud of you too." Then to his surprise and her own, she hugged him. Clayton was taken aback, then allowed himself to be just as vulnerable and wrapped his arms around her too.

Alexander placed a medal over Alicia's head.

"Congrats, Meteora," he beamed. "I told you the world would know your name."

Alicia fought the urge to cry and sniffled it back up. Though she was here, her mind was on her brother and all that he had taught her, without even being here.

Cedric, I promise. This is just the beginning.

"Thanks, Uncle Alex." She smiled.

"Thank you, Cadet." He offered his hand, and she shook it.

Tigris delicately laid a medal over Cooper's head. Though the big feline was wearing gloves to protect people from his claws, it didn't mean that his nails didn't poke out every now and then. His paws passed over Cooper's fluffy ears, and he gingerly let the medal go. He sighed with relief and felt his suit deflate around him.

"Hybrid pride," Tigris whispered to the young cadet.

"Hybrid pride," Cooper said, before pausing and asking, "Can I get you to sign my action figure?"

Tigris' face contorted for a moment as the question rang in his ears. Cooper panicked in the back of his mind. *Oh no. Oh no. I ruined the moment.*

"Are you kidding me?" he asked behind his fangs. "I was going to ask for your autograph."

Cooper smiled, despite the wave of worry, then Tigris patted his shoulder.

"Throw in some bamboo cupcakes, and we'll consider it a trade," the big man offered. Cooper smiled as his personal hero patted his back and, with a wave, celebrated him in front of legions of heroes.

Richa swayed over to Reuben, who bowed his head to accept the medal. She draped it so softly over his neck he didn't know it was there until he felt the gold bounce off his chest

"Let's show the world our true colors as heroes," he heard her say.

Reuben looked up, and Richa's appearance had changed. Her face was covered in brown and gold scales with thin slits over her eyes...

*She's...She's...*Reuben's mind raced...*She's like me?!*

Richa gave him an encouraging smile, and he returned it. He closed his eyes, let the hunger loose, and felt his body morph before the crowd. *Let go...*

Reuben opened his eyes, and they too were now thin slits. His arm was soon coated in black scales. It felt natural, yet so did the fear. He turned out to the crowd, and they didn't shrink, run, or boo. They cheered.

Jordan was last in line, and he bowed low for Darius to loop the medal down and over his head.

"Congrats, StarLion," Kinetic said.

"Thank you." Jordan weighed the medal in his good hand. *Phew, gold is heavier than I thought.*

He was pulled into a hug by Kinetic. After a moment, Jordan hugged him back.

"You're going to do great, kid," Darius whispered to him as he did weeks ago after Jordan "got hair in his eye." "I'm going to make sure of it."

They parted, and Kinetic waved the crowd on as they applauded for them. Jordan peered out into the crowd and saw a number of familiar and unfamiliar faces. His first glance was to Lucas, who stood clapping stoically, then to Carnage, who stood in the back, clapping with a thin smile. Jordan didn't mind though.

He was going to take this moment. Plus, there was a whole school year left. Enough time to get to know each of them, hero or villain.

"Ladies and gentlemen," Richa called out, "I present the cadets of the Freshmen Leo Regiment."

The crowd erupted in applause once more, and Jordan walked with his team to the forefront of the stage where the audience continued to applaud. With all they had gone through this month and survived, this was worth it. This shining moment under the sun, recognized by friends, family, and fellow Espers, was worth it.

Richa took to the mic once more. "This is Fort Olympus, where..."

Richa paused to allow the crowd, heroes, and cadets to sync together, before calling out in unison to the heavens above –

"Astra Inclinant."

The End

★ ARTWORK ★

StarLion Cover by A2T will Draw
Instagram.com/a2t.will.draw

Back Cover, Spine, Title Logo, and "Regulus" by Daniel Bretas
Instagram.com/calaboca.co

Profiles by The Chamba
Instagram.com/thechamba

"Shooting Stars Over Space City", "The Thieves Part 3", & "Red Titan Rock" by
Rodrigo Sanni
Instagram.com/rodrigosanni

"The Thieves", "Crescent Cutter", "The Thieves Part 2", & "[Young Lions] X [Rubicon]"
by Notus_49
Instagram.com/notus_49

"Repel // Demons", "Double-Barrel Fireworks", & "HUSH MODE" by Balasdan
Deviantart.com/balasdan

CPSIA information can be obtained
at www.ICGtesting.com
Printed in the USA
LVHW080449201022
731081LV00003B/35

9 781736 185025